BRIDGE OF THE SEPARATOR

BRIDGE OF THE SEPARATOR

HARRY TURTLEDOVE

Bridge of the Separator

This is a work of fiction. All the characters and events portrayed in this book are fictional, and any resemblance to real people or incidents is purely coincidental.

A Baen Books Original

Baen Publishing Enterprises
P.O. Box 1403
Riverdale, NY 10471
www.baen.com

ISBN-13: 978-1-4165-0918-9
ISBN-10: 1-4165-0918-6

Cover art by Tom Kidd

First printing, December 2005

Library of Congress Cataloging-in-Publication Data
Turtledove, Harry.
  Bridge of the Separator / Harry Turtledove.
     p. cm.
  ISBN-13: 978-1-4165-0918-9
  ISBN-10: 1-4165-0918-6
  1. Clergy--Fiction. 2. Refugees--Fiction. I. Title.

  PS3570.U76B75 2005
  813'.54--dc22

                                                              2005026424

Distributed by Simon & Schuster
1230 Avenue of the Americas
New York, NY 10020

Production & design by Windhaven Press, Auburn, NH (www.windhaven.com)
Printed in the United States of America

10   9   8   7   6   5   4   3   2   1

BRIDGE
OF THE
SEPARATOR

When a synod in Videssos the city named Rhavas prelate of Skopentzana, the priest thought he was being sent into exile. Not only that, he thought it an insult to the imperial family, for wasn't his grandmother sister to the grandfather of Maleinos II, Avtokrator of the Videssians? To put it mildly, he didn't want to leave the imperial capital for the city in the far northeast of the Empire of Videssos.

Old Neboulos, the ecumenical patriarch of Videssos, finally had to take him aside and talk sense into him. Gorgeous in a cloth-of-gold robe with Phos' sun picked out in shining blue silk on the left breast, Neboulos sat Rhavas down in the study of the patriarchal residence, close by the High Temple. The patriarch's long, bushy white beard wagged as he poured wine for both of them with his own hand.

"This is not exile," Neboulos insisted. "It is not—I swear it by the lord with the great and good mind. It is opportunity."

"Easy for you to say," Rhavas insisted. "You don't have to go." He was in his mid-twenties then, but remained unintimidated by Neboulos' rank and by his years. Rhavas was tall and thin, with a long, narrow axe blade of a face, a dagger of a nose, and brilliant black eyes under elegant, aristocratic eyebrows. His tonsure only made his forehead seem even higher than it would have anyway.

He was one of the most brilliant clerics, maybe the most brilliant, of his generation, and he knew it very well.

So did Neboulos, who made a placating gesture before lifting his silver goblet. "Drink, drink," the patriarch urged.

With an angry gesture, Rhavas took hold of his goblet, which matched the other. Both were decorated with reliefs of Phos, the god of light and goodness, triumphant over his eternal rival Skotos, who dwelt in eternal ice and darkness and worked evil. Rhavas and Neboulos raised their hands in reverence and intoned the good god's creed: "We bless thee, Phos, lord with the great and good mind, by thy grace our protector, watchful beforehand that the great test of life may be decided in our favor."

Together, they spat in ritual rejection of Skotos. Only then could Rhavas drink. Not even his ferocious temper kept him from noting that Neboulos had served him very fine wine. *He wants to soften me, to butter me up*, the younger man thought savagely. *Well, to the ice with me if I aim to let him.*

"Opportunity?" Rhavas laced the word with scorn. "Where is there ever opportunity outside Videssos the city?"

"By the good god, Rhavas, opportunity is where you find it." Neboulos sketched Phos' sun-circle above his heart to show he was serious. "You were born here in the capital; perhaps this is not so plain to you. But I come from Resaina, in the westlands. I rose there. Had I not risen there, I would not sit here now." He ran a hand down his glittering patriarchal vestments, which seemed out of place in the comfortably shabby, scroll-filled study.

"Yes, yes," Rhavas said, still full of rage and impatience. "But I *am* here. I can rise here. Does Skopentzana have a decent library? Does it have a library at all? How am I supposed to study the good god and his glory without the tools of scholarship?"

"Skopentzana will have books. Skopentzana is rich, rich in many things," Neboulos answered. "Among the things it is rich in is the chance for you to administer a major temple. You will not find *that* chance so easy to come by here in the capital, no matter how high your blood is."

"Oh." Rhavas was suddenly thoughtful. Now he had to fight to hold on to his anger. And fight he did. "Running a temple never did seem all that exciting to me. I'd sooner follow Phos than lead men."

"But, my dear . . ." For a moment, Neboulos seemed at a loss how to go on. He stroked his unkempt white beard. That seemed to give him whatever he needed, for he went on, "As you see, I am old. I shall not be patriarch much longer."

"Most holy sir, may you live a hundred and twenty years!" Rhavas exclaimed.

"You are kind to say such a thing. Believe me, I am grateful, but I shall not live a hundred and twenty years. At my age, one does not commence a long exegesis on Phos' holy scriptures. I do not know who will succeed me; that is for the synod and the Avtokrator to decide. But I have a good notion of who may succeed my successor."

"You do? How?" To Rhavas, the patriarch's speech was as opaque as if he'd suddenly started using the language of the sea-roving Haloga barbarians who dwelt beyond even distant Skopentzana.

Rhavas always remembered how Neboulos smiled at his naïveté. "Who? Why, you, of course." The ecumenical patriarch's right forefinger was bent with age, but not too bent to point straight at Rhavas' chest.

"Me?" Rhavas' voice rose to a startled squeak. "I never wanted to be patriarch. I never thought to be patriarch. Why me?"

"Your modesty does you credit, holy sir." Neboulos chuckled rheumily. "Why you? You are a learned man. You are a wise man. If you will forgive an old man's observation, you are wiser and more learned than you have any business being at your age. That is one side of the goldpiece. The other side is, you have a connection to the imperial family. The Avtokrator is likely to want a man who can run the temples well and is not inclined to quarrel with him."

"He may not get what he wants." Rhavas had a prickly sense of honor and an even pricklier sense of duty. "I will do what I find right and what I find proper, come what may."

"I understand," Neboulos said. "Blood calls to blood even so. My guess is, you *will* be patriarch—provided you do what you need to do before you don the golden robe. You must be watchful beforehand that the great test is decided in your favor." He smiled at using the words of the creed in a new context.

By contrast, Rhavas frowned. He suspected frivolity there. No matter what he suspected, he didn't let it deter him from his main point: "Why send me to Skopentzana, then?"

"How can you hope to run all the temples if you have not

shown you can run at least one?" Neboulos replied. "There is the reason behind it—to let you run a temple and to teach you to run one. Having proved you can do that, you will, I doubt not, be recalled to Videssos the city before too long. Someday, you will plop your fundament onto this ratty old couch. When you do, I pray you, think of me every once in a while."

For some little while, Rhavas didn't know what to say to that. At last, softly, he asked, "You believe in your heart I should do this thing?"

Neboulos sketched the sun-circle once more. "By the lord with the great and good mind, my son, I do. Videssos will have need of you in years to come. The faith will have need of you as well. I could command you. However proud you may be, I am still your superior in matters ecclesiastical. But I do not command here. I beg."

Rhavas bent his head. "So be it, then. Let the good god's will be done."

Fifteen years went by. After a few of them, Neboulos passed from this world, his spirit walking the narrow Bridge of the Separator to see whether it gained Phos' heaven or fell down, down, down to Skotos' eternal ice. His successor, a certain Kameniates, was translated to Videssos the city from the westlands town of Amorion, where he had been prelate.

So far as Rhavas knew, Kameniates remained in good health. That perturbed the prelate of Skopentzana much less than it would have when he first came to the far northeast of the Empire. He had made his peace with this, his new hometown. It was not Videssos the city. Nothing else in the Empire, nothing else in the world—not even Mashiz, the capital of Videssos' western rival, Makuran—came close to Videssos the city.

But Skopentzana was itself. Before coming here, Rhavas would have denied that any place outside the imperial city could have an identity of its own, a character of its own. Everything beyond the great, unconquerable walls was simply . . . the provinces, as far as he was concerned. The provinces were a dreary place where nothing interesting ever happened, where no one had or wanted to have a new thought, and where shepherds were likely to get to know their ewes altogether too well.

He had learned better now. Skopentzana had a lively life of

the mind, though not exactly of the sort he had known in Videssos the city. Here, they thought men from the capital provincial because those men knew nothing of what went on in Halogaland to the north or among the Khamorth nomads on the vast plains of Pardraya to the west. Even poetry was different here. Imitating Haloga models, it gave more weight to alliteration and assonance, less to rhyme, than verse did in the capital. Rhavas had tried his hand at the local style a few times, and won praise from men whose judgment he respected.

He hadn't expected that when he came. He also hadn't expected that Skopentzana would be beautiful. But beautiful it was, though beautiful in ways that had nothing to do with the majesty of the capital's seven hills. The River Anazarbos ran singing to the sea past this city. Every other poem in these parts talked about the river and its banks of golden sand. Rhavas would have got sick of the poetry if it didn't tell the truth. There were times when he got sick of the poetry anyway, but that was only because he had too much of the critic in him.

Dark woods of fir and spruce, winters that came early and lingered late, long misty days of summer when it seemed as if the sun would never set . . . The sunlight had a peculiarly rich tone in the north, one made more intense by the yellow sandstone from which so much of Skopentzana was built. Rhavas had to get used to the steep pitch of the roofs. As soon as he saw snow slide down them, he understood.

He also had to get used to preaching in the temple that, with the city eparch's residence, formed two sides of Skopentzana's central square. Most temples throughout the Empire, from what he had heard, modeled themselves after the magnificent High Temple in the capital. He'd expected one more provincial copy here, and braced himself to judge it by how nearly it approached its prototype.

What he hadn't expected was that the chief temple in Skopentzana was as old as the High Temple, and as different from it as bread and beer. (He'd had to get used to beer, too, as wine was an expensive import in these parts where grapes wouldn't grow. He learned to drink the bitter brew. He never learned to like it.) The High Temple's great dome mounted on pendentives was a wonder of the world. The marvelous mosaic of Phos stern in judgment inside the dome was another.

Skopentzana's chief temple had no central dome. When Rhavas first saw it, he exclaimed, "It looks as if someone used an upside-down ship for the roof!" Ships were on his mind then. He'd been seasick much of the way up from Videssos the city, and the vessel that carried him on the last leg of the journey had to outrace Haloga pirates to safety.

In fact, as he found out later, he wasn't so far wrong. One of the inspirations for the temple was a Haloga longhouse, and longhouses often were roofed with ships too decrepit to put to sea. It made for a different sort of building and, in some ways, a different sort of service. In the High Temple, the altar was at the very center of things, under the dome, with worshipers all around in equal numbers. Here there were worshipers in front and behind, but very few to the sides. The priests who served the altar necessarily adapted to the shape of the building they used.

On the day when Rhavas' life changed forever, he was standing in the central square, between the eparch's residence and the temple. Statues of locally famous Videssians crowded the square. Largest was a great bronze of the Avtokrator Stavrakios, the great conqueror of two centuries before. Surrounding him in bronze and marble and the local golden sandstone were lesser figures. They all seemed to look to him for permission to stand there. It was an illusion, but an effective one.

Rhavas happened to be looking up at Stavrakios, too. Even with a pigeon dropping on his nose, the old Avtokrator looked like a tough customer. By everything Rhavas knew of him, he had been a tough customer. He'd made both the Halogai and the Makuraners fear him, no mean feat when they dwelt at opposite ends of the Empire.

A pretty woman leading a toddler dropped Rhavas a curtsy. "Good morning, very holy sir," she murmured.

"And a good morning to you. May Phos bless you on it," Rhavas answered gravely. The woman walked on. He eyed her with the same careful consideration he'd given to Stavrakios' statue. Phos' priesthood was celibate. Some priests, being men like any others, flouted the rule. Rhavas scorned them. Some kept it, though it ate into their flesh like the iron shackles around the ankles of slaves and convicts condemned to the mines. Rhavas pitied them. He usually wore the shackles of celibacy lightly, even proudly. Every so often, though . . .

His mouth was never wide, nor particularly generous. Now it narrowed to a thin, hard line. He deliberately turned his back on the woman and her little girl. Out of sight . . . Out of sight did not mean out of mind, not here, however much Rhavas wished it would. Though he looked at the woman no more, he saw her perhaps more plainly than ever.

He knew sin in others. Part of his peculiar sort of pride was to know it in himself as well. He sketched Phos' sun-circle above his heart and murmured prayers against the weakness of his flesh. Despite those fervent prayers, the memory of the woman's smile and soft voice lingered.

And then, in an odd way, the good god heard his prayers and answered them. Up from the southern gate, the gate farthest from the river, came a dispatch rider on a horse he lashed into a gallop, though it wasn't far from foundering. "Out of my way! Out of my way, curse you!" the rider shouted at anyone in his path. He flicked his whip not only at the poor horse but also at anyone who did not move out of the way fast enough to suit him. Cries of rage and pain rose up in his wake.

Here was something out of the ordinary. Rhavas forgot about the pretty woman as he stared at the dispatch rider thundering across the square. The man leaped down from the horse and tossed the reins to one of the startled sentries in front of the eparch's residence. Then, still on the dead run, he dashed inside.

Out of the ordinary indeed, and not a good omen, not at all. Something somewhere in the Empire must have gone badly wrong. Frowning, Rhavas hurried toward the residence. The sentries, even the man holding the lathered horse's reins, bowed low as he came up. "Very holy sir," they chorused.

The horse's sides heaved. Its nostrils glowed red as coals. Over its panting, Rhavas asked, "Did the courier say anything before he went inside?"

"Only that he had to see the eparch right away," one of the soldiers answered. Like his comrades, he wore a conical helmet with a bar nasal, a mailshirt, and baggy wool trousers tucked into stout boots that rose almost to his knees. He held a grounded pike in his right hand; a sword in a worn leather sheath hung from his belt.

"Not a word more than that, the miserable dog," another sentry added irately. He was a swarthy man with a wide forehead, a narrow chin, and sharp cheekbones: a typical Videssian, in other words. His indignation at the courier's silence was also typical. Rhavas had preached sermons on the Videssian love for gossip. He feared they didn't strike home as well as some of his other sermons. He might as well have preached against eating. Lust for gossip and news was as much a part of the Videssian character as a craving for good food.

Embarrassment suddenly heated Rhavas' cheeks and his ears and the shaven crown of his head. *Why, here I am, guilty of the very sin I've thundered against from the pulpit*, he thought. He promised himself penitential prayers before an image of the good god. Even as he made the promise, though, he wondered whether carrying it out would suffice to uproot the sin he'd found inside his own bosom. He hoped and doubted at the same time.

Stiffly, he said, "If the most honorable Zautzes learns anything I should know, I hope he will do me the courtesy of calling on me at my residence."

"I'm sure he will, very holy sir," one of the sentries said.

Rhavas was also sure of it. The civil administration and the temples stood shoulder to shoulder in ruling the Empire. And even if they hadn't . . . Even if they hadn't, Zautzes would have been a fool not to consult the man who was not only prelate of Skopentzana but also the Avtokrator's cousin. Rhavas had no great love for Zautzes; the man was a lecher, and also overfond of wine, at least by the prelate's austere standards. But no one could ever accuse the eparch of being a fool.

Turning, Rhavas went back toward the temple. This time, he strolled instead of striding. As if he were a traveler from afar, he stopped dead and admired each statue in turn. He lingered longest at the great bronze of Stavrakios. He remembered doing the same thing when he first came to Skopentzana all those years earlier. He really had been a traveler from afar then. No more.

This time, his dawdling had method in it. The square couldn't have been more than a bowshot wide. Even so, Rhavas hadn't completely crossed it before someone shouted out his name from the direction of the eparch's residence. He turned, as if in surprise.

There stood Zautzes himself, waving and doing everything this side of jumping up and down to catch his notice. Gravely, Rhavas waved back. Zautzes hurried toward him. The eparch always put

Rhavas in mind of a frog. He was short and squat. He had a wide face, a broad mouth, a receding chin, and eyes that threatened to bulge out of his head.

Frogs, however, did not commonly wear fur-edged silk robes shot through with gold and silver threads. Nor did frogs wear boots trimmed with red. Those boots symbolized Zautzes' own connection with the Avtokrator. Only the ruler himself was allowed a pair all of red.

The two leaders of Skopentzana bowed to each other. "Very holy sir," Zautzes said, his voice a gravelly bass.

"Most honorable sir." Rhavas' voice was only slightly higher, but much smoother.

"You will know a courier has come to me with news. You will also know he came with, ah, a certain amount of urgency." Zautzes even blinked like a frog. The motion was slow and deliberate and involved his whole face.

"I had gathered something to that effect, yes." Rhavas was not about to let the eparch win a battle of understatements. "Of course, if it's none of my business I'll just go back to the temple and find out about it from my cook or the cleaning woman."

That made Zautzes blink again, even more extravagantly than before. "Well, very holy sir, it does have somewhat to do with you. Yes, somewhat, by Phaos." The eparch was from these parts, and pronounced the good god's name in the old-fashioned, two-syllable way. In the capital, they'd clipped it down to one. Zautzes gathered himself. "D'you know Stylianos, the grand domestikos?"

"I met him a few times when he came into Videssos the city, but he was usually on campaign even then," Rhavas answered. "I can't say I know him well, though. Why do you ask? Has something happened to him? I hope not."

He meant that. Stylianos was a good general, probably the best grand domestikos the Empire had had in at least a hundred years. His forays onto the Pardrayan plains had warned the Khamorth nomads that their raids into imperial territory would not be tolerated. Few Videssian commanders had ever hit back effectively at the plainsmen. Stylianos made a welcome exception.

But Rhavas didn't care for the way Zautzes stared at him: as if he were a fly to be snapped up with a flick of the tongue. The eparch said, "Something's happened to him, all right, very holy sir. He's proclaimed himself Avtokrator of the Videssians, and he's moving against the city." To Videssians from one end of the Empire to the other, the great imperial capital was *the* city.

"Phos!" Rhavas muttered, and sketched the sun-circle over his heart. "Maleinos will not take that lying down, most honorable sir. He will fight to hold the throne, and fight with everything that's in him. You asked if I knew Stylianos, and I don't, not well. But I know my cousin. I know what he will do." Bitterness filled his voice: "He raised Stylianos up to be grand domestikos. Is this the thanks he gets?"

"So it would seem," Zautzes said, an answer whose breathtaking cynicism left even the sardonic Rhavas at a loss. Into the prelate's silence, Zautzes went on, "It's been a while since the Empire's last civil war. I'm afraid we've got a new one on our hands."

"I'm afraid you're right," Rhavas said. "For that alone, Stylianos will be damned to Skotos' eternal ice." Now Zautzes was the one who didn't respond right away. Rhavas raised an eyebrow. In a very soft voice, he asked, "Or do you disagree, most honorable sir? Maleinos raised you up, too, you know."

"I want peace in the Empire," Zautzes said. "Whoever can give me that, I'm for."

That was an answer that was not an answer. Rhavas' tone grew sharper: "If the would-be usurper comes to Skopentzana, will this city welcome him or close its gates against him?"

"You would do better to ask Himerios than me." Zautzes sounded sullen, resenting being put on the spot.

Rhavas grunted. The garrison Himerios commanded was intended to protect Skopentzana from Haloga pirate ships rowing up the Anazarbos. It wasn't very big; the blond barbarians hadn't been troublesome lately. And Himerios had always seemed content enough with little to do and scant resources with which to do it. Now . . .

Now Rhavas and Zautzes might not be the most important, most powerful men in Skopentzana after all. That role might belong to the garrison commander. Rhavas nodded briskly to the eparch. "No doubt you're right, most honorable sir. I had better do that."

Zautzes looked no happier. Rhavas had a hard time blaming him. The eparch had to go on running Skopentzana as if nothing were wrong. He had to collect the head tax and the hearth tax as usual. He had to see that justice was done, that the city's walls and public buildings were repaired . . . and that whoever won the civil war wouldn't think he'd backed the other side.

With a curt bow, Rhavas turned away. He didn't want Zautzes to see how worried he was. Most prelates throughout the Empire would be making the same calculations as the local eparchs. Rhavas didn't have that burden—or was it a luxury? Stylianos would assume he was loyal to his cousin, the Avtokrator, and the rebel would be right.

Out of the corner of his eye, Rhavas saw Zautzes waddle back toward his residence. That gave the prelate the privacy he needed to swear under his breath. Maleinos had proved himself a reasonably good Avtokrator, and a reasonably able one as well. Rhavas wouldn't have worried about most rebels; he would have been confident his cousin could put them down in short order.

Stylianos? Stylianos was a different story.

A man with the broad shoulders, heat-reddened face, and battered hands of a blacksmith came up to Rhavas. "Is something wrong, very holy sir?" he asked. "You look like you just watched an oxcart run over your pup."

Rhavas looked at him—looked through him. The blacksmith's face got redder yet. *It isn't his fault*, the prelate reminded himself, trying to be charitable. Charity didn't come easy, not now. "I'm afraid, my good man, that it's nowhere near so trivial as that."

The blacksmith walked off scratching his head.

Himerios didn't boast anything fancy enough to be called a residence. He lived in an ordinary house, one just like the others along its street. Its ground floor was built of the local golden sandstone, its upper story of timber now pale with years of weathering. The only opening in the ground floor was the doorway, and the door, of thick planks reinforced with iron, could have done duty in a fortress. The upper story boasted a couple of windows with stout wooden shutters that could be closed tight against the biting cold of winter. As usual in Skopentzana, the slates on the roof were steeply pitched, so snow would slide off instead of sticking.

Rhavas knocked on that formidable door. Two boys kicking a ball back and forth in the narrow, muddy street gave him an odd look; it wasn't the sort of neighborhood where priests appeared every day. A scrawny stray dog rooting through rubbish paid no attention to him. He preferred the dog's attitude.

When no one answered, Rhavas knocked again, harder. This time, the door creaked open. There stood Himerios, who stared with even more surprise than the boys showed. "Very holy sir!" the garrison commander exclaimed. "To what do I owe the honor of this visit?" He didn't say, *What do you want from me?* but that had to be what he meant.

"May I come in?" Rhavas asked.

"Well, yes, of course." Himerios stood aside to let Rhavas do so. The garrison commander was as tall and lean as Zautzes was short and squat. He even overtopped Rhavas, who was far from small, by a finger's breadth or two. He had a long, angular face, with a sharp nose and a mole on his right cheek just above his neatly trimmed fringe of lightly frosted beard.

Several stools and a table furnished the front room, along with one wooden chair near the hearth. Himerios waved Rhavas to the chair. Rhavas shook his head. He perched on a stool instead; the chair was plainly Himerios' special place. Sure enough, the officer—who wore a loose wool tunic over baggy breeches tucked into boots like most men in this cold northern city—sat down there.

"Ingegerd!" he called back to the kitchen. "The prelate's come to pay a call. Fetch us some wine and honey cakes, please."

"Yes, I will do that," his wife answered. Her name said she came from the Haloga country. So did the sonorously musical accent that flavored her Videssian.

She brought out the refreshments on a wooden tray a couple of minutes later. She was almost as tall as Rhavas herself, and exotically beautiful: fair-haired, fair-skinned, with granite cheekbones and chin and with eyes bluer than the sky above Skopentzana. No matter how resigned to celibacy Rhavas was, his own eyes followed her emphatically curved shape as she served him and Himerios.

"Very holy sir," she murmured, and sketched the sun-sign. Unlike most Halogai, she'd given up the fierce gods of her homeland for the lord with the great and good mind.

After raising his hands to the heavens and spitting in ritual rejection of Skotos, Rhavas sipped the wine. It was sweet and strong and good—and he needed bracing. He took a bite from a honey cake. It was rich with walnuts and butter. He'd had to get used to that last; in Videssos the city, which favored olive oil instead, using butter branded one a barbarian. The stuff did stay fresh better here than down in the capital.

Himerios also ate and drank. So did Ingegerd, who'd sat down on a stool after setting the tray on the table. Haloga women had a reputation for forwardness of both the good and the bad sort; she evidently lived up to it. Rhavas clucked, but only to himself. Though her forwardness bent custom, it broke no religious law.

"Well, very holy sir, what's on your mind?" Himerios asked, setting his pewter goblet on his knee.

Before answering, Rhavas glanced toward Ingegerd. She looked back steadily, her sculptured features all serious attention. Himerios still gave no sign of sending her away. However strange it seemed to the prelate, the garrison commander evidently wanted his wife to hear. With a small shrug, Rhavas passed on the news: "The general Stylianos has rebelled against his Majesty, the Avtokrator Maleinos."

"Phos!" Himerios exclaimed, and then, hoping against hope, "You're sure?"

"As sure as needs be," Rhavas answered. "I have it just now from Zautzes the eparch, who has it from a courier up from the south. I saw the courier ride up to Zautzes' residence. He almost killed his horse getting here. He thought his news important. I did not hear it from his own lips or see the dispatch he bore, but I have no reason to doubt the eparch."

Ingegerd spoke with a man's, even a soldier's, directness: "This can only mean civil war. Who will win?"

Nine words, and she'd said everything that needed saying. Rhavas put the best face on things he could: "Maleinos has ruled for many years. Most people are loyal to him. And he holds Videssos the city. No one can claim to rule the Empire without ruling the capital, and Videssos the city is the greatest fortress in the world." Every word of that was true. It would have spelled the ruination of most uprisings before they were well begun. This one . . .

"Stylianos is Stylianos," Himerios said. "Videssos hasn't seen the likes of him for a long time." And that, unfortunately, was also true.

Ingegerd said something in her own language. Rhavas knew not a word of the Haloga tongue. He watched Himerios give him a sudden startled look. *Did she just remind him I am Maleinos' cousin? To the ice with me if I don't think she did.*

But Rhavas thought he would have stayed loyal to Maleinos even without a blood tie between them. He said, "You need to remember that the Avtokrator is Phos' vicegerent on earth. Maleinos is the legitimate ruler of the Empire; his father and grandfather ruled it before him. And what is Stylianos? A would-be usurper, someone who would topple Phos' vicegerent. Who would do such a thing? Only a man who has taken Skotos into his heart." Again, he ceremonially spat in rejection of the dark god.

So did Himerios and Ingegerd. All orthodox believers in Videssos had faith that in the end Phos would prevail over Skotos, good would prevail over evil. To believe otherwise was to fall into blackest heresy, and surely to forfeit one's soul to the ice of the dark god's hell.

All the same, Himerios said, "Suppose Stylianos wins, very holy sir? I'm not saying he will, mind you, but just suppose, all right? He'd become Avtokrator, right?"

"He would still be a usurper," Rhavas said stiffly. Maleinos' grandfather—his own grandmother's brother—had been a usurper, too, but he didn't bring that up. To be fair, he didn't even think of it.

"He wouldn't *just* be a usurper. He'd be the Avtokrator, too. He'd wear the red boots," Himerios persisted. "Wouldn't that make *him* Phos' vicegerent on earth?"

Rhavas was an honest man. He'd never imagined he would wish he weren't. Here, he did. Making a sour face, he answered, "Technically, yes, but the sin of rebellion would still lie heavily upon him. The patriarch might well require penance before he could worship in the High Temple."

Ingegerd spoke again in the Haloga tongue, sharply this time. Himerios gave her an impatient nod. Then he swung his attention back to Rhavas. "I do thank you for bringing me this news, very holy sir. Now, if civil war should come to Skopentzana, I will know what to do. Phos prevent it, but if it should . . ." He made the sign of the good god above his breast.

So did his wife. And so did Rhavas. The prelate left Himerios' house a few minutes later, certain the garrison commander had said he would act in Maleinos' interest. Rhavas had got all the way back to his own residence before he ran through Himerios' words in his mind once more. He stopped dead, his hand on the latch, realizing Himerios had in fact said no such thing.

"Trimmer. Accursed trimmer," Rhavas said scornfully. But how many others would also wait to see which way the wind was blowing before setting their own sails?

Preaching had never excited Rhavas. Studying the struggle between the good god and his wicked rival had always interested him much more than trying to put that struggle and what it meant across for layfolk. He'd never given *bad* sermons. No one as well organized and generally capable as he was could do that. But he'd been competent, not inspired, and he'd always felt the lack.

Now, suddenly, inspiration struck. When he spoke to Skopentzana from the pulpit in favor of Maleinos and against Stylianos, he spoke from the heart, not from the head. He used the same theme with his congregation as he had with Himerios and Ingegerd, but with fresh and vivid details thrown in at every sermon.

He found himself looking out at the sea of faces in Skopentzana's main temple as if they were so many pagan Halogai and he was trying to convert them to the worship of the lord with the great and good mind. (In reality, many priests had tried to convert Halogaland. A lot of them ended up as martyrs to their faith. Most of the Halogai remained stubbornly unconverted—Ingegerd marked an exception, not a rule.)

"Will you deny—can you deny—that the usurper seeks to overthrow the natural order of things?" Rhavas thundered from the pulpit, slamming down his fist. "Can you deny this is nothing but wickedness? Can you deny it leads only to the ice?" He stared out challengingly at the worshipers.

Zautzes was there. So was Himerios. If Ingegerd was, Rhavas couldn't see her; women had a separate gallery, upstairs from the men on the ground floor of the temple, which latticework screened off from prying eyes.

Neither the eparch nor the garrison commander presumed to quarrel with Rhavas or to shout out Stylianos' name. Nor did anyone else. Most of the people who came to Skopentzana's main temple were plump and prosperous and middle-aged; most of them would be just as well pleased to see things go on as they always had.

Skopentzana boasted more than one temple, of course. So did any Videssian city of decent size. Spires topped with gilded sun-balls sprang up from rooftops in every neighborhood. Other priests, men of lower rank in the ecclesiastical hierarchy, presided over them.

Everyone must say the same thing, Rhavas thought. *All of them must tell their congregations that Maleinos is the rightful Avtokrator and Stylianos only a rebel and a usurper. This is the truth; it must be made plain.*

The prelate's fervor worked its way into the usual prayers and hymns, too. Because of it, the congregation responded with more enthusiasm than they mostly showed. For one of the rare times in his life, Rhavas felt the power of his preaching. There had been times when he took less enjoyment from wine.

After reciting Phos' creed for the last time, he dismissed the worshipers. They filed out of the temple buzzing among themselves. Rhavas couldn't remember the last time he'd heard that kind of excitement among them. He couldn't remember if he ever had.

"Good sermon, very holy sir," said a man with a robe full of ornate—and expensive—embroidery. "You really sounded like you meant it."

"I always mean it," Rhavas said. That anyone could doubt his sincerity wounded him to the heart.

Plainly, the congregant had no idea he'd offended. "Maybe you do," he said, "but it doesn't always have that old oomph, if you know what I mean." The noise he made sounded as if he'd just been kicked in the belly. "You give it that old oomph"—there it was again—"and folks won't forget it."

"Oomph," Rhavas echoed in hollow tones. The man nodded. Rhavas fought the impulse to pound his head against the polished cedar of the pulpit. He knew how long and hard he labored over his sermons. He might not have been an inspiring speaker, but his logic was always clear and straightforward, his theology impeccably orthodox. And none of that had really struck home with his audience? Evidently not. Passion and vigor counted for more with them.

I could have preached for Stylianos instead, he realized. *I could have called down anathemas on my cousin's head. If I sounded excited while I was doing it, people would have praised me, the same as they're praising me now.*

He wondered why he'd spent so many years poring over Phos' sacred scriptures and the commentaries generation upon generation of theologians had written about them. Was that what made a successful priest? Again, evidently not. He might have done better joining a troupe of actors and mountebanks. That he postured in front of a crowd seemed more important than what he postured about.

Half a dozen more people praised his preaching as they left the temple. Their words left him colder by the moment. *Stylianos? I could have called on them to reverence Skotos! And if I did it with passion enough, they might obey.* He shivered. Surely the lord with the great and good mind would never let such a travesty of justice come to pass.

Soothsayers in Skopentzana were three for a copper, as they were in any other city in the Empire of Videssos. Like the witches and hedge wizards who sold fertility spells for livestock and love philtres and charms sworn to make an enemy itch in embarrassing places, many of them—maybe even most of them—were frauds. Some, though, some had a certain talent.

In all the years Rhavas had been in Skopentzana, he'd never felt the need to consult a soothsayer. He and the eparch had worked together to catch some of the worst frauds and send them out of town with stripes on their backs. A man couldn't hang around the edges of magic, though, without learning a little something about who was reliable as well as who was not. And so, when the prelate decided to learn what he could of things that lay ahead, he didn't hesitate. He summoned a certain Eladas.

The soothsayer was a man a few years older than Rhavas—closer to fifty than forty. His robe was of good wool, and clean. So many such people were desperately poor, which of itself disqualified them in Rhavas' eyes. If they couldn't see the future well enough to do themselves any good, how could they hope to help anyone else? Eladas passed that test.

He passed another immediately thereafter. The first words out of his mouth after he was ushered into Rhavas' study were, "Very holy sir, prophesying about the imperial succession is a capital crime. I do not break that law, nor would I ever. I tell you this only because there is civil war in the land. I do not ask what you would ask of me." He did not say he did not know.

"I will not make you worry about the headsman's sword. I will not make myself liable to it, either," Rhavas assured him. He'd intended to see whether Eladas *would* prophesy along those lines, but could hardly blame the man for ruling it out straightaway.

Eladas politely inclined his head. "You are gracious." His face was ordinary enough—except for his eyes. They were large and dark and haunted. Rhavas could well believe they saw things most men would never notice. Eladas sipped the wine a junior priest brought him. After that young man left the room, the soothsayer asked, "What would you know, then?"

Rhavas smiled, not least in pride at his own cleverness. "I hope to learn from you whether I shall become ecumenical patriarch."

"I see," Eladas said. No doubt he did, too. If Maleinos held the throne, his cousin's chances of promotion were excellent. If Stylianos overthrew the present Avtokrator, Rhavas would be lucky to stay where he was. But inquiring about the patriarchal succession wasn't against the law. Eladas sipped from the winecup again. Then he set it down and spoke in brisk, businesslike tones: "Give me your hand."

"Certainly." Rhavas held it out. Eladas took it between his own hands. They were warm and firm and dry: no clammy touch here, as soothsayers were often said to have.

No nonsense here, either. Rhavas also liked that; he was and always had been a man with no use for nonsense. Eladas chanted no mystic and probably senseless charms. He just studied Rhavas' hand as intently as the prelate might study a passage in the scriptures.

Slowly, he nodded to himself. Slowly, he looked up from Rhavas' hand to his face. He nodded again, this time to his client.

"You will—" he began, and then said no more. His grip suddenly tightened on Rhavas' hand, tightened with agonizing force. His eyes, those eyes that saw so much, opened wider than a man's eyes had any business doing. What was in them? Astonishment? Fear? Fear, Rhavas thought, for that crushing grip all at once went icy cold. Eladas took one hand away for a moment to point at the prelate. Accusation? Triumph? Again, Rhavas couldn't be sure. The soothsayer's mouth worked, but no sound came forth.

And then those staring eyes rolled up in Eladas' head. The man let out a last gasp and slumped over. At first, Rhavas thought he had fainted. Then, with a twinge of horror, he realized Eladas wasn't breathing. Now he was the one who seized the soothsayer's wrist. He probed for the point where the pulse pounded most powerfully.

He felt . . . nothing, nothing at all. He shouted hoarsely for the young priest who'd let Eladas in: "Matzoukes! Come quickly!"

A wet stain at the crotch said Eladas' bladder had let go. A stench said his bowels had done likewise. Matzoukes hurried into the study. He took in the scene at a glance. "Phos!" he exclaimed. Of itself, his hand moved in the sun-circle. "What happened here, very holy sir?"

"He's dead," Rhavas said dully. "Dead." Of that there could be no possible doubt. "I asked him a question, and he began to answer it, but he had a . . . a seizure, I suppose you would say. He fell over, and the rest . . . the rest is as you see."

"What did you ask him?" Matzoukes inquired.

Rhavas withered the youngster with a glance. Matzoukes turned very red and bowed his head in shame and discomfiture. Rhavas grew businesslike: "Help me get the body out of here. Did he have family? I think he did. We'll have to let them know. And we will have to make sure that the charity of this temple does not leave them wanting. This was not our fault"—he said that as much to reassure himself as Matzoukes and the dead Eladas, whose eyes still seemed filled with blind reproach—"but we shall make what amends we can."

"Y-yes, very holy sir," Matzoukes quavered. But he was steady enough as he and Rhavas manhandled Eladas' corpse out of the study. Afterward, panting a little out in the hallway, he said, "I do apologize for snooping. I meant no harm by it, and I certainly didn't mean that your question, whatever it was, could have had anything to do with . . . this." He sketched the sun-sign again.

Matching the gesture, Rhavas said, "Don't fret, my son. I took no offense." That was a lie, but a lie kindly meant. Matzoukes let out an audible sigh of relief. Rhavas stared down at Eladas. They hadn't closed the soothsayer's eyes, so he still seemed to stare back. Rhavas wished he could believe the man had suffered an unfortunate apoplexy or something of the sort. He wished he could, but he had no luck—no luck at all.

As far as he could tell, Eladas had heard his question, looked for the answer, found it . . . and died of terror when he realized what it was. Rhavas still didn't know the answer. The prelate only wished he hadn't asked the question.

★　　　　★　　　　★

Every time a courier came up to Zautzes' residence, Rhavas stared across Skopentzana's central square, wondering what news the man had in his head or in the waxed-leather dispatch tube he carried on his belt. And every time a trader came up from the south and set up a display of pottery or bronze vessels or perfume or spices in one of the city markets, Rhavas wondered what gossip he passed on to the traders and townsfolk.

Would Stylianos try to encourage rebellion here? Before long, Rhavas realized that was the wrong question. The right question was, why wouldn't Stylianos? What did he have to lose? Nothing. What did he have to gain? The crown—in other words, everything.

Rumor said Maleinos had won a battle, somewhere down in the south. Then a different rumor swept through Skopentzana, this one claiming that Stylianos had beaten the Avtokrator and sent him scurrying back to Videssos the city. Rhavas had no idea what to believe. Not believing anything seemed easiest.

He gathered the priests in Skopentzana together and spoke to them about the need to keep Maleinos on the throne. One of them said, "Stylianos will make you sorry if he wins."

"No." Rhavas shook his head. "If the rebel defeats the rightful Avtokrator, I will already be sorry, so he will not be able to make me so."

He wasn't the only Videssian to revel in quibbling for its own sake. The priest looked him in the eye and said, "In that case, very holy sir, he will make you sorrier."

"You are a worthy grammarian," Rhavas said sourly. "It is possible that he may make me sorrier. If the good god is kind, however, what is possible will not come to pass. And that is why I have asked all of you here to the temple today: to urge you to do everything you can to keep the usurper from stealing the throne."

None of the priests said he favored Stylianos. Rhavas would have been surprised if any man had, especially with so little reliable news coming out of the south. But Maleinos' support also seemed lukewarm. *Fence-sitters*, Rhavas thought unhappily. The lesser priests would see who was winning, and choose based on that. Rhavas knew nothing but contempt for such trimming. He would have preferred a man who dared to admit he backed the rebel. At least such a man would show himself principled, and so worthy of respect. His principles might be misguided, but they would be real. The expedient souls . . .

After they left the temple, Rhavas made a note to himself to send men he trusted to the other temples in the town. Hearing what the priests had to say from the pulpit when they thought he wasn't listening might prove worthwhile. They might pledge loyalty under his eye and go back on it as soon as they were out of earshot. With men who cared more about who was winning and who losing than about who right and who wrong, such things were to be expected.

A few days after his meeting with his fellow priests, Himerios called on him. Bowing, the garrison commander said, "Well, you won't have to worry about my loyalty anymore, very holy sir."

"No?" Rhavas asked cautiously, not sure what the officer meant.

"No." Himerios' voice was grave. "His Majesty has summoned the garrison here down to the south, to join his other forces in the fight against Stylianos."

"Ah?" Rhavas said: as neutral a sound as he could make. "And you are obeying his Majesty?"

"I am," Himerios replied. "Ingegerd will stay behind. A civil war's nothing to take a woman into, and Skopentzana's far enough out of the way that the fighting's unlikely to get here. If . . . if things go wrong, very holy sir, I'd count it a kindness if you see that she doesn't suffer on account of my choice—and if you'd look out for her generally."

Rhavas bowed to him. "What I can do, I will. How much that may be, I do not know. If things go wrong, they are likely to go wrong for me as well as for you. In that case, I doubt I will have much influence on events. You might do well to ask some other priest besides me."

Himerios shook his head. "You're an honest man. Priests are men like any others. Some of them, meaning no offense to you, I wouldn't trust to keep an eye on a sack of manure, let alone a woman."

That came too close for comfort to Rhavas' own thoughts about his fellow clerics. He said, "You do me honor by not including me in their number."

"You annoy people for different reasons," Himerios said. "You cling strongly to what you believe. I don't mean to offend you when I say that you cling strongly even where another man would think of changing his views. That can't help but upset those who hold their opinions less firmly."

You're a stubborn crank was what he meant. No matter how smoothly he phrased it, that would have offended many men. Not Rhavas. The prelate bowed once more. "Good is good and evil is evil," he said. "I will cling to the stronger one with all my might, and do that which I see as good in the sight of Phos. All men—and all women—should do the same. If they do less, they put themselves in peril of meeting the eternal ice when their days on earth are done."

"I think we all try to do right as we see it," Himerios said. "Not everyone sees it the same way, though."

"There is only one right path," Rhavas said stubbornly. "It always lies ahead of us. We must find it and travel it, for in the end it leads over the Bridge of the Separator and into Phos' eternal light. Choose the wrong path, and you will never cross the bridge. You will fall down into damnation instead."

For a moment, Himerios looked frightened. Rhavas was a more effective speaker talking to one man than he was from the pulpit. The garrison commander visibly gathered himself. "You're not talking about me in particular, eh, very holy sir? You mean *any* man who falls off the straight path."

"Yes, of course," Rhavas said impatiently, not seeing that it had been anything but *of course* to Himerios. "Do that which is right, and the good god will reward you. Do otherwise, and Skotos will see to it that you pay the price." He spat in rejection of Phos' dark rival.

So did Himerios. The Videssian soldier said, "I hope to come home to Skopentzana soon. If I do, that will mean the Avtokrator Maleinos has won and the rebellion is over."

"If you do, it will mean Phos has triumphed and Skotos is defeated," Rhavas said. "May the blessings of the lord with the great and good mind go with you."

"Thanks. That means a lot to me." Himerios turned to leave. "And if by some mischance things should go wrong, please . . . remember Ingegerd."

"What I can do, I will," Rhavas said again. "As I told you,

though, if things go wrong, she would be better off with some other protector than me."

Three days later, he watched the garrison commander ride out of Skopentzana through the south gate at the head of his men. Videssos' banner, a gold sunburst on blue, fluttered over the soldiers. Rhavas wondered how much good that banner would do during a civil war. Both sides would fly it then, and neither would be able to use it to tell friend from foe.

The soldiers setting forth from Skopentzana didn't seem worried about who their foes would be. The foot soldiers tramped along with shouldered pikes. They had swords on their hips to protect themselves in case their main weapons broke. Some of the cavalry were lancers, others archers. Foot soldiers and horsemen alike waved to friends—usually pretty friends—they were leaving behind. Ingegerd stood not far from Rhavas, her fair hair shining in the sun. Her face stayed stern as a warrior's till Himerios rode past. Then warmth flooded into it. She blew him a kiss. He took off his helmet and bowed in the saddle. It made a pretty picture . . . until Rhavas saw the tears on her cheeks.

Zautzes was also there to watch the garrison depart. The eparch looked like a very unhappy frog. Catching Rhavas' eye, he beckoned him over. The prelate elbowed his way through the crowd.

"What do we do now, very holy sir, if the Halogai swoop down on us?" the eparch inquired.

"Well, most honorable sir, I presume we do the best we can," Rhavas replied.

"Faugh!" Zautzes said, and Rhavas had never heard a more disgusted noise. Zautzes went on, "I can raise up a city militia, and I suppose I will, but asking militiamen to fight without soldiers to stiffen them is like taking a bunch of ropemakers, giving them a dead sheep, and expecting them to cook a tasty supper. You know what the Halogai are like."

Rhavas looked over toward where he'd last seen Ingegerd, but he couldn't spot her now; she must have gone home after her husband rode out of Skopentzana. Only after that half-involuntary glance did the prelate nod. The northern raiders were indeed very ferocious and very dangerous.

"We just have to hope they hold off till we sort through our own troubles," he said. "If Stylianos had stayed loyal, we wouldn't need to worry about any of this. The lord with the great and good mind will remember his treason."

"It's only treason if he loses," Zautzes said. Not for the first time, he was devastatingly cynical. Rhavas started to give back an irate reply, but before he could loose it Zautzes continued, "If Phaos didn't want him to win, he'd lose, right?"

That took things out of the realm of politics and into the realm of theology. Rhavas' anger faded; now he had the chance to teach. "It's not so simple, most honorable sir. We all believe Phos will finally prove stronger than Skotos, and will prevail at the end of days. Light will drive out darkness." He sketched the sun-sign. So did Zautzes. Rhavas plowed ahead: "But Skotos is also a god, and the end of days is not yet. Wickedness may triumph—for a while."

Zautzes stayed cynical, saying, "You do realize, very holy sir, that priests loyal to Stylianos will say it's his Majesty who's Skotos' tool? *I* do not say this, mind you, for I am loyal to Maleinos, but it's an argument with two edges, and it can cut both ways."

"They may say it, yes, but they will be mistaken." Rhavas spoke with great conviction. Doubt was no part of his makeup; once he formed an opinion, he clung to it through thick and thin. "The Avtokrator is Phos' vicegerent on earth, as I have said before. To rebel against him is to rebel against the good god himself."

"You are surely right." By the way Zautzes said it, he wasn't sure of anything of the sort. "His Majesty is a good and worthy ruler, and is bound to do Phaos' work, as you say. But what of the rulers who are wicked tyrants? The Empire of Videssos has known a few."

"As I say, Skotos can have his momentary triumphs." Rhavas spat on the cobblestones in rejection of the dark god. As Zautzes had with the sun-circle, he made haste to follow suit here. Rhavas continued, "You will notice, most honorable sir, that wicked tyrants seldom rule for long. A better ruler commonly takes their place—Phos gains the advantage in the struggle against darkness and evil."

The eparch nodded. His jowls wobbled when he did. "May it be so here," he said, and turned away.

"Yes. May it be so." Rhavas was on the way back to the prelate's residence before he realized Zautzes hadn't said that Maleinos' triumph and the good god's were one and the same. But Zautzes had said earlier that he was loyal to the reigning Avtokrator. He'd done nothing to make Rhavas disbelieve him . . . yet.

And the closer I watch him, the smaller the chance he has to get away with anything like that, the prelate thought.

Waiting for word wasn't easy. It never was. Rhavas tried to keep doing what he did every day, but routine had no flavor for him. He might have been mired in mud. Skopentzana, meanwhile, hurried toward high summer like a lover running to meet his beloved. Days stretched and stretched. The sun rose early in the far northeast and set late in the far southwest. During the brief nights, full darkness hardly came. There was always a hint of twilight in the north.

People said that in the Haloga country, farther north still, the twilight was even brighter, so that a man could read a book at midnight—not that many Halogai could read at any hour of the day or night. People even said that in the far north of Halogaland the sun never set at all during high summer, but skimmed low above the northern horizon and then began to climb again.

Rhavas didn't know whether to believe that. For one thing, it seemed unnatural. But if the sun stayed in the summer sky longer in Skopentzana than in Videssos the city—which it surely did—why shouldn't it stay there all day if one traveled farther north still?

Why? The prelate's chief objection wasn't natural but theological. As long as the sun lingered here in summer, it barely dared show its face come wintertime. On Midwinter's Day, the day of the solstice (and a great festival all over the Empire), it poked its nose up over the horizon, scuttled across the southernmost sky, and then sank again. The prayers that went up hereabouts to save the sun from Skotos were uncommonly sincere.

But suppose the sun never rose at all on Midwinter's Day. Suppose all remained in darkness. Wouldn't that give Skotos untrammeled sway over the world till it returned to the sky once more . . . if it ever did? So Rhavas feared. For that reason, he fought shy of believing in either everlasting summer daylight or unending winter night.

Couriers came to Zautzes and rode out of Skopentzana again. Sometimes the eparch would tell Rhavas what they said, sometimes he wouldn't. His silences made Rhavas fume, but the prelate knew he couldn't do much more than fume. Antagonizing the most powerful civil authority in the city struck him as a bad idea. If Zautzes declared for Stylianos and brought Skopentzana with him, that would be a heavy blow against Maleinos.

One of the ways Skopentzana differed from Videssos the city was that summer rain was common here rather than being a phenomenon talked about for years after it happened. One of Zautzes' secretaries squelched across the square on a drizzly, drippy day to summon Rhavas to the eparch's residence.

"Did he say what this was about?" Rhavas asked eagerly.

"No, very holy sir," the secretary answered. "He just told me to bring you back." Plainly, he couldn't have cared less what the news was. And why should he? Except for the sake of gossip, what difference did it make to him who ruled the Empire?

A hooded cape over his robes, Rhavas followed Zautzes' man through the square. The statues standing there seemed softened by the mist and rain. Even stern Stavrakios turned what felt like a benign eye on the prelate as he passed.

Zautzes bowed to him at the doorway. "Very holy sir," the eparch murmured.

"Most honorable sir," Rhavas replied politely. He tried to keep his tone light as he asked, "You have news?"

"I have news," Zautzes agreed. "Will you come into my office and take some wine with me before you hear it?"

"By your leave, most honorable sir, I would rather not. Tell me here and now and get it over with." Cape dripping on the mosaic floor, Rhavas stood there like a man braced for surgery without even the small balm of henbane and poppy juice.

But the eparch surprised him by giving him a large, froggy smile. Rhavas might have been a particularly delicious bluebottle buzzing around the lily pad. "The news is good, though, very holy sir," Zautzes said.

"Good?" Rhavas spoke the word with suspicion, as if it were not one commonly applied to news.

"Good," Zautzes repeated. "His Majesty has defeated the rebel near Develtos, not too far from Videssos the city, and sent him off in headlong retreat."

To Rhavas, born and raised in the capital, Develtos seemed some distance off to the east, but perspective counted for a good deal. Seen from Skopentzana, Videssos the city and the provincial town weren't that far apart. And the news . . . ! The prelate bowed. "I thank you, most honorable sir. You are right, of course. That is the best of news."

Zautzes' jowls wobbled when he shook his head. "Not quite the best, I'd say. The best would have Stylianos dead on the field and his uprising dead with him. Not quite the best, no, but good. And now, having heard the news, will you drink wine with me to celebrate it?"

"I will, and gladly," Rhavas answered.

He seemed to find a special beauty in the simple ceremony accompanying the wine that Zautzes' servant poured for them. Even spitting in rejection of Skotos took on a new meaning, a new truth. The change wasn't in the ritual or even in the wine, though that was very good. Rhavas needed a little while to realize it, but the change was in himself—he was all but giddy with relief.

"Tell me more," he kept saying to Zautzes. "By the good god, tell me more. Driven off in headlong retreat? Retreat in which direction?"

"Away from the capital, obviously," Zautzes repeated. Rhavas only snorted; that was too obvious even to need saying. The eparch went on, "I've told you everything the dispatch told me. Past that, I would only be guessing."

"Guess, by all means," Rhavas said expansively. Zautzes' eyebrows rose and his bulging eyes widened slightly. The prelate hardly ever offered invitations like that. Rhavas didn't care what he usually did. Today he would feast off the spun sugar of speculation if he couldn't bite down on the meat of fact.

"As long as you know I *am* guessing," Zautzes said, and Rhavas gave him an impatient nod. Screwing up his face in thought, Zautzes continued, "After a defeat like this, not many towns will want to open their gates to Stylianos. He'd have to flee for the frontier, unless I miss my guess. Maybe the soldiers who guard against the Khamorth nomads will keep their affection for him. It's a slim hope, but probably the best one he has."

"What about the barbarians themselves?" Rhavas asked.

"What about 'em?" the eparch returned. "If the frontier troops stay loyal to Maleinos, they'll keep the nomads out. And they'll probably keep them out even if they don't. Why wouldn't they? Stylianos won't want anything like pandering to the savages on his record."

"Yes, that's so. If he wins, he wouldn't want to win with barbarian backing. And if he loses, he only makes his rebellion worse by inciting the Khamorth."

Rhavas remembered that conversation for a long time. Every word he said made good logical sense. He almost always did. But what he reckoned logical and what Stylianos and Maleinos would reckon logical were not precisely the same. Just how far from the same they were would come out in short order.

Being the man he was, Rhavas did sometimes wish that Skopentzana boasted more in the way of books. The northern city had more than he'd expected when he came here, but not enough to satisfy him. Of course, even Videssos the city hadn't had enough to satisfy him. He sometimes thought all the books ever written wouldn't be enough to satisfy him.

One way to solve that problem was to write a book of his own. If he set out the precise relationship between Phos and Skotos and supported it with quotations from the sacred scriptures and from earlier theologians, no one else would need to tackle the job for years. Others had attempted it before him; it was, after all, one of the fundamental issues facing the faith. But none of those learned tomes was learned enough to satisfy him. He wanted his work to be suitable not only for a generation alone but for all time.

He'd finished the manuscript. Despite the trouble he'd had tracking down some of the more arcane references here in Skopentzana, he'd finally managed it. But finishing a book was only the first step in getting it into other people's hands. He had no trouble reading his spidery scrawl. As far as he could tell, that made him a minority of one.

Skopentzana did not boast the swarm of scribes who worked in Videssos the city. The capital also had swarms of secretaries and clerks and other bureaucrats who needed things written but often lacked the time to do the writing themselves. And Videssos the city had more people who could read than any other four places in the Empire put together. Add all that up, and it could support so many scribes. Skopentzana couldn't.

The one Rhavas had chosen to work with was a middle-aged fellow named Digenis. He peered shortsightedly at the prelate when Rhavas strode into his cramped little shop. Only a shortsighted man could stay a scribe once he got into his middle years. Men with normal vision whose sight lengthened lost the ability to read the small scrawl of a manuscript.

"Good morning," Rhavas said.

Digenis brightened. "Ah! Good morning, very holy sir," he said, recognizing Rhavas' voice where he'd had trouble knowing his face. "How are you today?"

"Well enough." Rhavas unbent enough to add, "Perhaps even a bit better than that."

"I am glad to hear it," Digenis said. "Is this on account of the news from the south, very holy sir, or do you also have other reasons?" He was as avid for gossip as any other Videssian. He also had good connections; the news of Maleinos' victory over Stylianos wasn't all through Skopentzana yet.

"I am certainly glad the news from the south is good," Rhavas replied. If he had any other reasons, they were none of Digenis' business. "Can you give me more news to make me happy? How is my book coming?"

"It's coming well, very holy sir," the scribe told him. "I do have to interrupt it every now and then to take on some small project that will put gold in my belt pouch, but I always return to it as soon as the other work is done."

Rhavas made a discontented noise. He'd paid Digenis in the usual way for a long work: half at the beginning, half when the book was done. That had been a while ago now; of course the scribe would have gone through most of the first installment by this time. Part of Rhavas wished he'd given Digenis the whole fee at the start. The rest, the cynical part, wondered if the other man would have lifted a finger to write if he had.

"How are you coping with my hand?" the prelate asked.

"It gets easier as I go along. I'm used to it now," Digenis answered. "Meaning no offense, though, I still think I'll make my second copy from my first, and not from your original."

"You may do that—after I've been through your first to correct your errors," Rhavas said in a voice like all the worst parts of Skopentzana winter.

He waited to see if Digenis would swell up with indignation and deny he would make any. Some scribes labored under the delusion that they were perfect. More wanted their clients to labor under that delusion. Rhavas knew better. He had yet to see a book with no scribal errors. Most of the books he'd seen held quite a few. He was ready to sound even icier than he had already if Digenis tried to claim *he* was somehow set above the common run of pen pushers. *Perfection is reserved for Phos alone* made a good opening. He could go on from there, too.

But he turned out not to need to. Digenis said only, "Well, I hope you won't find too many of them, very holy sir."

Rhavas felt like a trotting horse getting ready to gallop that was suddenly told it had to walk instead. "So do I," he said gruffly.

"Interesting, reading what you have to say," Digenis remarked. "Half the time—more than half the time—you know, a scribe doesn't pay any attention to what he's copying. The words go from your eyes to your hand. You don't think about them in between. I started out like that with your book, too. I couldn't keep it up. What I saw *made* me think about what I was writing. I couldn't help it."

"For which I thank you." Rhavas was flattered, but not particularly surprised. Videssians were mad for theology: not just priests but potters and farm wives coming into town to sell cabbages. The ones who had their letters—and some of the ones who didn't—could reason with surprising sophistication, too. Rhavas couldn't help asking, "And what do you think?"

"You argue very strongly," Digenis replied. "If anything, I think you make Phaos too strong in the world as it is. He will win in the end, surely—I am orthodox. But the end is not yet. Skotos remains a potent foe." He spat on the floor after naming the dark god.

"Good *is* stronger than evil. We see it every day," Rhavas declared.

"Anyone would know you come from a rich family, very holy sir," the scribe said in a low voice.

The prelate wasn't sure he should have heard that. He was sure it made no difference, which went some way toward proving Digenis' point.

✦ ▌▌

Day followed day. Rhavas never stopped exclaiming when fogs and rain came to Skopentzana even in the summertime. "Anybody would know you came from Videssos the city, very holy sir," Zautzes said when they met by Stavrakios' statue one misty morning.

The prelate frowned. Someone else had said something like that to him not long before. He couldn't recall who, or why. Not being able to recall annoyed him, as it always did. "What is the news?" he asked the prefect. His breath smoked when he spoke. That would never have happened in summer in the capital, either.

"Not much," Zautzes answered. "The only thing I'm sure I can truthfully tell you is that Stylianos hasn't given up the fight. The war goes on."

"Too bad." Rhavas meant that with every fiber of his being. "I'd hoped he would see he can't win and give up the fight."

"Even if he does see he can't win, he may not give up," Zautzes pointed out. "What can a rebel expect if he tries to surrender? The sword, little else. Maybe exile to a monastery if he's very, very lucky. With that to look forward to, why not hope for a lucky break?"

Rhavas frowned again, not because he didn't agree but because he did. "If Stylianos' followers see he cannot win, they'll abandon him," he said. "Then he'll have no choice but surrendering or trying to disappear."

"No doubt you're right," Zautzes said. "It hasn't happened yet, though—or if it has, I haven't heard of it."

"Nor I." Rhavas tried hard not to let his irritation show. News came slowly to Skopentzana. It was too far from places that mattered to expect anything else. The prelate knew as much. He'd understood it when he came here; it was one of the reasons he'd been so much less than delighted to come here. Through all the years since, it had bothered him less often than he'd expected it to. Of course, those years had been quiet. The Empire of Videssos was quiet no more.

"One good thing . . ." Zautzes said.

"I'd gladly hear anything good," Rhavas said. "What is it?"

"That the Halogai *are* quiet," the prefect answered. "You always worry that a rebel down on his luck will send lieutenants over the border and bring barbarians back into the Empire." Rhavas had seen that he wasn't a particularly pious man. The eparch sketched the sun-circle even so, to turn aside the evil omen.

Matching the gesture, Rhavas said, "What of the Khamorth? Stylianos always had more to do with the nomads than with the wolves of the north."

Zautzes looked west, toward the broad plains of Pardraya. Again, Rhavas did the same thing. No Videssian could say with certainty how far those plains ran, or what lay at the far end of them—if they had a far end. Writers with more imagination than sense peopled the distant steppe with dog-faced men and web-footed men who lived in the rivers and men with no heads but with faces in the middle of their chests. Rhavas didn't believe in any of those prodigies, but he couldn't prove they were only imaginary.

Slowly, the eparch said, "I can hope he wouldn't want to bring them into the fight. When you deal with Khamorth, you're always liable to get more than you bargained for."

Now Rhavas glanced toward the sun, which was trying to burn its way through the morning mist. The disc was dim enough to let him look at it without hurting his eyes. Just as it had more radiance than it was showing, so the steppe nomads could indeed cause more trouble than those who tried to deal with them often looked for. One clan chief, or two, or three, might sign their men up as mercenaries. That was all right. But if they found the pickings good, more nomads might follow, and still more, until Videssos had to try to drive them back beyond the frontiers. That had happened more than once since Stavrakios' day.

"How much of the Empire would be nothing but grazing land if the Khamorth had their way?" Rhavas asked.

"If the Khamorth had their way? Why, all of it, very holy sir," Zautzes answered.

Again, he was bound to be right. He was telling an unpleasant amount of truth this morning. Rhavas' gaze went to the great statue of Stavrakios. The conqueror seemed ready to go to war on the instant—or he would have if a pigeon hadn't perched on the palm of his left hand.

"Well, we wouldn't want our lives to be dull all the time, would we?" Rhavas inquired.

"My personal life? No," Zautzes said. "My professional life? My professional life is a very different story. If nothing happened in my professional life, that would prove I was doing an excellent job."

Rhavas raised an eyebrow, but the eparch plainly wasn't joking. Rhavas still had many things he wanted to accomplish in *his* professional life. That book Digenis the scribe was copying was only the beginning. He still aspired to more scholarship, and to donning the patriarchal regalia one day. Poor Zautzes! He had no hope of rising further. He would never become a provincial governor or a minister in Videssos the city. Torpor and inactivity were the most he had to look forward to.

Fortunately, the eparch had no idea what Rhavas was thinking. Long years in and around the imperial court had taught the prelate how not to let his face show what went on behind it—a talent that had its uses in the ecclesiastical hierarchy, too. Zautzes said, "I don't think we need to worry much about the plainsmen. Stylianos knows better than to summon them, and, ah, they know better than to come into Videssos on their own."

The little catch in his voice gave him away. He'd started to say that the rebel had taught them not to come into Videssos on their own—that or something very much like it. He'd checked himself, but not quite soon enough. Rhavas' somber countenance hid a smile now. Zautzes had just shown why he'd never rise higher than eparch.

"If the lord with the great and good mind is kind to us, soon this civil war will be gone and forgotten," Rhavas said. "Then we won't have to worry about an irruption of nomads off the steppe."

"May it be so, very holy sir." No matter what Zautzes thought, he couldn't very well disagree with the Avtokrator's cousin. And no Videssian, regardless of whether he favored Maleinos or Stylianos, could possibly want the Khamorth rampaging through the Empire. As the mist slowly cleared, Zautzes also looked up to the statue of Stavrakios. "*He'd* make mincemeat out of anybody who tried to cause trouble for the Empire."

"Wouldn't he just?" Rhavas agreed. The conqueror had had a driving intensity no Avtokrator since had been able to match. He'd beaten the Makuraners in the far west and sacked Mashiz, their capital. He'd smashed the Khamorth at the edge of the steppe. And his fleets of war galleys had trounced the Halogai again and again. No other Videssian ruler had given himself over to war so completely.

"But he's not here," Zautzes said, which was another obvious truth. "We have to do the best we can on our own."

"We can. We will. And it will be good enough." Rhavas spoke confidently. The eparch nodded.

Men and women lingered in the narthex of Skopentzana's chief temple after the divine liturgy. Husbands met wives descending from the women's gallery. Brothers met sisters. And young men and young women not formally related to one another got to look as much as they wanted, which didn't happen many other places in Videssian towns.

Rhavas knew all this, knew it and paid hardly more attention to it than to the air he breathed. *His* duty in the narthex was talking about the sermon and, with the more prosperous members of the congregation, about donations. This wasn't one of his favorite parts of the job. It was, he knew, one of the reasons he'd been sent to Skopentzana. If he couldn't do it here, he wouldn't be able to do it at the High Temple, either.

By now, he was good enough at it. He listened with half an ear, nodding in all the right places, as a plump fur merchant who'd got rich trading with the Halogai went on and on about the sermon. Like so many Videssians, the fur trader fancied himself a theologian. Like a lot of them, he was mistaken.

When Rhavas first came to Skopentzana, he would have pointed that out in biting detail. No more. He wanted the locals to stay happy with him. If they were happy with him, they were likelier to stay happy with the Avtokrator Maleinos, too. Skopentzana had no garrison inside it, not anymore. A citizens' rising could bring it over to Stylianos' side. Anything Rhavas could do to stop that, he would.

A flash of gilt hair distracted him from the long-winded fur trader. That was probably lucky for the merchant, who was drifting so close to out-and-out heresy that Rhavas had an ever harder time holding his tongue. Videssians were a swarthy folk, almost all of them brunets. Ingegerd always stood out among them.

"Excuse me, if you'd be so kind," Rhavas told the trader, and stepped away before the man had a chance to answer. He nodded to Himerios' wife. "I hope the sermon pleased you."

"As always, you speak well," Ingegerd answered seriously. "I still find it strange to have the good god's ways and powers spoken of so openly. In Halogaland, the gods are the gods. Everyone knows what they can do, but no one talks about it very much."

"This is not Halogaland, I am glad to say," Rhavas told her. "We want to know Phos' will as well as we can. This lets us precisely follow it."

"So you say. But I sometimes think you Videssians spend so much time arguing about the lord with the great and good mind for no better reason than that you like to argue." Ingegerd's smile took most of the sting from her words—most, but not all.

Rhavas might have got angry at her if he hadn't had the same thought himself while listening to the fur trader. "We will argue about almost anything," he admitted, "but some things are more important than others." He paused for a moment. "I hope you are doing well?"

"As well as I can be, with Himerios away," she answered. Those startling blue eyes darkened, as if a shadow had crossed across the sun. "But I have no word of him. All I can do is wait and worry."

"And pray," Rhavas said stiffly.

"And pray," Ingegerd agreed. "But so many prayers go up to Phos. Who can say whether he will have time to bother with mine? Will you pray for Himerios, too, please? You are a very holy man, very holy sir, so the good god is likelier to listen to you than he is to me."

Is she mocking me? Rhavas wondered. The playful way she used his title suggested that she was. She sounded serious, though. He wanted to scratch his head. He didn't understand her. He didn't understand women generally, but he also didn't understand how thoroughly he didn't understand. With her, unlike the general case, his incomprehension was clear to him. Voice gruff, he said, "I will pray for him."

Ingegerd dropped a curtsy. "I thank you, very holy sir." She swept away, majestic as a ship under full sail.

As Rhavas watched her go, behind him the fur trader grumbled out loud to a friend or perhaps to his wife: "Calls himself a holy man—expects other people to call him a holy man, by the good god—but he'd sooner talk to that foreign chippy than he would to me. Oh, yes! I'll bet he would! And that's not all he'd sooner do to her, either, or I miss my guess."

Slowly, Rhavas turned. He remembered the mosaicwork image of Phos stern in judgment in the great dome of the High Temple. No mere mortal could rest easy under that magnificent, unforgiving gaze. At the moment, he himself might have been its incarnation. Under his eyes, blood drained from the fur trader's face, leaving it corpse-pale. "Did you say something that had to do with me?" Rhavas inquired into sudden, vast silence.

He waited, clinically curious: how much nerve did the trader have? Enough to challenge him to his face? He didn't think so, and he proved right. Still pale and frightened, the man shook his head, muttering, "No, very holy sir, not me. You, uh, you must have heard wrong."

"Must I?" Rhavas gravely considered the notion. "Well, I suppose it is possible. Not likely, mind you, but possible."

He didn't quite call the fur trader a liar, but he didn't miss by much, either. The man scuttled out of the narthex, scuttled out of the temple. Rhavas would have been amazed if he ever came here to worship again. The prelate dared hope the man would go to some other temple to offer up praises to Phos. Rhavas didn't want to swing the trader's soul toward Skotos.

After starting to spit in rejection of the dark god, Rhavas arrested the gesture. The rest of the people watching him would think he used it to condemn the fur trader. Rhavas didn't want that; the man had done a perfectly good job of condemning himself.

Later—much later—Rhavas would wonder whether that moment hadn't been an odd sort of watershed. He would search his memory to see if he hadn't felt some small premonition. And, search as he would, he would come up empty again and again. He hadn't known. He hadn't even suspected. What sort of man could see into the future? A soothsayer? Yes . . . and no. Rhavas remembered too well what had happened to Eladas. If the man hadn't frightened himself to death . . .

For some reason, no one else that morning had much in the way of queries for Rhavas. The narthex, in fact, emptied with startling speed. A priest smiled at the prelate and said, "You should put the fear of Phos in them more often, very holy sir. We'd have more time to ourselves that way."

Rhavas looked through him, as he'd looked through the fur trader. "You tend to your business, Oriphas. I will tend to the temple's business."

Where the trader had turned white, Oriphas turned red. That showed a bit more spirit, anyhow. The priest's chin lifted in pride. "I meant no harm, very holy sir," he said. "Just—a bit of a joke, you might say."

"*You* might say so, perhaps," Rhavas replied, and Oriphas went redder yet. The junior priest bowed, as if to say he gave respect even where it might not be deserved. Rhavas bowed back, as if to say he cared not a fig for Oriphas' opinions—which he didn't. Seeing as much, Oriphas stalked away in a snit.

Sometimes Rhavas' temper would stay kindled for a long time. Sometimes, indeed, he never forgave at all. Here, though, he let out a long sigh. By then, the narthex was altogether empty, so there was no one to hear it. He knew he would have to find some way to come to terms with the priest. Oriphas hadn't been doctrinally incorrect, only impolite. If Skotos held power over every man who was impolite, then how few would cross the Bridge of the Separator and attain to Phos' heaven? Very few, Rhavas feared.

And if that was so . . . A logically trained mind pursued an idea wherever it led. If only a handful attained to Phos' heaven—so what? Would they not be all the more special for being an elect?

Rhavas liked the idea. But he frowned again, at himself this time. Was it theologically sound? Could Phos triumph in the end if most souls tumbled down to the eternal ice? How?

The prelate sighed. The alternative seemed to be making most men better than they really were. That was what the lord with the great and good mind always sought to do. What sort of success even the good god found . . .

Skotos, on the other hand, tried to make men worse than they really were. When Rhavas was in a gloomy mood, he thought the dark god found altogether too much success. When he felt more cheerful, he reminded himself that mere men were only men, and that they were not and could not be perfect. They did have to try, and—he supposed—most of them did most of the time.

When Rhavas walked back into the main hall of the temple and up the aisle toward the altar, he was the only one there. His sandals' soles slapped against the flagstones of the aisle. He never would have noticed the sound when the temple was full; now echoes came back from walls and ceiling.

His eyes went to the images of the good god that filled the temple. Phos stared back at him, again and again and again. Rhavas bowed his head, hoping to know the all-enfolding comfort communion with Phos could bring. But he'd returned to the temple in the wrong mood. Despite that multitude of images, he felt very much alone.

Every time Rhavas saw a courier ride up to Zautzes' residence, he worried. Couriers came fairly often. Civil war or no civil war, the business of the Empire went on. The eparch didn't bother telling him about most of the messages. In some towns, the prelate would have done as much governing as the eparch, but Zautzes was touchy about his prerogatives. Rhavas didn't push him; administering the temples and monasteries in Skopentzana gave the prelate plenty to do.

Rhavas was out in the square talking with a couple of merchants when a rider came galloping by and tied his horse in front of the eparch's residence. The man ran inside. One of the merchants chuckled and remarked, "Somebody put scorpions in his drawers."

That made the other trader—a dealer in amber—laugh, too. "He's got something that needs telling, all right," he agreed.

"I wonder what it could be," Rhavas said.

Both merchants shrugged. The one who'd spoken of scorpions said, "We'll find out pretty quick. Zautzes can't keep a secret to save his skin. And even if he could, his guards'll blab in the taverns."

They were thinking of ordinary things—of the duty on goods coming into Videssos from Halogaland, maybe, or a change in the rate of the hearth tax. Rhavas had other worries. When he saw a courier in a hurry . . . "Maybe it's news of the Avtokrator's fight against the usurper."

The merchants shrugged again. The amber dealer said, "What if it is? One of them will win, and then things will quiet down again." He plainly didn't care whether the winner was Maleinos or Stylianos.

His colleague nudged him and whispered in his ear. He turned red. Both of them said hasty good-byes to Rhavas. The prelate knew exactly what had happened there. The amber dealer had forgotten—or perhaps hadn't known—he was related to Maleinos. The other trader had set him straight, whereupon they'd both decided they had urgent business somewhere else.

It wasn't the first time time such things had happened to Rhavas. He knew it wouldn't be the last. What he didn't know was what news the courier had brought to the eparch.

He started across the square. He hadn't got far when one of the guards purposefully strode his way. The man waved. "Hello, very holy sir," he called. "The eparch would like a word with you."

"What a coincidence," Rhavas said dryly. "I would like a word with the eparch, too. I would like that very much."

Ignoring the sarcasm in Rhavas' voice, the guard nodded and said, "Then please come with me." He ceremoniously led the prelate in the direction he was already going. The other guards bowed to Rhavas as he went by. He responded with a dip of the head he'd cribbed from his imperial cousin.

In Zautzes' study sat a thin, travel-worn man who was improving his morning with a cup of wine. Zautzes himself was also drinking one. He had the look of a very unhappy frog. After shouting for a servant and sending the man after wine for Rhavas, the eparch said, "The news isn't good, very holy sir."

"By your manner, most honorable sir, I hadn't expected that it would be." Rhavas perched on a stool and swung toward the courier. "I presume you will be able to give me the details?"

"What I know of them, yes." The man looked weary unto death. How far and how fast had he ridden? He took a long pull at the winecup. The servant came in just then with another cup, this one for Rhavas. As he took it with a murmur of thanks, the courier went on, "The core of it is, the Avtokrator's been beaten. Badly beaten. It happened near a place called Imbros, northeast of Videssos the city."

"Oh, yes," Rhavas said quietly. "I know of Imbros."

"Then you'll know it's on the highway running back to the capital." The courier waited for Rhavas to nod, then continued, "It was a running fight most of the way there. Stylianos kept trying to get men around behind his Majesty and cut him off from Videssos the city. Maleinos' men had to fight their way through a couple of times, but the rebels never quite blocked their path."

"Phos be praised for that." Rhavas wanted to gulp his own wine, but made himself go through the usual ritual beforehand. He shivered, though Zautzes' study was warm enough. Had Maleinos been trapped away from the capital, Stylianos would be Avtokrator of the Videssians now, with no one to challenge him. The prelate said, "So Maleinos *is* safely inside Videssos the city?"

"He is, very holy sir, yes," the courier answered, and yawned an enormous yawn. "Excuse me. Like I say, he's back there now, but his army took a beating in the battle, and then took a worse one in the pursuit. He'll have to do some serious recruiting and mustering before he can face Stylianos in the open field again."

"The westlands . . ." Rhavas and Zautzes said the same thing at the same time. The lands on the far side of the strait called the Cattle-Crossing were rich in men, and rich in horses, too.

But the courier, instead of encouraging the two leaders of Skopentzana, only shrugged. "There's word Stylianos has lieutenants in the westlands himself. This fight fills the whole Empire."

It hadn't yet filled the far northeast. Indeed, it had already emptied Skopentzana of soldiers. Rhavas said, "If the Avtokrator can't recruit in the westlands, where will he draw more men?"

Another shrug from the courier, one that showed even raising and lowering his shoulders took effort. He said, "It's a good question, very holy sir. Too bad I haven't got a good answer for you."

"You're from the city, aren't you?" Rhavas asked. The man nodded, also effortfully. Rhavas wasn't sure what made him think so. Not the courier's accent—that intonation had spread from Videssos the city for miles around on both sides of the Cattle-Crossing. But the cheeky way he'd finished his reply: yes, that sort of attitude belonged to the capital alone.

"Where do we go from here?" Zautzes asked.

The courier yawned again. "Me, I'd like to go to bed," he said.

Zautzes called for a servant. The man took the courier off to a guest room. The eparch went out and spoke to the guards. They took charge of the rider's hard-used horse; Rhavas watched them lead the poor beast past the study window toward the stables. Zautzes came back shaking his head. He stared down into his winecup, as if the answer to the mystery of life might lurk inside. People uncounted had sought it in wine, but nobody had found it there. Plaintively, he repeated, "Where *do* we go from here?"

"By the good god, most honorable sir, I don't know what to tell you now," Rhavas replied. "Stylianos has proved stronger than I thought. All we can do is wait to see who wins. I still pray my cousin does. If he doesn't . . ." The prelate shrugged. "If he doesn't, the usurper will do with me as he wills. Since you aren't connected to Maleinos by blood, you should be safe enough either way."

"His Majesty appointed me. I am known to be loyal to him. I *am* loyal to him," Zautzes said. "If we were in the westlands, we could flee to Makuran if things didn't turn out the way we hoped."

Rhavas nodded. Videssians fleeing political convulsions often took refuge in the other great civilized empire. Makuraner Kings of Kings sometimes used them as cat's-paws and stalking horses against Videssos. In the same way, Makuraner grandees were known to flee to Videssos, and Avtokrators happily used them against their old homeland.

"If things go badly wrong, you could run off to Halogaland," Rhavas said.

By the face Zautzes made, he might have smelled stale fish. "All things considered, very holy sir, I do believe I'd sooner face the headsman's sword."

Rhavas nodded once more. He felt the same way. Videssians in dire straits *had* gone to live among the blond barbarians, but a man would have to be truly desperate to do such a thing. Rhavas tried to imagine himself living in a smoke-filled longhouse;

learning the slow, sonorous tongue of the Halogai; forgetting books, wine, good talk, and everything else that made life worth living. The picture refused to form in his mind.

If a fugitive fell in love with a blue-eyed woman, she might help him forget all he'd left behind. Rhavas tried to imagine *that* for himself: one more picture that wouldn't form. For him, falling in love with a Haloga woman—indeed, with any woman—would mean abandoning his priestly vows, in effect abandoning his god.

"You're right," he said to Zautzes. "Death is better than some ways of holding on to life."

Before the eparch could answer, his servant slipped into the study with a carafe of wine. Smooth and silent as a ghost, the man refilled the eparch's cup and, when Rhavas nodded, the prelate's as well. Then he disappeared again. Zautzes sipped and sighed. "Maybe it won't come to that. I hope it won't come to that. I pray it won't come to that."

"Yes." Rhavas intended to spend more time prostrated before Phos' holy altar in the temple, and in his bedchamber before images of the good god and the holy men who'd served him. But prayer went only so far. Maleinos needed action, too. "Where will his Majesty come by more soldiers if he can't get many from the westlands?"

"I wish I could tell you," Zautzes said. "If he ordered the garrison out of a distant city like Skopentzana, he will have summoned men from closer towns, too. That leaves . . . I don't know what that leaves."

"The men from the frontier posts," Rhavas said. Now he was the one to look as if he smelled something nasty.

"It's possible that Stylianos has already summoned them. Many of them will have served under him and will be well-disposed toward him. Maybe they gave him the help he needed to beat his Majesty in this latest battle."

"Yes, you could be right." Rhavas' face didn't lose that expression. "I am sad to think even a rebel would strip the frontier bare." He'd thought about it for Maleinos. He hadn't liked it, but he'd thought about it. Why was he surprised Stylianos might have thought about it, too, and might have done something about it?

Because Maleinos is the Avtokrator, and is blood of my blood. He answered his own question almost at once. *Stylianos is a man who would murder his way to the throne.* His own grandmother's brother had murdered his way to the throne. He knew that, but once more chose not to think about it.

Zautzes said, "Any man will worry first about the enemy closest to him. Once he beats that one, he will think he can take care of any other troubles he may have."

"You could be right there, too. I—" Rhavas broke off.

"What?" the eparch asked.

"Nothing. Nothing that matters." Rhavas seldom lied, and didn't do it as well as a lot of Videssians. Zautzes raised an eyebrow, sure the prelate wasn't telling the truth. Rhavas' ears got hot. With his tonsure, Zautzes might have been able to watch his blush rise all the way to the top of his head. Rhavas kept quiet even so. He'd started to talk about the soothsayer, and about the question he'd asked the luckless man. But no. Zautzes didn't need to know that.

Rhavas had thought about summoning another soothsayer and asking him the same thing. He didn't have the nerve. If one man died while trying to see whether he would be patriarch, it was happenstance, coincidence, chance. But Rhavas couldn't forget the terror on Eladas' face and in his icy grip as he died. If another soothsayer tried to see the same thing and also died trying . . . Rhavas didn't want that to happen, and didn't want to have to worry about it if it did.

Zautzes visibly thought about pressing him on it, and just as visibly decided not to. "Well, very holy sir, we'll just have to wait and see what happens down in the south, as you said yourself. Once we know that, we'll have a better notion of what we ought to do." The eparch's laugh held a hollow undertone. "Who knows? Maybe Halogaland won't look so bad after all."

"I may grow desperate enough to do a great many things," Rhavas said with as much dignity as he had in him. "By the lord with the great and good mind, I will never grow desperate enough to run away to Halogaland."

A time would come when he'd wish he had never said that.

Skopentzana went on about its business as if the civil war convulsing most of the Empire were happening in distant Makuran. That was the one advantage Rhavas had ever found in living in a city so far from the imperial heartland. Interesting things passed Skopentzana by, but so did troubles.

The prelate could walk through any of the city's markets and watch Videssians and tall, blond Halogai and even a few swarthy, stocky, bushy-bearded Khamorth haggling over amber and furs and wine and jewelry and horseflesh and weapons and a thousand other goods. Everything seemed the way it had the year before, when peace pervaded Videssos. He wished the reality matched the seeming.

As days grew longer with astonishing speed when spring burgeoned here, so the hours of light shrank quickly as autumn approached. Birds began flying south. Nights grew chilly. Days had never got hot, not to a man used to the scorching, muggy summers of Videssos the city. Now they had trouble feeling anything but cool.

On the farms around Skopentzana, peasants began bringing in the harvest of barley and rye and oats. Few dared plant wheat here, for the growing season proved long enough to let it ripen only about every other year. Autumn harvests still sometimes made Rhavas feel as if the world had turned upside down and inside out. Down around Videssos the city, fall and winter were the rainy seasons, and farmers brought in their crops in the springtime.

He often grew tired of rye bread and oatmeal and chewy barley cakes. He drank wine whenever he could. For a man of wealth, that was most of the time. Because he could drink wine so much, he didn't have to grow tired of the beer the locals brewed from barley. He could tolerate it, but he'd never got a taste for it. After wine, it was nasty, sour stuff. He and Zautzes didn't agree on everything, but they were in perfect accord there. Even praying for a good crop of barley smacked of hypocrisy to him.

Ingegerd, now, took barley altogether for granted. In conversations in the narthex, Rhavas learned she'd bought a lot of barley for brewing: more than for baking. "In Halogaland, beer was all we had," she told him. "I do not think I tasted wine above once or twice before I came down into the Empire. Wine was—is—only for the chieftains, the big men, there."

"What a benighted place!" Rhavas burst out, and only later hoped he hadn't offended her.

Fortunately for him, she answered with a matter-of-fact nod. "I know that now," she said. "I did not know it then. How could

I? Halogaland was all I had seen. If one place is the whole world to you, you cannot think it fine or dreadful, not in any real way. Would we know how good Phos is if we did not have Skotos to compare him to?" She spat.

So did Rhavas, for whom the gesture was almost as ingrained as breathing. He didn't answer at once. She'd framed the question in a way that hadn't occurred to him. As far as he knew, it hadn't occurred to any other Videssian theologians, either. After his pause for thought, he said, "Phos is goodness absolute. We deny that at peril to our souls."

"I do not deny it, very holy sir," Ingegerd said steadily. "But would we understand *how* good he is if we did not see what went on in the world where goodness is not? I have seen horrors. Surely you have as well."

Rhavas hadn't, or not many; he'd lived a sheltered, prosperous life. He nodded even so; he followed where she was going. He said, "You believe good seems sweeter after evil, as wine seems sweeter after a taste of, uh, salt fish." He'd started to compare it to beer. That would have been fine in the capital, but not even with most Videssians born in Skopentzana.

"Yes, that is what I mean," Ingegerd agreed.

"The wine would be as sweet even without the fish," Rhavas said.

"My point is not what it would be but how it would seem," she replied.

To Rhavas, things were what they were. How they seemed mattered much less. He and the woman from Halogaland eyed each other in exasperation tinged with respect. He was the one who changed the subject, asking, "Have you had word of your husband?"

She shook her head. Her unbound hair flew like a shower of gold. "Nothing," she said. "And, with the turning of the seasons, I doubt I will hear, not till spring. I pray he is safe."

"So do I," said Rhavas, who had indeed offered up prayers for Himerios.

"I thank you for that, very holy sir." With Haloga fatalism, Ingegerd added, "In any case, it will be as it is."

"It will be as the lord with the great and good mind wills it to be," Rhavas said, a touch of sternness in his voice.

Hearing him take that tone would have made any of the priests who served under him quail. Ingegerd only nodded, equal to equal. "We said the same thing with different words, I think."

"Well, maybe we did." Rhavas found he didn't want to get into an argument with her. She was no trained theologian. The prelate didn't know whether she could read and write. But she had a formidable native intelligence. She thought straight, too, which many couldn't do. She would follow her logic wherever it took her, and she would face without fear whatever she found at the end.

Would I challenge her more directly if she were a man? Rhavas wondered. He couldn't remember the last time he'd backed away from a dispute. Backing away wasn't usually in his nature. Slowly, he shook his head. It wasn't that she was a woman. He'd got into disputations with women who fancied themselves theologians both back in Videssos the city and here in Skopentzana. He'd sent more than a few of them off in tears, too; when he did argue, he pulled no punches.

What, then? Before he could find anything that might be an answer, Ingegerd dipped her head to him and swept out of the temple. A man who smelled of onions came up and bent his ear about something or other. He made responses that seemed to satisfy the odorous Videssian, and then forgot about him as soon as he took himself and his smell away.

When Rhavas got back to his residence, he found he couldn't remember any of the conversations he'd had after Ingegerd left. He'd been thinking about her, and about why he didn't want to argue with her, to the exclusion of almost everything else.

The answer, though, came to him as he was drifting toward sleep, when he wasn't thinking about it at all. He sat bolt upright in his dark bedchamber. "Phos!" he exclaimed, and sketched the sun-circle over his heart.

He'd asked himself the wrong question back in the narthex. It should have been, *Would I challenge her more directly if I didn't want her?*

There in the blackness—a blackness that reminded him too much of Skotos—he prayed and prayed and prayed, sleep forgotten. Celibacy had never been too hard for him, never till now. He'd scorned those who let their fallible flesh come between themselves and their devotion to the good god. Now, all unawares, he'd fallen into the same trap himself.

"She must never know," he whispered in the darkness. "No one must ever know." But the person who most needed not to know was himself, and he had no idea how to make that so.

Some of the troop of men who rode south through Skopent-zana were Videssians: soldiers of a sort Rhavas had seen many times. Some were Halogai, with whom he was also familiar—big, burly blond men with their hair swinging in thick braids behind them. They wore mailshirts and carried long-handled war axes. And some could have been one or the other or both—as on any frontier, there were men of mixed blood along the border between the Empire of Videssos and Halogaland.

A narrow-faced Videssian named Petinos commanded the troop. He came to Rhavas' temple to pray. The prelate invited him back to his residence for some wine. "Yes, we were ordered out of the frontier forts," the officer said in response to Rhavas' question. "We left behind what garrisons we could, but . . ." He shrugged.

"How soon before the Halogai take advantage of the border's being stripped?" Rhavas asked. "It won't be long, will it?"

Petinos only shrugged once more. "No one will move fast on the northern frontier after winter closes down, not even the blond barbarians. If the good god is kind, we may have those forts manned again by spring. Plenty of time for fighting down in the south, and that may give us an answer before the Halogai start stirring."

"And if it doesn't?" Rhavas said.

The borderers' officer shrugged yet again. "If there is no answer by spring, very holy sir, my men and I will still be down in the south. What happens up here won't be our worry anymore. But, I'm afraid, it will be yours."

Rhavas glared at him. Petinos looked back, imperturbable. Rhavas said, "This is not the feeling you should show for your fellow man."

"My fellow man sent me to the chilblain capital of the world," Petinos retorted. Rhavas wondered what he'd done to deserve getting sent to the farthest northeast. Zautzes might know; he paid more attention to that kind of gossip than Rhavas did. Petinos went on, "Now that my fellow man has seen fit to call me back to something approaching civilization, what can I do but thank him kindly? As for folk still stuck up here . . . I am sorry for you. The difference is, now I don't have to be sorry for myself, too."

That sort of ruthless pragmatism struck Rhavas as more typical of the Halogai than of Videssians. More of the north had rubbed off on Petinos than he was willing to admit—more, perhaps, than he knew. Rhavas said, "You do know the border troops have been pulled not just from this frontier but also from the one facing the Pardrayan steppe?"

"*What?*" Petinos started. His hand jerked so that wine almost sloshed out of his cup. He needed what looked like a distinct effort of will to steady himself. Slowly, he said, "No, very holy sir, I did not know that. No one had seen fit to tell it to me. Are things really so bad?"

"They aren't good, by all the signs." Rhavas didn't want to say even so much, but he didn't want to lie, either. "Even the rebel would not have done such a thing without gravest need."

"Meaning no offense, but it could be a need that puts a lot of people in the grave," Petinos said. "The Khamorth won't care whether it's summer or winter. They're on the move the year around, and live off the flocks they drive with them. If the frontier is empty, what's to stop them from swarming into the Empire? Once they're in, they'd be bloody hard to drive out, too."

In a low, troubled voice, Rhavas answered, "I'm afraid this thought also crossed my mind. I was hoping you would tell me it was so much moonshine, all wind and air—shadow, not substance."

"Phos! I wish I could, not for your sake—meaning no offense again, I'm sure—but because this could be the worst thing that's happened to Videssos in a very long time." Petinos tilted back his head, emptied the silver winecup at one long draught, and then poured it full again. "If Maleinos and Stylianos keep hammering away at each other, who will drive the nomads back to the plains where they belong? Will anyone?"

He didn't answer his own question. He didn't have to; the answer hung in the air regardless of whether he came out and said it. *No.*

Rhavas reached for the jar of wine, too. Most of the time, he was as stern with himself on such indulgences as he was with anyone else. Today? Today another cup of wine seemed not an indulgence but an anodyne. He wouldn't have begrudged it to a man facing the surgeon's knife, and felt himself—and the Empire—in much the same predicament.

The wine did help steady him. Setting down the cup, he said, "Phos must have prepared this great test of life for the whole Empire."

"Either that or Skotos is working something particularly nasty against us." Petinos spat.

So did Rhavas. "May it not come to pass!" he said. "Skotos may win battles, but surely everything we see in life proves that the lord with the great and good mind will triumph in the end."

"Surely," Petinos echoed. Rhavas sent him a sharp look. Petinos didn't sound as if he agreed. He sounded like a man pretending to agree so he wouldn't have to argue, or maybe like a man who said one thing but meant exactly the opposite.

Most of the time, Rhavas would have lit into him for such hypocrisy. Today, he let it pass. If Petinos wanted to endanger his soul, if he wanted to risk falling down to Skotos' eternal darkness and ice, that was his affair. Rhavas had more urgent things to worry about himself.

He worried even more when the detachment of frontier troops Petinos led marched out of Skopentzana. The gates swung shut behind the soldiers. The thud of those two great valves closing sounded dreadfully final in Rhavas' ears. It might have said the city would never again see imperial soldiers.

As a matter of fact, it said just that. No one knew it, though, not even Rhavas. Sometimes, as Eladas the soothsayer could have testified were he still among the living, *not* knowing what lay ahead was the greater mercy.

Spring in Skopentzana always seemed to last longer than it really did. It stretched ahead to the promise of summer. Autumn, by contrast, felt foreshortened. All that lay ahead of autumn was winter, and everyone in Skopentzana knew winter much too well.

Firsts came thick and fast in autumn. First leaves changing color. First leaves falling from the trees. First frost. First bare trees. They all came together in a few hectic weeks.

Some years, a hailstorm would wedge its way into the schedule. That could mean disaster and famine if it came early and ruined the harvest. This year, no natural catastrophe visited itself among Skopentzana.

That reassured Rhavas less than it might have. Skopentzana and the Empire of Videssos needed no natural catastrophes to be miserable, not this year. They had far more than their fair share of man-made catastrophes.

The first snowfall, nearly two months before the winter solstice, was slight and soon melted. Some years, weather almost summery came hard on the heels of a snowstorm like that. Sometimes it lasted for quite a while, too.

Not here. Not now. After the brief, halfhearted thaw, a real blizzard rolled out of the northwest. It was the sort of storm that made people fret about firewood, the sort of storm that didn't usually come till much later in the year.

Most folk clapped shutters over their windows, which only made the inside of their homes and shops darker and grimmer. Rhavas didn't have to endure that. The prelate's residence was one of the very few buildings in Skopentzana boasting glazed windows. Even in Videssos the city, they were far from common. Rhavas didn't think Skopentzana had had any till he put these into the residence. A few rich people and a few people who wanted to be on the cutting edge of fashion had imitated him since.

Rhavas didn't get the clearest view when he looked outside. The glass was streaked and bubbled and set in small panes separated by strips of lead. That bothered him not at all. It would have been no different in the capital. Glassmaking was an uncertain art.

Before long, clearly or not, he could watch snow whipping almost horizontally past his window. When winter came to Skopentzana, it settled in and made itself at home. Rhavas knew not much news from the south would come till the weather warmed again. That didn't mean no news would be made down in the warmer parts of the Empire. As Petinos had said, campaigning down there didn't have to stop so soon as it would in these parts.

Would Petinos ever come back through Skopentzana on his way back to the northern border. Would Himerios and the city garrison ever come back to Skopentzana? Rhavas wished he hadn't asked himself that second question. The part of him that cared about good governance hoped he would soon see Himerios here again. The part of him that cared about . . . other things had . . . other ideas.

That other part shamed him by existing. Prayer hadn't driven it from him, as he'd hoped prayer might. All he could do, it seemed, was try to pretend it wasn't there. What he thought, what he wanted—that was one thing. What he did—that was something else. Skotos might tempt a man. If the man didn't yield to temptation, he stayed in Phos' good graces . . . didn't he?

How could it be otherwise? By their very natures, men were imperfect. That left them vulnerable to temptation. But if they rose above it, the lord with the great and good mind would surely have to acknowledge their steadfastness.

Such things were easy to believe in the summertime, when Phos' light filled the sky almost the whole day long. After snow started falling, it was a different story. Light dwindled day by day. That happened in Videssos the city and all over the Empire, of course. Here in the north, though, the dwindling was dramatically magnified.

Midwinter's Day, the day of the winter solstice, was a great holiday throughout the Empire. People and priests proffered prayers to bring the sun back toward the north once more, to keep it from sliding ever southward and leaving the world cloaked in Skotos' eternal darkness.

In a place like Skopentzana, where the sun barely climbed over the horizon at the solstice, Midwinter's Day took on a special urgency, for Skotos seemed closer to triumph here than he did farther south. Towns and villages throughout the Empire reveled on Midwinter's Day after the prayers were done. The celebrations showed their confidence the sun *would* turn north once more—or so folk said.

In Skopentzana, though, the revels took on a special urgency. No one in this city had ever claimed people celebrated more heartily here because they had a greater fear that the sun might disappear for good. No one had ever claimed such a thing, no, but that was how it looked to Rhavas.

The prelate woke before dawn on Midwinter's Day. Considering how long the night before had lasted and how early he'd gone to sleep, that was hardly surprising. A lamp with a fat oil reservoir still burned on a table by his bed. Without that lamp, he might have thought Skotos had indeed conquered the world.

Lamplight let him see his breath smoke, even here indoors. A brazier did something to fight the cold—something, yes, but not much. Rhavas had heavy woolen drawers and a thick wool robe for winter wear. He also put on socks and heavy felt boots, not the sandals he would have worn in Videssos the city or any other place with even a semicivilized climate.

His robe had a hood, too. All priestly robes intended for winter use in Skopentzana did. A tonsured scalp bled heat into the air. Even the short walk to the temple was a torment.

No matter how cold it was, though, Rhavas lingered. No pink or even gray showed in the southeast; the sun would not rise for some little while yet. But the night was clear. Stars blazed in the sky. And the northern lights danced, across the sky from where the sun would eventually show itself. Shimmering curtains of gold and green streamed from the northern horizon more than halfway to the zenith.

Rhavas sketched the sun-circle above his heart as he stared at the marvelous, rippling lights. He'd heard of them when he lived in Videssos the city. He'd heard of them, yes, but he hadn't been sure he believed in them. They rarely showed themselves there, so rarely that he'd never seen them before coming to Skopentzana. He had now, more times than he could count. Their beauty and their strangeness took his breath away even so.

When he started to shiver and his teeth began chattering, he came out of his reverie and went on to the temple. Inside, it blazed with light. Lamps and candelabra all blazed away, hurling defiance at the darkness outside. So many flames burned, they helped heat the temple.

So did the swarm of people who packed the temple for Midwinter's Day services. They sang hymns with far more fervor than any congregation would have shown down in Videssos the city. They believed in eternal darkness in the capital; here, they really feared it. Because Skotos seemed so likely to get the better of the sun, their rejection of him seemed to mean more than it would have farther south.

As Rhavas preached his usual sermon on the turning of the seasons and the growing light that would come, he changed things so he could make an addition: "Some of you, coming to the temple, will surely have seen the northern lights." He waited for men here and there to nod, then went on, "Do they not show how Phos' light may appear at the most unexpected times and in the most unexpected way? Should this not be a lesson to us all?"

The Skopentzanans looked at one another. More of them nodded now. Some of them smiled, too, liking the figure of speech. Rhavas nearly smiled himself. He had always impressed them with his piety and his intellect. He knew that. He also knew they hadn't warmed to him. Few people did; his character was not of the sort that drew warmth. But he had here now.

People had a saying—*anything can happen on Midwinter's Day.* Maybe those smiles were proof of that.

For once, he didn't linger in the narthex after the service was done. Neither did anyone else. Everybody went out to the city square between the temple and the eparch's residence. By then, the southeast was going from pink to gold: the sun would make its brief appearance soon. The northern lights had faded almost to invisibility. Rhavas' sigh spewed fog out in front of his face.

As if to make up for the loss of the magic in the sky, half a dozen bonfires blazed in the square. Men and women of all stations and walks of life lined up at them, nobles next to barmaids, proprietors waiting peaceably behind pimps. Each in turn would run and leap over the flames, shouting, "Burn, ill luck!" in midair. One jump was suppose to be able to take care of a year's bad luck—not a bad bargain, or a small miracle, if true.

When jumpers came down on the far side of the fires, those who had already leaped would catch and steady them. Sometimes they would take a kiss as payment for their service. Sometimes they would go off and take more. Not all babies born nine months from now would look like their mothers' husbands. Anything could happen on Midwinter's Day.

Priests and monks got in the lines to jump the fires, too. They shouted along with everybody else. When wineskins and mugs of beer went through the crowd, they swigged from them along with everybody else. Some of them would break their vows of chastity before the day was done. That happened every Midwinter's Day. Some prelates and some abbots were inclined to look the other way. Rhavas wasn't one of them. To him, a sin was a sin, no matter when it was committed.

That didn't stop him from taking his place in a line and snaking up toward the nearest bonfire. Just before his turn to run and jump came, a cheer rose all over the frozen square: "The sun lives! Phos' sun lives!"

Rhavas looked back over his shoulder. Yes, there was the sun, sneaking up over the horizon at last. He murmured the creed—and then murmured again, in a different tone of voice, when he saw Ingegerd three or four people in back of him.

The woman ahead of him ran, jumped, and shouted out in midair. Someone beyond the fire steadied her. The heat haze rising from the flames made their shapes shimmer.

"Go on, very holy sir!" people near Rhavas called. "Go on!" Somebody pushed him, an indignity he would have suffered—in either sense of the word—on no other day of the year but this.

He ran. The chilly breeze blew into his face and pulled the hood off his head. He jumped, as strongly as he could. "Burn, ill luck!" he cried in a voice that rang across the square. His boots thudded down on the paving stones. He started to stagger, but someone caught his elbow. "My thanks," he said, panting a little.

"Happy to do it, very holy sir," answered the man who'd caught him. "Here—have a swig of this." He handed Rhavas a wineskin.

The prelate drank. The wine was sweet and strong. "A blessing from the good god," he said, and gave the skin to the woman who'd leaped just before him.

Another man jumped over the bonfire, and a woman with a wart on her cheek. Then it was Ingegerd's turn. She raced forward, arm's pumping like a man's as she ran. She soared high over the crackling flames. "Burn, ill luck!" she called, and came to earth again.

Rhavas stepped forward to make sure she didn't fall, but she needed no help, straightening on her own. He drew back a pace, disappointed—and disappointed at himself for being disappointed. Ingegerd dropped him a curtsy. "I thank you for the thought, very holy sir."

"Yes." Rhavas didn't thank himself for some of his own thoughts.

Ingegerd could not see that. She looked to the east, murmuring, "Another Sunturning come and gone."

"Yes," Rhavas said again, but the unfamiliar word piqued interest of a different sort. "Is that what they call Midwinter's Day in Halogaland?"

"It is." The yellow-haired woman nodded. Then she laughed. "I have not called it that, especially not in this tongue, for many years. Sunturning." She said something in the language she'd learned as a baby; Rhavas would have guessed it was the same word.

"How do the Halogai celebrate the day?" he asked—the scholar in him never slept for long.

"With great horns of beer and blood sacrifices and even more fornication than is the custom here," Ingegerd answered.

"I . . . see." Rhavas coughed a couple of times. He'd asked. She'd told him. She had a pagan—or at least a most un-Videssian—directness to her.

"What you Videssians do . . . This is all right," Ingegerd said.

"So glad you approve," Rhavas said dryly.

She laughed at him. He smelled wine on her breath. "As if it matters in Videssos what I think," she said. "You people here have your customs, as the Halogai have theirs. You think yours best because you are used to them, they think theirs best for the same reason."

Ours are hallowed by the worship of the lord with the great and good mind. Though Rhavas thought it, he didn't say it. Ingegerd was too likely to come back by saying her birthfolk thought their gods hallowed what they did. Anything could happen on Midwinter's Day, but a religious argument wasn't what he had in mind.

Ingegerd went on, "I do like the mime troupes who perform. We have nothing like that in Halogaland." Then, more girlish than Rhavas had ever seen her, she laughed and clapped her hands. "Here they are! I spoke of them, and here they are! Am I not a great wizard?"

Rhavas made himself nod, though the magic she'd worked on him was as old as mankind and had nothing to do with what anyone normally thought of as wizardry. He hoped he kept a sour expression off his face. No matter what Ingegerd thought of the mime troupes, he didn't much like them. To his way of thinking, they turned Midwinter's Day liberty into license. That everyone cheered when they did it meant nothing to him. There was a difference between popularity and right and wrong—and if there wasn't, there should have been.

The first troupe was a group of women dressed in men's clothes, which would have been scandalous—to say nothing of illegal—any other day of the year. They swaggered out, pretended to work for a couple of minutes, and then repaired to what was obviously supposed to be a tavern. There they got drunk with miraculous haste. When the barmaid came over, she proved to be a woman not only dressed as a woman but wearing little enough to threaten her with chest fever—and frostbite—in a climate like Skopentzana's. The women dressed as men gaped at her as if they'd never seen such a marvelous creature before.

Among the people in the square, the women laughed and applauded while the men jeered lewdly. Their skit done, the mimes hurried off onto a side street. A troupe of men dressed as women took their place. The men still wore beards and showed off hairy legs. That made their effeminate gestures and prancing all the funnier—to the men in the crowd, anyhow. Their skit was almost the mirror image of the one that had gone before it. From housework, they quickly switched to gossip and to pouring down improbable amounts of beer. The more they pretended to drink, the more licentious their gossip seemed to get, at least by the way they gestured and wagged their hips. The men watching them howled laughter. The women rained catcalls down on their heads. Everyone cheered as they minced off at the end of the skit.

A troupe of swarthy Videssians in mailshirts and blond wigs came out next. Everybody roared at them—they imitated drunken Halogai. They looked for love and looked for fights and ended up in a terrific free-for-all with one another.

Rhavas glanced over at Ingegerd. She was laughing as hard as any of the Videssians around her. She caught his eye, which he hadn't expected. "Halogai *do* act like that when they drink," she said, "and they *do* drink."

"You admit it?" he said.

"Why would I deny it, when it is true?" she answered. "Usually, though, we are not so funny as this."

The next troupe skewered Zautzes the eparch as a pompous fool. Zautzes did what he had to do: he laughed twice as loud as anyone else.

On every day of the year but one, lampooning the prelate would have been at least as risky for the person rash enough to do it as insulting the eparch. The rules changed on Midwinter's Day. No—the rules disappeared on Midwinter's Day. The mime troupe that came out after the one that mocked Zautzes mocked Rhavas. The man who played him wore a blue robe; he had a bald head that let him look tonsured. On his head he had a gold—more likely (much more likely) polished brass—coronet, to remind everyone of the prelate's imperial connections.

He also had a permanent frown, one doubtless enhanced by

greasepaint to be visible from a greater distance. He used it to disapprove of everything he saw, from a sausage seller to a pretty girl. He also thundered—silently, of course—from the pulpit. By the way the man impersonating Rhavas kept pointing to his coronet and sometimes even taking it off and pounding with it, he had to be thundering against Stylianos.

Zautzes' method made sense to Rhavas. Like the eparch, he laughed uproariously. He'd been doing it for years, ever since the first time a mime troupe went after him. Men in public life had to have, or at least to show, a thick skin. Those who couldn't got hounded the whole year through, not just on Midwinter's Day. Videssians were like wolves. When they scented blood, they hunted without rest and without mercy.

Out of the corner of his eye, Rhavas glanced at Ingegerd again. He might have hoped she would disapprove of watching a holy man mocked. He might have hoped that, but he was doomed to disappointment. She laughed at the teasing he got, just as she'd laughed at what the troupe before had done to Zautzes. Laughing when you were grinding your teeth was hard, but Rhavas managed.

He clapped and cheered when the mimes sashayed out of the square. If he was clapping and cheering *because* they were leaving . . . well, that was his business. No one else would know. No one else could prove it, anyhow, which was what really mattered.

Sure enough, anyone and everyone was fair game on Midwinter's Day. The next group of mimes that came out was enormous. It included not one but two men wearing imperial regalia. Each marched at the head of an army of men in armor: some ancient and rusty, the rest made from cheap sheet tin for the occasion.

Rhavas needed a moment to notice that the two rival Avtokrators were identical twins. They strode out in front of their armies to fight with each other. Somehow, the fight turned into a dance. One went back to one army, the other to the other. Had each man gone back to the army he'd had before? Had he traded armies with the other? Did it matter?

Wasn't raising that very question the point of the skit?

Most of the people in the square seemed to think so. They roared their approval. Some of them threw coins to the mimes. More than once, Rhavas caught the glint of gold in the air. Either some folk were already too drunk to know what they were doing or they knew exactly what they were doing and hated the civil war very much indeed.

The prelate had thought that would be the last skit, but it wasn't. One more came after it. Half a dozen men holding hands in a ring impersonated the walls of Skopentzana. Two men inside the ring showed it *was* Skopentzana: one wore a pasteboard model of the temple on his head, the other a model of the eparch's palace.

There was a spirited struggle outside "Skopentzana." Half the contestants wore blond wigs to impersonate Halogai. The other half wore bushy false beards and furs and leather to impersonate Khamorth nomads. What the struggle was about was which group would get to sack the city. They finally compromised and destroyed it together.

People laughed at that skit, too, but nervously. Like a lot of the others, it held an uncomfortable amount of truth. Skopentzana *was* vulnerable. How soon the barbarians beyond the border would realize that and how long the city would stay ungarrisoned . . . Not even Rhavas, who was usually an astute judge of matters political, had any idea.

The "Halogai" in the troupe swept off their wigs and bowed as the crowd in the square cheered them. Not to be outdone, the "Khamorth" swept off their beards and bowed even lower. Here and there, latecomers started jumping over fires again. Men and women who'd already done that began drifting out of the square. Taverns always did a roaring business on Midwinter's Day. Brothels didn't. On this day as on no other, men seldom needed to pay for that.

Rhavas' shadow stretched long before him. He glanced back over his shoulder at the sun. It stood about as far above the horizon as it would get, but that wasn't very far. The prelate shrugged. More than once, he'd celebrated Midwinter's Day here in the midst of a snowstorm. People leaped over bonfires then the same way they did in good weather. Mime troupes performed the same way, too. The only difference was, the audience had to crowd closer to see what sort of outrageousness they were perpetrating.

He looked around for Ingegerd, wondering if she would want to drink some wine with him. That wasn't sinful, especially since Himerios had asked him to look after her. If anything sinful happened later, he could blame it on the wine and on Midwinter's Day. Even his stern rectitude had, or could have, cracks.

But Ingegerd had slipped away. Ashamed of himself for the direction in which his thoughts had veered, Rhavas sketched the sun-circle over his heart. "Penance," he muttered. "Heavy penance."

He kicked at the paving stones, humiliated by his own weakness. He murmured Phos' creed again and again. He'd almost just failed a great test in his own life. He owed Ingegerd a debt of thanks for not staying with him—a debt he could never tell her about.

If he looked around a little, he could find some other woman with whom he might take his pleasure. That never occurred to him. He did not want a woman for the sake of having a woman. He wanted one woman in particular, a much more pernicious and dangerous affliction.

He never thought to wonder whether Ingegerd wanted him. That in itself was a telling measure of how little experience he had. Because he was so inexperienced, though, he didn't realize that it was.

"Phaos' blessings on you, very holy sir," somebody said at his elbow.

He started, then gathered himself. "And on you," he told the man. If he remembered rightly, the fellow sold fancy saddles.

The man eyed him for a moment, then breathed beer fumes into his face as he said, "It's Midwinter's Day, very holy sir. You're supposed to be happy. The way you look, somebody's just about to pound a live crawdad up your arse."

Part of Rhavas wondered how the saddler knew what sort of expression a man in that situation would wear. He almost asked, but at the last minute he held back. He was afraid the fellow would tell him. Instead, the saddler just stood there, awaiting his reply. Slowly, he said, "If the Empire were happier, I would be happier as well."

"Ah. The Empire." The other man had surely lived in the Empire of Videssos all his life. By the way he said its name, he might have heard of it for the first time from Rhavas' lips. "Well, now, very holy sir, that's a pretty big thought, that is. I don't know that I could worry about the whole Empire all by myself."

"There we differ, then," Rhavas said. For a wonder, the other man took the hint. He lurched off to bore someone else.

Rhavas thought about going to a tavern and drinking himself

blind. No shame attached even to a cleric who did that on Midwinter's Day. No public shame, that is—the prelate would have been ashamed of himself for such a lapse from asceticism. For one of the few times in his life, he stood irresolute.

He was still standing there, watching the sun scurry across the sky toward the southwestern horizon, when a courier came into the square. The rider made slow going against the throng celebrating Midwinter's Day. "What's the news?" a drunk bawled.

And the courier answered him: "The Khamorth! The Khamorth are over the border!"

III

A servant in Zautzes' residence lit lamps. Sunset was coming soon, and twilight wouldn't last long. Lamplight made a sorry substitute for daylight, but on Midwinter's Day daylight would not serve. Rhavas was glad he hadn't decided to soak himself in the sweet blood of the grape. With this news, he needed to be able to think straight.

Zautzes stared at the courier like a frog in a street puddle staring at a wagon bearing down on it. He plainly had been less moderate than Rhavas. He blinked and blinked, trying to make his wits work. Another servant brought wine for the courier and the prelate and more wine for the eparch. Zautzes gulped thirstily. Rhavas left his own goblet untouched. He asked, "Where have the nomads crossed the border?"

Before he answered, the courier sipped from his winecup. Unlike Zautzes, he'd earned the right to drink. "Where have they crossed, very holy sir?" he echoed. "Ask me where they haven't—that'll be a shorter list. From what I've heard, they're over it all the way from the Astris—not far from Videssos the city—up here to the northeast. They're over, and their cursed wheeled carts are over, and their flocks are over. They've come to stay, unless we can throw 'em out."

"Phos!" Rhavas muttered. He felt like drinking now, though

he still refrained. This was every Avtokrator's nightmare, come to life before his eyes.

"Throwing them back won't be easy," Zautzes said, "not with things, uh, being in the mess they're in." He still had his wits sufficiently about him to watch what he said and how he said it.

"Not with Maleinos and Stylianos at each other's throats, you mean." Rhavas had no compunction about telling the truth as he saw it. He seldom did. "This is a time when they need to set the needs of the Empire above their own ambitions."

"Good luck!" Zautzes said with a fine sardonic relish that wouldn't have been out of place even in the capital.

Rhavas scowled back at him. Zautzes gave back a stare more owlish than froggy. He might have said, *Go ahead. Tell me I'm wrong.* Rhavas couldn't, and he knew it, and he hated the knowledge. To a man with his eye on the throne, his imperial rival would loom larger than any foreign invaders.

The courier looked from the eparch to the prelate and back again. "Most honorable sir, very holy sir, what are we going to do?" he asked, showing a touching confidence that the two high officials would be able to tell him what he wanted to know.

Prelate and eparch looked at each other. Both men shrugged at the same time. Zautzes was never shy about talking, and the wine had done nothing to make him quieter. Where Rhavas kept quiet, he spoke up: "We'll just have to wait and see where the barbarians go and what they do. Then we'll be able to judge how best to deal with them."

That sounded good. The courier nodded, impressed by Zautzes' wisdom. Rhavas' orderly, logical mind noted that the eparch could just as well have said, *I don't know.* That would have meant exactly the same thing. Rhavas was willing to admit it wouldn't have sounded nearly so impressive.

The courier emptied his winecup, set it down on the table next to his stool, and yawned enormously. How long and how far had he ridden to bring his bad news to Skopentzana? Zautzes called for a servant. No one came. The eparch looked astonished. Rhavas said, "It *is* Midwinter's Day, most honorable sir. You're lucky you got anyone to come back and give us wine. Your men are probably out reveling again."

"Bah!" Zautzes said, and then, to the courier, "Here, come

along. I'll give you a bed for the night." A long night it would be, too.

"May the good god shine his light on you for your kindness," the courier said, sounding like a well-raised young man. He lurched to his feet. Half leaning on Zautzes, he left the eparch's study.

When Zautzes came back a few minutes later, he looked thoroughly grim. The wine he'd drunk might have made him mouthy, but it hadn't fuddled him. "What *are* we going to do, very holy sir?" he asked. "All the nomads have to do is follow the course of the Anazarbos. If nothing stops them, the river will lead them straight here."

"What could stop them?" Rhavas asked. "You watched the garrison leave, the same as I did. Nothing but villages and scattered farmers between the border and Skopentzana."

That made Zautzes look grimmer yet. "We have to keep them out," he said. "We have to. Can you imagine what they'd do if they got loose in the city?"

"I suppose I can imagine *some* of the things they'd do," Rhavas said judiciously. "I would really rather not discover how good my imagination is."

"A point," the eparch admitted. "Yes, unfortunately a distinct point. What *I* wonder most right now is, how am I supposed to enjoy the rest of Midwinter's Day? Anything can happen, they say, yes, but that doesn't usually include getting overrun by nomads who never bathe and who'd herd—and slaughter—people in place of cattle and sheep if they got half a chance. The Khamorth aren't my idea of fun, I fear."

"Nor mine." Rhavas looked west, as if he could see through all the miles of space between Skopentzana and the wandering clans of plainsmen. Not enough miles between them, not now. His formidable brow furrowed in thought. "We can't turn them back with soldiers, can we?"

"Not unless you've got some soldiers stashed in your basement along with the turnips and the beans and the barley," Zautzes said.

Rhavas didn't dignify that with a direct answer. Instead, he went on with his own train of thought: "Can we turn them back with magecraft, then?"

Zautzes' big, bulging eyes narrowed. "Well, I'm not the one to ask, very holy sir—you should talk with a real live wizard instead.

But I have to tell you something: I've heard ideas I like a whole lot less. How strong can the nomads' shamans be?"

"Not strong at all," Rhavas said firmly. "They reverence demons and devils, and come close to worshiping Skotos outright. Sorcerers who favor Phos must prevail against them them."

"All right, then." The eparch spoke as if everything were all settled. "We'll go out and give them what for. We've got plenty of sorcerers in this town. Let them earn their keep for something better than finding a little old lady's lost bracelet." He made it sound very simple.

Since Rhavas had never done any campaigning, it seemed simple to him, too. "Most honorable sir, this is a fine plan," he said.

"Glad you think so." Complacence at his own cleverness filled Zautzes' voice, even though the idea had been Rhavas'. Zautzes pointed at the prelate. "You should go with them, you know. Wizards are only men—sinners like anybody else. You, though, very holy sir, you really are a link between this sordid world and the good god."

"Me?" Rhavas said in surprise. Zautzes nodded. Rhavas thought it over. He'd never tried to travel in the northern part of the Empire of Videssos during winter, either. People did; he knew that. The courier now drifting toward sleep in Zautzes' guest room was living proof of it. Rhavas dipped his head in assent. "I'll do it. It's the least I can do for the Empire."

"Good man!" Zautzes exclaimed—by which he no doubt meant that Rhavas was doing what he wanted. He went on, "It will be something out of the ordinary for you."

Whatever else it would be, it would surely be that. Rhavas wondered what he'd just got himself into. Before long, he would find out. He took his leave of Zautzes and walked out of the eparch's residence. The sun, by then, had long since disappeared after its brief midday visit. The stars and the northern lights ruled the sky again, as they did for all but a little stretch of time at this season of the year.

The people of Skopentzana didn't seem to care. Midwinter's Day was Midwinter's Day. They intended to celebrate it. Not even the news of the irruption of the Khamorth could slow the revels. The nomads might have broken into the Empire, but they were nowhere near Skopentzana.

Yet, Rhavas thought. *They're nowhere near here yet.*

✳   ✳   ✳

People said the Khamorth were born in the saddle and spent their whole lives aboard their steppe ponies. People said they walked with a bowlegged waddle because they used their legs more for clutching the barrel of a horse than for getting around on the ground. People said all sorts of things about them, some of which might have been true and a lot of which were bound to be nonsense.

Rhavas wondered what people would have said about the expedition setting forth from Skopentzana on a bitterly cold winter's day. People could have said that he was one of the better horsemen in the expedition. That would have been true—and it also would have alarmed anyone who knew what sort of rider Rhavas was.

Most of Skopentzana's wizards, though, did make him look as if he'd been born in the saddle himself. Several of them were on horseback for the first time in their lives, having been in the habit of riding donkeys or mules when they rode at all. They kept complaining about how far off the ground they were.

"Don't worry," one of Zautzes' guards said cheerfully—he was a man who *could* ride. "If you fall into a snowdrift, you'll see it's nice and soft."

Even that wasn't quite true. The snow had a hard crust on it, one thick enough in spots for a man to walk on it without leaving tracks. Falling on that would be no bargain. Rhavas kept the hood of his robe up over his ears and his tonsured scalp. None of this was any bargain, not so far as he could see.

Ptarmigan took off with a whir of white wings. He'd never noticed them till they flew. In summer, the birds were mostly brown. In spring and fall, their plumage was brown and white. Now, in the wintertime, they were white but for eyes and wing-tips. Hares and ferrets and foxes went through the same color changes.

How do they know? Rhavas wondered. They had no calendars. They didn't pray and then roister on Midwinter's Day. But their changes were as reliable as the seasons themselves. The prelate shrugged, there in the saddle. He had no idea how the animals guessed the turning of the year.

"What is it, very holy sir?" A wizard named Koubatzes rode close by Rhavas. He had the highest reputation of any mage in Skopentzana. Many wizards went out of their way to impress those who saw them, wearing gaudy robes and long, elaborately curled beards and letting their hair grow long. Koubatzes didn't bother with any of that. He put Rhavas in mind of a clerk or a secretary. He was thin, middle-aged, and nondescript. His gray-streaked beard was closely trimmed; his robe, if of finer wool than most clerks could afford, was of an ordinary cut and dyed an unremarkable dark green.

Rhavas told him, finishing, "No theologian I know of has ever pondered this. Do sorcerers know more of it than priests?"

Koubatzes' eyes narrowed. His features sharpened. When he thought hard, his face was no longer ordinary. Wit shone from it like light from a lamp. More ptarmigan, frightened by the horsemen, rose into the air. Koubatzes' gaze followed the snowy birds till they came to earth again and disappeared.

"Well, well," the sorcerer said thoughtfully. His gaze swung back to Rhavas. "Isn't that interesting? No, very holy sir, I can't tell you how or why animals turn the color of snow when winter comes."

"Not all of them do." Rhavas pointed to the Anazarbos River, near whose southern bank the Videssians rode. The river hadn't yet frozen from bank to bank, as it would later in the winter. Some ducks floated on the icy water. Their plumage was duller than it would have been in summertime, but they hadn't gone white. Squirrels that gnawed on fir cones through the winter stayed red. Badgers and bears kept their color, too.

"Isn't that interesting?" Koubatzes said again, giving the ducks the same close attention he'd lavished on the ptarmigan. "The ducks are out on the water, mind you, while the ptarmigan live in the snow. A brown bird on a snowdrift wouldn't last long. That seems plain enough."

"What of ravens?" Rhavas asked, and the wizard winced. Rhavas went on, "Besides, you and I can see that changing color would might be to a bird's advantage, but how does the bird itself know that?"

"Beats me," Koubatzes admitted. "About the most I can tell you is that birds that turn white might—and I say it again: *might*—be likelier to live to breed. If the darker ones got eaten before they laid eggs . . ." He shrugged. "Take it for what you think it's worth, if you think it's worth anything."

"I don't know," Rhavas said. "Wouldn't turning white do a raven or a squirrel as much good as a ptarmigan? But ravens stay black and squirrels stay red."

"I told you I didn't have the answer," Koubatzes said, his breath smoking with every exhalation. "I just threw out an idea to see what you made of it. It's not likely to be true."

The horses plodded on. Their breath smoked, too. The day was bright and clear, but far below freezing. Even so far north, mild winter days were known, but this wasn't one of them. Birches and poplars and maples stood bare-branched and skeletal. Fir and pine and spruce stayed green the year around, but carried so much snow that they looked as if they were trying to turn white like the ptarmigan. Pleased with the conceit, Rhavas mentioned it to Koubatzes.

"Ah? Intriguing." The mage raised an eyebrow. "Now if you could get the trees to go white in winter *without* snow on them, very holy sir, you'd really have something."

"Mmp." Rhavas felt obscurely punctured.

He slept that night in a felt tent heated only by a charcoal-burning brazier. He wrapped himself in blankets and a fur robe and slept in all of his clothes, but remained cold and uncomfortable. He'd slept on the deck of the ship that brought him to Skopentzana—it was sleep on the deck or do without sleep. Since then, though, he'd lain in a bed every night. He would have complained more about the arrangements if the wizards and the guards weren't sleeping on the ground bundled in whatever they had, too.

Hot barley porridge sweetened with honey helped resign him to being out in the wilderness the next morning. So did hot mulled wine. Off in the distance, smoke rose from a peasant's hut. In this part of the Empire, peasants who couldn't keep a fire burning through the winter often didn't live to see spring.

Rhavas' thighs let out an unhappy twinge as he clambered up onto his horse. Some of the wizards groaned, too. Again, that made the prelate feel better. Yes, misery did love company.

"How long before we come across the nomads?" Rhavas asked the chief guardsman, a dour man named Ingeros whose gray eyes and light brown hair said he carried a good deal of Haloga blood.

Ingeros had grown up in Skopentzana, though, and was wholly Videssian in everything but looks. His shrug was a small masterpiece of its kind. It would have drawn admiration in Videssos the city. Here in this frozen wilderness, it struck Rhavas as being beyond praise. "We'll come across them when we do, very holy sir," he answered. "Or, if no band is making for Skopentzana, we won't. In that case, we go home."

That no band of Khamorth might head for Skopentzana hadn't occurred to Rhavas. The mere idea made him angry. *How dare they ignore my city?* went through his mind. He laughed at himself. He hadn't realized he'd become such a part of Skopentzana, or it of him. *I'm not just an exile from the capital, not anymore.*

A snowy owl slid silently across the sky. The big white birds flew mostly by daylight. Rhavas had had to get used to that on coming to the north country; down in Videssos the city and most of the Empire, seeing an owl by daylight was reckoned the worst of bad luck. It wasn't daylight here, not yet, but morning twilight said the sun was nearing the southeastern horizon.

Koubatzes saw the owl, too. Pointing, he said, "It's white all the time. What do you make of that?"

"We wouldn't call it a snowy owl if it were the color of mud," Rhavas answered gravely.

"Well—no." The wizard asked no more questions about animals after that, which suited Rhavas: he'd got more for his idle comment than he'd expected.

They rode west along the riverbank. In due course, the sun did come up behind them and pushed long shadows out ahead. Those shadows did not grow a great deal shorter as the brief daylight wore along. At this season of the year, the sun never rose high enough to cast short shadows.

More ducks bobbed in the Anazarbos. Rhavas also wondered how they could sit there all day without freezing: *he* wouldn't have lasted long in that frigid water. This time, though, he kept quiet about his curiosity.

The wizards and the guards and the prelate rode up to the top of a low rise. Ingeros was in the lead. He suddenly reined in and threw up a hand to halt the others. "What is it?" a sorcerer called.

"Sheep," Ingeros answered.

Never had Rhavas heard such an innocent word sound so sinister. "Khamorth sheep?" he asked.

"Sure looks that way to me," Ingeros said, and then, "Ha! Yes, there's one of the whoresons on his cursed pony."

Rhavas sketched the sun-circle over his heart. The plainsmen had traveled better than half as fast as the news of their coming. Their mobility had always plagued the Videssians, who'd had to defend a long frontier against them. Two or three times, imperial armies had come to grief going out onto the steppe in pursuit of the elusive Khamorth. From the time of Stavrakios to that of Stylianos, no Videssian army had tried it. But the rebellious general had won victories. *Not enough of them*, Rhavas thought.

Now Videssos' painfully perfect border bastions lay abandoned. The barbarians were inside the Empire—inside it on a vast front, in fact. Would they prove as hard to drive back as they had to contain on the plains? Rhavas spat in the snow, as if rejecting Skotos, in hopes of turning aside the evil omen.

Ingeros rode back to the men he shepherded. "Stay here," he told them. "Don't go over the rise and show yourself to the stinking nomads. Have you got that, sorcerous sirs?"

Koubatzes and the other mages nodded. Rhavas decided he had better do the same. One of the wizards asked, "What's to keep the Khamorth from coming over the rise themselves and finding us?"

"Well, it could happen, but I don't look for it right away," Ingeros replied. "Seems like the sheep have scraped off some of the snow there and found pretty decent grazing underneath. The Khamorth go where their flocks take them half the time—more than half, by the good god. If the sheep are happy, the plainsmen are happy, too. And so, sorcerous sirs, right now I'd say it's up to you."

"We'll do what we can," Koubatzes said. None of the other wizards disagreed or tried to take pride of place from him. They recognized that he was the best they had. When they weren't complaining about how high they were on horseback or how cold it was, they'd talked shop on the way out from Skopentzana. Rhavas knew something about sorcery. Few well-educated priests didn't; one order of monks, in fact, specialized in weather-working wizardry. That also involved astrology, or perhaps astronomy, in ways Rhavas didn't fully understand. He followed these mages well enough when they went on about the laws of similarity and contagion. As they got more technical, though, they might as well have started using the Haloga language.

Ingeros slid down from his horse. One of the other guards took the animal's reins. Ingeros reached into a saddlebag. He pulled out a white robe with a hood, which he draped over the clothes he already had on. He walked through the snow toward the top of the rise. As he neared it, he pulled the hood up over his head and crawled on his belly. The hood and robe did for him what white feathers did for ptarmigan and white fur for hare and ferret and fox: they made him disappear against the snowy background. He could spy on the Khamorth without their seeing him.

Koubatzes also dismounted. Before doing anything else, he paused to rub his hindquarters. Rhavas fundamentally approved of the gesture. "Methodios!" Koubatzes said, and pointed to a younger wizard.

"What do you need?" Methodios asked.

"You have a good deal of skill sniffing out wards," Koubatzes said. "Suppose you see what sort of protections the plainsmen are using."

"Right." Methodios took what looked like a stone with a stout needle through it from his saddlebag. "A lodestone," he remarked to his fellows. Along with the piercing for the needle, it had another for a fine silver chain. Methodios swung it by the chain, first this way, then that. He murmured a charm and made passes with his free hand.

Suddenly it seemed to Rhavas that the lodestone was swinging on its own, not through Methodios' agency. It described a complex pattern in the air. Methodios and the mages near him watched that path with careful—indeed, fascinated—attention. "How interesting," one of the wizards said, at the same time as another was remarking, "How unusual." The independent motion was interesting to Rhavas, too, but he could not have said if it was unusual.

"Well?" Koubatzes asked a minute or so later.

"Well, I would say there are some wards," Methodios replied, and the other mages who'd eyed the lodestone nodded. He went on, "How strong they are . . . I'm not quite sure, I'm afraid. I'd have an easier time gauging it if this were Videssian wizardry." He looked down at the lodestone again. "My feeling is that the sorcery we planned before we set out from Skopentzana should do the job."

"Excellent!" Koubatzes breathed out a small fog bank with the word. "This is also my belief. How can the Skotos-loving barbarians hope to stand against us when we have not only the lord with the great and good mind but also our hard-won learning, lore, and wisdom in the other pan of the balance?"

"That is well said!" Rhavas clapped his mittened hands together. His applause yielded only a muffled thump. A moment later, he realized that was just as well. Real clapping might have carried to the Khamorth shepherds on the far side of the rise.

"I thank you, very holy sir." Koubatzes bowed to him. "We will proceed as we planned and as we've discussed, then. I have the amulet here."

He drew it out from under the thick wool tunic he wore beneath a wolfskin coat that gave him something of the look of a nomad himself. Gold gleamed in the shape of the sun-circle. So did two of the three stones set into the golden disk: an emerald of a green to make meadows despair and a rainbow-shimmering opal. The third stone, by contrast, seemed no more than a small, glassy pebble. Pointing to it, Rhavas asked, "What is that stone, and why do you set so much store by it?"

"This, very holy sir?" Koubatzes set his finger on the non-descript stone. The prelate nodded. Koubatzes said, "This is an authentic diamond. I know it doesn't look like much, but the reason for that is simple: it is so hard, it cannot be polished or shaped. No other stone will so much as scratch it; only another diamond can do that. There are no more than three or four in all of Skopentzana, I believe."

Rhavas was ready to believe it, too. Even in Videssos the city, diamonds were surpassingly rare—and prized for their rarity more than for their beauty. The prelate understood that; this stone was nothing out of the ordinary to look at. He asked, "What is its special virtue? Come to that, what are the magical virtues of the other two stones?"

Koubatzes gave him a crooked smile. "So you'd be a sorcerer, would you?"

"Not I." Rhavas shook his head. "By your courtesy, tell me what someone not initiated into your mysteries may know."

"I'll do that, and gladly," the wizard said. "The diamond, which as you see is fixed to the left side of the amulet, is good against enemies, madness, wild beasts, and cruel men. The emerald drives away enemies and makes them weak. The opal conduces to making one victorious over his adversaries."

"These are all good choices, then," Rhavas agreed. "May Phos grant success to the spells you make from your stones."

"My thanks," Koubatzes said. "Pray for us."

Rhavas did. Surely Phos would favor those who reverenced him against the savages from the steppe. "We bless thee, Phos, lord with the great and good mind, by thy grace our protector, watchful beforehand that the great test of life may be decided in our favor." He repeated the creed over and over again, bearing down on *we* and *our*. He saw no harm in reminding the good god who his true followers were. Phos already knew, of course—but still, why leave such things to chance?

Koubatzes set the amulet not on the snow but on a square of blue silk he carefully laid out so its corners pointed toward the cardinal directions. Rhavas didn't need to ask what the square represented. What could it be but the sky through which the sun traveled? Koubatzes stood south of the square. Other wizards took their places to the north and east and west. They began to chant.

Power thrummed in the air as the incantation built. Rhavas could feel it, as he could feel lightning build up in the air during a thunderstorm before the stroke fell. The wizards' hands moved in quick, intricate passes, sometimes in unison, sometimes with each sorcerer playing his own role to help form a larger and more potent whole.

The mages not directly involved in the conjuration watched avidly. Perhaps the four casting the spell drew on their strength in some way Rhavas could not see, or perhaps they were pupils learning from the performances of masters. Methodios' eyes in particular were wide and staring. Next to this, the magic he'd worked was as a boy's playhouse measured against the imperial palaces in Videssos the city.

Quite visibly, Koubatzes gathered himself. "Now!" he said, and hurled the power toward the west. Then he and all three of the mages who'd helped him staggered; one crumpled to the snow. Wizards had great power, but did not wield it without a price.

"What magic can do, magic has done," Rhavas said. "May the lord with the great and good mind bless our endeavor and crown it with success."

"So may it be." Koubatzes sounded even more drained than he looked; his voice might have been that of an old, old man. Despite the cold, sweat stood out on his face. "Food. Wine. Something to restore myself somewhat."

"Sleep," the wizard who'd fallen in the snow said as he struggled to his feet. Koubatzes and the other two nodded.

The wizards carried honey cakes and wine in their saddle-bags along with their sorcerous impedimenta. They knew the men who made magics of this sort would need quick reviving. Koubatzes and the other three crammed their mouths with the sweets and gulped the strong wine as if afraid it would be outlawed tomorrow.

Ingeros drew back from the top of the low rise before calling to the wizards, "Well done, by the good god! The shepherd rode off like he had demons on his tail. Come to that, the sheep ran away, too."

Methodios, who had worked a smaller sorcery than the others, kept more of his strength. And, since he had been the mage concerned with what the Khamorth had in the way of wards, perhaps his sorcerous senses were already attuned to the nomads. Not half a minute after Ingeros spoke, the young wizard's eyes widened again, now in disbelief and alarm. "Counterspell!" he gasped.

"You're mad," another wizard said. "They couldn't possib—" He broke off. His face bore the same expression as Methodios'. "Phaos!" he gasped. "They could."

"We have to hold them." Koubatzes could barely hold himself up. Determination rang in his voice even so. "I don't know how they're doing this, but we can stop it. We *must* stop it. We—"

He got no further. He staggered as if someone had struck him a heavy blow. That wasn't because of his weakness from the spell he'd just cast. It came from a spell aimed at him—aimed at all the Videssian wizards, the guards accompanying them . . . and Rhavas himself.

Fear filled him. He might have been a winecup for all he could do to hold it out. He shivered. His teeth chattered. Ice ran up his back. All of that went on and on. It did not end, as it would have had the fear sprung from any natural cause. Some small part of him knew the terror was artificial, was sorcerously induced. Knowing mattered not at all.

The wizards who were on horseback dug heels into their mounts' sides. The horses bucketed off in all directions—most toward

Skopentzana, but not all. Some of the horses screamed in surprise and pain. Some of the wizards were screaming, too.

For all his weakened state, Koubatzes was better able to resist the Khamorth sorcery. Still staggering, he snatched up the amulet through which he'd launched the Videssian spell at the nomads. He clutched it as a drowning man might clutch a spar. But a spar would support a shipwreck victim. The amulet seemed to help Koubatzes not in the least.

"How are they doing this?" the sorcerer cried. "How, in the name of the good god?" His desperate eyes met Rhavas'. "In the name of the good god, very holy sir, make them stop!"

Rhavas thought it miracle enough that he hadn't fled with most of the mages and guards. Just staying where he was took every ounce of strength he had. He sent up another anguished prayer to Phos. It did no good that he could find. The fear the Khamorth shamans sent forth went right on lashing him.

With a low, terrified moan, Koubatzes jumped on his horse and fled. He was the last of the wizards to hold his place. The guards were gone, too. Ingeros had lasted a little longer than the others, but only a little. There sat Rhavas on the back of his horse, all alone.

Anger poured over him for a moment, anger almost hot enough to make him forget his sorcerously spawned panic. How dared the Khamorth strike back in defiance not just of the Empire of Videssos but also of the lord with the great and good mind? How *dared* they? It was an outrage!

That it was an outrage made it no less true. Rhavas' anger faded, as normal emotions will. The fear remained. If anything, it grew worse. Rhavas had no idea how the Khamorth were doing what they did. For that matter, even Koubatzes had had no idea how they were doing it, or how to stop them.

The prelate's courage—or rather, his resistance to the shamans' counterspell—at last collapsed. He booted his horse into motion. Had the animal chosen to run west, it would have carried him straight to the nomads, and that would have been the end of him. But it ran east, back toward Skopentzana, and so, though broken, he escaped the final disaster.

Koubatzes' horse had galloped east, too. Rhavas' caught up with the wizard after a while. "Why are we so afraid?" Rhavas asked through teeth that still chattered as if he'd been dumped naked in the snow.

"Because they have made us so." Koubatzes' face was a mask of terror. "I had not thought the wizard born who could put me in fear. I had not thought it, but I was wrong."

"How do we escape the sorcery?" Rhavas asked him.

"If I knew, I would tell you. No—if I knew, I would do it."

Little by little, as they bucketed on toward Skopentzana, the panic eased. Rhavas made what he could of that: "They cannot afflict us forever."

"No, but for long enough." Koubatzes reined in. As well he did; his horse would have foundered soon if he hadn't.

So would Rhavas'. The prelate let his mount blow out great gusts of steaming breath through distended, blood-red—almost fire-red—nostrils. "How?" Rhavas said in something close to physical torment. "How could the nomads, the barbarians, do this to us?"

"I do not know." Horror and rage filled Koubatzes' voice. They were aimed not at Rhavas but at himself. "Everything we did went as it should have gone. Their wards seemed nothing out of the ordinary. Our spell . . . Our spell, very holy sir, was a perfect specimen of its kind. We made no error in preparing the amulet. We made no error in the conjuration. I can tell you where we made the mistake."

"Where?" Rhavas asked.

"We thought the spell would be strong enough to rout the Khamorth, strong enough so they couldn't possibly reply. We seem to have been slightly in error there." The mage's laugh rode the high, ragged edge of hysteria. "Yes, just slightly, by the good god."

"But the good god should have watched over us, should have kept any such mischance from befalling us," Rhavas faltered.

Koubatzes laughed again, even more shakily than before. "What should have happened isn't what happened, very holy sir. Perhaps you noticed that. Aye, perhaps you did. If you would like to take that up with Phaos the next time you talk to him, I hope you'll be good enough to let me know what he has to say."

Such sarcasm stopped just short of blasphemy—if, indeed, it stopped short at all. Another day, Rhavas would have called Koubatzes on it. After the dolorous overthrow he'd just escaped, he barely noticed. He said, "I saw no sign the lord with the great and good mind rejected my prayers."

"No, eh?" The wizard raised an ironic eyebrow. "Our sorcery was routed. *We* were routed. If we hadn't got far away, I think I would have *died* of that fright. Might such things give you a hint?"

Even in Rhavas' present unhappy state, that was too much for him to stomach. "If you say Phos' power does not rule the world, sorcerous sir, you say Skotos' power does. *Do* you say that? I see no other choice."

"No, I do not say that." Koubatzes hastily backtracked. "Maybe the good god was punishing us for our sins. Whatever his reasons, though, he let the Khamorth triumph over us."

"Whatever his reasons . . ." Rhavas echoed. The civil war loomed large in his mind. Had the general with dreams of glory not risen against his cousin, none of this would have happened. The Empire of Videssos' armies would not have hurled themselves at one another. The frontier forts would not have been stripped of men to fling into the fight. The nomads never would have had the chance to swarm off the steppe.

"No help for it," Koubatzes said gloomily. "The cursed nomads can do as they please in these parts. Who can stop them? Who can even slow them down?"

"Despair is the one sin Phos will never forgive." Rhavas tried to use that to buck up his spirits as well as the wizard's. Had the Empire truly been sinful enough to deserve a barbarian invasion in this scale? Had the nomads been virtuous enough to deserve all the plunder and rapine they would take in Videssos? He had trouble believing it.

But Phos would do as he pleased, not as mere mortals wished him to do. Rhavas had to remind himself of that. The thought was chastening. He cared for being chastened no more than any other man would have.

Koubatzes eyed him now as if he had never seen him before. "You truly believe that, don't you?"

"What sort of priest would I be if I didn't?" Rhavas returned. "A sorry one indeed, I assure you. Shall we go back to Skopentzana and do what we can to get the city ready to defend itself?"

"I suppose we'd better," the mage said. "I don't think it will do much good, though."

"Do you say that as a man or as a foreteller?" Rhavas asked.

"As a man. I have not tried to look into the future. Sometimes one is better off not knowing." Koubatzes gave Rhavas a different kind of glance now, this one speculative. "What *did* you ask poor Eladas when he fell over dead trying to answer your question?"

"Whatever it was, I dare hope he crossed over the Bridge of the Separator and now enjoys eternal bliss with Phos." Rhavas sketched the sun-circle. The look of terror that had filled Eladas' face in his last living moments outdid even the fright the Khamorth shamans had just inflicted on his comrades and him.

Koubatzes grunted. "Did it have to do with the civil war?"

"Of course not." Rhavas did his best to sound offended at the very question. "Anyone who seeks foreknowledge about the Avtokrator stands to lose his head—a good law, I think, and a just one. I would not break it."

"All right, very holy sir. Don't get in a temper at me, please." Koubatzes made a placating gesture. His eyes, though, his eyes remained sharp and shrewd. He had no great physical potency, but lived by his wits—and they were formidable. "So you didn't aim to go against the law? Did you aim to go around it?"

Rhavas didn't answer right away. By not answering right away, he learned the truth of a proverb. He who hesitated *was* lost. "What I asked—whatever it was—is my business and not yours, sorcerous sir," he said, too late.

"Uh-*huh*," Koubatzes said. Rhavas had never heard such a disagreeable agreement. The mage added, "You made it Eladas' business, too, didn't you? Except Eladas took one look, and that was the last look he ever took."

"You don't know that. I don't know that, either." Rhavas was trying to convince himself more than Koubatzes. "Anything could have happened to him, anything at all. It didn't have to have anything to do with . . . with whatever I asked."

"Uh-*huh*," Koubatzes repeated, even more devastatingly than before. "Eladas was healthy as a horse. I happen to know."

"Horses die, too," Rhavas said. "Ours almost did, just now."

"So did we," the wizard pointed out. "But it didn't just happen to us. Somebody *made* it happen—those accursed Khamorth shamans. Are you telling me you don't believe something made it happen to Eladas?"

Not for the first time, Rhavas wished he were a better liar. He would have loved to tell Koubatzes he didn't think the one had anything to do with the other. He would have loved to—but he couldn't.

"What did you ask him, then?" Koubatzes rapped out.

"Whether I would become ecumenical patriarch." The answer flew from Rhavas' lips. He wondered whether the wizard had used some small spell to suck it out of him.

By the way Koubatzes blinked, that wasn't the question he'd looked for. He asked, "And did he answer it before he died?"

"No." Rhavas shook his head. "He may have seen the answer, but he did not give it."

Koubatzes grunted. "Too bad."

"Yes, I think so, too," Rhavas said. The question had eaten at him ever since Eladas expired in his study. What had the soothsayer seen? Would he be patriarch? Would he not? What disaster would spring from whatever the answer was?

He'd thought about giving gold to another soothsayer. Maybe Eladas' death was nothing but a coincidence. Maybe. Try as Rhavas would, he couldn't make himself believe it. The folk of Skopentzana assumed Eladas' passing had been a coincidence. They wouldn't think so if a second man died on the same errand.

With a worn, weary sigh, Rhavas urged his horse ahead. Koubatzes rode on after him. Neither of them said much after that till they came to Skopentzana.

Tears stung Rhavas' eyes. No, it wasn't Videssos the city. No other place in the world came close to Videssos the city, not even Mashiz, the capital of Makuran. Rhavas doubted even the Makuraner King of Kings would have quarreled with that. But, even if it wasn't what he had left, it was an outpost of civilization.

Men in helmets with spears on their shoulders tramped the walls. They weren't soldiers, not in any real sense of the word. They were artisans taking one morning or afternoon a week off from their regular work to keep up the illusion that Skopentzana was garrisoned. From a distance, they resembled the warriors who'd gone off to fight in Videssos' civil war. Maybe the Khamorth would take one look at them, decide Skopentzana was ready to fend off any attack, and go away to bother the nearby farms and villages. In that case, the local militia would more than have done its duty.

But what if the barbarians didn't?

Would the militiamen fight? Probably. Would they fight bravely? Some would, no doubt. Would they fight well enough to keep the Khamorth out of Skopentzana? How could anyone tell before they were tested?

Rhavas murmured Phos' creed, bearing down slightly on *watchful beforehand* and *the great test of life*. He'd spoken the creed when Koubatzes and the other mages aimed their spell against the Khamorth, too. Much good it had done him—or them—then. He prayed now that the good god would spare Skopentzana, which had had small part, if any, in the sins of those farther south.

The gates were closed. That relieved Rhavas' mind. Someone— probably Zautzes—was taking all this seriously. The great valves swung open wide enough to admit the prelate and the mage. Then, grunting with effort, the amateur gate crew swung them closed again and awkwardly lowered the heavy bars that secured them.

"How did it go, sorcerous sir?" one of the militiamen called cheerfully to Koubatzes. Rhavas knew the man, at least by sight. He made dishes and clay pots. He was very good at that. What sort of soldier he made . . . was all too likely to be a different sort of question.

Before replying, Koubatzes flicked a questioning glance toward Rhavas. The prelate nodded—not a showy nod, but a firm one. If Koubatzes didn't tell the truth now, it would come home to roost soon enough anyhow.

Perhaps seeing the same thing, Koubatzes sighed and said, "It went not well at all, I fear. The barbarians not only repelled our sorcery but struck back at us with strength we could not match. It was an evil day, and the nomads even now move toward the city."

The potter stared at him. "How could that happen?"

"It was easier than any of us dreamt it might be," Rhavas answered. "Easier for them, I should say." Ruefully, Koubatzes nodded agreement.

All the gate crew murmured. Another man—this one a woodworker famous not only for fine furniture but also for oars—said, "But what do we do now, if this be so?"

Wizard and prelate looked at each other. "Pray," Koubatzes said before Rhavas could speak. "Pray, and hope even prayer suffices."

"If prayer does not suffice, nothing ever will," Rhavas declared.

Koubatzes refused to back down. In light of the disaster that had befallen the sorcerers and their companions, that was perhaps less startling than it might have been otherwise. "So I said, very holy sir," he replied. "By what we have seen, it may be that nothing suffices."

"What prayer can do, prayer shall do," Rhavas said. "I, and this whole city, will pray as we have never prayed before."

Rhavas had many reasons to complain about Skopentzana. Winter there was a horror the likes of which he had never known before coming to the far north. The town was years behind the times. Even the local accent was old-fashioned. What most of the complaints boiled down to was that Skopentzana wasn't Videssos the city. The prelate had never complained of the Skopentzanans' impiety.

Nor could he complain of it now. Though days had begun to grow longer after the solstice, they still remained short and cold, so cold. Nevertheless, people began coming to the chief temple (and to the other temples in the city) well before the sun rose. Rhavas could complain about the architecture of the main temple—compared to what they were doing in the imperial capital, it was both provincial and archaic—but not about his congregation's size or enthusiasm.

People bowed to him and made Phos' sun-sign as he strode up the center aisle toward the altar. His robes were the most splendid he owned, almost wholly of cloth of gold and richly encrusted with rubies, emeralds, sapphires, and pearls. They were robes probably finer than any provincial prelate deserved to wear; they were robes fit for an ecumenical patriarch.

(He would not think of Eladas. He would not . . . except when, willy-nilly, he did.)

When he took his place at the center of things—as he had been at the center of things in Skopentzana for so many years—he raised his hands and his eyes to the heavens. The whole congregation imitated his gesture. Along with everyone else in the temple, he recited the creed: "We bless thee, Phos, lord with the great and good mind, by thy grace our protector, watchful beforehand that the great test of life may be decided in our favor."

Because Videssians spoke the creed so often, they sometimes spoke it in a perfunctory way, saying the words but not really feeling or caring what they meant. Not here. Not now. Every syllable burst from every throat achingly informed with meaning. Everyone in the city knew what had happened to the wizards who went out against the Khamorth. A few more came back to Skopentzana after Rhavas and Koubatzes. The rest did not come back at all. That carried its own message.

Rhavas lowered his hands, and the congregants sank back into their seats. He said, "Lord with the great and good mind, we know we are not a perfect people. We are men and women, and so Skotos afflicts us and makes us less than we ought to be." He turned his head and spat. His hearers carefully spat between their feet, so as not to foul their fellows.

"But we also know, O Phos, that we are ever mindful of thee, and that thy goodness is written on the doorposts of our hearts," Rhavas continued. "And we know that the savage barbarians who now afflict our lands acknowledge neither thy name nor the goodness that flows so bountifully from thy heart. They work evil for the sake of working evil, and they torment us both for sport and for the sake of evil. Therefore, if it please thee, keep them far from us. Turn them back toward the borders of our land, back toward the trackless steppe that is their natural home. So may it be, O lord with the great and good mind, if thou shouldst hear our prayer."

"So may it be," the congregation echoed.

Rhavas prayed on, with a sincerity and a passionate intensity he had never reached before. He knew what fueled that intensity: fear. Part of the fear looked ahead to what might happen if the Khamorth broke into Skopentzana, the rest looked back to the memory of what the plainsmen's shamans had inflicted on him and the other Videssians who'd ridden out to meet them.

Except for Koubatzes, Methodios, Ingeros, and a tiny handful of others, the Skopentzanans did not—could not—share the latter fear. *They are the lucky ones*, the prelate thought. But everyone in the temple could and did share the fear of a sack. Skopentzana had had no share in destruction for many years. The fear of enemies swarming over the walls and through the gates, though, was deeply ingrained in every city-dwelling Videssian.

That being so, Rhavas continued, "And we beseech thee, O lord with the great and good mind, to strengthen our right arms, that we may defend ourselves against the Khamorth and drive them back howling in defeat should they have the temerity to assail us. So may it be, O Phos."

"So may it be," his audience echoed once more, and signed themselves with the good god's sun-circle.

"In thy kindness and mercy, send us aid in our affliction," Rhavas said. "Let there be a swift end to strife internecine within the boundaries of the Empire of Videssos. Let the Avtokrator of the Videssians, thy vicegerent on earth, speedily send soldiers to deliver us from the barbarians and to protect us against all evil. O good god, O light of the universe, so may it be!"

"So may it be!" the congregation cried. Along with him, they raised their eyes and hands to the heavens in the hope that Phos would heed them.

When the service was over, Rhavas stood in the narthex to talk with the congregants who wanted to speak to him. Koubatzes gave him a grave bow. "What prayer may do, very holy sir, prayer has assuredly done," the mage said.

"I thank you," Rhavas replied.

"Whether you should is perhaps another question, for who knows what prayer may do?" With that cryptic utterance, Koubatzes bowed again and went out into the cold.

Zautzes waddled up to the prelate. Amusement—perhaps even admiration—sparked in the eparch's eyes. "You are a clever fellow, very holy sir, a most clever fellow," he said.

"I thank you for your kindness, most honorable sir," Rhavas said.

Zautzes chuckled as if he'd just caught a fat fly wafted along on a merry little breeze. "'Let the Avtokrator of the Videssians speedily send soldiers,'" he quoted. "Aye, let him indeed! And you managed to pray that he would without ever naming him. Well done! Very well done indeed!"

"As a cousin to Maleinos, I care a great deal about who rules the Empire," Rhavas said. "As prelate of threatened Skopentzana, I care not a fig. Whoever rules, let him send soldiers soon."

"That is well said." Zautzes bowed. As with most plump men, he needed some effort to do it. Straightening, he added, "You are an example to us all."

"I wish I were an example for the Avtokrator and the rebel,"

Rhavas said sadly. "They fight for the throne and forget the Empire they rule."

The eparch bowed again. "That is also well said." He paused for a moment, considering. "You being who you are, very holy sir, have you thought to write to his Majesty explaining your views?"

"Have I thought of it, being who I am? I have certainly thought of it, yes," Rhavas replied. "And I have decided not to do it. This has nothing to do with the difficulties of posting a letter in such unsettled times, either. It has to do with the difficulty of being who I am. One of the things a man in my position learns is that my cousin who is Avtokrator will brook more interference from a near-stranger than from me. He will presume the near-stranger knows no better, where he will presume I do know better and am seeking advantage in spite of what I know."

"I . . . see." Zautzes plucked at his beard. He let out a long sigh. "I must tell you, that makes more sense than I wish it did. You show yourself to be not unacquainted with the way the mind of a powerful man is likely to work." He turned as if to go, then paused and looked back at the prelate. "But it is a great pity all the same, is it not?" He didn't wait for an answer, but sorrowfully waddled away.

Balked of the chance to say anything, Rhavas found himself nodding. Zautzes told nothing but the truth there. Had Rhavas thought the Avtokrator would pay any attention to his pleas, he would not have hesitated an instant in making them. Only being sure they were pointless held him back.

For that matter, he had no idea whether Maleinos even had any men he *could* send to Skopentzana if he wanted to. Surely the Khamorth also menaced other towns closer to Videssos the city. How much of the Empire of Videssos were the barbarians overrunning? How much would still be in Videssian hands by the time this suicidal civil war was done? Would the Empire belonging to whoever finally won be worth having?

Maleinos and Stylianos think so, Rhavas thought gloomily. *As long as they do, no one else's opinion matters.*

Women came down from their gallery. Some of them visited the temple to be seen going in and out of it, even if custom kept them from being seen while they worshiped. Some of the younger men were every bit as much on display. But some of the women were as serious about what went on in the wider world as any of the men. And some were at least as shrewd as any of their male counterparts.

"Can we buy off the barbarians?" one matron asked Rhavas. "Can we send them gold to leave this city alone?"

"Perhaps," Rhavas said. "It is the weaker party's ploy in diplomacy, and usually a bad precedent, but perhaps. But what is to keep the Khamorth from taking our money and then attacking even so?"

"Why, the hope of getting more money from us later, of course," she answered.

"It is to be considered," Rhavas admitted. She gave him a brisk nod and strode out of the temple, wrapping her ermine stole around her neck as she went.

Ingegerd's bright hair made Rhavas imagine the noonday sun lit the narthex. She walked up to him with a grave nod of approval. "You spoke well, very holy sir," she said.

"For which I thank you," Rhavas said. "I wish I did not need to beseech the good god to aid us in such troubled times."

"We do what we must do," the Haloga woman said. "We beg the good god to help us, and we do all we can to help ourselves."

"You are a sensible woman." Rhavas shook his head. He did not want to patronize her. It suddenly seemed important that he not patronize her. "You are a sensible person. Himerios is fortunate in you."

With its granite underpinnings, the way her face softened was startling. "If you have room left in your heart after praying for Skopentzana, please pray for Himerios. Every time the Avtokrator and the rebel fight, I die a little more inside. And now Maleinos will have to face the barbarians, too."

Stylianos would also have to face them. Ingegerd said nothing about him, for her husband served the Avtokrator. Trying to console her as best he could, Rhavas said, "I do not think the Khamorth will attack the imperial army any time soon. They will do what is easy before they try anything hard."

"That puts off the evil day. It does not mean the evil day will not come," Ingegerd replied. Her cold, clear intelligence saw through to the heart of things. What she saw now with it made her own heart break. Struggling to hold the iron self-control Rhavas had always known in her, she went on, "I fear it will be long and long before Himerios comes home to Skopentzana once more."

"What will you do?" Rhavas asked.

Ingegerd hesitated. The prelate had not realized how he was hanging on her answer till he noticed he did not breathe while he waited. At least, she said, "I shall do the best I can, very holy sir. What else can I possibly do?"

And what is that? Rhavas thought it, but did not ask it. Being as sensible as she was, she would have told him she did not know now, but would have to find out as time went by. Why ask the question when you already know the answer? Instead, he said, "You are as wise as—" He broke off.

"As what, very holy sir?" Ingegerd asked, direct as usual.

As you are beautiful. But Himerios had asked him to keep an eye on her not for his own sake but for the officer's. And he had his own vows, his own knowledge of what he must not do, of what he had taken solemn oath he would not do, hedging him round. "As you are sensible," he said, hardly half a heartbeat later than he should have.

"My sense seems senseless. My wisdom, such as it is, fails me. He is not here; because he is not here, Midwinter's Day might as well not have come." Ingegerd gathered herself. "In your kindness, you might pray for me as well, but only after you pray for Skopentzana and for Himerios. They are more important." She dipped her head to him, then left the narthex, her back straight, looking only ahead, never behind.

Someone else came up to Rhavas after she had gone. The prelate must have said the sorts of things that needed saying. The man or woman must have been satisfied with whatever he did say. He had no memory of any of it. His thoughts were only on Ingegerd. *I will pray for you,* he thought. *Oh, yes.* And if Himerios was hacked to pieces by barbarian blades, if Skopentzana fell in fire and ruin, he would have prayed for what was important to him.

He realized that was wrong. Realizing it and being able to do anything about it were two different things. As long as he was praying, he would have to add some prayer for himself.

Not long after the prayer service, peasants began fleeing into Skopentzana from their outlying farms. Some told tales of horror, having barely escaped with their lives after the Khamorth plundered them and their neighbors. Others, wiser or simply more afraid of what might happen, ran off before disaster came down on them.

Zautzes began by putting the refugees in the barracks halls the garrison had occupied till recently. Before long, they filled those halls to overflowing. Skopentzana's temples housed some. The eparch quartered others on people who volunteered to help them. People stopped volunteering when one of the peasant fugitives got caught trying to sell his host's silver candlesticks.

That delightful news sent Zautzes to Rhavas' study. "What am I supposed to do now, very holy sir?" the eparch demanded in tones not far from despair. "I have people shouting at me to shut the gates against any more peasants. By the good god, I have people shouting at me to throw all the peasants already in Skopentzana out in the snow."

"Would you punish those who have done no wrong along with the guilty?" Rhavas asked. "Where is the justice in that?"

"The fellow who heads the militia we're using in place of real soldiers says they're eating up our food and not giving us anything in return," Zautzes replied. "He says they'll make it harder for us to stand siege if we have to, and so we ought to run 'em out."

"*Can* the Khamorth besiege us? Can we do anything at all about it if they do except pray and hope for the best? If they can and we can, can we last long enough for what these peasants eat to matter?" Rhavas was full of questions.

Zautzes only shrugged—once, twice, three times. "Very holy sir, I don't know the answer to any of those. I don't suppose anybody in Skopentzana does. I'll tell you this, though: I don't want trouble inside the city, especially now. I don't want these raggedy peasants stealing from people who are trying to do them good. And I don't want a mob going peasant hunting and murdering and raping for the fun of it, either."

"A point," the prelate admitted. "All right, then. Tell the head of the militia to come here before me. Maybe we can see eye to eye."

"I'll do it," Zautzes said at once. "I hope you can get him to see straight. Phaos knows I haven't had any luck."

The man who led Skopentzana's militia—the man who apparently had had the idea to form it—was a mason named Toxaras. He had a thick black beard with the first few streaks of gray in it, a face handsome in a rough sort of way, and the scarred, callused hands typical of his trade. Rhavas barely knew him; the man was not in the habit of worshiping at the chief temple.

Matzoukes showed him into Rhavas' study. Toxaras stared at the swarm of books in some surprise. The lesser priest had to cough to get him to bow to Rhavas. "Very holy sir," he murmured, his voice deep and rough. His wave encompassed the scrolls and codices. "Have you *read* all of these?"

Rhavas wished he had a copper for every time he'd heard that question. By now, the coppers would have added up to several gold-pieces—*for charity, of course*, he thought. "They aren't much good to anyone if he doesn't read them, are they?" he returned.

"Are they any good to anyone if he *does* read them?" Toxaras asked.

Before Rhavas could get angry, he realized the mason was serious. "I think so," he said. By the way Toxaras' mouth twisted, he wasn't convinced. The prelate continued, "I fear you are stirring up unrest in the city."

"Not me, very holy sir." Toxaras shook his head. "No, not me, by the good god. It's these cursed thieving peasants. They're the trouble. I just want to be rid of 'em."

"You want to leave them at the mercy of the Khamorth, you mean," Rhavas said, "the only trouble being that the Khamorth know no mercy."

Toxaras' bushy eyebrows drew down and together in a frown. "You make me out to be a villain, and a heartless man. I am no Skotos-lover." He spat on the floor. So did Rhavas. Frowning still, Toxaras said, "I am no villain. I am a man of Skopentzana. I want the best for my city. When I see these people eating up our food and stealing from the ones who took them in, when I see none of them in the militia, I think they put us all in danger. I don't see how anyone else could think any different, either." He glared defiance at the prelate.

In a struggle of good against evil, figuring out what to do was child's play. Not so when two conflicting visions of good collided. What *did* count for more, sheltering those peasants in Skopentzana or protecting the city against both them and the plainsmen? It was less clear-cut than Rhavas wished it were.

Sighing, he said, "If a man steals, no one can quarrel with forcing him out of the city. But how can you say the like when you speak of men who have done no wrong, of women who will have to suffer the nomads' lusts, of children who will be murdered while the nomads laugh? Where is the justice in expelling them?"

"They eat, very holy sir," Toxaras said patiently. "If Skopentzana holds twice as many people as usual, its food will last only half as long. That puts all of us in twice the danger we'd know otherwise."

"No." Rhavas' voice was sharp. "That *would* put us in twice the danger. But the peasants have not doubled our numbers, nor anything close to it. And since they have not, the danger has not come close to doubling, either." If Toxaras tried to chop logic with him, the mason would be sorry. Rhavas had been a prize student at the Collegium in Videssos the city.

But Toxaras didn't try. Shrugging broad shoulders, he said, "Have it your way. There's more people in Skopentzana right now than there ought to be. That means we're in more danger than we ought to be. And *that* means we ought to run those peasants out."

Rhavas folded his arms across the chest. "I say the risk is acceptable."

"Maybe it would be, if we had the garrison here," Toxaras said. "Now? I know the militia. I'd cursed well better, eh? We'll do our best, and that's the truth. But we aren't real soldiers, as much as I wish we were. We haven't got the weapons, we haven't got the armor, we haven't got the drilling regular soldiers get. We'll do the best we can, yes, not that those peasants will thank us for it. But I have to tell you, I don't know how good it will be."

"This also would be true regardless of whether we had refugees in the city," Rhavas replied. "Here is what I say to you as prelate of Skopentzana: if you expel people who have done nothing to deserve it, I shall anathematize you in the temple for all to hear. No one will treat with you after that, and Skotos' ice will await you on your death. You say you do not love the dark god. Now is your chance to prove it."

The mason's glare looked hot enough to melt all the snow for miles around. "All right. *All right*," he said heavily. "Have your way, very holy sir." He turned Rhavas' title into one of contempt, even of hatred. "Yes, have your way. But here is what I have to say to you: if Skopentzana falls, on your head be it. If the Khamorth sack this town, on your head be it. If they rape my wife and kill my kids, on your head be it. And if they slaughter all your precious peasants, too, on your head be it. I've done what I can for Skopentzana. You're doing what you can *to* Skopentzana." He sprang to his feet and stormed from the study. A moment later, the outer door to Rhavas' residence slammed thunderously.

Rhavas looked up past the ceiling to the heavens. Slowly, he nodded, as if at a bargain in the market square. "Lord with the great and good mind, I have done that which is right in my eyes," he said. "Grant the benefit of our salvation to this, the city I serve. And if Skopentzana should fall to the barbarians because I prove to be in error, let the blame be on my head. Let others be free of it. So may it be."

He waited, his head cocked a bit to the side, one eyebrow quizzically raised, as if expecting some answer from the good god. None came, of course. Phos was not in the habit of answering prayers in so many words. The play of events showed which were answered, which denied.

Not for me, the prelate thought. *Not for me, but for the city.* That part of the prayer stayed silent, but the good god surely heard it as well as he heard the part Rhavas had offered aloud.

Matzoukes poked his head into the study. "Am I right in guessing Toxaras was less than happy at what you told him?"

"I fear you are," Rhavas replied. "He disagrees with me down to his very bones, but he will do as I have asked him. The peasants will stay in Skopentzana. No one will be cast out of this our city without good cause. No one, do you hear me?"

"I certainly do, very holy sir." The young priest sketched the sun-circle over his heart. "May everything come to pass as you desire."

"Yes. May it indeed." Rhavas got to his feet. Weariness—not just of body but of spirit—shrouded him. He felt as if he'd been in a physical brawl with Toxaras, not just a battle of wills. He wasn't altogether sure he'd won it, either, even if the head of the militia had yielded to him. He was bruised inside, if not on his arms and shoulders and face.

Rhavas was used to getting his way in all things, partly because of who his ancestors were but more because of who he was. He'd got his way here, too, even if he'd had to threaten to hurl anathemas at Toxaras to do it. He'd got his way, but he hadn't

mastered the other man's will. Toxaras remained as convinced of
his own righteousness as Rhavas was of his.

The prelate sighed and stretched and sat down again. He said,
"Would you be kind enough to fetch me a cup of wine? I have
a bad taste I should like to wash out of my mouth."

"Of course, very holy, sir. I'll be right back." Matzoukes hurried away.

When Rhavas took the wine, he relied as much on the ritual
accompanying it as on the drink itself to calm his nerves. Raising
his hands to the heavens, rejecting Skotos with his spittle . . . How
many times had he done that before drinking? More than he
could count. That very familiarity—was it like what husband and
wife enjoyed after years together? He could not truly judge that.
He did know the ritual was the one thing he might have known
better than his own name.

Today, though, neither it nor the sweet wine soothed him as
he had hoped. Toxaras' defiance still roiled his spirit. *I am not
wrong*, Rhavas told himself again and again. *I am not wrong.*

Unable to sit still, he strode out of the study, draped himself
in his warmest robe, and left the residence. A man in ragged,
threadbare clothes was staring at the great bronze of Stavrakios
as if he'd never seen such a marvel. He probably hadn't—he had
to be one of the peasants Toxaras so despised.

You will stay here and you will be safe, Rhavas vowed to himself. *You will, or on my head be it.*

The Khamorth stayed away from Skopentzana longer than Rhavas or anyone else there would have dared hope after the local mages and the prelate came back defeated from trying to force them away by sorcery. Koubatzes came to Rhavas' study and said, "Maybe our magic did more good than we thought. They hit us, yes, but we hit them, too."

"It could be so," Rhavas replied. "I would not presume to tell you it is not so, sorcerous sir. But I would tell you this: I prefer to account for it with the prayers the whole city offered up to the lord with the great and good mind."

"It could be so, very holy sir." Koubatzes' tone of voice was almost identical to the one Rhavas had used moments before. It showed polite skepticism, but skepticism unmistakable for anything else.

"Why do you disbelieve?" Rhavas asked.

"I don't disbelieve." Now Koubatzes showed alarm. Understandably so: the whole weight of the ecclesiastical and governmental hierarchies fell on a man who descended into heresy or apostasy. "I do not disbelieve," the wizard repeated, with even more emphasis than before. "But men have offered up prayers on all sorts of things over years uncounted without having them heard. How can you be so sure these were?"

That was a legitimate question. Rhavas said, "I will answer you in two ways. First, this prayer was for something of extraordinary importance to the city and to the Empire of Videssos. We are the ones who worship rightly, and so we may hope Phos will hear us. We cannot demand anything of the good god, but we may humbly beseech him. We may, and we have." Koubatzes stirred on his stool. Rhavas held up a hand. "I had not finished. The other thing I would say is, if our prayers failed, where are the barbarians?"

"I already gave you one other possible explanation, very holy sir," Koubatzes reminded him. "But if you think I will quarrel, if you think I will complain, you can think again. I do not know where the barbarians are. I do know that I miss them not in the least."

"Nor will I quarrel or complain over that, sorcerous sir," Rhavas said. When Koubatzes went his way, the two men were on good terms.

Rhavas began doing something he had not been in the habit of doing till then: strolling along the walkway atop Skopentzana's walls whenever the weather was good enough to let him see out into the distance and whenever it wasn't too bitterly cold to keep everyone indoors who didn't have the most urgent reasons for venturing outside.

Militiamen marched regardless of the weather, of course. Some of them greeted Rhavas with jokes when he did appear. "No wonder you didn't show up yesterday," one of them called after a day bitterly cold even by Skopentzana's stern standards. "You'd have frozen the top of your head right off."

Rhavas flipped back his hood and let his tonsured scalp shine forth for a moment. This day was also anything but warm. "Still seems to be there," he said, and the militiaman laughed.

Toxaras and some others, though, did not smile and joke when they saw the prelate. They couldn't be openly rude, not when Rhavas might punish them with anathemas. But they made a point of staying as far away from him as they could, and of being selectively deaf when he asked them questions. They remained convinced he was mistaken.

Because of that, he was surprised when Toxaras came to his residence one afternoon and said, "Please walk out to the wall with me, very holy sir, if you'd be so kind. There's something you need to see."

"Oh?" Rhavas got to his feet. "Yes, of course I'll come. Can you tell me what it is?"

"You'll know it when you see it," the mason answered, glowering at Rhavas from under his bushy brows. Rhavas feared he knew what that meant. But he was also sure Toxaras was waiting for him to ask again, so he didn't. He refused to give the militia leader the satisfaction.

By the way Toxaras kept scowling as they tramped out from the heart of Skopentzana to the western wall, he'd expected Rhavas to probe harder, and was annoyed when he failed to. Toxaras' anger was the least the prelate had to worry about.

Up the stairs they climbed, Toxaras not breathing hard, Rhavas panting a little by the time they got to the top. The militiamen atop the wall seemed much more alert than they had the last time Rhavas saw them. Nobody joked with him now. The grim-faced men were staring out to the snow-covered ground beyond the city.

"Well, go on," Toxaras said roughly, all but shoving Rhavas toward the outer perimeter. "So much for all your fancy prayers, very holy sir. There are the Khamorth. Have a look for yourself."

Like a man trapped in a nightmare, Rhavas strode out to the edge of the wall. Against all logic and reason, he hoped till the very last instant that Toxaras would prove mistaken. The leader of the militia wasn't wrong, of course. There were the nomads, just as he had said. They wore fur hats and fur jackets and unkempt beards that blended in with the one and the other. They had leather trousers and felt boots that were supposed to keep their feet warm no matter how cold it got. The small steppe ponies they rode were shaggy of mane and tail and coat in general, which only added to the animal impression the barbarians created.

"Yes, I see them," Rhavas said quietly. "They are there."

"Are you satisfied with your handiwork now?" Toxaras demanded.

"My handiwork?" Rhavas shook his head. "I had nothing to do with bringing them here. You must blame that on the civil war. I did everything I knew how to do to keep them away from Skopentzana. Obviously, I failed."

Toxaras blinked. He'd blamed Rhavas for so much, he'd plainly included some things for which the prelate was not responsible.

He shrugged now. "They're there, and we've got all those stinking peasants in the city. How are we supposed to stand siege?"

"I don't know," Rhavas answered. "How are they supposed to lay siege to a city like this? I've never heard that they were the masters of rams and catapults and siege towers."

"Who says they need to be?" Toxaras returned. "All they have to do is stay around while we get hungrier and hungrier."

Rhavas looked out at the plainsmen once more. None of them was within bowshot of the walls, or even within catapult range. They just sat on their horses, eyeing Skopentzana with, perhaps, as much thoughtful—even speculative—interest as Rhavas and Toxaras and the rest of the militiamen were giving them.

"They have to eat, too," Rhavas said. "What will they live on while they wait for us to starve?"

"Their flocks. Whatever they can steal from us," Toxaras answered.

"Will it be enough?"

"How do I know? How do you know it won't be? We'd have a better chance if we had fewer useless mouths in here."

"Who are the barbarians?" Rhavas asked. "Those outside the walls, or those within?"

"Very holy sir, I'm not going to argue with you about that. You can talk rings around me. We both know it," Toxaras said. "But I'll tell you one other thing I know: I know which side I'm on. And I know you haven't done my side any good." He spat on the paving stones, rejecting Rhavas as if he were Skotos.

Propriety and holiness forgotten, Rhavas swung at him. The blow was clumsy and unpracticed. Toxaras ducked under it. Rhavas swung again, in a blind fury. Toxaras blocked with his left forearm. Then *he* swung. The next thing Rhavas knew, he was sitting on his backside on those paving stones, gasping and fighting for breath, the pit of his stomach one vast ache.

"Get up," Toxaras said, breathing hard. "Get up and get out of here, Skotos eat you. I didn't want to do that. I've got all the witnesses in the world that you tried to slug me first, but I still didn't want to do that. Go on. Get out. If I see you up here again, I'm liable to try and murder you."

Rhavas couldn't get up right away—not till that horrible feeling of being unable to breathe eased a little. Then, slowly and painfully, he rose. He hobbled all bent over for a few steps, like a sick old man. Pausing then, he made himself straighten. He still moved slowly, but he moved the way he should have moved. It hurt as much as anything he'd ever done, but he did it. Pride could be a terrible thing for any man, and all the more so for a priest.

As he got to the head of the stairs, he turned back and pointed at Toxaras. "I curse you as you have cursed me," he said.

The head of the militia fleered laughter. He gave Rhavas a gesture nasty boys had used on the streets of Videssian towns since time out of mind. Rhavas started to return it, then checked himself. He'd already lowered himself to Toxaras' level once. That was quite bad enough.

He went on down the stairs. Each footfall hurt. He was biting the inside of his lower lip against the pain by the time he got to the bottom. But he stayed straight. Yes, pride could be a cruel master indeed.

"Very holy sir?"

"What?" Rhavas didn't want to talk to anybody right now. He wanted to go back to his residence and pretend everything that had happened lately was only a bad dream. He knew better, of course, but the worst nightmare seemed better than this dreadful reality.

But the peasant in front of him didn't, couldn't, know anything about that. His colorless clothes, his colorful, rustic accent, and his hangdog manner all proclaimed him for what he was. "Phaos bless you, very holy sir, is all I wanted to say," he went on now. "I've heard how you done stuck up for us, and I reckoned you should ought to know we're right grateful."

Rhavas had never felt less blessed by the lord with the great and good mind. He didn't tell the peasant that. The man was being as pleasant and gracious as he knew how, and deserved to be treated the same way himself. The prelate stiffly inclined his head. "I thank you."

"No, very holy sir. I thank *you*." Awkwardly sketching the sun-sign, the peasant turned away.

"Phos bless you as well," Rhavas added—he should have said that first. The other man waved to him and went to do whatever such people did with their time. An aristocrat since birth, Rhavas had no real notion of what that might be.

He was still moving stiffly when he got back to his residence. "Are you all right, very holy sir?" Matzoukes asked.

"The Khamorth have come to Skopentzana," Rhavas answered. "How can anyone in the city be all right now?" The young priest exclaimed in dismay. He didn't ask Rhavas anything more about himself. That came as a little relief, or maybe more than a little.

Bit by bit, the bruise on Rhavas' midsection faced from purple to greenish blue to yellow. The bruise on his spirit took longer to heal. He wondered if it would ever fully fade.

When he and Toxaras saw each other on the streets, they both turned away at the same time. It was as if neither trusted himself in the presence of the other. Rhavas knew he didn't.

No matter what Toxaras had said, he would go up on the wall every so often to look out at the plainsmen. Somehow, the militia leader was never nearby when he did. The Khamorth would occasionally ride up and shoot a few arrows at the men on the wall. The defenders shot back. A few people got hurt, but only a few. It was a desultory sort of siege. But no one came into Skopentzana, and no one seemed eager to try to go out of the city, either.

Zautzes began rationing grain. The rations were smaller than people would have liked, but not small enough to make them suffer. They soon got used to them. Toxaras, however, scowled fiercely at the idea of food being rationed at all. And he scowled whenever he saw peasant refugees lining up to get their allotted amount of grain along with folk whose families had lived in Skopentzana for generations.

Rhavas affected not to notice that, or the whispers that followed him around. Toxaras was not the only man who resented his stand on behalf of the peasants. *To the ice with all of them*, the prelate thought fiercely.

He was just coming back to the residence after getting his own ration—he was too proud to have Matzoukes pick it up for him—when someone called his name. He turned and stared through spatters of snow. It was Voilas, a potter who'd become Toxaras' second in command in the militia.

"Yes? What is it?" Rhavas' voice was colder than the weather. Voilas had never made any secret of agreeing with Toxaras.

Now, though, the militia officer sketched the sun-sign on his breast before speaking. "P-p-please come with me, very holy sir."

He had to try three times to choke out the first word. His face was white as the snow on the wind.

"Why should I?" Rhavas snapped. "What will you show me to lacerate my spirit now?"

"By the good god, very holy sir, this you must see." Voilas drew the sun-sign again, more vehemently this time.

Glaring, Rhavas said, "If you are fooling me, you will pay." Voilas violently shook his head. He had the air of a man rocked to the core. *Something* had happened. The prelate grudged him a nod. "Wait till I put my grain away, then."

"Yes, very holy sir. Whatever you say, very holy sir." If Voilas was only pretending to be rocked, he made a better actor than any Rhavas had seen in the mime troupes on Midwinter's Day.

When Rhavas came out again, the potter led him toward the western wall. Rhavas' suspicions flared again. That was where Toxaras had shown him the Khamorth after he began to hope Skopentzana had fended them off. "How now?" he growled as they neared the wall.

"You'll see for yourself in just a moment, very holy sir." Voilas kept repeating the title as if it were some kind of charm.

They came around the last steep-roofed building. A crowd of men—mostly militiamen, but a few ordinary townsfolk, too—stood near the base of the stairway Rhavas had used to reach the wall and descend from it on the day when he quarreled with Toxaras.

"Phaos! Here's the prelate!" somebody in the crowd said. The men scattered. Some of them hurried back up onto the wall. Some went into Skopentzana. Some seemed to flee almost at random, as long as they were moving away from Rhavas. That left . . .

"You see, very holy sir," Voilas whispered.

"I see." Of itself, Rhavas' hand shaped the sun-sign. There lay Toxaras, his head twisted at an unnatural angle, the right side of his face and of his skull crushed. Blood pooled beneath his ruined head. It still steamed—this had just happened. But, though his blood might still be warm, he was only too plainly dead. "How?" Rhavas asked.

"You ought to know, very holy sir," Voilas told him.

"What do you mean?" the prelate demanded irritably.

"You cursed him up there—right up there, very holy sir." Voilas pointed to the top of the wall. More militiamen were staring down at Toxaras' body. Some of them signed themselves when their eyes met Rhavas'. Voilas went on, "You cursed him up there, very holy sir, and he was coming down the stairs, and he slipped on some snow or some ice, and he fell—and there he lays."

"Lies." Rhavas made the correction without conscious thought.

He made it, and Voilas didn't understand it. "No lies, very holy sir. Nothing but the truth, by the good god. Your curse bit, and he's dead. No one's going to quarrel with you now, very holy sir. You tell us what to do, and we'll do it. You'd best believe we will. We want to keep on breathing, we do."

"Why don't you curse the Khamorth, very holy sir?" a militia-man called from the top of the wall. Several others nodded.

"This is nonsense," Rhavas said. "This is chance. Men curse one another every day. This is nothing but Toxaras' bad luck. Anyone can slip on snow or ice. I had nothing to do with it."

"Not likely, very holy sir." Voilas shook his head again. "No, not bloody likely. Bad men call on Skotos"—he spat—"and the dark god listens. Everybody knows that. If a good man calls on Phos, won't he listen, too?"

Rhavas still stared at the crumpled corpse. He didn't remember calling on the good god when he cursed Toxaras. He'd just retaliated for the mason's curse on him. He said, "I have prayed to the lord with the great and good mind to send the barbarians far away. I will go on praying for that, you may be sure."

"That's not enough. That's not anywhere close to enough," Voilas insisted. "You have to curse them, very holy sir. Then we'll be rid of them."

"You think I can do more than I can," Rhavas told him.

"I know you can do more than you think." Voilas pointed to Toxaras' body. "Doesn't that tell you anything?"

"Phos! Don't just leave it lying there. Have some men take it away," Rhavas said. They wouldn't bury Toxaras for some time—not till the ground thawed out. "Does he have family? They'll need to know."

"He has a wife and four little ones," Voilas replied. "It won't be easy for them without him."

He was bound to be right about that. Even so, Rhavas said, "It's not my fault. I had nothing to do with it. I'm sorry he's dead. You can't blame me for that, and neither can his family." A wife and four children! They would have had a hard time without their breadwinner even if the Khamorth weren't prowling outside Skopentzana.

Voilas said, "Everybody knows you cursed him, very holy sir. You can say whatever you want now, but everybody knows. Everybody will know how he died, too. It's no secret."

"You told me himself how he died—he slipped on ice or snow. What has that got to do with me?" the prelate demanded.

"How many times had he been up and down those stairs before you cursed him? Did he fall down them then? Nooo." Voilas stretched the word. "Did anybody else fall down them? Nooooo." He stretched it even further.

"How many times was he up and down them *after* I cursed him?" Rhavas said frantically. "He didn't slip right away. This is all madness, I tell you."

"Yes, very holy sir." That wasn't Voilas agreeing with him. That was the potter being too afraid to contradict him.

The prelate stared at the body one more time. Toxaras' blood had stopped steaming now. There should have been flies. So Rhavas told himself, anyway. But Skopentzana in winter had no flies. Insects knew better than to venture out in this weather. Had they tried, they would have frozen.

Did Toxaras think the curse had struck home, too? Had his last horrified moments been spent in blaming Rhavas? No one would ever know.

No news came up from the south. News in Skopentzana was often sketchy in the wintertime, but this winter it was not sketchy. It was, in a word, nonexistent. How widely had the Khamorth spread through Videssos? Rhavas couldn't know, but he could make guesses, and he liked none of them.

Zautzes began reducing the grain ration as winter wore along. It got small enough to pinch, though not to threaten people with actual starvation. *Not yet*, Rhavas thought gloomily. He prayed every day for the Khamorth to abandon the city. They didn't. The not-quite-siege dragged on.

The militia sent a mounted party out through a postern gate. If Skopentzana didn't know what was happening in the wider reaches of the Empire, odds were the rest of the Empire didn't know what was going on here in the northeast, either. The militiamen hoped a garrison in some nearby city would come to Skopentzana's rescue.

Rhavas suspected that was a forlorn hope. If Skopentzana's garrison had marched off to fight in the civil war, wouldn't others have done the same? It only stood to reason, or so it seemed to him. With Voilas leading them, though, how much did the militiamen care about reason? Not much—that was how it looked to the prelate, anyhow.

He prayed for the riders' success all the same. Bad odds didn't make things impossible, just unlikely.

Day followed day. No imperial soldiers marched or rode into Skopentzana from the south. None of the men who'd ridden away from the city ever came back. No one could be sure what had happened to them. No one could be sure—but, again, Rhavas liked none of the guesses he made.

People began talking behind his back. They would point at him when they thought he wasn't looking, then quickly turn away when they thought he was. Some people who'd attended the divine liturgy at his temple for years suddenly began worshiping elsewhere. Some he'd never seen before began coming to the services he led. He reckoned the trade a bad bargain. The new worshipers eyed him as if hoping he would curse someone else so they could watch the luckless victim expire before their eyes.

He felt like cursing *them*. He didn't do that, either. Curses were a serious business, even if they didn't seem to understand that. Or if curses weren't a serious business, then they were of no account at all, which also wasn't what the newly arrived ghouls in the congregation wanted to hear.

Rhavas tried to keep his preaching and his prayers as close to what they would have been without the civil war and the irruption of the Khamorth as he could. It wasn't always possible. He did have to keep mentioning the peasant refugees and to keep reminding his audience that the peasants were just as much Videssians as were people whose forebears had lived in Skopentzana for the past 150 years.

Not everybody appreciated being reminded. Militiamen would sometimes get up and walk out in the middle of a sermon. So would some of the more prosperous merchants and landowners in the city. When Rhavas went out to the narthex to talk informally with people after the divine liturgy, he would notice that some of the women had also left their gallery earlier than they might have.

Ingegerd was never one of those. Because of her sun-bright hair, he would have noticed if she'd been among the missing. "You do well," she told him after one of his more impassioned sermons.

He bowed as if she and not he were the one with the imperial connections. Did her good opinion matter so much to him? Plainly, it did. "I thank you very much," he told her, doing his best not to show how much that came from the heart.

"We would be fools to stir up strife inside the city when the barbarians outside trouble us so," she went on.

Some in Skopentzana would have called her a barbarian, even though she was married to a Videssian. Before he got to know her, Rhavas might have done that himself. That people would be fools to stir up strife inside Skopentzana had never occurred to the prelate, which didn't mean Ingegerd was mistaken. Rhavas said, "We would be *wrong* to seek to cast out the refugees."

"Well, yes. That, too, of course," Ingegerd said. The practical issue mattered more to her than the moral one.

That disappointed the prelate. Ideally, Ingegerd should have thought just the way he did. He said, "If we do not help one another, who will help us when we need help the most?"

"Even so." She nodded briskly. "I wish Phos would have made the rebel and the Avtokrator ask this same question of themselves."

She had to know Rhavas was Maleinos' cousin. He couldn't remember speaking about it, but it was anything but a secret in Skopentzana. Yet she did not hesitate to criticize Maleinos and Stylianos in the same breath. Did that make her naïve or simply confident in her own sense of what was fitting?

Not everything Maleinos had done since the rebellion broke out was something Rhavas would have done had he worn the red boots in his cousin's place. He couldn't possibly have claimed otherwise. He said, "It is sad but true that a man will do what he thinks to be to his advantage, and then will find—or invent—all manner of reasons to explain why what he did was the only possible moral thing to do."

"Phos will judge those who act so." Ingegerd sounded as stern as the grimmest theologian Videssos the city had ever spawned.

"Phos will judge all of us," Rhavas agreed. "Any man—or any

woman—who forgets the Bridge of the Separator and lives for this world alone is bound to pay the price through all eternity."

"Even so," she said again, and dropped him a curtsy no noble-woman would have been ashamed of. "And now, very holy sir, if you will excuse me . . ." Wool skirt billowing around her legs, she swept out of the temple.

Rhavas did not think he watched her with particularly close attention. He did not think so, but he could not deny he missed the first half of what a still-plump merchant said to him, and had to ask the man to repeat himself. The merchant chuckled as he did. "Aye, she's worth looking at, isn't she?" he added. "If she warmed your bed, you wouldn't have to worry about winter nights." His elbow dug into Rhavas' ribs.

Penance. I need more penance, the prelate told himself. *Any man who forgets the Bridge of the Separator . . .* Had he condemned himself out of his own mouth?

He'd done nothing incorrect. He hadn't tried to seduce her. He hadn't even tried to touch her hand or stroke her hair. But his thoughts were not what they should have been. Admitting as much was better than trying to pretend he was pure—wasn't it?

Usually, the temple seemed a refuge from the hurly-burly of the secular world. Now Rhavas was glad to escape it. He felt impure, unclean, unworthy of the high ecclesiastical rank he had won and the even higher rank to which he aspired. If he could not master his own animal nature, what good was he?

In the square between the temple and the prefect's residence was some sort of commotion. People came running toward the trouble from all directions, shouting as they might have when a couple of schoolboys squabbled. But these were no schoolboys. They were men, men shoving and cursing at one another. Even as Rhavas began to run that way himself, the first sword came out, its sharp edge gleaming in the sun.

The prelate needed no more than a moment to recognize what was going on. Militiamen were squaring off against peasants who'd sought refuge in Skopentzana. The sword he'd seen was in a peasant's hands. A moment later, blades also leaped from militiamen's scabbards.

"Hold!" Rhavas shouted in a great voice. "By the lord with the great and good mind, hold! Put up your blades, all of you! Put up, I say!"

They *did* put up, a measure of the power Rhavas had in the city even among the militiamen who despised him. As in a schoolyard fight, each side pointed at the other and shouted, "They started it!" Then they both shouted, "Liars!" at the same time and almost started brawling again.

"Who laughs when we fight among ourselves?" Rhavas demanded. "Who gains when we act like fools? I can tell you, if you are too blind to see for yourselves. The Khamorth gain, and Skotos laughs." He spat on the ground. "Can you not hear him? Do you seek to have him triumph over the good god? *Do* you?"

"No, very holy sir." Peasants and militiamen spoke together, in small voices. They might have been boys caught out by the schoolmaster.

But then one of the peasants said, "We're sick of having these sacks of dung stare down their snoots at us and call us names because we grow food to keep them alive and don't make our living by cheating our neighbors."

That brought forth howls from the militiamen. The peasant would have done better not to call names when he was complaining about other people calling him and his friends names. The militiamen pointed that out in angry detail.

"Enough!" Rhavas said. "Enough from both sides, by the good god! For there should be no sides inside Skopentzana. We have to face out, against the barbarians beyond the walls. If we battle among ourselves, what do we do? We make matters easier for the nomads."

"Better the barbarians than these bastards," a peasant said. "At least the plainsmen'll treat *everybody* bad."

"Traitors!" the militiamen shouted. "Polecats!" They yelled out as many other choice epithets as they could think of, too. The peasants shouted back. Yet again, men on both sides started reaching for weapons.

Rhavas thought of invoking Zautzes' authority. Had the eparch still had a garrison of loyal imperial regulars, the prelate would have done it. But, had the eparch had a garrison like that, there would have been no militia to begin with. Rhavas sighed. Whatever happened here, it was up to him.

He pointed first to the militiamen, then to the peasants. "You *will not* raise weapons against each other. You *will not* insult or revile each other. We are all Videssians. We are none of us savage plainsmen. We will act like what we are. Do you understand me? *Do you?*"

Sullenly, both peasants and militiamen nodded. "They're out to land us all in trouble," a militiaman said, in spite of nodding.

"That will be enough of that. That, in fact, is too much of that," Rhavas said. "You do not seem to want to take me seriously. I will tell you how serious I am about this business, gentlemen. If you do raise weapons against each other, my curse will fall upon you. If you do insult or revile each other, my curse will fall upon you once again. Do I make myself plain?"

Before Toxaras plunged to his death, they wouldn't have paid any attention to Rhavas. He knew that. He knew it all too well. But he was not ashamed to exploit their superstition for the good of Skopentzana. And the threat worked better than he'd dreamt it could. Militiamen and peasants all gasped in horror and dismay. They sheathed their weapons. They backed away from one another.

And they pulled away from the prelate. So did the townsfolk who'd gathered to watch the fight. When Rhavas spoke of cursing, no one wanted to be anywhere near him. All at once, he stood by himself in the middle of the square.

He was sad—and yet, at the same time, he wasn't. He'd done what he'd set out to do: he'd persuaded the militiamen and the peasants to stop fighting each other and to stop baiting each other. As long as they all stood foursquare for the defense of the city, he was sure all would be well.

I put the fear of Phos in them just in time, he thought. If that peasant thought the Khamorth a better bargain than the militiamen, then things in Skopentzana had come to a pretty pass indeed.

When next he preached at the temple, half the seats were empty. The men sitting in the others eyed him as the folk of Videssos the city eyed one of the elephants occasionally imported from the barbarous lands across the Sailors' Sea: as a strange, dangerous, and clever beast now apparently harmless but liable to break loose and devastate its surroundings at any moment. When they sketched Phos' sun-sign above their hearts, he got the feeling that they were aiming it at him.

He spoke of the need for reconciliation. "We are all followers of the lord with the great and good mind," he declared, something not far from desperation in his voice. "We are all Videssians.

When we face the barbarians beyond the walls, surely this counts for more than all our differences."

Surely. The word echoed mockingly in his mind. He knew better. Every man—and every woman in the upper gallery—who heard him knew better. Faction fights were meat and drink in the Empire of Videssos. The present civil war was only the biggest symptom of the disease. At a pinch, Videssians would form factions and passionately back them regardless of the nature of the argument: theology, racing horses, which street they lived on. They reveled in controversy. If they couldn't find anything old to argue about, they would invent something new. This latest squabble between militiamen and peasants was a case in point.

After the sermon, Zautzes waddled up to him in the narthex. "By the good god, very holy sir, every word of that needed saying," the eparch told him. "Every single word. People need to hear these things, to the ice with me if they don't."

"I'm glad you think so, most honorable sir," Rhavas replied. "I am afraid people hear these things every day. What they need to do is listen to them."

"Well, if they won't listen to you, they won't listen to anybody." Zautzes chuckled. "After all, if they don't pay attention to you, you'll make them sorry, in this world and the next."

Rhavas wanted to despair. "Don't tell me you believe in that idiotic nonsense about curses! That's all it is—nonsense. Any rational man knows as much."

"No doubt," Zautzes said. "But then, how many men are rational?" He walked away before Rhavas could find an answer for that. The prelate wasn't sure he liked the answer he found.

A matron descending from the women's gallery told him what a charming sermon he'd preached. He'd thought of a lot of words for it, but that wasn't any of them. On the other hand, she seemed to have no idea that so many townsfolk feared him. A rational man himself—or so he believed, at any rate—he hadn't dreamt mere ignorance could be so comforting.

Because he *was* so comforted, he listened to her longer than he would have otherwise. Even so, he turned away when Ingegerd came toward him. The matron muttered something about barbarians and sluts, not quite far enough under her breath. She never knew how close Rhavas came to cursing her then and there—or how lucky she was that he didn't.

"You spoke well, very holy sir," Ingegerd said. "But then, you commonly do."

Rhavas bowed. "I thank you. I thank you very much. Do you think anyone will heed me? That is the true measure of speaking well."

The garrison commander's wife only shrugged. "I cannot tell you. I wish I could. Folk have a way of hearing what they want to hear—no more and no less. And you Videssians, meaning no offense, have a way of quarreling amongst yourselves."

"How can I take offense at what is so plainly true?" Rhavas asked.

Ingegerd shrugged again. "Plenty of people have no trouble at all." That was also true, even if, once more, he wished it weren't. She went on, "You are trying to take these folk in the direction they ought to go. You deserve the credit for that, and they deserve the blame if they will not follow."

"I am not the one who will punish them if they do not," Rhavas said. "The Khamorth will lash them with whips of scorpions."

"So they will, if Phos decides they should." Ingegerd was a convert to faith in the good god, but her belief was firm.

"Yes, if Phos decides they should," Rhavas agreed, ashamed that she should have to remind him the lord with the great and good mind lay behind the barbarians' actions.

Ingegerd sketched the sun-sign. If Rhavas paid more attention to her smoothly rounded bosom than to the sun-sign itself . . . if he did, he was the only one who knew it. And he had already given himself penance for a wandering eye. He could always give himself more.

Yes, go ahead, he jeered silently. *You care for the sin more than you care about the penance. The more you prostrate yourself and pray before the altar, the more you wish you were doing other things.*

He hoped none of what he was thinking showed on his face. It must not have, for Ingegerd did not pull back from him in anger or disgust. She did ask, "Very holy sir, has this city done anything to ready itself if the Khamorth should break in?"

"Not so far as I know," the prelate replied. "Everything that has been done, has been done to hold them out."

She nodded. "We must do everything we can to hold them out. But we should also try to be ready in case everything we do is not enough. Or do you think I am wrong? Do you think I see doom where doom looms not?"

"I don't know," Rhavas said heavily. "By the lord with the great and good mind, I just don't know. Nor am I any sort of fighting man. You might do better to speak to Zautzes or to Voilas. You are the garrison commander's wife, and can be expected to know somewhat of these matters. As for me . . . I am the man who, they think, cursed their commander. Whatever I say to them, they are not likely to heed me."

"They may not love you," Ingegerd said, "but I think they will heed you. They would be fools if they did not." She gave him the beginnings of a curtsy and walked out of the temple.

Not for the first time, Rhavas had trouble paying attention to the Videssian who came up to him next.

After what Ingegerd said, Rhavas had trouble seeing Skopentzana's walls as barriers against the Khamorth. Might they not also be traps? If the barbarians did break in, how would the folk of Skopentzana protect themselves, defend themselves, escape the foe? Though he had told her he wouldn't, the prelate went to Zautzes with the question.

"If they break in, very holy sir?" Zautzes stared at him. "If they break in, we're ruined. It's as simple as that. We can put up the best fight we know how, or we can hide the best way we know how, but it isn't likely to make much difference one way or the other. Or do you say otherwise?"

"No," Rhavas answered unhappily. "I wish I could."

"Holding them out is what walls are for." The eparch warmed to his theme. "Walls keep the savages out and the civilized folk in. That's what makes Videssos the city such a special place: it has better walls than any other city in the world. Folk there don't have to lose any sleep worrying about whether barbarians will slaughter them in the streets."

"No, indeed," Rhavas said with politeness as frigid as the weather. "They can worry about Videssian rebels slaughtering them in the streets instead. See the progress our wonderful civilization has brought us?"

Zautzes gave him a reproachful look. "You haven't got the right attitude, very holy sir."

"No?" Rhavas shrugged. "And all the time I thought that was the

Khamorth and the Videssian traitors. Only goes to show you never can tell, doesn't it? Good morning, most honorable sir." He left the eparch's office with no ceremony whatsoever. He felt Zautzes' eyes boring into his back, but the other man said not a word.

An icy breeze brought tears to Rhavas' eyes as he started across the square toward the temple and his own residence. Winter would have been hard enough without the barbarians prowling beyond the gates. Knowing the Khamorth were out there added a different sort of chill to the air.

There beyond the statues in the center of the square, two small groups of men were moving toward each other. Because his eyes were tearing, Rhavas couldn't tell just who was in either group. He didn't get much of a chance to look, either. When the men, whoever they were, spotted his robe of sky blue and sun gold, someone exclaimed, "Phaos! It's the prelate!" Both groups promptly dissolved. In the blink of an eye, Skopentzana's central square emptied—except for Rhavas himself.

He sighed, shook his head, and kept on walking. He didn't know for a fact that militiamen and peasant refugees had been about to square off against one another again. Because he didn't know it, he didn't have to do anything about it. No curses would fly on either side.

He did wish he could have taken Voilas and the most prominent peasant and knocked their stubborn, empty heads together. That might have done more good for Skopentzana—and certainly would have done more good for him—than all the curses and anathemas he could have hurled.

Two days later, Voilas sought him out in his residence. The new militia commander gave him a venomous stare. "Have you heard the latest, very holy sir?"

"Probably not," Rhavas admitted. "But, since you obviously came here to enlighten me, that won't matter much, and it won't matter long. Go ahead; tell me the latest. Be my guest."

"Some more of those stinking peasants are saying they'd sooner live under the savages than in here," Voilas said venomously. "Why would they say such a thing? Why? Tell me why, by the lord with the great and good mind!"

"Because they hate you?" Rhavas suggested. "Because you militiamen have treated them worse than the barbarians would have?"

Voilas gaped as if the prelate had just spat in his face. "But that's crazy!" he exclaimed. "What have we done?"

"Item: you tried to keep them from coming into Skopentzana in the first place. Item: you tried to throw them out once they did take refuge here." Rhavas ticked points off on his fingers as he spoke. "Item: you don't think they ought to get rations, even though they grew the food you're eating. Item: militiamen harry them every chance they get. Item . . . Shall I go on?"

The new head of Skopentzana's militia lacked Toxaras' imposing physical presence. He was a shrewder man, though; Rhavas watched the calculation in his eyes. "What do you suppose we ought to do about that?" he asked, licking his lips.

"Not much you can do about it now, is there?" Rhavas said. "If all of you had let up on the peasants after Toxaras had his accident"—he wouldn't call it a curse, or think of it as one—"that might have done some good. If you leave those people alone from now on, that may help some, but to the ice with me if I think it will do a whole lot."

"If they're traitors, we *ought* to put 'em out of the city, by the good god," Voilas said viciously. "How else are we going to keep Skopentzana safe?"

"Don't you think that would make matters worse?" Rhavas inquired. "Can you be sure you'd hunt them all down? Can you be sure none of them has kin living inside the walls? Don't you see? You'd make those people hate you, too, but you wouldn't know who they were so you could watch out for them."

"You're no help at all, very holy sir," Voilas complained.

"Why? Because I don't give you leave to do what you want to do anyhow? I intend to lose not a minute of sleep over that," Rhavas said. "The most you can do is keep an eye on the noisiest troublemakers—and maybe on some of the quietest one, too, since they might be smart enough to cause trouble without trumpeting out a warning ahead of time. Do you see what I'm saying?"

Plainly, Voilas didn't want to. Just as plainly, he recognized that he had no choice. His hand fell to the hilt of the sword on his belt. But he also recognized that wouldn't do what he wished it would. Voice choked with fury, he said, "Remember, very holy sir, you called down a curse on your own head if anything went wrong. If I were you, I'd be praying hard that it doesn't come true."

He stormed away, and was gone before Rhavas could even try for the last word. The prelate made a horrible face, though no one was in the study to see it. Even had Voilas stayed to listen, how could he have responded? He had no idea. His right hand shaped the sun-sign. "I have prayed," he said. "I do pray. I intend to keep on praying." Every word of that was true. How much good would it do him—or Skopentzana?

He hated Voilas for making him think such thoughts. When he came to this distant place, he'd never dreamt a potter could shake his faith worse than any of the clever, even brilliant, theologians in Videssos the city.

For the first six weeks after Midwinter's Day, or even a little longer, the weather in Skopentzana remained mild by northern standards. Oh, there was snow on the ground, and it seemed bitterly cold to anyone who'd grown up in the capital, but no great blizzards came roaring through, as sometimes happened every other week in winter in this part of the world.

And then all that abruptly changed. For three days, howling wind and swirling snow filled the air in Skopentzana. At first, when the snowstorm descended on the city, Rhavas hoped it would either drive the Khamorth away or freeze them in place. He didn't need long to realize that was a forlorn hope indeed. The nomads endured dreadful winters on the Pardrayan steppe. Just because a blizzard afflicted Videssian soil instead wouldn't make it anything out of the ordinary for them.

It wasn't anything out of the ordinary for the Skopentzanans, either. They simply started digging out, as they did whenever winter dealt them a buffet. They took a sardonic pride in enduring the worst the season could throw at them.

"Still alive, are you?" one man would greet another as they shoveled their walks clear.

"Oh, no, not me," the second Skopentzanan might reply. "I froze to death day before yesterday." They would both laugh and get on with their work.

After two days' respite, another blizzard slammed the city, and yet another two days after that. By then, even the longtime inhabitants weren't laughing anymore. Even in a city as ready for it as Skopentzana was, too much winter could kill.

Had the Khamorth set scaling ladders against the walls when

the snow was at its worst, they might easily have gained the top—who could have seen them till they were there? But they didn't. Truly, they knew nothing of siegecraft. *A good thing, too*, Rhavas thought.

Yet another blizzard dumped still more snow on Skopentzana a few days later. Had Videssos the city faced such weather, everything in the capital would have ground to a halt. Hundreds, maybe thousands, of people would have frozen. In Skopentzana, it happened almost every winter. No one got too excited about it. Men and women had furs and thick woolen blankets. They had houses made snug against the worst winter storms could do. Even with less firewood than they might have liked, they got by.

When that latest snowstorm blew itself out at last, one of Zautzes' servants came across the square to the prelate's residence. "Very holy sir, the eparch would like to talk with you about the ration," the man said.

"I'll come," Rhavas said at once; the ration was serious business. "Is he going to cut it again?"

"Sir, that's what he wants to talk to you about," the servant replied.

Rhavas decked himself out in his warmest hooded robes. Zautzes' servant wore enough clothes to keep himself warm in Skotos' frozen hell. The blizzard might have stopped, but it remained bitterly cold outside.

Despite the hood, Rhavas felt the weather more than a secular man might have; as soon as he got outside, heat poured from the top of his head like water out of a cracked pot. He refused to let it get him down. "Good to see the sun again," he remarked.

"That's the truth, very holy sir," Zautzes' servant agreed.

Drifts of snow clotted the square and made the statues at the center of it hard to recognize. The sun shone dazzlingly. Rhavas squinted against the glare. The servant's footprints were almost the only marks in the smooth expanse of white. "Shall we follow your track back to the eparch's?" the prelate asked.

"Suits me," the servant said. "I got here, so I expect we can get back."

Almost like sled dogs, he and Rhavas plunged into the snow. The going was hard. No crust had frozen yet, so they had to flounder through the drifts instead of surmounting them. Before Rhavas got anywhere near the statues, he began to sweat. The perspiration started to freeze on him whenever he slowed, even for a moment. But he needed to pause every so often to catch his breath.

At one such halt, he pointed to an odd-shaped lump in the snow near the base of Stavrakios' statue. "What's that?"

Zautzes' servant shrugged. "Just a drift. The wind can do all kinds of funny things—you'd better believe it can."

"Oh, I know it can, but that doesn't look like anything the wind shaped to me." Rhavas started shoving snow aside with mittened hands. Even through thick felt, the cold bit into his hands.

The servant, a younger man, stood watching him for a little while, then, with an exaggerated sniff, started pushing snow around himself. "You'll see," he said. "There won't be anything except—"

"Oh, but there is." Rhavas' mittens had just bumped something firmer than the soft, fluffy snow. "It's . . . Phos!" He sketched the sun-sign. "It's a body, dumped into the drift."

Eyes wide enough to show white all around the iris, the servant signed himself, too. "You—you were right, very holy sir," he stammered. "Who—who could have done such a wicked, sinful thing?"

"Let's find out who's dead," the prelate said grimly. "That may tell us something about who killed him."

He and Zautzes' servant dragged the corpse out of the snow. "I don't recognize him," the servant said, gulping.

"I do." Rhavas sounded grimmer than ever. "He's one of the peasants who got here a jump ahead of the Khamorth. He was one of the men quarreling with the town militia just before the snowstorms started, too." Figuring out what had killed him wasn't hard, either, not with the left side of his head smashed in. He'd lain there for a while; his blood had frozen into ruby ice.

The servant turned away and was noisily sick in the snow. Steam rose from the vomit. The servant stuffed fresh, unfouled snow into his mouth and spat it out. He repeated that several times, then choked out, "Who would want to do such a horrible thing?"

"There are certain . . . obvious possibilities, shall we say?" Rhavas replied. "If this is the work of a militiaman—I don't say it is, but there we find one of those obvious possibilities—he has a great deal to answer for, not just for his own soul's sake but also for the danger in which he has placed Skopentzana."

"That'd be sweet, wouldn't it?" the servant said. "Just what we'd need, eh? Our own little civil war inside the city."

"Yes." Rhavas said no more. Really, the servant had said everything that needed saying. Videssians *would* fight among themselves.

"What are we going to do, very holy sir?" the servant asked, and then answered his own question before Rhavas could: "We ought to cover the body over with snow again, is what we ought to do. Then we could pretend the whole thing never happened, and nobody else in town would have any idea."

Reluctantly, Rhavas shook his head. "I'm afraid it wouldn't work. Someone will miss this fellow"—for the life of him, he couldn't come up with the peasant's name—"and then they'll find him, and then the trouble will start. And it will be worse if the peasants find him than it will if we go tell your master what happened and let him get after the killer."

"Get him after the militia, you mean," the servant said. Rhavas muttered something highly untheological under his breath. Militiamen were Skopentzana's main—no, Skopentzana's only—defenders right now. Could Zautzes afford to antagonize them?

On the other hand, could the eparch afford to ignore coldblooded murder? Looking down at the red ice clinging to the dead man's head, Rhavas shivered. That was the right word, sure enough.

"Nothing good will come of this," the servant said mournfully. As mournfully, Rhavas reflected that Phos need not have granted the man the gift of prophecy to make that a very good guess.

They slogged across the square to the eparch's residence. Rhavas winced when he saw two militiamen in front of it instead of Ingeros or others from Zautzes' remaining handful of regulars. Ominously, they hadn't come out to see what the prelate and the servant were doing. Did they already know someone lay there dead? Did they know who? Had they put him there? Those were all good questions. Rhavas discovered he wasn't so sure he wanted the answers to any of them.

Zautzes gave him mulled wine spiced with cinnamon. Whatever reductions in the ration the eparch was contemplating, he himself still lived well. Before he could start talking about anything so mundane, Rhavas told him about the corpse in the snowbank.

The eparch made a noise down deep in his throat. It sounded

as if it wanted to be a word but didn't know how. Then Zautzes gulped a gobletful of the hot wine. That done and downed, he did speak: "Why does the good god hate me so much that he gave me a city infested with idiots to govern? Can you tell me that, very holy sir?"

"Most honorable sir, I would call it a city stuffed with sinners," Rhavas replied. After a moment's thought, he added, "We may not be so very far apart after all, you and I."

"No. We may not," Zautzes said bitterly. "And much good may our concord do us, for it's all too likely to be the only concord in Skopentzana these days."

"What will you do?" Rhavas asked.

"Pray that his wife broke his head because she caught him buggering a goat," the eparch answered, which startled laughter not far from hysterical out of Rhavas. Zautzes went on, "Barring anything so, ah, convenient, I suppose I'll have to try and catch the whoreson who did do him in." He paused again, while his wits caught up with his mouth. "And if that whoreson's a militiaman, as he's only too likely to be . . . Well, isn't that just the loveliest mess you ever saw?"

"I thought so when I found the body," Rhavas said. "I was hoping you would tell me I was wrong." Something else occurred to him. "And the body was meant to be found, too. Otherwise, there are countless better places to hide it."

"You're full of good news today, aren't you?" Zautzes said.

"Do you want more?" Rhavas told him how indifferent his guardsmen were.

The eparch laughed a sour laugh. "Why am I not surprised?" He heaved his bulk up from behind his desk. "Well, those good-for-nothings won't be able to ignore it if I rub their noses in it. By Phaos, I'll make 'em sorry if they do!"

He lumbered out toward the front. He wasn't a tall man, but he was wide. Even with rationing in Skopentzana, he hadn't lost his protuberant belly. Following him—as Rhavas did—was like following a boulder rolling down a mountainside. But no boulder could have given the performance he did when he got outside. He shouted at the militiamen. He screamed at them. If they hadn't dodged smartly, he would have kicked them in the backside.

They all but dove into the snow to escape him. Rhavas noted that they didn't have to ask him where the body was. They knew, all right. They just hadn't cared till the eparch lit a fire under them.

For his part, Zautzes preened. Out there at the entrance to his residence, he strutted and swaggered. He was a frog having a very good time on his lily pad. And, unless Rhavas was vastly mistaken, he was doing his best not to think about all the unpleasant possibilities he'd outlined back in his study. The prelate had a hard time blaming him. Trouble would come all too soon. Why brood on it when it wasn't quite here?

His guards dragged the dead peasant through the snow back to the residence. It was hard work; neither of them looked happy when they got back. The peasant, of course, would have been even less delighted had he still been in any condition to express an opinion.

Glaring at the militiamen, Zautzes snapped, "Do you know who this poor lunk is?—was, I should say."

They both shook their heads. "Never seen him before, most honorable sir," one of them said. The other's head stopped going back and forth and started going up and down to show he hadn't seen the dead man before, either.

Zautzes' glare grew more menacing. "You're both lying. Skotos' ice"—he paused to spit—"I've seen him around. I just can't put a name to him. It's the same with the very holy sir here. Are you two deaf and blind? Wouldn't surprise me one bloody bit."

"He's a country clodhopper," one of the guards said sulkily—not the one who'd spoken before, but his partner. "Who gives a flying futter what his name was?"

That was too much for Rhavas. "He was a man. He was a Videssian. He was murdered, foully murdered," he thundered. The guards both blinked at his vehemence. Still full of rage, he went on, "One of your friends—or maybe one of you, for all I know—smashed in his skull. What sort of riots and bloodshed will that spawn in this city? At what time could we afford such trouble less?"

Both guards spoke together: "Wasn't us who done it."

"Who did?" Rhavas and Zautzes shouted the question at the same time. The militiamen shrugged identical shrugs.

"We'll get to the bottom of this with or without you—and Phos give you more mercy than you deserve if we find you're *at* the bottom of it," Zautzes snarled. He shouted for the servant who'd found the body with Rhavas. When the fellow came, the eparch said, "Go fetch Koubatzes the wizard. We'll see what he has to say about this sorry business."

Before the servant returned with the mage, a man pushed his way through the snow up to the eparch's residence. He stared at the body at the base of the stairs. "Phaos!" he exclaimed in a rural accent. "I was going to ask if you folks knew what became of poor Glykas, but now I see for my own self. Some o' them militia bastards done for him, sure as sure."

Both guards growled. Rhavas and Zautzes kept them from doing anything more than growl. *The fat's in the fire now*, Rhavas thought gloomily. Glykas was dead, the other peasant refugees knew it, and they had no trouble at all figuring out who'd killed him. What would they do for revenge?

"Should have let us knock him over the head, too, most honorable sir," one of the militiamen said as the peasant floundered off through the snow. "That would've kept things quiet a while longer."

"You chucklehead," Zautzes said in a deadly voice. "I'm going to do you the biggest favor I ever did: I'm going to pretend I didn't hear that. But if Koubatzes tells me you had anything to do with this, you'll end up envying this dead bastard here."

Rhavas thought he was taking a chance. If his guards did know something about the killing, they were liable to turn on him now—and on the prelate as well. But they just stood there muttering to themselves. To Rhavas, that was evidence, if not proof, of their innocence.

The servant and Koubatzes took a long time coming back. Zautzes muttered and fumed while he waited. Rhavas was more philosophical. With all the snow on the ground, anybody needed a long time to get anywhere. At last the mage followed Zautzes' man back to the residence. Koubatzes carried his sorcerous paraphernalia in a leather sack.

He nodded greetings to the eparch and the prelate. "A murder, is it?" he said crisply, and then, looking down at Glykas' corpse, "Well, so it is."

"What can you tell us about it?" Rhavas asked. "If you can find out who did the deed and why, that may help keep the city quiet. We need to punish the guilty here, and we need to be seen to be punishing the guilty. If no one has any doubt we are doing what needs to be done, that will help keep the lid on. We can hope it will, anyhow."

"I understand," Koubatzes said. "I'll do what I can. Don't know how much that will be, not till I have a go." He opened the leather sack and started muttering to himself: "Marigold, pennyroyal, and mistletoe." He took dried leaves and flowers—Rhavas supposed they were the plants he named—and set them in dead Glykas' mouth. Zautzes' guards muttered, too, in disgust. Koubatzes took no notice of them. He found another leaf and set it on his own tongue. Indistinctly, he said, "Sage."

Chanting with the herb in his mouth couldn't have been easy, but he managed. Perhaps the charm he was using was specially adapted to the circumstances. His passes were, as usual, swift and sure. Watching him work, Rhavas couldn't imagine him failing—and yet he had, and dreadfully, against the Khamorth.

The spell ended. Koubatzes stood in front of Glykas' body. He did not seem a happy man. "Well?" Rhavas asked, though he did not think all would be well.

"Well, very holy sir, magecraft won't tell anyone much about this business, I'm afraid," the wizard answered. "Whoever did the deed cast a spell on the body afterward, to shield it against magical investigation. If I'd come across the body just after it died, I might have got around the spell. When he's been lying out in the snow for the good god only knows how long . . ." He shook his head and spread his hands. "Sorry, but no."

"Wouldn't the snow preserve him, the way it would a fish?" Zautzes asked.

"I'm afraid not, most honorable sir," Koubatzes replied. "The longer ago that spell was laid, the longer it had to cling, and the snow hasn't got anything to do with that."

"How are we supposed to catch the killer, then?" Rhavas asked.

"Usual way, I would say," Koubatzes answered. "Find out who didn't like him, find out who owed him money and to whom he was in debt, find out if his woman was unfaithful, find out if some drunken fool is boasting of breaking his head in the wineshops. No magic to any of that, but it usually works well enough, even if it takes a bit of time."

"We'll do it," Zautzes said. "Yes, we'll do it, all right, but I was hoping you could make things quick and easy." The corners of his wide mouth turned down. "Nothing these days is quick or easy, worse luck." Koubatzes only shrugged and spread his hands again.

Rhavas said, "I don't know whether finding Glykas' killer will be easy or not. I do know it had better be quick. If it isn't, we'll have a war inside this city. That would be bad enough any time. With the Khamorth outside..." He didn't go on.

Zautzes looked unhappier still, like a frog that had swallowed a bee and was suddenly repenting of the decision. The prospect of civil strife didn't seem to bother Koubatzes—but then, his features were less mobile than the eparch's. He bowed to Zautzes and Rhavas in turn, then started back along the path he and Zautzes' servant had broken.

"I don't suppose you're interested in talking about the ration now, are you?" Zautzes said plaintively.

"Most honorable sir, I would say you'd be a fool to cut it. You would do better to wait till the fuss over this murder dies down—if it does," Rhavas replied. "If you catch the killer, then you have some hope of reducing it without stirring the city against you. Some."

"I wish I could tell you you were wrong, very holy sir. As things are..." As things were, Zautzes' sigh sent a cloud of fog into the chilly air.

Rhavas felt like sighing, too. Glykas' body tempted him to despair. Some folk said despair was the only unforgivable sin, the sin that opened a man's soul to Skotos' cold and greedy hand. He remembered saying it himself, in fact. Maybe it was true. But he'd never before seen folly on a scale to match this.

After bowing to Zautzes, he started back across the square toward the temple and his residence next door. As he slogged through the snow, he wondered if it concealed other corpses. He almost hoped a dead militiaman lay under it. Then, at least, dishonors would be even. Both sides in Skopentzana would have equal reason to feel ashamed—or, if the dark god had hold of them, to feel proud.

He saw no signs of other bodies. Since that meant no other Videssians had died, he supposed he should have been glad. And he *was* glad—in a way. But he would also have been glad, or at least relieved, to see the scales balance.

Just before he got to his residence, the light dimmed. He looked up in surprise. Sunset still came early, but not this early. And indeed, the sun hadn't set. Grayish yellow clouds had covered it, though, and were getting darker and thicker every moment. Another storm was coming. Rhavas grimaced. Hadn't Skopentzana already gone through enough?

He wondered whether Phos was trying to see how much the city could endure. The good god was piling things on thick. But Phos could send troubles when and as he wished. It was up to mankind to endure.

"Trouble, very holy sir?" Matzoukes asked when Rhavas came inside.

Rhavas didn't ask how the young priest knew; his own face had to be as grim as the growing storm outside. "Trouble?" he echoed. "You might say so. Yes, you just might say so." In a few words, he told the other man what had happened in the central square.

Matzoukes sketched Phos' sun-sign. "That's . . . dreadful, very holy sir!"

"It is indeed. The exact word, in fact, for I am filled with dread," Rhavas replied. "I think all of Skopentzana should be filled with dread. All of Skopentzana, I fear, cares very little for my opinion. The most I can hope for is that we do not fly at one another's throats."

"Surely it can't be as bad as that, very holy sir," the other priest said.

"It can be that bad. It can be worse. It can be, and I am afraid it is," Rhavas said. Shaking his head, Matzoukes left the room, as if he didn't even want to imagine such a thing.

Rhavas didn't want to imagine such a thing, either, which didn't mean he could avoid it. He was altogether too good at seeing disasters before they happened. He was not glad to possess such a knack. He would, indeed, have given almost anything not to have it. But it was part of his character—he preferred to think of it as a gift from Phos. Why the lord with the great and good mind had chosen to give him such a gift . . . Rhavas had often wondered, but never yet found an answer that even began to satisfy.

Snow started sifting out of the sky again later that afternoon. The wind didn't howl as it had in some of Skopentzana's earlier blizzards. This was a businesslike storm; it seemed to announce it was here to stay. The snow fell, and piled up, and went on falling. Rhavas was glad his residence had a steeply pitched roof that would shed most of what came down on it. He worried more about the temple, whose roof rose at a shallower angle. If the snow that stuck there got too heavy, the roof might come down.

He worried more when the snow was still falling just as hard and just as steadily two days later. People trapped in their homes without firewood would surely start to freeze. But maybe the latest snowstorm was also a sort of backhanded gift from Phos. In weather like this, militiamen and refugee peasants couldn't possibly clash. Nobody could do much of anything in weather like this.

So Rhavas thought, at any rate. Once again, he proved he hadn't been born in the Empire's far northeast. He'd learned a great deal from dwelling here so long, but he was no native, and did not think as a native would.

He had to take a shovel with him when he went to the woodshed behind the residence. He was no more immune to worries about fuel for the fire than any other Skopentzanan. But, to his relief, he seemed to have plenty.

Some sort of outcry made him pause on the way back. The falling snow seemed to muffle everything. He'd noticed that even back in Videssos the city, where it happened much less often. But the noise here swelled despite the snowstorm. Soon, cupping a hand behind his ears, he could make out words: "The Khamorth! The Khamorth are in the city!"

For a long moment, Rhavas simply stood motionless, as if the storm had frozen him in place. It was not so much that he didn't believe his ears: much more that he didn't want to believe them. The ice that grew inside him had nothing to do with the frigid weather. Here were his own words, coming back to haunt him.

If Skopentzana falls to the Khamorth, on my head be it. That was what he'd told Toxaras, that or something so close as to make no difference. The mason who'd commanded the militia was dead and couldn't see his revenge. But the horror of it closed round Rhavas' heart like a vise and squeezed and squeezed and squeezed.

How had the barbarians broken in? He didn't know. Maybe it didn't matter (though some frightened, foreboding part of him said it was liable to matter very much). In certain ways, it surely didn't. If they were in, the Videssians had to drive them out again if they could. And those who were not fighters had to look to their safety—again, if they could.

The prelate hurried back inside the residence. When he got there, Matzoukes greeted him with, "What's that racket, very holy sir? Why is everybody yelling in the middle of this dreadful storm?"

Rhavas told him why. The young priest went white as the clean snow outside. Rhavas went on, "I know you're from this city, holy sir. You will have kinfolk for whom you are concerned. See to your loved ones. I don't mind, not now."

Matzoukes bowed. "Thank you, very holy sir. May the good god bless you for your kindness. But by the vows I swore, my place is at your side, not my family's. I'll stay."

"No, not now," the prelate said. "Were things different, I might seek to hold you to those vows. Not now. In the name of the lord with the great and good mind, I release you."

"Are—are you sure, very holy sir?" the young priest quavered. Rhavas nodded firmly. He drew Phos' sun-circle over his heart to reassure Matzoukes, who said, "The good god bless *you*. After all this is over, I'll come back and care for you the way I always have. I swear I will, very holy sir!"

"Of course," Rhavas said gently. "Now go." Matzoukes dashed away. Rhavas thought he would likely be killed in the sack. *Better he should die with his family*, the prelate told himself. He feared the militiamen couldn't oust the nomads, not after they'd gained an entrance.

You'll likely die in the sack yourself—that was the next thing that occurred to Rhavas. He confronted the notion with regret but, he was proud to discover, without much fear. He remained convinced he had done what he could for Skopentzana. If the good god willed that he should die a martyr at the hands of the demon-worshiping Khamorth, he was ready to face the perilous journey across the Bridge of the Separator. He drew himself up very straight, bracing himself to face his end with as much dignity and courage as he could muster.

And then dignity dissolved and courage took on a new shape. "Ingegerd!" he exclaimed. He had sworn to Himerios that he would do all he could for the garrison commander's wife. If he had less noble, less altruistic reasons for hoping she safely came through this ordeal, he did not have to admit them to anyone, even to himself.

He started to race out of the residence, as Matzoukes had done. The young priest had had the sense to take a shovel with him, to dig his way through the worst of the drifts. Rhavas realized he would have to do the same. Matzoukes had even left the better shovel, the one with the smoother handle and the broader blade, for him. That was generous of the youngster.

Shouldering the shovel as if it were a spear, Rhavas left the residence. He had trouble seeing very far through the swirling snow. Some of the cries he heard, though, were not cries that would have sounded from Skopentzana were all well.

Digenis pushed past him toward the temple. Pointing that way, the scribe said, "We'll have sanctuary there, eh, very holy sir?"

"I doubt it," Rhavas said. "I doubt the Khamorth know the meaning of the word. You would do better either to hide or to fight." Digenis stared at him as it he'd suddenly started spouting the plainsmen's speech. Then the man went on into the temple regardless of what he'd said. Rhavas sighed. He didn't know why he was surprised, but somehow he was.

Others, men and women, were also heading for the temple. Did they think a building would save them? If they did, Rhavas feared they were doomed to disappointment—and probably just doomed.

"You! Prelate! You stinking, bald-arsed, very holy sack of horse turds!"

Rhavas had been insulted before. He didn't think he'd ever been reviled with such crude excess. Drawing himself up with angry wounded pride, he demanded, "Who speaks to me so?"

"I do, by Phos!" Voilas strode out of the swirling snow. The militia leader carried a spear with fresh bloodstains dripping down the ash-wood shaft from the gore-clotted iron head. "I do, and if you want to curse me, go right ahead. I don't even care anymore. You've already cursed Skopentzana, you poxy, pious pissweed!"

"You lie," Rhavas said furiously.

"In a pig's pizzle I do," Voilas retorted. "Who said, 'Let the peasants come in. They won't work any harm'?" He pitched his voice to a mocking whine nothing like Rhavas', but perfectly designed to get under the prelate's skin. Pointing with the spearhead, he went back to his normal tones to say, "Well, very holy sir? Was that you, or wasn't it?"

"What if it was?" Rhavas changed the grip on his shovel. If Voilas came after him with that spear, he vowed to himself that the other man would get the surprise of his life.

But Voilas didn't thrust with the spear or throw it. He just gestured with it. Videssians habitually talked with their hands; since his were full, he used what he was holding as an extension of them. "What if it was? I'll tell you what if it was, and may you take knowing what it was to the ice with you. You'll have been by the postern gate near the main west gate?"

"Yes?" Rhavas hadn't meant to make the word a question, but found he couldn't help it. Apprehension sent a chill up his spine that had nothing to do with the snowstorm in which he stood. "What about that postern gate?"

"What about it? I'll tell you what about it." Voilas' fury was so volcanic, Rhavas half expected to see the snow clinging to his beard and eyebrows puff into steam. The militiaman went on, "Here's what about it. One of your fornicating peasants—one of the peasants Toxaras wanted to toss out, one of the peasants *I* wanted to toss out, one of the peasants *you* said we bloody well had to keep on account of they were all such wonderful fellows—one of *those* peasants, very holy sir, snuck out at first light or maybe a little before, opened up that postern gate, and waved to the stinking barbarians to come on in. And you know something else? They did."

"No," Rhavas whispered. Again his own words tolled in his mind, harsh as the clangor of an iron bell. *If thus-and-so happens, on my head be it.* Thus-and-so had happened, had happened at the hands of one of the people he'd tried to help. Where was the justice in that? *On my head,* Rhavas thought dizzily.

Voilas laughed in his face, remembering those words, too. "You cursed Toxaras, and for what? For doing what he could to save this city and the people who live in it. And then you went and cursed yourself, and now it's come back to bite you, and I hope it bites you even harder than it bit him, if a curse can bite harder than killing a man. Serves you right, very holy sir. You're getting just what you deserve. It's just a pity the city's suffering on account of you knew everything there was to know." He spat at Rhavas' feet as if he were rejecting Skotos, then stormed away.

Rhavas wanted to shout after him, wanted to tell him it was as much the militia's fault as his. If the militiamen hadn't harried the peasants every chance they got, if they hadn't left Glykas dead in the snow . . . But if the peasants hadn't been in Skopentzana to begin with, none of the other troubles could even have begun. *On my head be it.* There it was, not only on his head but on his shoulders, pressing down as if he were trying to carry the weight of the world. He'd asked for this. He didn't know he'd asked for it at the time, but he had.

And now he'd got it.

He wanted to sink down into the snow. How could Phos have let this happen? Or was it Skotos? The god of light and the god of darkness were eternally at war. Only the blackest heretics and lovers of evil believed Skotos could be the stronger. With this disaster staring Rhavas in the face, he was tempted to wonder why.

He spat. If he came to believe the dark could be stronger than the light, then everything he'd lived for became meaningless. *I will not do that. I must not do that*, he told himself. What he had to do now was everything he could to salvage good from this catastrophe.

On toward the house where Himerios had lived, the house where Ingegerd still dwelt. Sometimes he forced his way through the snow, sometimes he used the shovel to clear a path for himself. By now, people all through Skopentzana were crying that the Khamorth were loose in the city. So far, though, Rhavas had seen none of the barbarians.

The prelate rounded a corner and almost fell over a body lying in the snow. The corpse was very fresh. Only a little snow lay on it, and its blood still stained the snowdrift in which it lay. An arrow stuck up from the dead man's back. Hastily sketching the sun-sign, Rhavas hurried on.

More Videssians came out of their homes. Some shouted at others to get back inside. Others called for getting away however they could. Even in the midst of chaos, Videssians still argued with one another. A couple of them turned to Rhavas. "What do we do, very holy sir?" they called.

"Fight if you can," he answered. "If you can't, pray." That left them quarreling over which they ought to do. He might have known it would.

Finding his way was a nightmare. He knew Skopentzana well, but the snowstorm was enough to confuse anybody. The town's twisting streets were confusing enough when he could see farther than the end of his nose. Now . . . Now he went down two or three blind alleys and had to double back on his track.

As he was coming out of the mouth of an alleyway, people on the street into which it opened fled past him, crying, "The Khamorth! The barbarians!"

He looked in the direction from which they were running.

Up the street after them came a plainsman on a pony: a burly, broad-shouldered man with a big nose and a bushy beard. The Khamorth wore furs and leather. He held a curved sword in his right hand. Intent on his prey, he paid no attention to the prelate—if he even realized Rhavas was there.

Rhavas swung the shovel—not at the barbarian, but at the pony forcing its way forward through the snow. The blade smashed into the horse's right foreleg. With a horrible scream of surprise and torment, the beast crumpled. Its rider also cried out in surprise. Rhavas hoped the horse would crush him under it, but he kicked free and scrambled to his feet. Somehow, he hung on to his sword.

He shouted again. This time, the cry had words in it, though Rhavas did not understand his guttural language. The Khamorth advanced on him past the thrashing pony. The barbarian was badly bowlegged, which might have been funny under less frightening circumstances. As things were, it just made his clumping, purposeful gait all the more menacing.

"Get back!" Rhavas shouted, hefting the shovel.

Plainly, the barbarian knew no more Videssian than Rhavas did of his language. Just as plainly, the Khamorth wouldn't have been inclined to listen even if he had understood. Rhavas set himself. He had more reach than the Khamorth, but a shovel was only a clumsy makeshift weapon, while a sword was made to let the life out of foes.

Fast as a striking snake, the Khamorth slashed at Rhavas. The prelate barely blocked the blow with the shovel's shaft. The nomad cut again. Again, Rhavas turned the stroke. He lashed out with the shovel, as much to keep the barbarian busy as for any other reason. The Khamorth tried to use the sword as Rhavas had used the wooden handle of the shovel. The edge of the shovel blade caught the sword squarely—and broke it, sending all the sword but a short stub and the hilt flying through the air.

The plainsman stared in horrified astonishment at what little he had left. He threw the stub at Rhavas' head. Rhavas ducked. The Khamorth turned to run. Rhavas pursued him. Neither of them could move very fast. When the Khamorth floundered into deeper snow and slowed even more, Rhavas swung the shovel again.

This time, the blade bit into the side of the plainsman's head. The barbarian wore no armor, only a fur cap. The shovel smashed in his skull as it would have smashed an earthenware wine jar. He crumpled; all the bones in his body might suddenly have turned to water. A harsh stink fouled the air—his bowels had let go. He twitched for a little while, then lay still. He would never get up again.

Rhavas stood over him, panting harshly. The prelate stooped. Yes, the Khamorth had a knife on his belt. Rhavas took it and walked back to the pony he had crippled. He stooped again. This time, he cut the suffering animal's throat. The steppe pony let out an amazingly human sigh as its life rivered out of it. The smell of blood—all hot iron—reminded Rhavas of the inside of a smithy.

He realized nothing good would happen to him if the barbarians found him standing near the bodies of one of their friends and his horse. He hurried away. He was lucky no other nomad had happened by.

He shook his head and swore as foully as he knew how. If he were lucky, the Khamorth never would have broken into Skopentzana at all. If he were lucky, they never would have surged across Videssos' frontiers, either. If he were lucky, Stylianos never would have rebelled against Maleinos. What he had here wasn't good luck. It was only luck a trifle less disastrously bad than it might have been.

Still Skotos' luck, he thought. He shook his head and spat in the snow. The Khamorth were welcome to the dark god. "Phos!" Rhavas said. "I follow Phos, and none other." By the way he spoke, someone might have claimed he did.

More bodies lay in the snow. A few were plainsmen. More, far more, were Skopentzanans. Shouts and curses said fighting still went on here and there. And despairing screams said the Khamorth were amusing themselves in other ways besides simple slaughter.

Rhavas squeezed the shovel more tightly. If that happened to Ingegerd . . . "No," he muttered. He'd told Himerios he would protect her from such things.

An arrow thudded into the door of a house behind him and stood there thrilling. He waited for another one to pierce his heart or his belly. But the plainsman who'd shot at him just rode on by. Why not? The barbarian would have plenty of other targets later.

Here was Ingegerd's street. Three Videssians lay dead in it, their blood staining the snow. One was a woman. Her skirt was hiked up to her waist. Rhavas bit his lip and turned away. He was not supposed to see such things.

He knocked on the door. Only silence answered him. He knocked again. A little panel in the center of the door swung open. For a moment, he stared into one of Ingegerd's pale eyes—so startling to a man used only to brown.

The panel shut. The door opened. "Come in, very holy sir, and quickly!" Ingegerd said. "What are you doing here? It's madness in the streets."

He went inside. She closed the door behind him and set the bar in place to hold it closed. He said, "I told Himerios I would do what I could for you if things went wrong. Things have gone wrong. Here I am. What I can do, I will."

She looked at him. For a moment, he thought she would say she was likelier to be able to look out for him than the other way around. Had she said that, she might well have been right. That would have made it more humiliating, not less. But what she did say after that quick appraisal was, "There's blood on your robes, and on the spade as well."

He looked down at himself. Yes, he was splashed with red. He shrugged. "It's not mine." He told the the story of the fight with the nomad in a few bald sentences.

When he was through—even before he was through, in fact—Ingegerd's eyes lit with more warmth than he'd ever seen in them before. "That was bravely done, very holy sir, bravely done indeed."

"Was it?" Rhavas only shrugged. He hadn't thought about bravery. He hadn't thought about anything, except that the Khamorth would kill the people he was pursuing and then that the barbarian would kill *him*.

"Here. Wait." Ingegerd opened a chest of polished cedarwood. Out of it she drew something wrapped in oily rags—a sword, Rhavas saw when she removed the swaddling. "Take this. Himerios had his best blade on his hip when he hied southward, but this spare will serve you better than a spade."

Even when she spoke Videssian, she did so with the cadences and rhythms of the Haloga language she'd left behind. She held the sword out to Rhavas. The hilt fit his hand as if made for it.

Men had been making tools for murder as long as any other sort, and had turned that trade into art no less than any other.

"Thank you," Rhavas said, even though he was no swordsman. Then, as he would not have with a Videssian woman, he added, "But what of you?"

"Here is another blade," she said, reaching into the chest once more. "If need be, we shall battle back to back." By the way she held the sword, she knew what to do with it. She might not have a man's strength, but she would not lack for skill.

"For now, perhaps the best thing we can do is stay where we are and hope the barbarians will not trouble this house," Rhavas said.

"Yes, that is wisdom—for a while," Ingegerd said bleakly. "If the Khamorth gain mastery of the city, though, they will leave no home unravaged."

"They will have to slay me before they trouble you," Rhavas declared.

That was the strangest sort of gallant speech a priest of Phos might give. Again, he waited for Ingegerd to mock him. She did nothing of the sort. Her eyes warmed again. "You are gracious, very holy sir," she said. "Maybe it will not come to that. I hope it will not come to that." She didn't say she thought it would not come to that.

As if to explain why she would not say such a thing, several horsemen thundered down the street past the barred front door. They shouted to one another in their throaty, guttural tongue. Though Rhavas could not understand what they were saying, their tone of voice told him they were having the time of their lives. More than anything else, he hated them for the obvious pleasure they took in destruction.

Ingegerd's face twisted. "So much for the militia. A fine set of heroes they turned out to be."

"It is . . . not quite so simple as that," Rhavas said. *On my head be it.* He told her how the peasant had opened the postern gate and let in the Khamorth.

"Oh," she said in a flat, almost dead, voice when he finished. "And it was at your urging that the peasants stayed in the city."

"Yes." Rhavas answered with one pained word of his own. He might have known she had the wit to cut straight to the heart of his anguish. *On my head be it. Those* words, he feared, would torment him to the end of his days. He bowed his head. If Ingegerd chose to swing that sword, he would accept the stroke from her with a sort of despairing joy. It would free him from the blame, from the curse, he'd called down on himself.

But she said, "Very holy sir, you could not have known ahead of time how it would turn out. We have to do what we can now for Skopentzana and for ourselves."

It wasn't absolution. No one save possibly the ecumenical patriarch could give him that. But it came closer than anything else he was likely to find in Skopentzana. "Thank you," he whispered.

"For what?" Ingegerd spoke in honest perplexity. "You did what you thought best. What else could you do?"

More Khamorth galloped past outside, shouting in their own language. More screams and cries of pain and shrieks rose from all over the city, and the ones that had words were in Videssian. Rhavas bit the inside of his lower lip till he tasted blood. No, he would not find absolution in Skopentzana, if he ever found it anywhere. And what he had thought best had proved worst. How could he forget that? How could he pretend it was not so? He couldn't, and he knew it. A talent he lacked was the one for self-deception.

And then he stopped worrying about what he had done, what he hadn't, and what he might have, for a new cry rang through the city: "Fire!"

Ingegerd's eyes went very wide. Rhavas suspected his did, too. They both said the same thing at the same time: "We can't stay here now." Flames would race through Skopentzana. Fire was always a dreadful danger because it was so hard to fight once it got loose. If anything, it was worse in winter. Some wells would be frozen, which mattered little when people could make do with melted snow but a great deal in fighting flames. The drifts in the street would thwart bucket brigades, too—and so would rampaging barbarians with swords and bows. To the Khamorth, fire was a tool for driving their quarry from its hiding places. And it was all too likely to prove a brutally effective tool, too.

"What food do you have that we can take with us?" Rhavas asked. Then he bowed his head again. "If you care for my company, I should say. If not, I will find my own way as best I can."

"Two together are better than one alone," Ingegerd said—not a ringing endorsement, but an endorsement. She turned away.

"Let me see what I can bring—for you are right, and we will have to flee the city if we can." When she came back, she had a blanket slung over her shoulder—a makeshift knapsack. "Bread. Cheese. Sausage."

"Good." The prelate scowled. "As good as it can be, anyhow. Good would be having the barbarians beyond the walls where they belong."

Ingegerd opened the panel in the door again and looked out. "No horsemen, not this minute," she said. "Bodies in the street that were not there when you knocked . . . Come on." She unbarred the door and went outside.

Thick, choking smoke already fouled the air. How many fires had the Khamorth set? How fast were they spreading? Too many and too fast—those were the only answers that mattered to Rhavas. He needed a moment to orient himself, then swung toward the south. "The closest gate, yes?"

She nodded. "Yes. What else can we do?"

"Nothing." Rhavas was far from sure even fleeing would help, but it was the only hope they had.

He hadn't gone far before he thrust the sword Ingegerd had given him into his belt and went to work with the shovel—not against the Khamorth, but against drifted snow that blocked their way. Shovelful after shovelful flew. In other times, it would have been great sport: either that, or it quickly would have worn Rhavas out. Now it was only one more thing he had to do.

He fought through the drift, and he and Ingegerd went on. The way was easier for a little while—others fleeing ahead of them had partly cleared it. But that meant it was easier for the Khamorth, too. A bearded barbarian on foot came out of a house. He dropped the silver candlesticks he'd been holding and ran toward Rhavas, swinging back his sword for a killing stroke.

The prelate had no chance to drop the shovel and draw his—Himerios'—blade. He'd won once with his unorthodox weapon. Maybe he could again. But the Khamorth was dreadfully close and looked dreadfully fierce—and then looked dreadfully surprised as a fat snowball caught him full in the face. He coughed and sputtered and brought up a mittened hand to get snow out of his eyes and nose.

Rhavas hit him in the face, too, but with the iron blade of the shovel. The nomad roared in pain. Blood spurted from his broken nose and from a great gash on his cheek. It spattered the snow, horribly red. Rhavas hit him again, this time in the side of the head. He crumpled, sword falling from nerveless fingers.

"Well done!" Ingegerd said from behind the prelate.

Rhavas' heart thudded. "I thought I was a dead man," he said. "Phos bless you for your quick wit—and for your strong arm."

"That was . . . not so much," Ingegerd answered. "Halogai know what there is to know about snowballs and the throwing of them. I only wish I had been able to put a rock in the heart of that one."

"Even without, it did what it needed to do," Rhavas said. Ingegerd nodded. They pressed on.

They had to turn back from one street. Fire had got there ahead of them. Flames and black smoke billowed up, blocking the way. Through the clouds of smoke, Rhavas got brief glimpses of bodies sprawled in the snow. They all looked Videssian. He sketched the sun-sign, wishing them a safe journey over the Bridge of the Separator to a happy, joyous afterlife beyond.

When Rhavas and Ingegerd turned south again, they came up to a temple the plainsmen were plundering. Three blue-robed priests lay outside in pools of blood. Rhavas sketched the sun-sign again. "They dare!" he whispered in outrage and shock that seemed ridiculous in retrospect—of course the barbarians dared. But knowing of it and seeing it proved two different things. "They dare to rob the house of the lord with the great and good mind!"

"To them, it is but a store of gold and jewels," Ingegerd said.

She was right, of course. A laughing Khamorth carried an icon of Phos out of the temple—not for its beauty but for its gold leaf. Maybe he thought it was gold all the way through, though the weight should have given that away. Other nomads brought away better spoils.

"Quick," Ingegerd hissed. "Past them while they care more for booty than for blood."

She was also right about that. The Khamorth were happy with what they'd taken, and briefly sated. They let the prelate and the woman get past them without more than a glance. A few doors down, other barbarians had broken into a tavern. Wine and beer delighted them as much as gold had pleased their fellows at the temple.

What Rhavas dreaded was half a dozen of them coming after him and Ingegerd at once. Even if he beat back the first couple of attackers, it would only enrage the rest—and he could not afford to lose at all. Ingegerd, perhaps, could afford it even less than he could, for the Khamorth were more likely to kill him cleanly.

She might have plucked that thought from his mind. "Do not fret," she said as they hurried past the tavern. "They will have no sport over me. I know how to draw the blade across my own neck if fortune fails us."

"May the good god prevent it," Rhavas muttered.

"Yes, may he indeed," Ingegerd answered calmly. "But in case he does not, I can look after myself."

That should have bordered on blasphemy: how could mortals presume to set their will against Phos'? And suicide normally sent someone falling from the Bridge of the Separator down to the eternal ice. Suicide under such circumstances, though . . . Rhavas could not find it in himself to condemn such a thing, and could not believe the lord with the great and good mind did, either.

"Quickly," the prelate said as they went past the tavern. "If they notice you are a woman . . . things become more difficult." And anyone who would not notice that Ingegerd was a woman was not paying attention.

But Rhavas got her round a corner before a startled shout rang out from the direction of the tavern. The barbarians had been too intent on the drink they'd found to think of other pleasures right away. "Here, let me lead," Ingegerd said then. "I think I can lose them in the maze of streets."

"Go ahead, then," Rhavas said. "Try not to use any ways where the snow has not been trodden, or they will trail us the more easily."

She nodded. "A thought of weight . . . Down here now." She turned left. "Now through this alley." Only a few people had gone through it; she and Rhavas did their best to step in the tracks that were already there. She pointed to the right. "Now that way—and we should be close to the gate."

The next interesting question was whether they would be able to get out. Were the gates open? Did plainsmen swarm around them? Even if he and Ingegerd could escape Skopentzana, what then? Could they make their way across country to the closest village, or even to the closest farmhouse? How could they keep from leaving a trail wherever they went?

That wasn't one interesting question—it was more like half a dozen. Unless they could find answers to all of them, they would find answers to other questions, the ones of the sort where no one who learned them was in any position to pass them on to anyone else.

The gates were open. Rhavas breathed out a sigh of relief and a young fog bank to go with it. He and Ingegerd weren't the first ones to flee this way. He saw no great swarm of plainsmen, either. The Khamorth were having better sport inside Skopentzana than they would have had outside the city. Odds were they thought they could hunt down escapees at their leisure. Odds were they were right, too, but Rhavas refused to dwell on that.

"Out!" he said to Ingegerd.

"Out!" she echoed. They both ran for the gate. They ran out through it. Once beyond bowshot from the walls, they paused for a moment, panting. If anything was more exhausting than running through snow, Rhavas could not imagine what it might be.

He turned back toward Skopentzana and shook his fist at the strong stone walls and at the barbarians inside them. "My curses on the Khamorth!" he shouted. "May they suffer what they have made others suffer! May they die as they have made innocent Videssians die! May they burn as they have made Skopentzana burn! And may pestilence destroy any of the murderers my other curses do not overtake!" He spat in the snow.

Ingegerd nodded somber approval. "That is an excellent curse, very holy sir. I do not think any of my own people could have laid a stronger one on the plainsmen. May it bite deep. May it bite as deep as the one you set upon the man who commanded the militia."

Rhavas wished she hadn't spoken of Toxaras. And then, all at once, he wondered why. If he *had* cursed Toxaras, maybe he really could curse the Khamorth, too. And he *wanted* to curse the barbarians. "May it be so," he said, accepting the possibility. "And now, I think we had better find shelter for ourselves."

"Yes, that would be a very good thing to do," Ingegerd said. "Hard to tell where the road is with so much snow on the ground."

When the snow finally melted in spring, the road would disappear into a sea of mud for a few weeks. Mosquitoes and gnats would make Skopentzana and the countryside miserable. But that time lay in the distance. For now, winter still reigned supreme here. Rhavas pointed toward a grove of bare-branched apple trees ahead. "That is an orchard. Where there is an orchard, there will be a farmhouse. If people still live there, perhaps they will take us in. And if it should be empty, we can rest for a while, build a fire—"

"Better not," Ingegerd broke in. "The smoke would draw more eyes than we want to see."

He bowed. "You are right, of course, and I am wrong. But the day is cold, and the night will be colder."

"I have a thick blanket here." She patted the makeshift knapsack. "If we lie under it together, we can stay warm, or warm enough."

For a moment, the prelate was shocked. Then he realized she meant exactly what she'd said: that and no more. He sighed heavily. Lying down together with any woman would tempt a priest. Lying down with a woman he'd long admired . . . He sighed again. "Let's get to that farmhouse," he said, his voice perhaps rougher than he had intended.

On they went. Here and there ahead of them, Rhavas saw other people also trudging through the snow, singly and in small groups. When he looked back to Skopentzana, he saw a few more. Maybe others had escaped from different gates and gone in other directions. Even so, the city that had been the pride of the north, the city that had stood second or third in all the Empire of Videssos, stood no more. Skopentzana had fallen.

"There." Ingegerd pointed with a mittened hand. "That will be the path to the farmhouse." The wind that had scoured away some snow and the lie of the land made it easier to recognize than Rhavas had thought it would be.

The farmhouse itself and the nearby barn might almost have been snowdrifts themselves. No smoke rose from the hole in the roof. The buildings seemed intact, though. The plainsmen hadn't burned them.

"I wonder if anyone else has taken shelter here," Rhavas said.

They'd drawn to within fifty yards of the farmhouse when a low rumble filled the air and the ground began to shake beneath Rhavas' feet. *Earthquake*, he thought—he'd been through several of them in Videssos the city, though he couldn't remember any since coming to Skopentzana. Half a heartbeat later, he thought, *This is a big earthquake.*

Half a heartbeat after *that*, the quake knocked him and Ingegerd off their feet and into the snow. He knew he cried out. He thought Ingegerd must have screamed. But he couldn't hear his voice, let alone hers, through the great bass roar that surrounded them.

While it was going on, the earthquake seemed to last forever. Afterward, he supposed it couldn't have shaken for more than a minute or two. That was plenty. That was, indeed, excessive. He wondered if the ground would open and swallow him up. He had heard that sometimes happened. It didn't happen here. Sullenly, the shaking subsided.

Rhavas scrambled to his feet. Ingegerd was already upright, but her face was gray with shock. She said something in the Haloga language, as if forgetting that he didn't understand it. Only little by little did reason return to her eyes. "That was . . . very bad," she choked out.

"Yes." Rhavas had to force the word past his lips, too. Then he screamed again, and so did Ingegerd, for another earthquake started. This one was smaller than the monster they had just survived. It didn't knock them off their feet, and he could hear their cries of terror.

"Phos!" Ingegerd exclaimed when the second round of shaking eased. She sketched the sun-sign over her heart.

"It will do that," Rhavas said. "After a good-sized quake, the smaller ones will go on for months. After one like this . . ." He shuddered. "After one like this, they'll go on for years."

Ingegerd looked as if he could have said nothing more horrible. Some of the aftershocks from a quake like this would be big enough to shake down things that had survived the first jolt. They would do more damage. They would kill more people.

Rhavas stared at the farmhouse and barn he and Ingegerd had been approaching. Both had fallen into rubble. The house, which was built all of stone, was only a heap of stones now. If they'd sheltered there before the earthquake struck, the collapse would have crushed them.

The barn had been stone up to about the height of a man's shoulder, with planking above that. It had come through better than the farmhouse. It too was wrecked, but not so badly. Taking refuge in what was left of it might help shelter the fugitives.

And . . . Rhavas started to laugh. Ingegerd stared at him as if he'd lost his mind.

He pointed to the timbers, some of which had been scattered like jackstraws. "We won't lack for firewood," he said.

"Oh." She managed a nod of sorts. "Yes, very holy sir, that is true. And no one will think anything special of fires now—not after that."

Another aftershock rocked them. Rhavas thought this one was stronger than the first. He didn't shout this time, though. Maybe all the terror had been knocked out of him. Ingegerd also stayed silent—grimly silent, if her expression was any guide. After a few heartbeats, the shaking and the roaring stopped—until they decided to start again.

Only after that did the prelate's stunned wits begin to work again, at least after a fashion. Of itself, his hand shaped Phos' sun-sign. "By the lord with the great and good mind!" he burst out. "What's happened to Skopentzana?"

He couldn't see well. Even though the earthquake had knocked the snow off the branches of the trees in the apple orchard, they still blocked his view. He went back the way he and Ingegerd had come to get a better look. She followed.

"Phos!" Rhavas whispered once he had it. The walls of Skopentzana had fallen to the ground, all except for a few stretches that stuck up like teeth in an almost empty jaw. Through the smoke and the cloud of dust the quake had shaken into the sky, the great gaps in the wall let him see how many buildings had fallen down. The bulk of the temple, which had dominated Skopentzana's skyline, stood no more. That felt like a knife in his heart.

He had to look away. If he stared at the place where the temple had been, he would start to weep. In this weather, the tears would freeze on his face and freeze his eyelids together.

It was, perhaps, not surprising that his gaze settled on Ingegerd's face. What did surprise him was that she was staring not at the ruination of Skopentzana but at him.

As he had a moment before, she whispered, "Phos!" With her, though, it was not a sound of horror or dread but one of awe. She went right on staring. "Truly, very holy sir, you *do* have the power to curse," she went on. "Look at what you just visited on the Khamorth!"

"Nonsense," Rhavas said. He'd said the same thing when Voilas accused him of causing Toxaras' death with his curse. Now, though, he sounded more uneasy than he had then. Dismissing two unlikely sets of coincidence was much more than twice as hard as dismissing one.

And Ingegerd shook her head. "No, very holy sir. You should not say such a thing. You should be proud. Phos has given you great power. See the vengeance you have visited upon the vandals. Relish the revenge you have worked."

Rhavas shook his head. Before he could answer, another aftershock rumbled through and rocked him. He had to fight to hold himself upright. So did Ingegerd. Seeing her swaying there made him wish she would fall into his arms. But the trembling stopped, and she straightened.

"It is not Phos' power," Rhavas said stubbornly. "I have prayed to the lord with the great and good mind, again and again, beseeching him on bended knee. Had he hearkened to my prayers, Skopentzana would stand yet, and the plainsmen would wander well away from her walls."

Like many people, he often spoke in the style of those who impressed him. When he heard himself alliterating like that, he realized yet again how deeply Ingegerd had got under his skin.

She said, "It is a great power. Surely even you will not deny that. If it comes not from Phos, whence comes it?"

"I do deny, and will deny, that it is anything past happenstance." Rhavas denied that more to himself than to the yellow-haired woman standing beside him. If he denied it, he did not have to think where that power might come from.

Ingegerd made an impatient noise—more than a sigh, less than a word. But she let it rest there, as she might have if Rhavas had insisted on talking about fashions in tunics and nothing else. She was very pointedly putting up with an eccentricity, not agreeing with anything the prelate said.

Instead, she looked back toward the battered barn. She said, "Will it be safe to shelter there, or is it likely to come down on our heads while we sleep tonight—if we sleep tonight?"

Rhavas eyed the barn, too, with more than a little relief. "I think we will *need* shelter tonight. Do you not agree? Also, even now I would not care to start a fire in the open so close to Skopentzana. It might bring us more company than we would care to have."

She thought for a moment, then nodded crisply. "Very true.

There are risks of one sort as well as risks of another. Shelter it shall be."

The barn still smelled like a barn. There was no livestock inside. Had there been, the animals would have burst out during or right after the earthquake. But the Khamorth or Videssian stragglers had plundered the place after the owners abandoned it or were killed—or maybe the owners drove the animals into Skopentzana. In that case, the quake might have done what raiders hadn't.

A hatchet no one had bothered to steal lay almost at Rhavas' feet when he ducked into the damaged barn. It had probably been hanging on a wall and escaped notice in the gloom. He gladly grabbed it now and used to to chop up some of the barn's planking for a fire. That was when he realized he had nothing with which to start one. He had never made fire by rubbing sticks together. All he knew about the operation was that it required more patience than any three normal human beings possessed.

As if she camped out in battered barns every day, Ingegerd took flint and steel from her blanket-knapsack along with the food she'd brought from Skopentzana. "O pearl among women!" Rhavas exclaimed.

She didn't even answer that. She just gathered straw from the dirt floor of the barn for tinder and began striking the flint and steel together above it. Before long, sparks made the straw catch. She and Rhavas both fed first splinters and then real pieces of wood into the growing fire.

Except for what came from his own exertions, the heat from the flames was the first Rhavas had felt since escaping Skopentzana. He and Ingegerd toasted chunks of sausage over the flames, then ate them and some of the bread and cheese she had brought. She looked at what was left. "This will serve for tomorrow, and maybe the day after," she said. "Past that . . ."

"We are free of the city," Rhavas said. "We are luckier than most who were in it when the barbarians broke in and when the earthquake struck."

"When the earthquake struck . . ." Ingegerd shook her head. "Say rather, when your curse struck."

"I will say no such thing." Rhavas pointed to the flames. "I will say, with regret, that we should let this die out after all. If it shines through the night, it is only too likely to draw two-legged wolves this way. The barn does not shield the light well enough to hide it."

Ingegerd considered, then nodded. "Like as not, you are right. Well, it was not large enough to give us much warmth. Here in a partly closed space, we will do well enough in all our clothes and under the blanket."

"Yes," Rhavas said, though he was thinking, *No.* Lying down with a woman, even if they were both fully clothed, even if there was neither lovemaking nor any intention of it, bent his vows somewhere close to the breaking point. How close? He would have to discuss that with some other ecclesiastic one of these days. But if the only way to survive to discuss it was by lying down with the woman now . . . *Then I will, that's all.*

And he did. By then, the fire had already shrunk to embers that gave no more than a dull red glow. Under the thick, scratchy wool, he and Ingegerd turned their backs to each other. But they still touched. They needed to, to share each other's warmth. Trying to pretend it wasn't happening, trying to pretend everything was normal, he murmured, "Good night."

"Good night," she answered. They both started to laugh. It might have been the worst night either one of them had ever known—and things would get no better when morning came. But they stayed polite just the same.

Rhavas wondered whether he would sleep at all. Then exhaustion coshed him. Every Khamorth in the world could have paraded by the tumbledown barn in the next few hours. Every Videssian ecclesiastic in the Empire could have peered into the ruin, stared disapprovingly at the spectacle of a respected prelate under a blanket with a woman, and gone off muttering. Rhavas would never have known any of it. Every aftershock in the world could have . . .

But that turned out not to be quite true after all. No matter how weary he was, no matter what horrors he'd seen, endured, and escaped the day before, some of the aftershocks might have wakened a dead man. And one of them eventually succeeded in waking him.

Even after his eyes flew open, he wasn't sure they had. The fire was out, so he lay in darkness absolute, as if Skotos had conquered the world. The ground shook beneath him. The stones of the barn's lower walls groaned around him. The partly tumbled timbers creaked above him. For a long, horrid moment, he had no idea where he was. The eternal ice seemed the likeliest explanation.

To make things worse, or at least stranger, someone was breathing in his face from very close range. A hand and arm were draped across his shoulder. His own hand rested on a smooth curve under rough wool. He jerked it away with a gasp of horror—that could only be a woman's hip.

"It's all right, very holy sir," Ingegerd said softly. "I know you meant nothing by it. We twisted around while we slept, that's all."

Full memory returned to Rhavas at last. "Yes, so we did," he answered, and hoped his own voice sounded less shaky to her than it did to him. Another quake, a smaller one, made him put *shaky* in a new perspective. "The aftershock woke me."

"I know. You slept through two or three that roused me," Ingegerd said. "You must be more used to them than I am."

"I don't believe anyone ever gets used to them," Rhavas said. He wanted to roll away from her, but the only warmth anywhere was where they touched. She didn't roll away from him onto her other side, either. They were left with each other, and nothing else. He shook his head. This was not how things should have been, but he was powerless to change it. "We should try to go back to sleep." If he was asleep, he wouldn't have to think about what he was doing here.

He could not see her nod, but he felt the motion. "That is surely the sensible thing to do, very holy sir. In the morning, we can go on."

"Yes." Never had Rhavas longed for Phos' light as he did now.

What he had was darkness. Ingegerd began to breathe slowly and regularly. He wondered how she could drop off like that. She never had taken her hand from his shoulder. It felt warm. It felt more than merely warm, in fact. It might have been on fire.

Rhavas knew that was only his inflamed imagination, his out-raged conscience. Knowing didn't mean being able to do anything about it. He lay there, not wanting to move for fear of disturbing her. Another small aftershock rattled the planking over their heads. Ingegerd stirred and muttered, but did not wake. Rhavas wanted to sign himself as he prayed, but he couldn't; she lay too close to him. He hoped the good god would take the thought for the deed.

He must have dozed off, though he never remembered falling asleep once more. When he woke the next time, gray predawn light was leaking down through the riven roof. But that was the least of his worries. He and Ingegerd lay breast to breast, her head on his shoulder, their arms and legs entwined as if they clung from love rather than cold.

He had never held a woman so. He had never thought he wanted to hold a woman so, not till he came to know Ingegerd. And now he could not free himself from the temptation she represented, not without disturbing her—and that, he told himself, would be unforgivable after the day they'd endured. Yes, so he told himself.

After somewhere between a quarter and half an hour of that sweet torment, yet another aftershock rattled the barn. Ingegerd's eyes flew open. "Only an earthquake," Rhavas said, to remind her where she was and what had happened.

She managed a shaky laugh. "Only an earthquake," she echoed. "Someday, maybe, I will be able to say that and not feel my marrow freeze when I do. You are a brave man, very holy sir."

Brave enough to fight what you do to me? I wonder. By the good god, I truly do. But Rhavas held that in, as he held in so much. He said, "*Our* marrow did not freeze in the night, despite earthquakes and snow and everything else."

Ingegerd nodded. "That is so. The blanket warmed us, and we warmed each other."

She had warmed him, sure enough. If he had warmed her the same way, she gave no sign of it. She disentangled herself from him. He turned a sigh into a cough and plucked at his beard. "Have I got straw in it?" he asked.

"Not much," she answered. Her hands flew to her hair. "What of me?"

Greatly daring, Rhavas plucked out one or two pieces. Instead of scowling, she nodded her thanks. He said, "There may be more, but your hair is so fair that it is hard to see."

"A drawback of Haloga blood I had not thought of until now," she said, smiling. But the smile faded as she went on, "One of my folk living among Videssians is seldom left unaware of other drawbacks for long."

"I hope I have not been one to give offense," Rhavas said.

"Oh, no, very holy sir. You are a true friend," Ingegerd said. The prelate would have been glad to bask in that for an eon or two, but she continued again: "And Himerios, of course, is far more than friend. But many Videssians are not shy about thinking me a barbarian and saying what they think."

"No doubt," Rhavas said tonelessly. He tried to keep his mind on the matter at hand, not on the hopeless memory of her pressed against him. She hadn't even known she was doing that, and had withdrawn as soon as she woke up. "We should eat, and then we should put as much distance between us and Skopentzana as we can. Later today, we will need to find another place where we can pass the night."

"What you say makes good sense," Ingegerd said. "But then, what you say generally makes good sense. Shall I start the fire afresh, or do you fear smoke too much?"

"We got away with it once. I am not sure we could hope to do it twice," Rhavas said after a little thought.

Cold, cold sausage sat like a lump in his stomach. Cold, cold bread proved not much better. He wished he would have risked a small blaze. By Ingegerd's expression, so did she. But she did not reproach him for the choice. With his scant experience of women, he thought them all scolds till proved otherwise. Her forbearance raised his opinion of her even higher.

After eating, they started south again. Rhavas had feared they would run into hordes of Khamorth swarming toward the fallen, the shattered, Skopentzana, but they saw hardly any plainsmen all that day, and those only at a distance. Maybe the earthquake had disrupted the nomads even more than he'd suspected.

Aftershocks kept making the ground shake under their feet. Some were barely perceptible, others considerable quakes in their own right. Each time the earth trembled, Rhavas knew a fresh spasm of panic. How long would the shaking last? How bad would it be? Even when he was in the open, where nothing could possibly fall on him, the unthinking terror would darken his wits.

And not his alone—after one of the harder aftershocks, Ingegerd said, "This is one of the hardest things I have ever borne. Hard winters I know, and likewise war. But when the very ground beneath my feet betrays me . . ." She shook her head. "Such a thing should not be possible."

"They do happen." Rhavas tried not to admit his own fear even to himself. "They are more common in the south, but they can come anywhere."

Ingegerd looked at him with awe in her eyes. "And this one came at your command, very holy sir."

"I do not believe that. You too would do better not to believe it." Even more than aftershocks, the prelate feared that what she said might be true. If his curse had stricken Toxaras, if his curse had called up the quake and crushed the Khamorth, what had his curse done to *him*? What *would* it do to him?

"Very well. Let it be as you say. I will not believe the earthquake came at your command," Ingegerd answered obediently. But mischief sparked in her eyes. "Only because I do not believe it, that does not mean it is untrue."

"Heh." Past the chuckle that came from him involuntarily, Rhavas didn't dignify that with a reply. Ingegerd looked smug, as if she knew she had won the point. Maybe she did. And maybe she had, too.

They trudged on. Rhavas had only a vague notion of where the next town would be. He hadn't gone far from Skopentzana all through his tenure. He was a city man both by birth and by inclination. Even Skopentzana hadn't been city enough to satisfy him fully, not when he'd come from the imperial capital. But he'd never seen any reason to leave it for the semibarbarous countryside—not till now.

The sun slid across the sky. Days were still short, though noticeably longer than they had been right around the time of the solstice. "We had better look for shelter," Ingegerd said as afternoon drew on toward evening. "I would not care to sleep in the snow tonight."

"Nor I." Rhavas' shiver was not altogether artificial. "That would all too likely mean our deaths."

"Oh, no." The Haloga woman shook her head. She looked surprised. "A man with only a cloak can pass the night well enough. Do you not know how?"

"I fear not," the prelate answered.

"Well, it is so." Ingegerd spoke with an assurance that compelled belief. "And with the warmth of two of us and with all we have, it would be easy." If sleeping in the snow meant no choice but sleeping in each other's arms, Rhavas suddenly hoped all barns and farmhouses would disappear. If he had to do it to survive, it could not possibly be sinful for him . . . could it? Ingegerd went on, "But, easy or not, it would not be so comfortable as a farmhouse, or even a barn."

"No doubt you are right." Rhavas hoped he didn't sound too mournful. Evidently not, for Ingegerd just nodded briskly and walked on.

When Rhavas spotted the farm off to the side of the snow-covered road, he pretended for a few heartbeats that he had not. It availed him nothing, of course, for Ingegerd saw the place, too. "If anyone dwells there, we can beg a place by the hearth," she said. "If not, it is ours to do with as we will."

"So it is," Rhavas said resignedly.

"Do we halloo?" Ingegerd asked as they drew near.

"I see no horses tied close by," Rhavas said. "Where there are Khamorth, there will be horses." He paused to see if she would disagree. When she didn't, he went on, "This being so, I think we may safely call."

They did. No one answered. Ingegerd found another question: "With these cursed quakes continuing, dare we shelter there this night?"

"You were the one who said you would rather not spend the night in the open. Neither would I," Rhavas replied. "The risk is worth taking. If the farmhouse hasn't fallen yet, it probably won't."

When they went in, they found the Khamorth had been there before them. The plainsmen had butchered the family that lived on the farm; only the winter weather kept the bodies from stinking. By all the signs, the nomads had amused themselves with the farm wife and her daughter before killing them. Rhavas and Ingegerd both sketched the sun-sign without realizing they did it. Neither said a word as they dragged the dead outside. As silently, Ingegerd set the woman's clothes, and the girl's, to rights before moving them.

Even after the corpses were gone, bloodstains made the place grimmer than Rhavas cared for. As much to herself as to him, Ingegerd remarked, "We do not what we would, but what we needs must."

"Just so," Rhavas said heavily. "Yes, just so."

The fire in the hearth was as dead as those who had kindled

it. Unlike them, though, it could be brought back to life. Rhavas brought in wood from the pile behind the farmhouse. As twilight quickly faded toward night, Ingegerd fumbled with flint and steel. At last, she got a fire going.

"Shut the door, very holy sir," she told Rhavas. "It will hold the heat in and not let the light leak out. And no one in the dark is likely to see the smoke."

Rhavas obeyed. He and Ingegerd both sat close by the fire, eating of the food she had brought out of Skopentzana and letting the warmth soak into their bones. Whenever they moved, the flickering flames sent their shadows swooping along the rough stone of the walls. Two or three aftershocks brought straw sifting down from the thatched roof, but worked no worse than that.

Before long, they were both yawning. Rhavas rose and turned the peasants' wool-stuffed mattress over. That did not get rid of the stains on it, but did mean he and Ingegerd would not have to lie on them.

"I would have done the same, but you were there before me," she said.

As they had the night before, they lay down under the blanket back to back and, with odd formality, wished each other good night. As Rhavas had the night before, he fell asleep as if someone had hit him over the head. He could feel how soft he was. He'd lived too quietly for much too long.

When an aftershock woke him in the middle of the night, the fire had died back to embers. The farmhouse had got colder, and he and Ingegerd had responded by snuggling together and wrapping their arms around each other. She only half woke, and murmured something in his ear. He couldn't tell what it was; she spoke in the Haloga tongue. But the moist warmth of her breath on his skin kept him awake long after he should have slipped back into unconsciousness.

He didn't realize he had gone to asleep till he jerked awake, this time abruptly enough to wake Ingegerd, too. "What is it?" she whispered. "Is it trouble outside?"

"No," he answered, absurdly angry at the world. "A bedbug bit me." He needed a moment to remember to add, "I'm sorry I bothered you."

She shrugged against his shoulder. "You cannot be blamed for that. Like as not, the same will befall me next."

"You are charitable," he said. As long as she was awake, he scratched—it wouldn't bother her. A moment later, she did, too. She laughed about it. Rhavas didn't. He was not accustomed to bugs. He wondered whether the poor peasants had them or the Khamorth brought them. Either, he supposed, or maybe both.

He did some more scratching and then, bedbugs or no, dozed off. When he woke again, morning twilight was seeping through the slatted shutters in place over the farmhouse's windows. He and Ingegerd lay face to face again, and in each other's arms. He knew he ought to get away, if he could do it without rousing her.

Instead, of their own accord—or so it seemed to him—his arms tightened around her. That didn't rouse her, or not quite; she muttered, but then went back to breathing deeply and regularly. But it roused him, much more than he'd imagined it would. The soft pressure of her breasts against his chest, her belly against his . . .

Then there was pressure from him against her belly, and not soft pressure, either. She laughed softly. "Himerios," she murmured. She knew what that pressure was, all right, and was used to it, even welcomed it—from her husband.

Her eyes opened, bare inches from Rhavas'. For a moment, she plainly had no idea who he was or where she was. He waited for her to pull back in horror, even in disgust. And she did draw back, but slowly and deliberately.

She sighed and nodded. "I might have known this would come up," she said, more to herself than to Rhavas. And it *had* come up; it throbbed almost painfully. But that wasn't what she meant. She looked Rhavas in the face, her eyes still too close to his for him to look away. "You are a man, and I am a woman."

"Yes," he answered miserably. By the way she said what he was, he might have been a child. As far as experience went, he *was* a child.

Still as if he were one in truth, Ingegerd went on, "I am a wedded woman, and glad to be such. And you, very holy sir, you are a priest, and you know and I know what a priest's vows are."

"Of course," he said, and closed his eyes. That was the only way he could avoid her gaze.

But her voice softened as she went on, "I know what those vows are, and I admire you for holding to them. It cannot be easy for a man. I know of no Haloga who would willingly undertake them."

"There was the holy Kveldoulphios, a couple of hundred years ago during the reign of Stavrakios." Even in his embarrassment, Rhavas could no more help showing off his scholarship than a jackdaw could help stealing a bit of bright, shiny metal on the ground.

"Kveldulf." Ingegerd said the name in the northern fashion. None of the vowels stayed quite the same. "Well, you are right, very holy sir. I have heard of him, as who in Skopentzana has not?" She refused to let herself be distracted. "But we were not speaking of him, but of the two of us. I know your body will do what it will do. It cannot help being what it is. But by your vow—and by the promise you gave my husband—what it would do, you will not do."

Eyes still closed, Rhavas whispered, "You shame me."

"I do not mean to. If I do, I cry your pardon," Ingegerd answered seriously. "We need each other here. Two together have a better chance than two ones apart. I am not angry at you. Your body said you wanted me. So be it. You did not try to work anything against my will. The one I can forgive—indeed, it needs no forgiveness. The other? That would be different. But it has not arisen, and I trust it will not. Shall we go on from there, then?"

"I think we had better," Rhavas answered. He spoke severely to what had arisen. He was a man of stern, almost ascetic, discipline, and did not anticipate how strongly it would answer back. Priests were taught that desire was a poison. Rhavas had always believed it. No one had ever told him what a sweet poison it could be.

For a moment, he wondered why not. But that was only too easy to figure out. Such teaching would weaken ecclesiastical discipline. Oh, priests succumbed to the lusts of the flesh all the time. But if the hierarchy did not admit as much, it could punish them or transfer them as seemed best, and otherwise ignore the question. It was so large—and so inflammable—that everyone judged it better ignored.

Rhavas always had—till it happened to him.

Ingegerd got out of the bed. She opened the shutters. Gray light filled the farmhouse. The bloodstains on the floor and the furniture seemed almost black, but gained more color as sunrise drew closer. Ingegerd scratched and made a wry face. "Bugs," she muttered, and then, "I wonder if the Khamorth stole all the food here, or if they came but for the sport of slaying."

"We have little left of our own, do we?" Rhavas said, and his stomach snarled like a hungry wolf.

"We will have *nothing* left of our own after we break our fast here, and a meager breakfast it shall be," Ingegerd said. "And we needs must have food. Tramping through the freezing cold wears one down faster than almost anything else."

She rapidly searched the house, and exclaimed in delight when she turned up four loaves of bread. The cold had preserved them against mold and insects. They were the last things the farmwife had baked before she became a victim of the nomads' lusts.

As Rhavas broke chunks of bread and warmed them in his hands before eating them, his gaze kept sliding to Ingegerd. *I would have made her a victim of my lusts*, he thought unhappily. But then he shook his head. He would sooner not have had her a victim. He would sooner have had her willing, even eager, even wanton.

He glanced at her again. And if she weren't willing, let alone more than willing? He was grimly honest enough to realize he wanted her anyway. *But I didn't do anything*, he reminded himself, and salved his conscience.

They each ate one loaf along with the last of the cheese she'd brought from Skopentzana, and set aside the last two for later. "We had best be off, and make what use we can of the light," Ingegerd said.

"Yes," Rhavas said, and laughed at himself. After another day struggling through snow, he would be too weary to threaten anyone's virtue by the time nightfall came.

They had just left the farmhouse when a strong aftershock staggered them. They clung together for a moment, not from lust but from fear. "I hate this," Ingegerd said when it ended. "Once something is over, it should be *over*."

"I wish it were so." Rhavas meant that from the bottom of his heart. "But it will go on. The quakes will mostly grow smaller as time goes by, and will come less often. Come they will, though."

He and the Haloga woman slogged south. She pointed to a dark smudge on the horizon. "I think that will mark a town."

"The good god grant that you be right," Rhavas said. "May he grant also that it still be in Videssian hands." If its walls had fallen in the earthquake, it would make easy meat for the Khamorth. How far *had* the barbarians spread through the Empire? Was anyone doing anything to try to hold them back? Rhavas pondered the blood-mad folly of his cousin and of Videssos' best and most famous general. If their war was not madness, what would be?

Quietly, Ingegerd said, "I fear me we have a problem, very holy sir." She pointed to the west.

Rhavas turned his head that way. As quietly, he answered, "Well, I'm afraid you're right." Four Khamorth on their ponies were trotting purposefully toward the two of them. They weren't within bowshot yet, but they would be before long. Without looking over his shoulder at Ingegerd, Rhavas said, "Run. I'll hold them as long as I can."

"Thank you, very holy sir, but there is no place to run," Ingegerd said. And she was right: there weren't even any trees close by. She went on, "As you have stood with me, I will stand with you. If I fail and you have the chance, kill me quickly at the last. And if even that cannot be"—her pause might have been a shrug—"sooner or later, everything ends."

Fury burned through Rhavas. Just when they had hope of safety, the barbarians came upon them. They were close enough now for him to see the snow spurting up from their horses' hooves, and to see them set arrows to their bowstrings. One let fly. The shaft fell short, but others wouldn't.

"Curse you!" Rhavas cried with all the rage he had in him. "Curse the lot of you!"

One by one, silently and without any fuss, the Khamorth fell off their ponies and lay motionless in the snow. The horses trotted on for a few paces, then stopped in what looked like confusion. Rhavas gaped at the dead bodies in astonishment and disbelief.

He slowly became aware that Ingegerd was gaping at *him*. "By the good god, very holy sir," she whispered. "You saved us."

✦ VI

Rhavas and Ingegerd rode up to the town of Tzamandos on two of the plainsmen's ponies. They led the other two. Neither of them was much of an equestrian, but they both saw they could travel faster mounted than afoot. They carried the barbarians' bows and arrows, and they wore wolfskin caps that kept their heads warmer than anything they'd had before.

"Phos spoke through you, very holy sir," Ingegerd said as they neared Tzamandos. "What else could it have been?"

The prelate didn't answer. His own thoughts were all awhirl. He had not believed his curse had anything to do with Toxaras' death. He'd figured that for nothing but an unfortunate coincidence. He had not thought the earthquake that leveled Skopentzana sprang from his curse of the Khamorth, either. How could any man imagine he might command an earthquake?

But what had just happened, out there in the snow-covered field... How could he ignore that? How could he claim it had nothing to do with him? He couldn't, and knew it all too well.

How could he believe Phos had had anything to do with it? He couldn't, and he also knew that all too well. The knowledge terrified him as nothing ever had before.

Phos had been the furthest thing from his mind when he called down the curse on the Khamorth. It hadn't been a prayer.

151

Prayer hadn't had the first thing to do with it. That curse had been a cry of outrage, a cry of hate, wrung from the very depths of his being.

He'd done a lot of praying. What had it got him? An Empire riven by civil war, a city fallen to the savages, disaster almost beyond reckoning. If the lord with the great and good mind heard his prayers at all, he had an odd way of showing it.

His curses, on the other hand, struck home. He didn't care to think about what that might mean.

And, to his vast relief, he didn't have to. "Who comes?" shouted a man on the wall. "If you're as barbarous as you look, you'd better steer clear. We're still ready to put up a fight, by the good god."

Taking off the wolfskin cap, Rhavas called out his own name and station. He continued, "With me is Ingegerd, wife to Himerios, garrison commander of Skopentzana. If you have refugees from our city within the walls, they will vouch for us."

"No need," the man said. "You speak Videssian like a native, and I see your head was shaved. Come in and be welcome, holy sir—uh, very holy sir—and the woman with you as well."

Was shaved? Rhavas set a hand on top of the organ in question. Sure enough, he felt stubble there. He shook his head in bemusement. He'd kept his scalp smooth since taking the vows of priesthood. But he'd had no chance to shave it the past few days. *One more thing to tend to*, he thought.

With much creaking of hinges that needed oiling, Tzamandos' gates swung open. Rhavas and Ingegerd rode into the town. The militiamen closed the gates behind them. The amateur soldiers were full of questions: "How bad is it in Skopentzana?" "Did the barbarians really break in?" "How could they take such a strong city?" "What did the earthquake do up there?" "Do you people aim to stay here?" "Where will you go if you don't?"

Rhavas answered as best he could. Ingegerd seemed content to let him do the talking, maybe because he had more rank than she did, maybe because Videssian was his birthspeech and not hers, or maybe just because—like a lot of Halogai—she thought Videssians liked to talk for the fun of it.

The locals exclaimed in horror when they heard how Skopentzana had fallen. "Some folk who got here ahead of you said the same," one of the militiamen said gloomily, "but we didn't want to believe 'em. Now I guess we have to."

"We've got farmers and their kin in here, too," another added. "Don't like to think we've got to keep a special eye on 'em."

You probably don't, Rhavas thought. Up in Skopentzana, the refugees and the militia had become foes from the start. If that hadn't happened in Tzamandos, the militiamen didn't need to fear that the farmers would prefer the barbarians to them.

He spoke as little as he could of the earthquake. Especially now, he didn't know what to say. To fend off the locals' questions, he asked questions of his own. "It shook us hard," a militiaman answered. "Shook some buildings down, killed some people. But we didn't have bad fires the way we could have, and the walls stayed up, Phos be praised." He drew the sun-circle above his breast.

So did Rhavas, though his head still whirled. How much had Phos had to do with the earthquake? Any more than with any other part of Rhavas' curses? If Phos hadn't given those curses the power to bite, *who had?* The prelate shied from that like a horse shying from a snake.

No sooner had he thought of horses than one of the locals asked, "How did you come by the Khamorth ponies, very holy sir?"

It was only natural that he should ask. Perhaps the biggest surprise was that the militiamen had had so many other questions ahead of that one. Rhavas coughed. He had no good answer. Then Ingegerd spoke up: "The prelate killed the barbarians to whom they belonged. They are ours now, as spoil of war."

Her slow, sonorous speech only made the words seem more impressive. The militiamen eyed Rhavas in a new way. A priest—a not particularly impressive-looking priest—who'd slain four Khamorth? Rhavas thanked the good god she hadn't said *how* he killed them. That would have taken more in the way of explanation than he had in him.

"Where is an inn that will tend to the garrison commander's wife?" he asked. "I can beg shelter at a temple, of course, but she may not."

"We're pretty full up, but we'll see what we can do," a militiaman said. "Since she came with you, though, I expect we'll manage."

"I thank you for your kindness," Ingegerd said. Her voice, or perhaps her way of speaking, had something in it that commanded attention. The militiamen almost came to blows deciding which inn would be best for her. At last they decided only the one run by Evtherios would do. One of them appointed himself guide, and self-importantly led the way.

Rhavas came along. He asked her, "Now that you have come here, will you stay? It might be safer if you did."

She shook her head. "No. I will seek my husband. And as for safety, I see none anywhere. With Skopentzana fallen, who can doubt that the like mischance might befall Tzamandos, or indeed any town?"

"As I promised Himerios, I will help you if you can." Rhavas hesitated, then added, "Unless you would sooner have seen the last of me. I can understand how that might be so, and you need not say otherwise for politeness' sake."

Ingegerd shook her head again, this time with a smile on her face. "I would not keep silent for politeness' sake; anyone who knows me will know this is so." Rhavas believed her; whatever she was, she was no hypocrite. Hypocrisy was a Videssian vice, not one from which a Haloga was likely to suffer. She went on, "Nothing untoward happened, nor do I look for anything untoward to happen if we travel together."

"Then we will go on when we can," Rhavas said. Right then, he had no idea whether he looked for the same thing. He also suspected that what he thought of as untoward right now might differ from Ingegerd's notions of the same thing. He did not ask. He did not want to know.

"Here we are," the local militiaman said proudly. "Evtherios' inn—the finest in Tzamandos."

No doubt it was. It actually boasted two stories, the lower one of stone, the upper of timber. In Skopentzana, it would have been ordinary. In Videssos the city, it would have been a shocking hovel—Rhavas didn't think any buildings there still had thatched roofs. For a third-rate northern town, though, it wasn't bad.

"Uh . . ." The militiaman hesitated. "You do have money?"

"I do," Ingegerd answered calmly. The man looked relieved. So, no doubt, did Rhavas. He had little of his own. He was not a priest who cared nothing for gold; he scarcely could have been, coming from the family that had given him birth. But when he got the shock of learning the Khamorth were in Skopentzana, he'd thought of escape first and everything else afterward. That might well have saved his life, but was liable to cause some embarrassment now.

"Very holy sir, if you'll come with me, there's a temple around the corner," the militiaman said. "If you and the lady are traveling together, you'll want to stay close by each other."

Rhavas gave him a sharp look. Was he implying . . . ? But no, he wasn't. He plainly accepted the situation for what it was—for what part of Rhavas (and a very specific part, too) wished it weren't. The prelate fought to hide that wish even from himself. He nodded to the local. "My thanks."

The priest who presided over the temple surely wouldn't have said it was the finest even in Tzamandos. The fellow's name was Tribonianos, and he didn't seem to have much to say about any-thing. He blinked a good deal, and smelled of stale wine. Had Rhavas come to inspect his temple and not to take shelter in it, he would have had some harsh words for the priest. He *did* have them, but made himself hold them in. It wasn't easy—unlike a lot of Videssians, he usually said what he thought.

"You're a lucky man, very holy sir, to come out of the downfall of Skopentzana alive," Tribonianos said.

"Maybe," Rhavas answered. Standing in front of the fire in the priest's hearth felt wonderful. He almost bathed in the wonder-ful warmth. But he found he couldn't leave it at the one word. "Had we been truly fortunate, Skopentzana never would have fallen. The foolish feud between militiamen and peasant refugees spelled her doom."

"We?" Tribonianos echoed. "You got out with others, then?"

"With another," Rhavas replied reluctantly. "With the wife of the city's garrison commander, he having been summoned some time since to join in the civil war now wounding the Empire."

He'd hoped that long phrase would distract the other priest from the meat of the sentence. No such luck, though. "You came away from Skopentzana . . . with a woman?" Tribonianos said, raising bushy eyebrows. However unwillingly, Rhavas had to nod. The local priest leered at him. "Then you *are* a lucky man, very holy sir."

"By the good god, nothing untoward passed between us." Rhavas let some anger come into his voice. Part of it was anger at himself, for wishing something untoward had passed with Ingegerd. But Tribonianos did not need to know that, and what Rhavas said was true, even if incomplete. He went on, "I would take oath of this at the altar in the High Temple in Videssos the city."

Tribonianos had never been to the capital. He probably couldn't even imagine what it was like. But the High Temple's fame reached all through the Empire of Videssos and beyond. The priest muttered, "Of course, very holy sir," and Rhavas couldn't have proved he meant it sarcastically.

Hot porridge with bits of smoked pork in it was also wonderful, partly because it was hot and partly just because it was *food*. Rhavas felt emptier than he ever had in his life before. He'd done more, and done it on less, than he'd ever had to do. Even a second helping wasn't enough to make up for all he'd gone through on the way down to Tzamandos—but it helped. So did the wine he drank with the porridge.

Tribonianos offered the prelate his own bed, but Rhavas declined. The priest got him blankets, and he rolled himself up in them by the hearth. A soft mattress did not seem to matter so much as the warmth from the embers.

When he woke the next morning, the embers had gone cold. The floor was still hard. He got to his feet and stretched, feeling elderly. The way his joints and tendons crackled when he did made him feel no younger.

It was time for morning devotions, but Tribonianos was still snoring. Back in Skopentzana, Rhavas would have booted the other priest out of bed to join in them. Here, he hesitated. He still outranked the local, but this was Tribonianos' temple. Rhavas decided to let him sleep.

He went through the devotions himself. The prayers and hymns felt strange in his mouth—almost wrong. Even as he praised Phos, he wondered if the lord with the great and good mind had had anything to do with his curses. None of his *prayers* had been answered, but the curses . . . The curses had brought down Toxaras, had flattened Skopentzana, had slain the barbarians who were about to attack Ingegerd and him.

What did that mean? It surely meant something; things didn't happen for no reason. But what?

Tribonianos came up to the altar as Rhavas was finishing his prayers. "Do you aim to shame me?" he asked sourly.

"No," Rhavas answered, meaning yes.

The local priest did what ritual required of him. He did it by rote, with no spirit behind it. Had things been otherwise, Rhavas would have had a good deal to say to him about that. But things were as they were, and the prelate, his own thoughts confused, his heart heavy, let the priest get by with what was technically correct and otherwise meaningless. When Tribonianos finished, he eyed Rhavas with what couldn't have been far from hatred. "You're not going to stay here, are you?" he demanded.

"By the good god, no!" Rhavas knew leaving meant putting his life, and Ingegerd's, in danger. But he also realized that Tzamandos, even if the people inside kept breathing, was already dead—if the place had ever been alive.

His vehemence won the first approving glance he'd had from Tribonianos. The local didn't want him here any more than he wanted to be here. "I'll fix us breakfast," Tribonianos said. "After-ward, you can go up on the wall. If you don't see any of the barbarians up there, why then, you're off." Oh, yes. Tribonianos wanted him gone.

Well, I want myself gone, the prelate thought. Breakfast was more of the porridge with bits of salt pork in it. Again, Rhavas ate as if he expected food to be outlawed tomorrow. By Tribonia-nos' expression, that was just one of the reasons to be glad when he left. Rhavas drank a cup of wine with the meal. Tribonianos drank several. Did he do that all the time? Rhavas wouldn't have been surprised.

After breakfast, Rhavas did go up on Tzamandos' wall and look out. The wall itself was laughable next to that of Videssos the city or even Skopentzana. Besiegers who knew what they were doing would have breached it in short order. But it sufficed to keep the plainsmen out.

Rhavas saw snow and trees and occasional bits of bare ground where the snow had blown away. He saw no Khamorth, and hoped he never did again. When he went back to the temple, he found Ingegerd waiting for him there and Tribonianos staring at her in what looked like a torment of hopeless lust. Rhavas felt an odd mix of sympathy and disgust. *It's not as if I don't know how he feels,* the prelate thought unhappily.

Ingegerd ignored the hunger on Tribonianos' face. *Why not? She ignores mine, too,* Rhavas told himself. The Haloga woman said, "A dozen or so now at the inn purpose leaving for points south, and would have us join them. Most are men. Some have weapons, and mayhap a notion of what to do with them. What think you, very holy sir? Are we safer in company or by ourselves?"

"My guess would be in company," Rhavas replied, even if he would rather have been alone with her. "If you think I am wrong, I will listen."

"No." She shook her head. "I think you are right. They plan on leaving later this morning. In the meanwhile, I will buy us what food I can."

"Everything will be repaid you when we come to a richer temple than . . . this," Rhavas promised, not quite able to hide his distaste.

"That is well said, and surely well meant, and all the more surely needless to fret over," Ingegerd said. "We are comrades, you and I, and do what we do as comrades do for each other. I will see you at the inn before long." She dropped a curtsy and left.

"Comrades." Tribonianos spat it.

"That is the truth. Any other words, and any of your wicked thoughts, would be a lie." Rhavas waited to see if Tribonianos would challenge him. The priest didn't, which left Rhavas some little while to contemplate his own wicked thoughts.

Out through Tzamandos' southern gate went the men and women seeking better refuge from the barbarians. Some were Skopentzanans, others Tzamandans who feared their town would not hold. "A good thing we have you with us, very holy sir," said a Skopentzanan who recognized Rhavas. "With the good god listening to your prayers, we'll have nothing to fear from the barbarians."

Rhavas and Ingegerd looked at each other. The prelate knew they were thinking different things. She believed his holiness and his piety were what had let him curse the Khamorth. He wished he could believe that, too. To the expectantly waiting Skopentzanan, he said only, "May it be so."

"Good luck," a militiaman called as they left Tzamandos. "And here's hoping you won't need it."

May that *be so*, Rhavas thought. The gates of Tzamandos closed behind them with an echoing thud. All at once, out there in the open, Rhavas felt like an ant scurrying across a platter. He had some other ants for company, but how much could they help if danger came? They were only ants, after all.

His hindquarters and inner thighs ached, proof of how unaccustomed to riding he was. He didn't complain; some of the other travelers were slogging along on foot, as he and Ingegerd had been doing till those plainsmen . . . perished. The steppe pony he rode kept looking back at him. It had had a Khamorth in the saddle, a man born to horsemanship; it probably wondered how it had got stuck with such a blunderer.

Horses' hooves and men's boots crunched on snow. Somewhere not far enough in the distance, a carrion crow called harshly. That was the last thing Rhavas wanted to hear. Carrion, these days, too likely came from the Khamorth.

On they went. One of the men from Skopentzana said, "Better this way than with no company. I got out of Skopentzana by myself, and I never thought I'd make it to Tzamandos. Now I figure I've got a real chance, anyway."

That made no logical sense. Rhavas almost pointed it out to him. Plenty of bands of plainsmen were big enough to overwhelm this party of fugitives. And it would draw more eyes than a man traveling alone.

The prelate kept quiet. If the other man needed hope to cling to, he could cling to whatever he wanted. It wouldn't hurt. There was nothing doctrinally wrong with it. If he died having made that kind of mistake, it wouldn't hurt his chances of crossing the Bridge of the Separator.

What of your own curses? Rhavas' shiver had nothing to do with the winter weather. He didn't ignore that, but he didn't take so much notice of it. He had clothes that were warm enough, and he'd eaten well. The chill in his spirit was something else again. No steaming bowl of porridge, no blazing hearth, could drive it out.

All that day, the travelers saw no Khamorth. They stopped for the night in what had been a peasant village. Most of the houses in it had been burned. The ones that still stood were empty. The three women in the traveling party slept in one of them, the men in two more. They chose sentries to take turns watching through the night, a luxury Rhavas and Ingegerd had not enjoyed.

The man who shook the prelate awake sounded apologetic. "Awfully sorry to bother you, very holy sir, but it's your turn," he said.

"It's all right," Rhavas answered around a yawn. He did his

best not to disturb the other snoring Videssians as he got up
and went outside.

Somewhere, an owl hooted. Somewhere much farther off—
fortunately—a wolf howled, and then another and another,
till they might have been a distant chorus of demons. Rhavas
shuddered; that fit in too well with his own worries. The moon
peered through rents in the clouds every now and again, spilling
pale light over the dead village and turning shadows to blots
of living midnight.

He carried a spear. He wasn't sure how dangerous that made
him. The answer, he feared, was *not very*. But if he could shout an
alarm and try to fight back, that would do the others some good.
Hurrah, he thought unhappily. Some Videssian clerics—the holy
Kveldoulphios, for instance—courted martyrdom as secular men
courted beautiful women. But that longing was not in him.

Thinking of Kveldoulphios made Rhavas think of the Halogai,
who had slain the convert to Phos' faith although he was of their
blood. And thinking of the blond barbarians to the north made
Rhavas think of Ingegerd. He reckoned that a great and astonishing coincidence, though the truth was that almost anything would
have made him think of Ingegerd just then.

His eye went to the peasant hut where she sheltered with the
other two women. As if on cue, the moon came out again and
bathed it in cold silver light. Rhavas sighed gustily. Two nights
earlier, he'd held her in his arms—oh, not in the way songs sang
of, but in his arms nonetheless. And now . . . Now she might as
well have been on the far side of the moon.

Padding like a wolf himself to escape the thoughts he carried
with him, he prowled through the deserted peasant village. Once
something scurrying across the snow made him gasp. But it was
only a mouse dashing from one burned-out hut to another. The
priest breathed again.

Frightened of a mouse! How Toxaras and Voilas would have
laughed! But Toxaras was dead—*under my curse*, he thought, and
shuddered. And if Voilas hadn't died when the Khamorth entered
Skopentzana, he likely had when the earth trembled and walls
and houses fell. Try as Rhavas would, he couldn't make himself
believe he missed either man who'd led Skopentzana's militia.

Something glided by all ghostly overhead. The prelate's heart
leaped into his mouth, but it was only an owl, sailing along on

silent wings. *Too late. The mouse is already hiding again.* But there would be others.

The moon disappeared. Darkness came down like a cloak. In Videssos the city and in Skopentzana, lamps and fires would have leaked lights through shutters. Some streets even had torches flaring after the sun went down to hold night at bay. None of that here, nor stars, either. This might have been Skotos' realm come to life on earth.

Rhavas' hand shaped a gesture said to hold the evil god at bay. He did not like the way Skotos kept cropping up in his thoughts. He looked around, not that he could see much. Moving carefully in the gloom, he made his way back toward the houses where his companions sheltered.

He was almost there when yet another aftershock rattled the peasant village. It was a strong one, strong enough to stagger him. Men and women cried out; horses squealed in terror. But unlike the quake that had leveled Skopentzana, this one did not go on and on and on. A few heartbeats and it was done. The animals fell silent. Inside one of the men's huts, somebody said, "That was nasty." A couple of others laughed in agreement.

Another man stuck his head out of the hut and called, "You all right?"

"Well enough," Rhavas answered. The man waved and disappeared again.

Little by little, Rhavas' heart stopped pounding. Aftershocks were wearing. They constantly threatened to turn into great earthquakes, and no one could know they wouldn't till they didn't. The fear was that they would never let up.

A motion from the women's hut. Rhavas' hands tightened on the spearshaft. That was absurd, as he realized a moment later. No danger would come from there—none that a spear could rout, anyhow.

Rhavas recognized Ingegerd even in the darkness. The other two women were short and on the dumpy side; next to them, she was a fir beside spreading oaks. "Are you all right?" the prelate called to her, as the man from the other hut had to him a moment earlier.

Her head swung toward him. He didn't think she'd known he was there. "Is that you, very holy sir?" she asked.

"No one else," he said.

"Then as friend to friend I may freely tell you I am *not* all right," Ingegerd said. "Whenever the earth shakes, my heart freezes within me. I want to scream. I want to run. And I know none of that would do me the least good in the world. Mine is a warrior folk. I feel shame in owning to such cowardice, but shame at lying would be worse."

"No one is a hero against an earthquake," Rhavas said. "How can any man oppose something so much stronger?"

"I know that." Ingegerd hesitated, then resumed: "How can any man summon something so much stronger?"

"I do not know that I did," Rhavas answered. "And if I did"—something he would not have admitted even to himself before watching four Khamorth slide from their horses and die—"I know not how I did."

The moon came out. It turned her golden hair to shining silver. Her eyes gave back the light almost as if they were a cat's. She took a few steps toward him. "If you were not a very holy man, surely you could not have done it."

His laugh rang harsh as a raven's croak. "If I were as holy as you would make me out to be, you would not have had to pull away from me after we slept under the same blanket."

To his amazement, Ingegerd laughed, too. "Does that still distress you? It bothers me not at all. Even the holiest man is yet a man, with the desires of a man. You did not violate your oath, and you did not seek to violate me. Let it go. It is forgotten."

Maybe by you, he thought. He would not forget the feel of her against him, or of his rising to the occasion, for the rest of his days, however long those might prove. He would not forget the red fury that had fired his curses, either. What did that have to do with holiness? Nothing he could see.

"I think you can safely go back inside again," he said. "If that aftershock did not shake down the hut, none is likely to."

"No doubt you are right. You are a sound and sensible man," Ingegerd said. Rhavas had tried for many years to be exactly that. Never had he so regretted succeeding. She went on, "I tell myself all will be well, but I cannot make myself believe it."

"With all the Empire turned upside down and with the very ground trembling beneath our feet like a beast in pain, hope comes hard," Rhavas replied. "Yet to deny hope is to deny the lord with the great and good mind and to give oneself into Skotos' hands."

"This I will not do, then," Ingegerd said with a sturdy determination alien to most Videssians. She nodded to Rhavas and went back into the hut as if about to slay a dragon inside it. Had a dragon dwelt there instead of a pair of dumpy Videssian women, she would have slain it, too. That Rhavas did not doubt.

And what of me? he wondered. Somehow, he feared dragons less than he feared either Ingegerd or himself.

The party plodded south. Even on a Khamorth pony, Rhavas felt as if he were struggling through mud. He and Ingegerd had to hold their pace to that of those on foot. He did not think any good would come of that. The only thing he could do about it, though, was abandon the dismounted travelers. He didn't want to do that, either.

Three Khamorth looked them over from a long way off, far out of bowshot. The barbarians did not try to attack. Instead, they wheeled their horses and rode off.

"They go to bring back their fellows, very holy sir," Ingegerd said urgently. "You should curse them, that they may not do this."

Rhavas raised his arm toward the retreating Khamorth. After a moment, though, he let it fall. "The power is not in me," he said.

She stared at him. "Why not?"

"I don't know, but I can feel the curse would fail," he answered. She bit her lip but did not push him. That made her a paragon among women, even if he did not realize it. He was lost in thoughts of himself. Why was he so certain any curse he launched now would surely fail to bite?

The only thing that came to him was, *I am not angry enough.* He had been in a great fury when he cursed Toxaras, when he called the earthquake down on Skopentzana, and when he felled the Khamorth who rode at Ingegerd and him.

Now . . . How could he be passionately furious at men who were riding away? If they came back and attacked, that would be different. He hoped it would, anyhow. For the moment, he had no fire in his belly.

Other Videssians had spied the plainsmen, too. They knew the Khamorth hadn't trotted off because they were going to let the refugees escape. One of the men said, "We'd better find a place we can fight from."

That was easier said than done. The snow-covered ground they were crossing held no farmhouses, no barns, no fences. It was simply . . . ground. A small clump of pines off in the distance offered the only break in the monotony.

Ingegerd pointed toward them. "There we must make our stand, and quickly. If our main hope fails, we can make the best fight we may." By *our main hope* she meant Rhavas, even if the others did not fully grasp that. Some of them muttered about a foreign woman telling them what to do, but what she said was such obvious truth that they could not mutter long.

"Our trail in the snow will lead the barbarians straight to us," one of the dumpy Videssian women said sorrowfully.

"What difference does it make?" a man replied. "If we don't go there, they'll find us like so many bugs on a plate." That also seemed much too true, and painfully reminded Rhavas of his own thoughts after they left Tzamandos.

They were within about a hundred yards of the trees when someone looked back over his shoulder and said, "We'd better hurry."

Rhavas looked back, too. Strung out across the horizon were Khamorth riders. They came forward at a businesslike trot. Experimentally, he raised his arm again. He still felt no sudden access of power. Rage fueled it, yes, rage and fear—not the emotions he would have thought Phos would put in a man's heart. He was afraid now, and he was angry, but neither emotion bubbled in him the way they both had before. Maybe he'd been through too much, and lost for the moment the ability to feel deeply. Whatever the reason, there would be no curses any time soon.

Ingegerd saw what he did, and what he did not do. "No, very holy sir?" she asked.

"It seems not," Rhavas said.

"Then we shall fight." She sounded unafraid. "If you can, remember the boon I asked of you before and grant it me at the last."

"If I can," Rhavas said. "If I must."

Then the Videssians got in and under the pines. The spicy, resinous smell of them filled Rhavas' nostrils. Some of the men strung bows and nocked arrows. The prelate had no idea how much good that would do, or whether it would do any good at all.

He looked out past the trees. The Khamorth still came on. He searched for rage and fear in himself—searched for what might let him curse them and kill them or drive them off in dismay. Searching, he found . . . not enough. He felt curiously detached, removed from the scene, as if it were happening to someone else. He knew it wasn't, but couldn't make himself believe it.

One of the Videssian men said, "The women ought to get as far away as they can. You, too, very holy sir. Meaning no offense, but you're not going to be much help in the fight."

"I'll stay," Rhavas said, very conscious of Ingegerd's eye on him.

"No, go on," the man said, while his comrades nodded. "I don't fault your spirit, but you've no skill with weapons. Save yourself if you can. Maybe we'll hold out long enough to let you get away. Go on, curse it. The longer you argue, the worse your chances get."

His curse had no power to bite, not the way Rhavas' did—or could. Ears burning in spite of the cold, the prelate turned away. The two Videssian women were already stumbling deeper into the stand of trees. Ingegerd waited. "I will stand beside you, if you like," she said.

"Go on," he told her. "You might be worth more in a fight than I am, if—" He gestured instead of saying *if I cannot curse*. She nodded. He went on, "Even so, though, they are liable to kill me quickly if they take me alive. They will have their sport with you before they let you die." *Sport I wish I had.* He fought that thought down.

Not knowing it was in his mind, she took his hands in hers. "Then you come, too. No shame to you that you are not a man of your hands, not when you chose the good god's path rather than the warrior's. Come. We will save ourselves if we can."

No one else was likely to have persuaded him. Ingegerd he obeyed as if he were a little boy listening to his mother. Behind him, an arrow thudded into a tree trunk—the Khamorth were close enough to have started shooting. A moment later, someone let out a bubbling scream. *That* arrow had struck flesh, not wood.

It all seemed very far away, very unimportant, to Rhavas. If the barbarians cut him down—well, so what? What was he but a priest shaken in his faith? Wasn't Videssos better off without a man like him?

Shouts and curses in Videssian and in the harsh, guttural Khamorth language erupted behind him. He looked back over his shoulder—and tripped over a snow-buried stone, measuring himself full length on the ground. "Oof!" he said: a singularly undignified noise.

Almost man-strong, Ingegerd hauled him to his feet. "Come *on*, very holy sir," she panted. "If you are going to flee, you must *flee.*"

"I am—doing my best," Rhavas said.

He kept trying to listen as he stumbled through the snow. He did not look back again, though. He'd learned one lesson. *If you are going to flee, you must* flee. *She is right.* The shouts and screams at the edge of the trees were fewer now. What calls there were came mostly in the Khamorth tongue. The Videssians might have sold their lives dear, but not, he feared, dear enough. The barbarians were coming after those who had got away.

Ingegerd could have outdistanced him. He waved for her to do just that. She either did not see him or pretended not to. Boots thumped behind the two of them. Rhavas tried to go faster. He had little luck. The skin on his back tightened, as if that could ward off an arrow or the bite of a sword's honed edge.

He dodged behind a tree—and just in time, for an arrow surely aimed at him slammed into the trunk. He did peer around then, in fearful fascination. Two Khamorth were shouting at a third—the one who had shot. Maybe they'd realized Ingegerd was a woman, and didn't want this fellow to take the chance of killing her right away.

Now they'd seen the prelate from the front, and knew he could be no woman. All three of them smiled very nasty smiles. They could have flanked him out and shot him. Instead, two of them drew their swords and advanced on him. They'd have fun getting rid of him while their friend circled around him and caught Ingegerd. Then they would all have more fun, and then they would kill her.

Rhavas' own fate mattered little to him. That he'd let down the Haloga woman mattered enormously. He pointed at the barbarian who was going after her and screamed, "Curse you! Curse you, curse you, *curse you!*"

The Khamorth threw up his hands, screamed, and crumpled to the snow, dead before he touched it. The other barbarians stared.

So did Rhavas. That he could bring forth such power, wherever it came from, still astonished him.

Howling what had to be curses of their own, the other two Khamorth swung up their swords and rushed toward him. "Curse you!" he shouted at them. His blood was up now, not for his own sake but for Ingegerd's. Their faces twisted in pain. They staggered, groaned, and collapsed. They thrashed in the snow for a little while, then lay as motionless as the first plainsman.

"Very holy sir?" Ingegerd's voice behind Rhavas almost made him scream. He whirled in something not far from panic. "They are dead, very holy sir," Ingegerd said. "They are dead, but others will live yet. We have not escaped. Hurry away, before more Khamorth find the trail."

Her calm good sense restored order to a world that had seemed to be coming apart at the edges. "I come," Rhavas said, and he did.

A couple of minutes later, women's screams rang out from elsewhere among the trees. Some of the barbarians had caught the other two, then. "Can you curse them, as you did the three you slew?" Ingegerd asked.

Rhavas felt of himself, as he might have if he tried to decide whether he had the strength to lift some heavy load. He found that strength wanting, and shook his head.

She sent him a curious look. "How did you do it just now, then?"

"How? Because one of them threatened you," Rhavas said simply.

Ingegerd said nothing to that for some little while. Then, in a voice most carefully neutral, she asked, "And the other two?"

"Aftershocks." In the earthquake-scarred north country, the word came naturally to his lips.

She said something in her sonorous birthspeech. Rhavas made an inquiring sound. She started to answer, then checked herself. "It does not translate well into Videssian. And I think we are making a mistake in fleeing deeper among the trees now."

"What would you rather do?" Rhavas asked.

"Go back for our horses," she said, "and for those the Khamorth will have left behind. We can travel quicker with them, and keep the foe from coming after us."

"If they have not left a guard," Rhavas said.

"If they have, belike you can dispose of him. He will threaten both of us, after all." Ingegerd thought for another moment, then nodded to herself. "It is the best plan we have, anyhow." Rhavas did not contradict her. She went on, "If it works, we win much. Let us try it."

They hurried back toward the edge of the trees. The screams in the little wood went on and on. Rhavas wondered how Phos' might could be consistent with such evil, and with the good god's inevitable triumph. Maybe Skotos was stronger than Videssian theologians imagined. He shook his head. He could not, *would* not, believe that.

He and Ingegerd came around the bole of a tree as thick as he was tall. Behind it lay the body of one of the Videssians with whom they'd been traveling. Of itself, Rhavas' hand shaped the sun-sign. The man's blood stained the clean white snow. Half his face had been hacked away. He must have been one of the archers who'd shot at the plainsmen, for they'd pulled down his drawers and thrust an arrow up his . . . Rhavas dared hope he was already dead when they did that.

Ingegerd said, "May he safely cross the Bridge of the Separator. Those who did this to him will surely suffer forever in Skotos' ice."

"Yes," Rhavas said, wondering how she, who'd been born outside the Empire's beliefs, had more faith than he did. He made himself add, "We had better go on." She nodded, her mouth a thin, pale slash that both admitted and defied what she had seen.

They passed other bodies and more scarlet splashes and streams on the snow. The barbarians hadn't just slain; they seemed to have cut and slashed for the sport of it. One dead Videssian was gutted like a boar brought down in the hunt, his entrails not only spilled out onto the snow but then chopped to bits. Rhavas' stomach lurched. The man couldn't have lived long while that was going on . . . could he?

And this was surely not the only such slaughter the Khamorth had worked. Wherever they caught Videssians, they must have amused themselves this way. If nothing else, the practiced skill of the atrocity proved as much. They must also have been work-ing such evils on one another out on the Pardrayan steppe for centuries uncounted.

How? Rhavas wondered. How could the lord with the great

and good mind have tolerated wickedness, viciousness, on such a scale for so long? The prelate wondered whether any Videssian theologian had ever seriously addressed the question—and, if so, what answer he had found. With the sour taste of nausea in the back of his mouth, Rhavas saw one ominous and obvious possibility: that Skotos really *was* stronger than the theologians living comfortably in Videssos the city, the richest and grandest city in the world—or even in Skopentzana—had imagined or could imagine.

If priests who speculated learnedly on Phos' sacred scriptures saw how things could be in the real world—well, then what? Would the real world matter to men consumed with the spirit and the world to come?

It mattered desperately to Rhavas right now, if he wanted to go on living in it. "We're getting close," he said in a low voice.

"I know," Ingegerd answered, even more quietly. "Can you see? Have the savages left a sentry behind?"

"I don't know. . . . Wait." Had that been movement behind a tree? It had—no doubt about it. "Yes. There is one."

"Curse him, very holy sir. If you have Phos' holy power in you, curse him."

Rhavas had no true notion of what sort of power lay within him, or from whom it sprang. Before, when he'd tried to bring it out without great stress, he'd always failed. *Could* he turn it into a weapon as reliable as bow or spear? He pointed toward the plainsman. "Curse you," he said, wondering what would happen next.

The Khamorth fell in the snow, face first.

Ingegerd seized Rhavas' arm and squealed like an excited little girl. "You did it, very holy sir! By the good god, you did it!"

"So I did," Rhavas said, still more surprised than not. He was not sure—he was far from sure—he'd done it through Phos' power, but at the moment he wasn't inclined to be fussy, either. He'd cursed the plainsman, and the plainsman was dead. What else mattered? Nothing he could see. Roughly, he went on, "Let's get the horses, and let's get out of here."

"That is good advice," Ingegerd agreed, still looking at him as if she thought he was the most wonderful thing in the world. Seeing that awe on her face made Rhavas feel twice as tall, twice as wide, and eight times as strong as he really was.

They quickly hitched the horses together, then mounted the ones they had been riding. All the Khamorth ponies followed without any trouble; they were used to being led in long strings. Rhavas said, "I hope the rest of the nomads are properly surprised when they come back and find their mounts gone."

"I think they will be," Ingegerd said warmly, and then, "Maybe you ought to curse the whole wood."

He thought about it. He aimed his arm as he might have aimed an arrow. Then he shook his head. "Whatever may be in me, that is not."

"Too bad," Ingegerd said. "The Khamorth within deserve whatever may befall them."

"I can only do what I can do," Rhavas said. "I did not know I could fell that one man until I tried."

"I do not blame you," Ingegerd said quickly. "I would never blame you. That you can do what you can do is a wonder past compare. But, having seen so much, am I to be blamed for wishing I might see more?"

The prelate shook his head. "Not by me. I would never blame you."

Now she eyed him with something besides almost adoring admiration. "Back among the trees, you said you cursed the one barbarian because he was going after me," she said slowly.

"I did," Rhavas agreed.

Even more slowly, Ingegerd went on, "I thank you for it—do not mistake me, very holy sir. But mayhap it would be well to remind you once more that I am Himerios' wife, and still have every hope of finding my husband once more."

"I hope you do. I am with you to help you do it, as Himerios himself charged me to do," Rhavas said, and most of that was true. The first four words? Perhaps not. He thought of asking her what she would do if she could not find Himerios, or if she found he had fallen in the fighting. He thought of it, but kept silent. The question, he judged, would make her angry or make her wary. He wanted neither.

He looked back over his shoulder. The woods were well distant now. One Khamorth came out into the open and stared south, no doubt wondering how all the horses could have disappeared. That made Rhavas laugh, but only for a moment. If mounted plainsmen found the others, they might all pursue.

Ingegerd looked back, too. She saw what Rhavas had not. "The clouds are boiling out of the north," she said. "Another storm is coming. I was hoping we were through with them."

"We had better look for shelter, then," Rhavas said. "I would not want to be caught in the open." If his voice was troubled, who could blame him? He saw nothing that looked like a refuge, not even more trees ahead.

"With all these horses to keep us warm, we can shelter in the snow if we must." Ingegerd sounded more confident than Rhavas felt. But she went on, "Still, you are not mistaken, very holy sir. Shelter would be better."

Rhavas pointed ahead, to a low swell of ground. "Maybe we will be able to see something from there." He did not really believe it, but sometimes hope had to do. He and Ingegerd rode forward. Even as they did, the wind began to freshen. The air had a raw feel to it, a feel of storm, of snow, of sleet.

And when they reached the top of the hillock, the prelate and the Haloga woman both exclaimed in glad surprise. There not too far ahead stood a farmhouse and a barn. Whether anyone lived on the farm these days was liable to be a different question, but the buildings would help hold out a blizzard either way.

Snow started swirling around the travelers before they reached the farm. When they came up to the farmhouse, Rhavas saw it was fire-damaged. He hallooed, but only silence answered him. He and Ingegerd got the horses into the barn, which had also seen the touch of flames. That didn't worry him so much. Khamorth ponies endured all sorts of hardships out on the steppe. He doubted one more snowstorm would faze them.

By then, he also doubted whether one more snowstorm would faze him. Had he been back behind Skopentzana's walls, he would have grumbled about the dreadful weather. All the natives of the place would have laughed at him as an effete southerner. Everybody would have been happy.

These days, happiness involved smaller things—or rather, larger ones. Staying alive another day kept people happy. Escaping enemies made them happy. And seeing those enemies fall over dead . . . Yes, Rhavas knew he had rejoiced when the Khamorth sentry crumpled.

Not finding any frozen corpses inside the battered farmhouse also made him happy. The folk who'd lived here must have got out before the plainsmen set fire to the place. Rhavas prayed they'd reached the shelter of a walled town before barbarians came upon them.

Even as he asked that mercy of Phos, he wondered how much good the prayer would do. The good god seemed to have ignored every other prayer he'd sent up. He did not know why Phos had turned his back on Videssos and on him in particular, but only a blind man, he thought, could have doubted it was so.

Outside, the wind began to howl in earnest. Snow blew by almost horizontally. The stone walls and what was left of the farmhouse's roof did give some protection, though.

"I think we will have to break up some of the furniture to build a fire on the hearth," Ingegerd said.

"Lucky it didn't all burn already," Rhavas said, and she nodded. They tore a couple of stools to pieces. She used flint and steel to start a small blaze, then put more wood on it. And then she produced strips of smoked meat and a leather sack full of coarse flour. Rhavas gaped. "Where did you come by those?"

"I searched the saddlebags on some of the steeds we took," she answered. He bowed, honoring her good sense. He wouldn't have thought of that—he *hadn't* thought of it. She found an iron griddle the nomads hadn't bothered stealing. "Let me get some snow to melt into water and I can make wheatcakes," she said. "They will not be of the best, but they will fill our bellies."

She had that exactly right. The wheatcakes were anything but delicious, ending up both bland and burnt. The meat was tough enough to challenge Rhavas' chewing. But all of it was ever so much better than going hungry.

After that unlovely but still satisfying supper, Rhavas glanced toward the bed against the far wall. The night would be cold—it was already cold. Even so, he said, "I will sleep here on the floor by the hearth if you like."

That Ingegerd even paused to think about it wounded him. But she quickly shook her head. "No need for that, very holy sir, for we can both use the warmth we give each other." Her smile held just a hint of mischief. "Not *that* sort of warmth, as you will understand. We are both enjoined against that, even if each for different reasons."

"Yes," Rhavas said. "I do understand."

"I thought you did." Ingegerd's smile grew warmer; firelight danced in her eyes. "I told you before that you were not to blame for what happened a few days ago, and I meant it. Would I lie down beside you if I did not?"

"Not if you were wise, as you plainly are," Rhavas replied.

"No doubt you give me too much credit," she said in a low voice, looking away from him as she spoke.

"No doubt I give you not enough." Rhavas started to say more, but saw that even so much flustered her. Had her husband never praised her many virtues? If Rhavas told her she was as wise as she was beautiful, he got the feeling he *would* sleep on the floor.

Surely no harm can come from lying beside a woman. We are cold, and we are decently clothed, he told himself. His ecclesiastical colleagues might—would—have a different opinion about that. He knew as much, even if he did his best to pretend to himself he didn't.

But his ecclesiastical colleagues weren't here, and were in no danger of freezing to death. Rhavas and Ingegerd lay down on the narrow, lumpy bed. As usual, they started out back to back. "Good night, very holy sir. I hope you sleep sound," Ingegerd said with the odd formality they'd both used before.

"Good night. May you also sleep well." Rhavas used the same scrupulous politeness.

Ingegerd sighed. Lying there beside her, Rhavas felt her go limp. Her breathing grew slow and regular. She started to snore. Rhavas, closer to the wall, stayed wide awake. He was much more conscious of her as a woman than he had been when they first escaped from Skopentzana. And the more he tried not to be, the more he was.

Outside, the wind howled and moaned. The fire guttered down to a last few embers glowing red as blood. Rhavas lay alone with his thoughts: alone, but not alone. Suppose that in spite of everything—in spite of aftershocks, in spite of civil war, in spite of invading barbarians—he succeeded in bringing her safe to Videssos the city. Suppose he did not touch her *that* way in all the long journey. How many priests in the capital would believe he hadn't? Any at all?

The more he thought about it, the more he doubted it. They would be sure he'd fleshed his lance to the very hilt. And why would they be so sure? Because they would have done the same thing themselves. They took the vow of chastity, yes—took it and spent the rest of their lives regretting it.

Rhavas hadn't really regretted it, hadn't felt it chafe him, till he came to know Ingegerd. The lord with the great and good mind must have had a cruel streak in him, to leave the prelate alone with—in bed with!—a woman he wanted but could not have.

She didn't want him. She'd made that plain enough. Resentment bubbling up inside him burned hotter every moment. She'd been glad enough when he cursed the barbarians and saved her (and, not so incidentally, himself). Oh, yes. That had made her happy. But was she ready to give him the most sincere reward a woman could give a man? Not likely!

Your vows, he reminded himself. But, like everything else before Skopentzana fell—and before he found out he could get his own back by calling down curses on the heads of those who'd wronged him—his vows seemed something from another world, another time. They might have been calling him from a mile beyond the moon.

Doing his best not to disturb Ingegerd, he rolled over so that he faced her. She stirred and muttered something, but did not wake. If she had, he would have pretended to be asleep himself.

She trusts you. She wouldn't lie down with you, wouldn't go to sleep beside you, if she didn't. Rhavas waited for a blast of shame to scorch him. And the shame did come, but not nearly so much of it as he'd looked for. Maybe resentment curdled most of it. *You fool!* He wanted to wake her and shake her and shout at her. *Chances are your precious Himerios is dead anyhow.*

However true that was, it would not bring her into his arms. He still had enough sense left to understand that. If he told her she was likely a widow, she would only hate him for it. She wouldn't look to him for a widow's consolation. If, on the other hand, she learned from someone else . . .

Resentment flared again, sour as heartburn. And Rhavas' heart was burning. Wasn't he a better man than the garrison commander, anyhow? Wasn't he wiser and more clever than Himerios? And, with the power to call down curses on his enemies' heads, wasn't he a more deadly warrior than the Videssian officer, too? *Of course I am.* Answering his own questions was easy. *To the ice with her if she can't see that for herself.*

She started to roll away from him, as if the fierce violence of his thoughts repelled her. On that narrow bed, though, rolling away would have meant falling out. Still sleeping, she checked herself. Still sleeping, she laughed a little at what she'd almost done. And, still sleeping, she rolled back the other way—rolled straight up against him, her head nestled against his shoulder. One leg slid up and over his.

"Phos!" he whispered, calling on the god of light there in the darkness. But he felt no light in his own spirit—far from it. Lust rose up, a great choking, blinding cloud. When she and Himerios lay in the same bed, did they sleep like this? How could Himerios let her go on sleeping when she did something so provocative? If, she having roused him, he roused her in turn so he could do what he wanted, would she be angry? Would she let out another one of those sleepy laughs and let him have his way, hardly caring herself? Or would she kindle, too?

Rhavas knew what he hoped the answer was.

Carefully, not wanting to disturb her, he slid his arms around her. He didn't squeeze. He didn't need to squeeze; she was already pressed tight against him. And what could he do about that? Nothing. A maddening nothing. It seemed terribly unfair.

He feared he would spend all night awake. That would leave him a wreck when morning came. They couldn't stay here and let him rest during the day. They had to keep pushing south and west. Sooner or later, surely, they would come to country where the Khamorth had not yet penetrated.

The prelate flinched. Of all the words he could have found, that one had to come to mind now. *Are you trying to drive yourself mad?* he wondered. But he wasn't mad. He knew that perfectly well. He was only a man who wanted a woman.

But it is a sin for me to want a woman. He reminded himself— and needed to remind himself—of that. Pressed against him, Ingegerd's warmth did not feel sinful. It felt like something he should have been able to enjoy all the days of his life. *What have we done to our priests by making them swear celibacy?* The answer seemed painfully—in the most literal sense of the word—clear.

Slowly, the ache in his loins receded. He found himself yawning. No matter how aroused he was, he was also exhausted. Still holding Ingegerd, he yawned again . . . and did fall asleep.

When he woke, he didn't realize for a few heartbeats that he had been sleeping. He and Ingegerd still lay close together; her breath was warm on his cheek. But he could see her now, though dimly. The fire had gone out during the night, but morning twilight was leaking in through the windows and through rents in the roof.

He hoped sleep had cooled his ardor, but needed only a moment to discover how naïve that was. The fire might have gone out, but he still burned. He burned hotter than ever, in fact; for the moment, weariness didn't weigh down his spirit.

Ingegerd sighed in her sleep. Rhavas sighed, too. He didn't know why she exhaled louder than usual. His own sigh was all unrequited lust, though he thought of it as love.

Before long, she would wake. It wasn't that she wouldn't want anything to do with him then. That would have been easier, or at least more merciful. But she would treat him as one friend treated another, and as intimately as one friend treated another. Had they been two men on the road together, that would have been fine. As things were, he found it either too intimate or, more to the point, not intimate enough.

Just once, he thought, halfway between wistfulness and fury. *Yes, just once would be enough. Just so I know what it's like.*

He didn't know what anything was like. He'd lived his whole life cut off from what drove the people who listened to him when he prayed and preached. He'd lectured them about it. He'd threatened them with Skotos' eternal ice if they broke the rules the temples and the Empire had laid down. A soft, pained snort of laughter escaped him. He'd had his nerve, hadn't he? All the priests in the Empire of Videssos had their nerve, didn't they?

And even more amazing was that people listened to them. People obeyed them. Why didn't men and women laugh like loons and tell them exactly how much nerve they had? For the life of him, he couldn't imagine.

How much nerve do I have? There lay Ingegerd, her face not a palm's breadth from his. *How much nerve do I have?*

Rhavas' heart thuttered, not only from lust but also from fear. He did not want to break his vows. The ice threatened, the ice beckoned, if he did. But he did not want to go through all his days not knowing what it meant to be a man; he did not want to die alone, having lived alone his whole life long. If he held to the oath he'd sworn while a youth, wouldn't he do exactly that? So it seemed, with perfectly logical clarity.

Heart still pounding—pounding so loud, he marveled that she could not hear it—he leaned forward and brushed his lips lightly—so lightly!—across Ingegerd's. She smiled in her sleep ... and then she opened her eyes.

Rhavas had pulled away by then, but it didn't matter. She knew what had happened. She wasn't so angry as she might have been, but she was far from pleased. "Very holy sir, this will not do," she said.

This when I have saved her half a dozen times lately. Rhavas was angry, whether Ingegerd was or not. *This when she still lies in the circle of my arms.*

Some of what he thought must have shown on his face, for Ingegerd said, "Our ways had better part after this. I will take my own chances from now on. With a horse under me and another to carry supplies, I will do well enough."

"No." Rhavas shook his head. "Your husband charged me to care for you, and care for you I shall."

Ingegerd shook her head, too. "That will not do. You want to ... to care for me in ways only Himerios should."

"Is that the thanks I get?" Rhavas demanded.

"You have my thanks. You have all my thanks," Ingegerd said. "But I see you want more than that now, and more than that I cannot give."

She started to pull away from him. His arms tightened around her. It took him almost as much by surprise as it did her. "One kiss—one proper kiss," he heard himself say.

Ingegerd's eyes opened very wide. She started to move toward him—and then brought up a knee toward his crotch. No doubt she intended to leave him writhing in pain, and to take a horse and leave before he could do anything about it.

And that would have worked, except he was also bringing up a leg, and her knee banged into his instead of going home. He realized exactly what she'd intended, and his anger turned to rage. "Is *that* the thanks I get?" he growled.

"You get what you deserve," Ingegerd retorted. "Now let go of me!"

"What I deserve? By the good god, I'll *take* what I deserve!"

Rhavas said, everything but his own fury and his own fever forgotten.

Ingegerd tried to knee him again, then hit him in the face. She was a large, strong woman. The blow hurt. It made him see stars. But it also made him angrier yet. He hit her, too, as hard as he could. Her head snapped back. She kept on fighting, but after that she was slightly woozy, slightly slow.

"I'll *take* what I deserve," Rhavas repeated, and flipped up her long wool skirt. The sight of her legs only inflamed him, though she went on trying to kick him and knee him. He might have been a man in the grip of fever or madness as he hiked up his own robes.

Ingegerd screamed, but there was no one to hear her cries. She and Rhavas tumbled out of the narrow bed. Straw-stuffed mattress or bare earth—it mattered not at all to him. However much she thrashed, he poised himself over her. "Ahhh!" he said as he began, an exhalation more of triumph than of pleasure.

She bit his hand. *He* screamed then, and hit her with the other one till she let go. His blood was on her face, and so was hers. He didn't know what she called him in the Haloga language. He doubted the words were endearments. He doubted it, but he didn't really care, not while he thrashed above her.

"Ahhh!" This time, the cry meant he had spent himself. It was less than he had thought it would be and more, both at the same time. What it was for Ingegerd . . . did not cross his mind until after delight blinded him.

Now the fever he might have had was gone. He pulled away from her and set his robes to rights. She lay huddled on the ground, her skirt still drawn up, her legs still bare. He looked down at his hand. It was still bleeding. He shook his head in wonder. Had she really done that to him? Had he really done *that* to her? The answer seemed only too obvious.

"Maybe you are right," Rhavas said. "We would do better traveling separately." It was as close to an apology as he could come. He knew he had sinned, but he did not feel as if he had sinned. Even with the pain from his hand to remind him of exactly what he'd done, he felt fine, or better than fine.

Ingegerd rolled away from him. In a voice like ashes, she said, "Who shall make you pay for your folly?"

"Folly?" Some of Rhavas' anger returned. Couldn't she see why he'd done what he'd done? "It was a . . . a compliment to your womanliness."

Her head came up. "Did I not ask you to slay me before you let the Khamorth pay me such compliments?"

"I am no Khamorth!" Rhavas said indignantly.

"No, indeed. You are worse than a Khamorth. They would only have done what they did. You not only did it, but tell lies about it, too. Truly Skotos has his claws deep in your soul."

"That is not so!" Rhavas' voice went as high as hers, and much shriller. She'd put a finger on his greatest secret fear. But it could not be true. It *must* not be true. If he'd cursed, it must have been through some other power, any other power, than the dark god's. "I will not hear your lies," he added, and strode away from her.

Her voice pursued him. "There will be vengeance, in this world or in the world to come."

"No! Liar!" His back still turned, he heard Ingegerd get to her feet. Then he heard something else: a small sound. She might have lifted something. He turned back. She had a knife in her hand, and advanced on him with terrible purpose.

"There will be vengeance," she repeated.

"No!" Rhavas flung out his bitten hand, perhaps only to ward her off, perhaps for some other reason he did not care to admit even to himself till the moment was there—or past. Fear and fury filling his voice, he cried, "No! Curse you, no!"

Ingegerd's eyes rolled up in her head. The knife fell from nerveless fingers. Her own rage faded from her face, replaced by a dreadful blankness. She swayed, tottered . . . crumpled. Rhavas knew death when he found himself in its presence. He knew death now.

"No!" he screamed, trying to cast out not just the moment but everything that had led up to it. But where to begin? When he'd raped Ingegerd?—for that was what it had been. When they'd escaped Skopentzana together? When he'd called down curses on his own head if the peasant refugees harmed the city? When the Khamorth swarmed into Videssos? When Himerios charged him with watching over Ingegerd? When Maleinos and Stylianos went to war?

The woman he'd cared for—the woman he'd imagined he'd loved—lay at his feet, not only dead but ravished. And how had she died? When he cursed her, of course. And how could he have cursed her—how could he have cursed anyone—save through the power of the dark god?

Skotos heard me, he thought. *Yes, Skotos heard me, and showed he heard me. Maybe Phos has heard me, but he never gave any sign of it. Which, then, truly is the stronger god? Yes—which indeed?*

VII

Rhavas rode away from the farmhouse by himself. It was still snowing, but not so hard. That didn't matter; he would have ridden away had the blizzard got worse instead of easing. He hoped riding away would let him leave his sins and his mistakes behind.

He didn't need long to find what a forlorn hope that was. Ingegerd's body lay in the farmhouse—yes. Rhavas hadn't had the heart to touch it again, even to drag it out and cover it over with snow. But the memory of what he'd done to her—both the rape and the curse—still burned inside his mind. However much he wished he could, he couldn't escape his sins so simply. He took them with him wherever he went.

She had it coming, he told himself. *If she'd only yielded to me, the way she should have, none of this would have happened.*

He knew he was trying to salve his conscience. Knowing it didn't stop him from getting angry at Ingegerd as well as himself. Before long, it didn't stop him from getting angry at her instead of himself.

When he realized as much, he sketched the sun-sign over his heart. "Phos!" he exclaimed. "Don't let me behave this way!"

But the prayer seemed feeble and useless and empty, the way all his prayers sent up to the lord with the great and good mind had seemed lately. What had Phos done to answer his increasingly desperate petitions? Anything? Anything at all? Not so far as he could see.

And what did that mean? He'd asked himself the question again and again, and shied away from the answers that sprang to mind. Now, jouncing south aboard a steppe pony across a snow-covered plain, he began to grapple with them, really for the first time.

This world was the battleground for the struggle between Phos and Skotos, between light and dark, between good and evil. So he had been trained to believe since childhood, and so he did believe now. Not a Videssian from the borders of Makuran to those of Halogaland would have failed to agree with him.

Videssians reverenced Phos. They prayed to the good god. They all believed Phos would triumph in the end, that he would confine Skotos to the eternal ice, and that good would reign in the world. Rhavas, again taught from childhood, had always believed the same thing. He'd believed it without thought, as anyone would believe a childhood lesson.

Now, rather than simply believing it, he thought about it. What was the evidence? "Phos' holy scriptures, of course," he said out loud, as if someone—perhaps his horse—had denied it.

That was all very well . . . until you measured the holy scriptures against what you saw in the world. Sin was as rampant as it had ever been—probably more so. Civil war consumed the Empire of Videssos. The Khamorth were loose inside the Empire. They wandered where they pleased and did what they would. Magic and prayer had proved powerless to stop them.

"And Phos turns a deaf ear to my petitions. Not one of them does he hear," Rhavas told the steppe pony. "Or it could be that he hears, but has not the power to respond. Yet I can curse, and when I do, the curse strikes home."

He remembered Toxaras' body lying in the snow. He remembered the ground shaking under his feet and the walls of Skopentzana falling to the ground. He remembered plainsmen tumbling from their horses, plainsmen falling dead in the forest. And he remembered Ingegerd crumpling to the farmhouse floor, Ingegerd whom he'd . . . loved? Ingegerd whom he'd given most excellent good reason to hate him. Ingegerd who'd done her best to kill him.

No, ride where he would, he couldn't get away from what he'd done. He took it with him, everywhere and always. The memories would never go away. What they meant, to him, to the Empire, and to the wider world . . . he was still working on that. He suspected he would be for a long time, if, in a world gone mad, he had a long time left *to* work on it.

Meanwhile, he rode south and west. As long as he was out in the open, he feared little. For better or for worse—for better *and* for worse—his curses would protect him from the barbarians as long as he saw them before they came into bowshot. Only when the track went through forest did he worry. There assailants could strike from ambush before he knew they were near.

But he came through safe whenever he passed through such places. Little by little, he decided the Khamorth did not haunt them. The nomads *were* plainsmen; forests had to seem strange and crowded and dangerous to them. Rhavas started to relax when he went through woods. A second, slower, realization made him wary again. The Khamorth might not prowl forests, but there were bound to be Videssian brigands on the loose as well, and tall trees and deep shadows would not bother them at all.

He camped for the night in the lee of a stone fence, the best shelter he could find. If he did not make a fire, he might draw wolves; if he did, he might draw men. Deciding men were more dangerous, he let darkness cloak him. Only after nightfall did he think of himself as under the dominion of Skotos' realm.

He ate smoked meat and coarsely ground flour moistened with snow that melted in his mouth. Ingegerd was the one who'd thought to plunder the Khamorth ponies' saddlebags. She'd taught him any number of things—a good many of which, perhaps, he would have been better off not learning.

"It's done," he said. The sound of his own voice startled him. But for arguments with himself, he'd spoken little since setting from the farmhouse where Ingegerd still lay. But he repeated, "It's done," and then added, "It can't be changed now. Nothing can be changed now. I go on from here."

Wrapping himself in all the clothes and blankets he had, he lay down in the snow. But for the horses close by, it might have been Skotos' hell: a dark and frozen wasteland. If he froze to death here, would the world to come seem much different? Or would something like this be all there was, now and forever?

His shiver had nothing to do with the weather. He was almost afraid to fall asleep, for fear he might not wake.

But wake he did. He started to praise Phos for letting him come through the long, cold night. However familiar the words were, they stuck in his throat. They might have been frozen there. What had the good god done for him, for Skopentzana, for Videssos? Nothing he could see. No, the disarray around him had to be Skotos' work.

Should I praise the dark god, then? he wondered. He shied away from the thought, as one of the steppe ponies might have shied from a scorpion. But once the notion lodged in his mind, it refused to leave.

After a breakfast like his supper, he rode away. Again, he would sooner have left behind the idea of praising Skotos. Again, he carried it with him whether he wanted to or not. *If I do come down to Videssos the city, how much will I be fleeing by then?*

But what choice did he have? If he didn't try to go on to the capital, what was he to do? The only other thing that occurred to him was to throw himself off a cliff. Then he would be free of the world, and the world would be free of him.

He shook his head. He had too much pride for that—too much pride, and too much fear of what would happen if he faced the Bridge of the Separator with all his recent sins still freshly seared on his soul. No, the only thing for him to do was to go on.

And by the time he got to Videssos the city, he might have a thing or two—or maybe more than a thing or two—to say to the proud and clever theologians who never thought to stick their noses outside the walls of the imperial capital. They had seen the world from one perspective—had seen it that way, in fact, for hundreds of years. He had a different viewpoint, one he thought held more truth.

They would not want to hear him. He was sure of that. Those arrogant little manikins were so sure they had all the answers. But if he showed them the truth, if he rubbed their noses in the truth, how could they deny it? They'd known he was a master theologian when they shipped him off to Skopentzana. He'd needed no seasoning in that, only in his knowledge of how to administer a temple. Well, he had that knowledge now, and more besides.

"Yes, and more besides," he told the steppe pony he rode. The pony paid no attention to him. But the priests and prelates in Videssos the city would. They would have to. Even the ecumenical patriarch would have to. Oh, yes. Even he.

* * *

Two days later, Rhavas rode into the town of Kybistra. He'd cursed one band of Khamorth raiders who tried to attack him. He'd done it man by man. When the first nomad tumbled from the saddle, the rest must have thought he'd had a seizure, or something of the sort. They'd kept coming. Losing a second man hadn't halted them, either. But when the third died as soon as Rhavas aimed a forefinger at him, the rest wheeled their horses and galloped away faster than they'd come after him. He'd felled a fourth man as they fled, more for the sport of it than for any other reason, and let the others make good their escape.

Kybistra was larger than Tzamandos. Here in the provinces, it counted for a city, though it was hardly more than an anthill when set beside the capital. Guards on the brown stone walls called a challenge to Rhavas as he rode up: anyone on a steppe pony made them nervous. But he was only one man, and he answered them in Videssian distinguished from their own only by the accents of Videssos the city—*he* didn't sound as if he'd been raised in the back of beyond. The gate crew swung the valves wide, then closed them again after he rode into the town.

One of the men from that crew gave him directions to an inn; after his unpleasant time in Tzamandos, he didn't want to lodge with another priest in a temple. The place wasn't far. In Videssos the city, it would have had some branches from a grape vine hung above the door. Here, a sign painter had daubed a bunch of purple grapes on a board. No vines grew anywhere close to Kybistra; winters here were far too savage, summers far too short.

A boy, perhaps the owner's son, took the pony he rode and the other one he'd led. He gave the lad a copper, and got back a bow and a polite, plainly memorized speech of thanks.

When he opened the door, warmth from a great fire blazing on the hearth greeted him. He hurried inside and closed the door behind him so none of the lovely heat could escape. Before even speaking to the innkeeper, he went over to stand in front of those crackling flames.

"Very holy sir!" called someone sitting at a table not far away.

Rhavas turned; he didn't want to draw away from the fire. "Koubatzes!" he said, and nodded to the mage. "Good to see you. Good to see anyone from Skopentzana. I had not known you got away."

"By the good god, very holy sir, I hadn't known you did, either," Koubatzes replied. The opening phrase was in a Videssian's mouth a dozen times a day. Hearing it, though, felt strange to Rhavas now. It was as if the wizard were telling him a clever lie. Koubatzes went on, "I almost didn't get away. A house fell in on me when that cursed earthquake hit us. If I hadn't jumped under a table, the roof would have smashed me flat."

That cursed earthquake. Koubatzes was righter than he knew. "I am glad you are safe," Rhavas said.

Koubatzes looked bleak. "I don't believe anyone is safe, not these days," he said. "I'm still breathing, though, and that puts me ahead of a lot of people." He tapped a stool by the one on which he perched. "Sit down with me and have a cup of wine. You look like you've earned it."

"Let me get a little warmer first," Rhavas said. Koubatzes grinned and nodded. The prelate turned to warm his back, then his front again, and then his back once more. He kept turning till he stopped feeling like a cold man and started feeling like a joint of meat on a spit. Then he did go over and sit down by the mage.

A barmaid walked up to him and asked, "What can I bring you, holy sir?"

Rhavas didn't bother correcting her about his rank. "Red wine," he answered. She went back to get it, swinging her hips. Rhavas' eyes followed her.

Koubatzes noticed him noticing her. "Must be hard to look all the time and never touch," he remarked.

That made Rhavas remember Ingegerd, Ingegerd whom he'd taken against her will, Ingegerd who lay dead north of Kybistra because of him. "Temptation is bad," he said seriously. "Yielding to temptation can be worse."

"I suppose so. Sometimes, though, it's fun," Koubatzes said.

Before Rhavas could reply, the barmaid brought him his wine in a cheap earthenware cup. "Here you are, holy sir." Did the smile she gave him say she wouldn't care about his vows if he didn't? That was how it looked to him. When he didn't respond, she swayed away.

Automatically, Rhavas went through the ritual every Videssian used before drinking. He spat on the ground in rejection of Skotos, then raised his eyes and his hands to the heavens. Most of the time, he hardly noticed what he did when he followed the ritual. Now . . . *Is the lord with the great and good mind really heeding me?* he wondered uneasily.

Shrugging, he drank. The wine ran strong and sweet down his throat. Koubatzes said, "You must have had some narrow escapes yourself, eh, very holy sir?"

"Anyone from Skopentzana who still lives has had narrow escapes," the prelate answered.

"Phos! That's the truth!" Koubatzes emptied his winecup and waved to the barmaid for a refill. She waved back to show she saw. Koubatzes continued, "Me, I almost died half a dozen times the first couple of days. Things seem a little better down here anyway, don't they?"

"Maybe a little." Rhavas didn't want to talk about it.

Koubatzes plainly did. He told Rhavas a couple of stories that showed how clever he was, and one that also showed what a good wizard he was. "Hadn't been for the confusion spell, they would have had me," he finished.

"A good thing you got away," Rhavas said.

"Well, *I* think so." Did Koubatzes sound complacent? To Rhavas' possibly jaundiced ear, he did. He went on, "How about you, very holy sir? You had no magic to ward you. How did you manage to stay free?"

"I managed," Rhavas answered, thinking Koubatzes wasn't so smart as he thought he was. Rhavas drank from his cup of wine. The less he had to say about what had happened to him since the Khamorth got into Skopentzana, the better he would like it.

But Koubatzes didn't want to leave it alone. "What happened to that blond woman, the officer's wife?" he asked. "You were sort of her guardian after he went off to fight in the civil war, weren't you?"

Rhavas silently cursed the Videssian penchant for gossiping about everything under the sun. How much of Skopentzana had known Himerios asked him to watch over Ingegerd? Too much of it, that was plain. He had to answer. He did, as briefly as he could: "She's dead."

"Pity," Koubatzes said. "She was a striking woman—and a good one, too, by all I ever heard. The two don't always go together, but they did with her. The barbarians got to her before you could, did they?"

"There was nothing I could do," Rhavas said, which, while not quite the lie direct, was not the truth, either. He wished Himerios hadn't half entrusted Ingegerd to him. Then he wouldn't have had to become more closely acquainted with women and their temptations than he was before.

If not for the civil war, it wouldn't have happened. Stylianos was the rebel, but Maleinos was the one who'd pulled garrisons out of the cities to go against him. Then Stylianos stripped the frontier forts, and then the Khamorth came in. Which claimant was the greater villain? Rhavas only shrugged, there on his stool. They both had so much to answer for.

"Pity," Koubatzes said again. "That must have made you sad. I know you're a man who takes his duty seriously."

The prelate nodded, not trusting himself to speak. Oh, yes, hadn't he just taken his duty with Ingegerd seriously! Seriously enough that he'd taken *her*, seriously enough that he'd left her dead on the farmhouse floor! Well, she would have left him dead there if she could.

He finished his wine at a gulp and waved to the barmaid as Koubatzes had done. She fluttered her fingers when she waved back. *Slut*, he thought. *Do you think I'll throw my vows over the side so easily?* But then, what vows hadn't he thrown away when he came down from Skopentzana? What difference did how he behaved now make? Hadn't the good god already turned away from him in disgust?

The girl brought him a fresh cup. "Happy to serve you, holy sir," she purred. How did she mean that? Was she so glad to fetch him wine? Or did she want to serve him some other way?

In his mind's eye, he saw Phos sternly staring down at him. The good god had the face he did in the mosaic in the dome of the High Temple in Videssos the city: a long, somber face made for judgment and always ready to condemn the transgressor. That Phos held a book in which all a man's deeds, good and ill, were recorded. Rhavas shuddered to think what the book said of him right now.

That shudder must have been more visible than he thought, for Koubatzes asked, "Are you all right, very holy sir? Are you well?"

How can I answer, Rhavas wondered, *when the good god has turned his back on me, when I am surely damned to the eternal ice?* But then he stiffened. His own back straightened. Wasn't everything he'd been through—wasn't everything Videssos had been through—lately a demonstration that the Empire's theologians had been getting things wrong, getting them backward, for hundreds of years? Wasn't it a demonstration that Skotos truly was stronger in the world and more likely to prevail at the end of time than Phos?

There. That was the thought he'd been shying away from for all this time. That was the thought he'd been afraid to face. And now he'd faced it—and nothing had happened to him. Phos hadn't slain him in a fit of fury. Did Phos really have the power to do any such thing? That wasn't how it looked to Rhavas.

And if Phos didn't . . .

"Are you all right, very holy sir?" Koubatzes asked again.

How to answer that? Rhavas wondered once more. To his own amazement, a laugh escaped his lips. "I'm very well," he said. "I'm much better than I thought I would be, in fact."

Koubatzes eyed him curiously. "I'm glad to hear it. You looked . . . rocky there for a while, if you don't mind my saying so. You do seem better now."

"Good. I feel better now. No doubt the wine helped," Rhavas said. The wine hadn't had anything to do with it. Seeing the way things worked in a new light mattered much more. Like most Videssians, Rhavas was a proselytizer at heart. Once he'd seen something, he wanted all his countrymen—indeed, the whole world—to see it the same way. He imagined the ecumenical patriarch's face when he propounded the new doctrine. That was enough to set him laughing again.

"No doubt the wine has," Koubatzes agreed—as polite a way of calling him a drunk as any he could imagine.

"I've been through too much lately," Rhavas said, more to throw the sorcerer off the scent than for any other reason. "I've almost died. I've seen my city die. I've seen the barbarians outdo us at war, and I've seen them outdo us at wizardry. Is it any wonder I'm less than I wish I were?"

The wizard winced at being reminded how the Khamorth had thrown the Videssian spell of repulsion back in his face. Rhavas had counted on that; he smiled to himself to see that he'd got it. "I'm sorry, very holy sir," Koubatzes murmured. "Indeed, you have every excuse to feel even more battered than I do—and that, believe me, is saying a great deal."

Rhavas finished the second cup of wine, then got a second-story room from the landlord. It was about what he expected: a cubicle with a bed, a stool, a lamp on the stool, a battered pine chest for whatever belongings a guest would put into it, and a pitcher and basin on top of the chest. For a night or two, it would be all right. Anyone who had to stay there longer would want to throw the shutters wide and jump out the window headfirst.

After a while, the prelate went down to the taproom. To his relief, Koubatzes wasn't there anymore. Rhavas ordered bread, half a capon, and another cup of wine from the barmaid who'd served him before. She winked at him when she brought him the food. How shameless was she? How shameless did she think he was?

At first, anger threatened to overwhelm him. That she should think him such a creature . . . But what if he was? What difference did it make? The world seemed a different place from the way it had a few hours before. Rhavas shook his head. No, that wasn't so. The world itself hadn't changed. Its overlord, or his understanding of who its overlord was, had. So why was he behaving as if he still believed what he'd believed for so long? Was it anything more than force of habit?

Though he'd found another place close by the fire, he shivered. If Skotos was the stronger, what were Phos' commandments worth? Anything? It didn't seem likely. And what commandments would the dark god have? No one had ever thought to write them down, not so far as Rhavas knew. That didn't mean he had no ideas. If Phos opposed something . . .

Darkness fell, out on the streets of Kybistra. *Skotos' time*, Rhavas thought, and shivered once more. The bonfire blazing on the hearth and torches set in bronze sconces on the wall held night at bay in the taproom. Smears of soot above the sconces spoke of how many torches had burned in them.

Even the brightest flames couldn't come close to matching daylight. People started yawning and going off to their rooms. Rhavas had worried all the meat off the capon's bones. He licked his fingers clean and got to his feet. "Can I give you anything else, holy sir?" the barmaid asked.

"No." But instead of leaving it at that, he added, "Not here." The barmaid got a fit of the giggles. How many priests had said something like that to her? *None who knew what I know*, Rhavas thought.

He carried a burning twig up to his room and used it to light the lamp. One small flame did not drive out the darkness; indeed, it barely pushed back the gloom. Rhavas' shadow, huge and black, swooped across the walls and ceiling. *Is that an image of Skotos, come to watch what happens here?* Rhavas shivered yet again.

He jumped when someone tapped softly at the door. For a heartbeat, he hoped it was Koubatzes or the innkeeper or anyone but . . . He worked the latch. The door swung open. The barmaid stepped into the room and quickly closed the door behind her. "You won't want people seeing," she said, a world of experience in her voice.

Later, he realized he could have sent her away even then. She might have laughed at him; she probably would have. But he could have done it. Scornful laughter would not have been too high a price to pay for virtue—had he still held his old notions of virtue uppermost in his mind.

Maybe the barmaid had wondered if he would think twice. Some panicky priests probably did. When Rhavas didn't, she laughed a little. "Well, then," she said, a meaningless phrase that felt like a complete sentence.

She pulled her shift off over her head.

Rhavas undressed as fast as he could. "It's cold," he said foolishly when he stood there naked. This time, the barmaid did laugh out loud. She pointed to the bed.

When Rhavas ravished Ingegerd, he'd been so inflamed he hardly knew what he was doing. He knew exactly what he was doing here, and why: to show himself such things were no sins regardless of what he'd been taught. If he was going to do them, he should not do them filled with shame, but with all his heart and will behind them. Better to savor them than to shun them.

He tried his best. The barmaid, with experience of other clumsy clerics, no doubt helped more than he knew. "Ahh!" he said at the end: both delight and understanding. "*That's* what it's supposed to be!"

"That's what it's supposed to be." The barmaid sounded altogether pragmatic; maybe it hadn't been everything it was supposed to be for her. "Can you slide over a little, holy sir? You're squashing me."

He did. Then he said, "You'll want something for this, won't you?"

"I didn't do it for nothing, by the good god!" she exclaimed.

By the good god. Did that mean anything? Had it ever meant anything? Generations uncounted thought it had, still thought it did. *But I know better*. Yes, Rhavas had the missionary urge. *I know better, and so will they*, he thought.

That would have to wait, though. The barmaid hadn't come to his room to be converted. She'd had a much simpler transaction in mind. He gave her a silverpiece. She seemed contented enough when she left the room.

As for Rhavas, he realized how far he was from ousting all the old belief when a spasm of guilt wracked him. Not only had he sinned, he had sinned deliberately. If he was wrong about what his recent experience meant, he'd gone a long way toward damning himself.

"I am not wrong," he said, there alone in the chamber. He had always been the most brilliant of theologians; Neboulos had said as much when sending him to Skopentzana all those years ago. He understood Phos' doctrine better than any other priest now living—he was sure of it. Why should he not understand Skotos better than anyone else as well?

He rose from the bed. As he'd expected, a chamber pot sat under it. He used the pot, then walked over to the lamp and blew it out. Darkness filled the room. *As it should*, Rhavas thought. *Yes, exactly as it should*. Two steps took him back to the bed. He lay down and went to sleep.

Sunlight sliding between the slats on the shutters woke Rhavas. By where the beams struck the floor, the prelate had slept soundly—more soundly, perhaps, than he'd intended. Rhavas started to sketch the sun-circle over his heart, as he had on waking every morning for as long as he could remember. But wasn't that one more habit to throw on the rubbish heap? So it seemed to him, and so he checked his hand's all but automatic motion.

Yawning, he got up and used the pot again. Then he opened the shutters. "Coming out!" he called, and chucked what was in the pot into the street. Anyone down below had to watch out for himself. No angry shouts rose, so Rhavas didn't suppose he'd given some luckless passerby a rude surprise.

He went down to breakfast. The barmaid on duty wasn't the one with whom he'd lain the night before. Koubatzes was already spooning up porridge, and talking with a man whose back was to Rhavas. After a bit, the mage's companion turned his head. Rhavas had thought he looked familiar: he was one of the men with whom the prelate and Ingegerd had traveled south from Tzamandos. For the moment, seeing him just made Rhavas glad that some of the party had managed to get away from the Khamorth in the stand of pines.

Rhavas called for a bowl of porridge and a cup of wine to wash it down. The barmaid brought him what he ordered. The bowl, chipped along the edge, was of the same cheap earthenware as the cup. The spoon was of horn. As for the porridge . . . It was hot, and it would fill him up. Having said that, he exhausted its virtues.

Nothing was wrong with the wine, though. He drained it and waved for a refill.

The barmaid had just brought him the fresh cup when Koubatzes came over to his table. "May I join you, very holy sir?" the mage inquired.

"Why not?" Rhavas said, a trifle grandly.

Koubatzes settled himself on a stool. It creaked under his weight. He drummed his fingers on the stained, battered pine of the tabletop. "I was talking with Arsenios there for a while," he said.

"Yes, I saw you. What about it?" Rhavas inquired.

"Well, I don't quite know," Koubatzes said. "He tells me he was traveling with you. As a matter of fact, he tells me he was traveling with you and the Haloga woman up until a couple of days ago."

"Oh." Rhavas sent Arsenios a look that should have melted most of the snow in Kybistra. The merchant, oblivious, stayed on his stool. He seemed to be chewing his cud like a cow. Rhavas thought hard about cursing him—he was angry enough—but reluctantly held back. If Arsenios fell over dead, Koubatzes would wonder why, and the wizard was wondering about too many things already. Rhavas just looked at him. "What about it?"

"You said she was dead, very holy sir," Koubatzes reminded him.

"She is." Rhavas knew perfectly well that was true. He knew the details, too, and no one else ever would.

But Koubatzes knew too much already, and knew it straight from

Rhavas' own lips. "You led me to believe she died in Skopentzana, when the barbarians sacked the city. How could she have traveled with you if that happened?"

"Simple." The word came out of Rhavas' mouth before he had the least idea of what would follow it. Whatever it was, it would have to be a lie. He did his best to make it a good one: "You must have heard me wrong. I said she died *after* Skopentzana, not in it. In fact, a Khamorth arrow hit her in the back as we were riding out of the woods after the plainsmen attacked us there."

Koubatzes frowned fearsomely. "By the lord with the great and good mind, that isn't what you told me before."

"By the lord with the great and good mind, sorcerous sir, it is." Rhavas swore the false oath without hesitation. It was all of a piece with everything else that had happened since Videssos' troubles started. So he told himself, anyhow.

The mage's frown only got deeper. "That is *not* what I remember you saying." But he sounded more puzzled than outraged or suspicious. Rhavas' rank and his manifest holiness argued powerfully that he should be believed. Koubatzes doubted himself at least as much as he doubted the prelate.

Rhavas tried to make his smile seem sympathetic. In fact, it was mocking. He sipped from his cup of wine, laughing, as it were, behind his hand. He said, "We were both very tired last night, and we'd both drunk wine. Who knows what you thought you heard?" He did not mention what he'd said then, but left the impression he was very sure of that.

That impression of certainty struck home, too. "Maybe." Koubatzes sounded doubtful, but of himself rather than Rhavas. "I would have taken oath—I *did* take oath, to Arsenios—you told me something different, though."

"You know how these things are. You've dealt with people," Rhavas said easily. "Let five men watch an accident in the square. Ask them what happened an hour later and you'll hear six different stories."

"Maybe." Now Koubatzes might have been arguing with himself. Part of him wanted to believe Rhavas: that was plain. Part of him still knew something was wrong, but didn't quite believe what it knew. He slowly got to his feet. "All right, very holy sir. I won't trouble you anymore."

"No trouble at all," Rhavas said to the sorcerer's retreating back. When he was trapped in the worship of Phos, he would have had trouble sounding so genial; most people would have called him stern and harsh. He thought he still might be stern, but in the service of a new master.

Koubatzes sat down with Arsenios once more. The merchant said something. Rhavas couldn't make out what it was, because the man's back was to him. Koubatzes came back sharply, so sharply that Arsenios flinched. Koubatzes got up again and stalked out of the taproom.

He still wonders, Rhavas thought. *Well, let him. What can he do about it? Not a thing, and he has to know it.*

Even if Rhavas came right out and told the wizard what he'd done with and to Ingegerd, what could Koubatzes do about it? Not much, not now. Before the Khamorth invaded, before Videssian administration here in the north—and through how much of the rest of the Empire?—fell apart, Koubatzes could have had him arrested and interrogated. These days? Each town remaining in Videssian hands might as well have been a separate tiny kingdom. Leave the walls behind and you left its jurisdiction behind as well.

Rhavas went out to the stables. The little horse he'd ridden and the other he'd led as a pack animal had been brushed and seemed happy enough. The stable boy expectantly looked his way. He gave the youth a couple of coppers.

"Phos' blessings upon you, holy sir," the stable boy said.

"And on you," Rhavas replied, trying not to notice his own hypocrisy. The stable boy seemed to have trouble deciding whether to feel pleased at getting a priest's blessing or disappointed at not getting another copper. Rhavas shrugged. That was the boy's worry, not his. He put the steppe pony's trappings on it, clambered up into the saddle, and rode away from Kybistra.

It was still cold. The snow would stay on the ground a while longer. But the sun rose earlier than it had in deepest winter, and set later. It climbed higher into the sky at noon and shone brighter day by day. Not spring yet—oh, no. But a place from which, if you looked ahead, you could see spring.

When Rhavas looked ahead, he saw the usual white-swathed landscape. No plainsmen roamed across the snow-covered fields. He would not have worried even if they did. He had their measure—he could point a finger and fell them well before their arrows could reach him.

Not wanting any nasty surprises, he also looked back over his shoulder. No nomads behind him, either. No nomads, no, but someone riding out from Kybistra along the same track. Whoever the horseman was, he was pushing his mount hard, gaining on Rhavas with every stride it took.

The man waved. "Very holy sir!" he called, his voice thin in the distance. Rhavas watched the smoke of his breath stream out around his head. "Wait, very holy sir!"

Koubatzes. Rhavas muttered to himself. He wondered whether he should rein in. The mage would catch him whether he did or not, so he did. He tried not to seem too surly as he raised a hand and said, "Hail."

"Hail." Koubatzes rode a Videssian horse, a beast two or three hands taller than a steppe pony. That let him look down on Rhavas. By his expression, he was looking down on the prelate metaphorically as well as literally. Pointing an accusing forefinger at Rhavas, he said, "You lied to me, very holy sir."

"In Phos' holy name, I did not." Even more easily than he had back at the inn, Rhavas brought out the lie with the force of truth.

Koubatzes sadly shook his head. "You lied, and you swore—and still swear—falsely in the good god's name. I thought long and hard on what you said last night, and on what you said this morning, and on what Arsenios told me. You lied, and I fear something truly evil has befallen the Haloga woman."

"Do you?" Rhavas' voice was silky with danger.

If Koubatzes heard that danger, he gave no sign. He persisted, "Yes, by Phos, I do. Will you make a clean breast of it and tell me the truth? It may win you mercy in the next world, if not in this one."

Rhavas laughed in his face. "You know nothing of this world or the next, wizard—nothing at all."

"I know what any Videssian may know. My belief is orthodox." Koubatzes sketched the sun-sign. His eyebrows leaped when Rhavas failed to imitate the gesture. Voice heavy with sarcasm, the sorcerer said, "You will tell me you know better?"

You will tell me you have fallen into heresy? was what he meant. Rhavas had fallen further—lower—than heresy. He not only knew it, he took pride in it. "Yes, I will tell you I know better," he said, and proceeded to explain exactly what he knew. Koubatzes was an intelligent man; Rhavas expected him to see the truth once it was set forth for him.

When the prelate finished, Koubatzes stared at him in what could only be horror. The wizard drew the sun-sign again, this time with great care. "Either you seek to lure me into misbelief, very holy sir, or you have gone mad," Koubatzes said. "Only you can say for certain what you've done with the woman. But I can say for certain that doctrine like this will send you to the flames. Nothing less could cleanse you of it."

"I give you the truth, and this is how you reward me?" Rhavas had realized there was a chance Koubatzes would not be persuaded. But that the mage would dare call him a madman, dare suggest he ought to go to the stake . . . Well, Koubatzes would pay the price for his folly. Rhavas pointed a finger at him. "I will show you who is right and who is wrong."

"You will not, nor can you, for you have already condemned yourself out of your own mouth," Koubatzes said.

Outrage tingled through Rhavas. He did not need it to do what he did, not anymore, but feeling it remained reassuring. "Curse you, Koubatzes," he said, and waited for the wizard to fall off his horse.

Koubatzes' eyes opened very wide. He breathed out a foggy plume of vapor. His face twisted in pain. But, to Rhavas' horrified dismay, he remained very much alive. "Phos!" the mage whispered. "That was as rude a stroke as the Khamorth shamans gave me."

Something close to panic struck Rhavas. He'd had a curse fail once before, but never like this. This curse had struck, and done what it could do—but what it could do turned out not to be enough.

"What did you do to the Haloga woman?" Koubatzes demanded, and then shook his head. "No don't waste my time with more lies. Whatever it was, it must have been very bad, or maybe worse than that. What you've done to me, or tried to do to me, will be plenty to see you dead."

Rhavas' heart raced in fear. *Phos help me*, he thought. But no—Phos would not help him, not now. That the idea had flashed through his mind was only a measure of how he'd thought for so long, how he'd thought before he knew better. If Phos would not help him, though, who would? No sooner had the question occurred to him than the answer formed in his mind. *Skotos help me*, he thought, for the first time deliberately calling on the dark god.

Did new strength come to him? How could he know till he tried to find out? "Curse you, Koubatzes," he said again. "Death be your portion."

Koubatzes' eyes widened again. Maybe he thought he'd withstood everything Rhavas could throw at him. If he did, now he discovered he was wrong. A groan escaped him. "You . . . can't . . . do . . . this," he ground out.

"I can. I am. I will," Rhavas retorted. "Curse you—curse you to death."

The sorcerer tried to make the sun-sign once more, tried and failed. He started some sort of counterspell aimed at Rhavas. He started it, but he never finished. Instead, his eyes rolled up in his head. He went limp and slid off his horse into the snow. The horse snorted, sidestepping nervously.

"I can, you see," Rhavas said. "Oh, yes, indeed." He dismounted and knelt by Koubatzes. His fingers found the wizard's wrist. He felt no pulse. The mage's chest did not rise and fall. Rhavas nodded to himself. He had cursed Koubatzes to death, and dead Koubatzes was.

Before getting back on his steppe pony, Rhavas went through the saddlebags Koubatzes' horse carried. He took food and a carefully copied grimoire and a large leather wallet full of sorcerous paraphernalia. Koubatzes would not need any of that again, and Rhavas' packhorse would have no trouble carrying it.

When Rhavas rode south, he felt oddly liberated. He had finally succeeded in leaving behind everything in and from Skopentzana: Ingegerd, Koubatzes, his temple . . . and his god.

"I am free!" Rhavas said. "Free of everything that held me back! Free to tell the truth I've found!"

He rode on. He still had a long way to go before he came to Videssos the city. When he got there, though, he would have a lot to say. And people there would listen to him. They wouldn't be officious, sanctimonious fools like Koubatzes.

"Or if they are, they'll be sorry." The horse's ears twitched as Rhavas spoke. Rhavas booted it forward. The capital might still be distant, but he was on his way.

*   *   *

He stopped for the night at a farmer's house that was anything but deserted. The man, a plump, middle-aged fellow named Illos, said, "Yes, we've heard there's trouble around. Uncommon lot of folks on the road, that's certain sure. But we've seen not a one of these barbarians, and we don't aim to worry about it till we do."

"That's a fact," agreed Marozia, his wife. But for lacking a bushy gray beard, she looked a lot like him. "Come on in, holy sir, and I'll feed you." She nodded briskly. "I'll feed you, all right. I'll feed you till you can't hardly walk."

"I can pay," Rhavas said. "I'd be glad to pay."

"Don't you worry about that," Marozia said. "Maybe you'll pray over the livestock before you ride on, something like that."

Rhavas nodded, not trusting himself to speak. Of course peasants still believed Phos hearkened to their worthless, futile prayers. Such stubborn, stupid folk would never listen if he tried to give them what he saw as the truth. All he could do was go through the motions they expected, no matter what he thought of them.

Illos and Marozia had a swarm of children, ranging down from a couple of boys with beards of their own beginning to sprout to a girl just starting to toddle around. Large families were often hungry. Not here, though. Marozia gave Rhavas a stack of barley cakes, a bowl of chicken stew thick with meat and peas and beans and chunks of turnip, and a mug of fruit-sweet blackberry wine. "Eat up," she commanded. "Plenty more where that came from." She might have been defying him to eat more than she could provide.

Eat he did, till he was groaningly full. "May I read by your fire for a little while before I sleep?" he asked.

"Go right ahead. We've got plenty of wood," Illos told him. "Nobody here has his letters, but if you want to study the holy scriptures, you go right ahead. I know that's what priests do."

Again, Rhavas did not enlighten him. He got Koubatzes' grimoire out of the saddlebag and began to study it. He had never tried to work magic before, but he could see it might be useful. His first look at the book of spells was not reassuring. It was written in a cramped, allusive style: Koubatzes writing to himself, for himself. To an outsider like Rhavas, one word in three, one idea in three, seemed to be missing. He wondered if he *could* cast a spell with a guide like this, or if disaster would eat him up because he didn't know enough about what he was doing.

"Look at him," Marozia whispered to one of her strapping sons. "See how holy he is?"

"He's something, all right," the young man agreed, also in a low voice.

Yes, I am *something,* Rhavas thought, *but what?* He didn't know. Whatever he was, the thing was newly hatched. *What will I be when I finish turning into whatever I'm turning into?* That was a better question. The only trouble was, he didn't know the answer.

I have the truth, he told himself. *If I didn't have the truth, would Koubatzes lie dead in the snow?* He remembered Ingegerd lying dead, too, but quickly shied away from that. *If she hadn't tempted me, if Himerios hadn't thrown her at me, it never would have happened.*

"Pray for us, holy sir," Illos said.

"I will pray that you and your whole family get exactly what you deserve," Rhavas said. Illos and Marozia and their children beamed. They thought he meant a prayer like that in a kindly way. He knew better. With the Khamorth on the prowl, what was likelier than that this farm would be overwhelmed before long? If Illos and Marozia couldn't see that, they were fools, and they would get what fools deserved.

He had his robes and his hooded cloak and his blankets. Marozia handed him another one, plainly the best in the house, of thick, soft wool. "I wove it myself," she said shyly, pointing to the disassembled frame of a loom leaning against a wall.

"I'm sure it will keep me warm," Rhavas said. Marozia bobbed her head and drew back. One of her sons set a mattress on the floor by the hearth. Rhavas lay down and spent as warm and comfortable a night there as he had anywhere since Skopentzana fell.

When he went out to the barn after a filling breakfast the next morning, he found his horses had been well brushed. The youth who had done it said, "They snapped once or twice, but I learned 'em who was boss pretty quick, I did."

"Good for you, and my thanks," Rhavas said. He blessed the animals in the barn, not because he thought it would help them but because the farm family had made it plain they expected it of him.

They still believe in good, he thought as he rode away. *They still believe in it, yes, and how much help will it give them?* Not much, he judged, not when they saw the barbarians riding toward them—or when they didn't see the plainsmen, but woke in the middle of the night to find the farmhouse, loom frame and all, burning around them.

Rhavas shrugged. It wasn't his worry. Illos and Marozia had made their choices. They'd made them, yes, and now they would pay for them.

He looked back over his shoulder a couple of hours later, and saw a column of smoke rising into the air about where that farm would have been. Illos and Marozia were liable to be paying for their choices even sooner than he'd expected. He shrugged again and rode on.

Lykandos was, or had been, a town not to be despised: a long step down from Skopentzana, two even longer steps down from Videssos the city, but still a place that thought of itself as a local center. It had thought of itself so. Now it was dead.

The north gate stood invitingly open. Only when Rhavas drew close did he see how fire had scarred the valves. He rode into the town. The reek of burning still hung in the air, though most of the smells of death still waited on the thaw that now was not far away.

A dog trotted out of a side street and started at Rhavas, its tongue lolling out of its mouth. The animal looked happy and well fed. Rhavas' stomach did a slow lurch when he thought about what it had probably been eating.

Another dog came up beside the first one, and another, and another, and then several more. More slowly than he should have, he realized a pack of dogs could be as dangerous to him as a pack of wolves. To them, what were he and the horses but more meat?

"Go away," he called to them. They paid no attention. He might have known—he *had* known—they wouldn't.

He wished he had a rock or something else he could throw at them. Wishing failed to produce one. And he didn't think he had long to figure out what to do, because the dogs were starting to edge forward. Rhavas no longer liked the way their tongues hung from their mouths. It didn't look friendly. It looked hungry.

He pointed at the first dog that had come out. "Curse you!" he said, and the dog fell over and died.

That did him less good than it might have. He could have intimidated a crowd of men by knocking down one of their number. The dogs had no idea he'd done it. A couple of them sniffed the dead one, but how could they understand Rhavas had slain it? They couldn't, and he couldn't tell them.

He pointed at another dog, one that looked as if it was at least half wolf. It fell over, too. Then he knocked over a big brown dog with floppy ears. They lay there in the snow. The others kept growling, working themselves up to attack.

"Curse you all!" Rhavas gasped. He had no idea whether that would help him. If it didn't, though, he feared nothing would.

A couple of the dogs yelped. A little one, at the very back of the pack, stayed on its feet. Most of them just quietly died. Rhavas eyed them in amazement and relief. He looked at the tip of his finger, as if it were a bow or a ballista through which he shot his curses. He knew better: it was only the way he aimed whatever was inside of him. The illusion remained powerful, though.

The little dog stopped growling and smiled a doggy smile at Rhavas. It wasn't about to attack on its own. As part of the pack, it would have been dangerous. By itself, it turned back into a lapdog. Rhavas threw back his head and laughed. Dogs didn't seem much different from people. A mob could destroy everything and everyone in its path. As individuals, the members might be ordinary men and women who wouldn't hurt a fly. Only the swarm of their fellows gave them strength and let them unleash their savagery without fear or even thought.

Rhavas urged his mount and the packhorse forward. They seemed glad to get away from the dogs even if those dogs were dead. Most of Lykandos had been burned. The deeper into the town Rhavas got, the worse it looked. Bodies lay in the street. Sure enough, dogs and carrion birds had worried at them ever since the town fell, however long ago that was.

A few of the corpses wore furs and leather, not cloth. The locals had put up a fight, then. Much good it had done them.

Even in a dead town, a destroyed town, a sacked town, there was bound to be food and bound to be money. Rhavas rode through Lykandos without looking. The Khamorth would have taken everything that was easy to find and that the flames hadn't swallowed. He didn't care to linger here. He didn't care to linger anywhere. The urge to get down to civilization burned in him. If anyone would hear him, his fellow ecclesiastics would.

Koubatzes should have. That the wizard hadn't still enraged him. Well, Koubatzes had paid for his folly. Anyone else who refused to hearken to the truth he brought would also have to pay. No Videssian of any theological stripe would have thought differently. But the others, all the others, were wrong. Rhavas was sure of it. He was sure enough to bet his life. He was sure enough to bet more than his life: he was sure enough to bet his soul.

Lykandos' south gate also sagged open. Rhavas rode out through it. He wondered what would be left of Videssos here in the northlands when all this fighting was done. Anything? Lykandos was an empty ruin. Skopentzana had been sacked and then destroyed in the earthquake. How many other towns had been burned, how many peasants either run off their lands or killed? *Could* the Empire restore itself here?

Rhavas shrugged yet again. What difference did it make, really? Videssos had lived a lie for hundreds of years. If the Empire was dead in these parts, maybe the barbarians would do a better job of things here. Why shouldn't they? However rude they were, they had some feel for where power truly lay.

The prelate laughed. "Maybe I ought to preach to them, not to the blind fools in blue robes," he said. But then he shook his head. He was a Videssian himself, after all. His own people deserved the first look at everything he'd found. If they turned away from it . . . But they wouldn't. They mustn't. "Curse them if they do," Rhavas muttered. "I'll fight them forever." He kept riding.

Smoke rose from Podandos, but it was a cheerful kind of smoke: smoke from hearths and cookfires and forges and torches and lamps. Lykandos was dead—had been murdered. Podandos still lived. Podandos, by all appearances, still thrived.

A militiaman on top of the wall shouted, "Who comes?" to Rhavas as he neared the north gate.

He gave his name and that of slaughtered Skopentzana and flipped back his hood so the guard could see his head had been shaved. He hadn't been able to tend to that lately. It didn't worry him much, either, though by all the rules it should have.

"Come on in, holy sir. You're welcome, by the lord with the great and good mind," the guard said. He called down to the gate crew: "Open up there, you lazy buggers! This fellow's safe as houses." The men who tended the gate shouted back. The wall muffled their reply, but Rhavas doubted it was a compliment. The man up on top of the wall just laughed.

As Rhavas rode in through the gate, he asked, "Have the Khamorth troubled you here?"

"They tried to break in, holy sir," one of the gate crew answered. "They tried, but we ran 'em off. This for 'em." He spat on the ground, as if rejecting Skotos.

"Good for you." Rhavas had to struggle to get the words out. The gate guard's casual, unthinking gesture reminded him how hard persuading his fellow Videssians might be.

That, though, was a worry for another day. For now, he needed a place to spend the night. He wanted an inn, a tavern, not a temple. He needed to talk to educated, thoughtful clerics, not to some backwoods bumpkin of a priest.

He found an inn without much trouble. After a stable boy led away his horses, he went into the taproom to buy supper and drink some wine and get a room for the night. He wasn't even thinking of luring a barmaid into his bed. No matter which god ruled the world, no matter how that god wanted and expected people to behave, a man could just get tired.

But as Rhavas asked the man behind the bar for a cup of red wine and some bread and cheese, a cheery voice called out, "The blessings of the good god upon you, my friend. You're a colleague, unless I miss my guess."

Rhavas turned his head. He hadn't even noticed the plump priest till the man spoke up. If that didn't prove how tired he was . . . He made himself nod. "That's right," he said.

"Pleased to meet you," the other priest said. "My name's Tryphon. Who are you, holy sir, and where are you from?"

Before Rhavas could answer, the tapman gave him what he asked for. That let him go through ritual—the ritual he no longer believed in—before saying, "I'm called Rhavas. I was lucky enough to get out of Skopentzana."

"Were you?" Tryphon's eyebrows rose. "In Phos' holy name"—he actually said, *In Phaos' holy name*, proving himself a backwoods bumpkin—"you're a lucky man. Not many got out, by what I've heard."

"Yes, I'm afraid that's so," Rhavas agreed. He paused to eat some of the bread and cheese. When he paused, Tryphon was still waiting expectantly. Rhavas felt he had to add, "Between the Khamorth and the earthquake, I fear Skopentzana will never be the same again."

"Too bad. That's too bad." Tryphon swigged from his own cup of wine. By his red cheeks and redder nose, he knew wine well—maybe a little too well. "We felt the earthquake here, too. Things fell off shelves. Some walls cracked. It was worse farther north?"

"You might say so," Rhavas replied. "Yes, you just might say so." He sipped instead of swigging. With the wine the taverner had given him, it didn't much matter. Nothing could make the stuff tasty.

"A terrible business. Everything that's happened lately is a terrible business." Tryphon drank again, then said, "My mug's gone dry. That's a terrible business, too, by Phaos." He set the cup on the counter. The tapman reached into a wine jar with a dipper and filled the cup again. After spitting in ritual rejection of Skotos and raising his hands to the heavens, Tryphon took another swig. "It makes you wonder what everything means, it really does."

"Well, I won't tell you you're wrong," Rhavas murmured, wishing the other priest would shut up and go away.

Tryphon did nothing of the kind, of course. Obnoxious people never had the faintest idea they were obnoxious. The local man said, "I think I know what's behind it all."

Rhavas realized he had to pay attention. "Tell me," he urged, wondering whether the bumpkin had by some accident hit upon the same truth as he'd found himself.

"Don't mind if I do," Tryphon said. "I always like to talk shop when I get the chance. Don't you?"

"When I get the chance," Rhavas answered, doubting this would be one of those times.

Tryphon leaned forward confidentially. "I think the lord with the great and good mind is testing us," he said.

"Testing us? In what way?" Rhavas inquired. Several people in the taproom came closer so they could hear better. Others craned their necks to listen in. Layfolk in Videssos enjoyed hearing their priests argue theology. They often weren't shy about jumping in themselves, either.

"Why, to see whether we stay loyal to him in adversity," Tryphon said. "Here in Podandos, we have." He sketched the sun-sign above his heart. So did most of the audience, including the tapman and a nearby barmaid.

Rhavas drew the sun-circle, too. People would have . . . wondered about him if he, a priest, had not. But all the same, he said, "I'm not so sure, holy sir, meaning no offense to you or your town."

"No? How not?" Tryphon sounded belligerent. Rhavas wondered how long it had been since anyone told him, even politely, that he was wrong.

"Think of Phos' creed," Rhavas replied, warming to the disputation. "Does it not say the good god is 'watchful beforehand that the great test of life may be decided in our favor?'"

"It does. It does indeed. Of course it does." Tryphon made the sun-circle again. "Which proves my point, I would say. Is this not the great test of our lives? Is our faith in the good god not being tested?" He smiled out at the men and women in the taproom—men and women who had surely heard his arguments before.

"You tell him, holy sir!" one of them called, which only made the local priest's smile broader and more confident.

"Very ingenious." By the way Rhavas said it, he plainly meant *very obvious*. Realizing as much, Tryphon bristled. Ostensibly ignoring that but in fact enjoying it, Rhavas went on, "I am afraid you have not taken all the creed into account. Consider the phrase 'that the great test of life may be decided *in our favor*.'" He stressed the last three words.

"Well? What about it?" Yes, Tryphon was all but snorting and pawing at the ground, ready to charge with head lowered and horns aimed straight ahead.

"What about it? Look around you." Rhavas waved. "*Is* the great test of life being decided in our favor? It doesn't seem so to me. Civil war is tearing Videssos to pieces. Can you deny that? Because of the civil war, the barbarians have come over the border and are settling where and as they please. Can you deny *that*?"

"Not here, by Phaos!" a man from the crowd said in a wine-blurred voice. Tryphon nodded emphatic agreement.

"No, not here." Rhavas' exquisite bow was also exquisite in its irony. "Podandos of course being the one great and true center of life in the Empire of Videssos, and all the campaigns of the Khamorth having been completed."

Several people smiled and preened, thinking him serious. They were fools, of no account. Rhavas paid attention to the ones who growled and muttered, the ones who knew sarcasm when they heard it. Again, Tryphon was one of their number. "What are you driving at?" he barked, his voice tense.

"Videssos is riven by civil strife," Rhavas repeated. "Skopentzana is fallen—Skopentzana is destroyed. Lykandos, not far north of here at all, is likewise but a corpse. Who can say how many other cities and towns have been ravaged? You will know for yourselves that the nomads are busy laying the countryside waste. What will the harvest be come fall? Will there *be* a harvest come fall? What will you eat, with no grain in the storerooms? Your dogs and cats? Each other? *Is* the great test of life being decided in your favor?"

Silence answered him. He'd touched the deepest secret fears of the folk in the taproom. Even the man behind the bar, a bruiser with a scarred, surly face, signed himself with Phos' holy sun, and he was far from the only person who did. Slowly, very slowly, Tryphon again asked, "What are you saying?"

"I am not saying anything in particular," Rhavas answered. "But I am asking a question I think needs asking."

"You are asking whether Phaos or Skotos is the stronger god." Tryphon spat on the rammed-earth floor.

Rhavas did, too. No, this would not be easy. He said, "Don't you think the question needs asking these days?"

Tryphon glowered at him, smiling and cheerful no more. "I think asking that question is heresy. By the good god, I think even *thinking* that question is heresy."

Heads bobbed up and down all over the taproom. Rhavas said, "Don't you think the most important thing about doctrine is that it should be true?"

"I think our holy and orthodox faith *is* true, just as the synods have defined it over the years," Tryphon said. "Will you deny that? If you do, you will show you are no true priest, but a heretic indeed, and deserving what any heretic deserves." He got more nods for that.

"How many Videssians have slaughtered one another? How many more have the plainsmen maimed and raped and murdered?" Rhavas asked. He'd done his own raping and murdering, but he did not speak of that. "Could this have happened if our holy doctrine were correct? *Is* Phos watchful beforehand that the great test of life will be answered in our favor? I ask you that, holy sir. I ask all of you the same thing. If he is, how do you know? All the evidence seems to point against it."

"Not all the evidence." Tryphon struck a proud pose. "If Skotos is the greatest power in this world"—he spat again—"may he strike me dead this instant."

Rhavas did not need to point when he knew exactly who his target was. He did not need to speak aloud, either, not when the curse all but formed itself in his mind. He just looked at Tryphon, and that only for an instant.

The other priest groaned. His eyes slid shut; his mouth dropped open. He crumpled to the ground. The barmaid and another woman screamed. A man standing by him knelt and grabbed his wrist. After a little while, the fellow let it fall. It did, limply. "He's dead," the man said, fearful wonder in his voice.

More screams and cries of dismay filled the taproom. Someone pointed at Rhavas. "It's *your* fault. *You* did this!"

"Me?" Rhavas shook his head. "I just stood here. You all saw me. I did nothing. I didn't touch him, I worked no spell. . . . He called a challenge, and perhaps it was answered."

"I think maybe you'd better get out of here, stranger," the tapman said slowly. "I don't want you dropping dead on the floor yourself, or anybody else, either. Tryphon was a good man. We'll all miss him. I don't suppose anyone would miss *you*, though, not even a little bit. You ought to go while the going's still good."

"All I did was ask some questions and try to find the truth," Rhavas said. "Where is the harm in that?"

"I don't know, and I don't care." The tapman reached under the counter and took out a stout bludgeon. "All I know is, we liked Tryphon, and now he's dead. We don't like you. The more we see you, the less we like you, too."

"Think on what you saw. Think on what it means." Rhavas set silver on the bar. "Here. This for my supper."

"No, thanks." The tapman shoved the coin back at him. He didn't touch it; he used a rag to keep from touching it. "On the house."

"You don't want my money?" Rhavas was amazed. He'd never known anyone in an inn who didn't want everything he—or she—could get.

Stolidly, the tapman shook his head. "Might bring bad luck. Never can tell." He turned away from Rhavas and toward the silently staring customers. "Come on, friends. We've got to get poor Tryphon out of here. What happens if a stranger walks in and sees him?"

"A stranger did walk in." One of the men pointed to Rhavas. "Look what came of that, curse him."

His curse was useless, harmless, as most men's were. Rhavas knew *his* was not. He also knew the crowd might nerve itself to mob him. If it did, he would show everyone what *his* curse could do. But all he said now was, "I wanted no trouble when I came in here. I still want none."

They let him leave. They let him reclaim his horse and the packhorse. Some of them followed him, though, till he rode out of Podandos. "Don't come back, either," one of them called from the gateway.

He almost cursed the whole town. That would teach them a lesson. But they would not be in a position to appreciate what they'd learned. He refrained. With luck, some of them would draw the proper conclusions from Tryphon's untimely demise. They might not only draw them but pass them on to other people. Rhavas wanted them to. He did indeed have the missionary instinct.

What he didn't have was anywhere to spend the night. It would be cold—but he wasn't so afraid of cold as he had been before breaking out of falling Skopentzana. One way or another, he expected to get by.

And he did. He found a place where a storm had toppled two or three trees onto one another, creating not only a windbreak but something almost like a lean-to. He tried to start a fire by ordinary means, but had no luck. Then he tried a word of command stolen from Koubatzes' grimoire. In no way was it a proper sort of spell. That didn't mean it didn't work, for the flames crackled to life.

Shelter. Warmth. He hadn't been orthodox in getting them, but so what? He had them. And he hadn't been orthodox coming at the way the world worked—but, again, so what? *I know what I know*, he thought, there alone in the woods.

 **VIII**

fter Podandos, Rhavas did no more preaching for a
while. He did not care for the reception he'd got there.
Yes, backwoods bumpkins, sure enough, and a priest
who'd thought he knew it all. Better to save the truth he'd found
for those who could best appreciate it. Rhavas went on toward
Videssos the city.

He kept hoping he would outdistance the Khamorth and their
irruption into the Empire. He kept hoping, and he kept being
disappointed. Wherever he went, he found the barbarians there
ahead of him. They'd sacked and plundered farms and villages
and small towns and a few more cities. They hadn't gone back to
the Pardrayan steppe afterward, either. They'd come into Videssos
to stay. Their flocks and herds wandered across land that should
have had wheat and barley springing up from it after the spring
thaw came.

And the thaw was almost here. Rhavas could feel it. One day
soon there would be a *snap!* in the air, and all the winter's snow
would start to melt. After that, the going would be slow till the
land dried out again, but then, for a few weeks, glory would
shine out over the world. Spring in the northlands was much
more dramatic than it was down by the capital.

Rhavas noticed he was traveling with his head cocked to one

side, listening for that *snap!* Trouble found him before he found it. A troop of nomads rode toward him across a broad, snow-covered expanse that would probably be a meadow once the thaw began. He wasn't unduly afraid of the Khamorth, but they could be a nuisance, maybe a dangerous nuisance.

To them, he was just a Videssian they'd caught out in the open. He could tell when they got close enough to realize he was riding a steppe pony and leading another. They booted their mounts up from a trot to a gallop. They assumed—rightly—that he must have killed other Khamorth to get their horses, and it looked as if they intended to pay him back.

He pointed at the closest nomad, who was still well out of archery range. The Khamorth tumbled off his horse and sprawled in the snow. The rest of the barbarians kept coming. Rhavas pointed at another one. He fell, too. So did another, and then another. If the plainsmen came any farther, he realized he would have to kill them all. Otherwise, they would be able to shoot at him with their fearsome, horn-strengthened bows, a prospect he relished not at all.

But they reined in then. They had to see he was a wizard of sorts, and that he could go on killing them if he chose. He waited as they put their heads together. At last, after some argument, one of them ostentatiously threw his bow down in the snow. For good measure, he also threw down the leather case in which the nomads carried their bow and arrows. Then he slowly rode toward Rhavas, plainly doing his best not to seem threatening.

Rhavas pointed at him nonetheless, but did not form the killing thought in his mind—not yet. "That's close enough!" he shouted. If the barbarian turned out not to understand Videssian or just ignored him, the fellow was a dead man.

But the nomad stopped. And he not only understood Videssian, he also spoke it after a fashion. "How you do?" he shouted back.

"How did I do what?" Rhavas said.

"Kill." The Khamorth came straight to the point.

"By the power of my god," Rhavas answered.

"You lie." The plainsman's voice was full of scorn. "Phaos do nothing. Phaos sit there like horse turd on ground. Videssos—wizards all bad. But not you. How you do?"

"My god is not Phos." There. Rhavas had said it. He waited for the world to fall to pieces around him. All he'd believed since he was a boy . . . That had already fallen in ruin. Despite his words, nothing special happened now. The breeze tugged at his beard—that was all. He licked his lips and said the rest of what needed saying: "Skotos is my god."

Even after saying it, he had to fight the urge to spit, for he'd spat for so many years every time he named the dark god. "Skotos?" the Khamorth echoed. He nodded, a plain token of respect. "This is strong god. We leave you be." He wheeled his horse and rode back to his comrades. They listened to him. Then, after rounding up the horses of the fallen men and heaving the corpses up onto them, they trotted off. Rhavas watched them, fearing some trick, but there was none. They were gone.

He rode on, too, tasting fear and exultation and a kind of helpless contempt for his own folk. Videssians could not see what was right in front of their faces. The Khamorth had no trouble grasping it. Didn't the world make plain that Skotos was mightier than Phos? So it seemed to Rhavas, and so it seemed to the barbarians as well.

And Rhavas had named Skotos as his god, and the sky had not fallen. Phos had not smitten him with a lightning bolt from the heavens. Things went on as they always had. Was Phos too busy elsewhere to pay attention to his blasphemy? Priests never tired of proclaiming that Phos saw everything everywhere. Rhavas couldn't guess how many times he'd hammered that point home himself, down in Videssos the city and then in Skopentzana.

If the lord with the great and good mind wasn't busy elsewhere, why didn't he punish Rhavas? Was he too weak? If he was, didn't that mean Skotos was the more powerful of the two? Everything else Rhavas had seen lately led him to believe it did. Wasn't this one more fagot on the funeral pyre of good?

"And my own folk, purblind fools that they are, will not see it," Rhavas muttered, his breath making puffs of fog around him. "The barbarians know the truth. Who would have imagined that?" He shrugged. "Well, those who do not care to see will just have to be shown." He rode on, leaving the meeting with the Khamorth behind him. He did not think that troop would trouble him again, and he proved right. He usually did.

* * *

When spring came up around Skopentzana, road traffic stopped dead for several weeks. All the snowdrifts seemed to melt at once, turning the landscape into bogs and swamps. The mud time, people called it. Hard on its heels came the mosquito time; bugs of all sorts bred in the countless puddles and ponds the yearly thaw spawned.

By the time the spring thaw came this year, Rhavas was a long way south of Skopentzana. Snow still covered the ground, but not to the depth it would have had up there. Though roads turned muddy, they remained roads. His travel slowed, but it did not stop.

That was all to the good. He would not have wanted to get stuck in some provincial town for most of a month. The priests there would have wanted to discuss matters theological with him, as Tryphon had in Podandos. They would have ended up regretting it—again, as Tryphon had. Rhavas had been able to leave Podandos. If the thaw kept him in some other town . . . That could be difficult.

He might have solved the problem by wearing ordinary clothes, letting his hair grow out, and trimming his long, shaggy beard. Later, he was amazed at how long that took to occur to him. He kept his blue robe. He paused in one town so a barber could shave his head. He'd been on the road for a couple of days afterward before he paused and wondered why he'd done it.

The answer didn't take long to find. "I *am* a priest," he said, as if someone had denied it. Plenty of people would deny it before long. He knew that. Once he started preaching, he probably would not persuade everyone of what he saw as the new truth.

But if I persuade the ecumenical patriarch, if I persuade the leading prelates in Videssos the city . . . They were the ones who made doctrine for the whole Empire. If they saw things as he did, before long everyone in Videssos would see them that way, too. That was what he aimed for. *And that is what I will have.*

As he rode toward the capital, the land turned green around him. Trees cloaked themselves in leaves. New grass sprang up from fields and meadows. Woods were suddenly silent no more. Insects buzzed—there were mosquitoes in these parts, too. And birds, newly arrived from the strange lands beyond the Sailors' Sea, sang to seek mates as they hunted the mosquitoes and other flying things. They caught them by the thousands, by the tens of thousands. But the bugs bred by the millions.

Mountains rose on Rhavas' right as he got farther south. They weren't tall, jagged peaks, but low and round and smoothly curved. They might almost have been women's breasts. The snow that clung near their summits after it had melted farther down their slopes only added to the impression. Rhavas wondered if that would have occurred to him before . . . *Before things changed*, he thought, and nodded to himself. Yes, that sounded right.

If he remembered straight, more mountains would lie in his path as he went on toward Videssos the city. The Paristrians were a more formidable range than these overgrown hillocks, too. They might even serve as a barrier to keep the Khamorth out of what lay beyond them. Or, of course, they might not. Rhavas could only guess now. He wouldn't know till he crossed them.

A few days later, a troop of horsemen came north up the road toward him. *Khamorth*, he thought, and resolved to curse them one at a time, as he had with the last band, till the survivors got the idea that he and the power protecting him were too dangerous to toy with.

He needed longer than he should have to notice that these men wore chain mail, not leather boiled in wax. They had iron helmets on their heads, not fur caps. They rode full-sized horses, not steppe ponies. And their standard-bearer carried a blue banner with a golden sunburst. They weren't plainsmen but Videssians—Videssian soldiers, in fact.

Rhavas had thought that breed all but extinct. They didn't seem to know what to make of him, either. They pointed ahead when they spotted him. Some of them kicked their horses up from walk to trot. They seemed bemused when he didn't try to get away.

Only afterward did he realize they might have robbed him even though they wore the Empire's livery. The line between soldiers and brigands was a fine one, especially in times of civil strife. They wouldn't have got much if they had taken everything he owned, but they might have tried to kill him as part of the sport. They might have succeeded, too, because they would have taken him by surprise.

One of them called, "Halt, in the name of the Avtokrator!"

He reined in. *Which Avtokrator?* he wondered. He almost asked them, but checked himself at the last moment. If they favored

Stylianos, they might want to seize him—or worse—because he was Maleinos' cousin. Instead, he raised his right hand in a gesture of benediction and said, "Blessings upon you." If he had to, he would name Phos—hypocrisy could be useful. If he didn't, he wouldn't.

Some of the troopers sketched the sun-circle. The man who'd ordered him to halt asked, "Where are you from, holy sir?"

"Skopentzana," he answered truthfully.

"Skopentzana!" the soldier exclaimed. "You're a cursed long way from home, then, aren't you?"

"A cursed long way indeed," Rhavas said. Even naming the northern city could have been dangerous if they were after its prelate. But Skopentzana was big enough to have—to have had—many priests. He could easily have lied about his own name and station.

"Is it true what they say? Has Skopentzana fallen to the barbarians?" the soldier asked.

"That is true. The barbarians sacked it and an earthquake laid it low," Rhavas replied. "I do not know when it will rise again, or if it ever will. Many other cities and towns and villages have also fallen."

The soldiers muttered among themselves. The man who did the talking for them said, "That's hard news, holy sir. I feared it would be so, with all the garrisons gone from that part of the Empire. To the ice with Stylianos for starting his cursed rebellion."

Rhavas almost acclaimed Maleinos then. At the last moment, he held back. Civil wars were hard times, and times full of trickery. These men might revile Stylianos to see if he would agree with them—and then seize him or kill him if he did. He didn't think that was likely, but he didn't think it was impossible, either. Instead of declaring himself, he just asked, "You favor Maleinos, then?"

"By the lord with the great and good mind, we do," the soldiers' spokesman said. "Stylianos stinks of Skotos—doesn't he, boys?" As he spat in the dirt, his comrades shouted obscene agreement. He glowered at Rhavas. "And what about you, holy sir? Whose side are *you* on?"

Had he come out for Stylianos after that, Rhavas would have been a fool—and, in short order, a dead fool. But he didn't intend to. "I told you before I knew which side you leaned to that I come from Skopentzana. I am Rhavas, who was prelate there, and cousin to his Majesty, the Avtokrator Maleinos."

"Very holy sir!" The horseman bowed in the saddle. "Will you bless us before we go on?"

"Gladly," Rhavas lied, and did what the soldier asked. He laughed at himself as he spoke the words and made the gestures. If he'd said what he wanted to say, it would have had more effect. But if he'd said what he wanted to say, the men would have done their best to kill him.

"We thank you, very holy sir," the soldiers' spokesman said when Rhavas had got through his ordeal. "Where are you bound, if you don't mind my asking?"

"Videssos the city," Rhavas answered. "How far have the plainsmen penetrated? And where is the fighting between the Avtokrator and the rebel?"

"You're liable to run into Khamorth almost until you get down to the Long Walls, maybe even beyond 'em," the cavalryman answered, and Rhavas grimaced. The Long Walls lay only a couple of days' journey outside the capital, and protected the farmlands close to it. The soldier went on, "And who knows where our men and Stylianos' are at? They want to get at each other, yes, but they've got all the cursed barbarians in the way. You'd better be careful—that's all I've got to tell you."

"I've come this far," Rhavas said. "If my prayers are answered, I'll make it the rest of the way."

"Phos will heed you. I'm sure of it," the soldier told him. Rhavas had said nothing about to whom he might pray. He said nothing now, either, and nothing on his face showed what he thought. The soldier looked back at the rest of the troop. "Come on, boys! We've got our own job to do. We don't need to bother the very holy sir anymore."

Away they rode. Their horses' hooves thudded. Their chain mail jingled. The sunburst banner snapped in the breeze. Rhavas watched them over his shoulder for some little while before kicking his own horse into motion once more. They were the past, the dead past. The future?

He laughed and set a hand above his heart. "*I* make the future. I make it right here!" he said softly. And what would he make it into? Why, whatever he wanted, of course.

Laughing still, he went on toward Videssos the city.

*   *   *

Rhavas had never seen the Paristrian Mountains till they heaved themselves up over the southwestern horizon: he'd traveled up to Skopentzana by sea, and sailed around the peninsula whose northern rampart they were. They proved less impressive than he'd expected. They were taller and sharper than the ranges farther north, but not the grand, jagged things he thought of when the word *mountains* came to mind.

Khamorth roamed near the Paristrians. Videssian soldiers—some loyal to each claimant to the throne—also patrolled that part of the countryside. Here, at least, the land was debatable. Farther north, Rhavas doubted whether the Empire's sovereignty would ever return. The barbarians had simply swamped that part of Videssos.

When Rhavas went into a town, he mostly just said he was a priest coming down from the north. Sometimes he would talk about the adventures he'd had getting to wherever he chanced to be. He steered clear of arguments with local priests. The tale of what had happened to Tryphon hadn't come south with him or ahead of him. He suspected it was on its way, though. He didn't want to add anything to it.

Part of him felt more at home as he traveled through lands that hadn't been so badly ravaged. This was what the Empire of Videssos was supposed to be like. So his old way of thinking said, anyhow. But was that so? Wasn't all of this doomed to fire and destruction, whether at the hands of the barbarians or of those who battled in the mad and endless civil war?

Now that Rhavas was in the midst of green, growing springtime, believing in ice for all eternity came harder. It came harder, but he managed—especially after he rode up to a battlefield where the armies of Maleinos and Stylianos had clashed the year before.

Even after so much time, the stench of death still floated above that field. Rhavas could tell where most of the soldiers had fallen, for that was where the grass grew tallest and most luxuriantly—the rotting bodies had manured it well. Through the rich green, white bones leered out.

Rhavas looked up and down the dirt road along which he was riding. No one but him was on it now. One army must have come up the road, the other down it, till they met here. Eyeing the boneyard the field had become, he could not tell which force had supported which rival Avtokrator. That went a long way toward explaining the monumental unimportance of the civil war—but not to the men who fought it.

"Fools," Rhavas muttered. He dismounted and tethered his steppe pony and the packhorse to a bush not far from the side of the road. Maybe that was the point. As he walked through the grass and looked at the bones from close at hand, he grew ever more convinced of it. Here lay a skull that had been split, there a rib cage with an arrow through the breastbone. What *were* men but wicked fools who slaughtered one another for the fun of it and for no better reason?

Were they anything more than that? Not so far as Rhavas could see.

He bent and picked up a rusting saber. The hand bones of the corpse that held it came apart as he took it from the dead grip. The useful pattern they had once made fell back into randomness. *As do all useful patterns, the proof of which I see before me,* he thought.

He hefted the sword, then let it fall once more. It clanged off a stone hidden in the grass. The blade snapped in two. Rhavas nodded to himself, as if that also proved his point.

Both the horse he was riding and his packhorse were grazing when he went back to them. Except perhaps for the smell surrounding it, the field meant nothing to them. Being only beasts, they did not know when they were well off.

Remounting, Rhavas rode on toward the mountains. How many mournful fields like that one were scattered across the Empire of Videssos? How many more of them would fatten vultures and ravens and crows before the civil war finally ended, if it ever did? On both sides, warriors had gone and would go into battle shouting Phos' name, sure that it was holy.

But how could the good god's power coexist with savagery such as this? It seemed impossible. Slowly, Rhavas nodded. What else could it be *but* impossible? Good, if it existed at all, had to be nothing more than a lucky accident, one sure to shatter when struck by evil. For evil surely endured forever.

As far back as written records in the Empire of Videssos went, Phos' priests had inveighed against evil, against Skotos. Was the world any better now than it had been when they started their denunciations? Rhavas laughed all the more harshly because the smell of death still lingered in his nostrils. If he didn't laugh over that question, he would have to burst into tears on account of it.

Somewhere not too far away, a band of Khamorth off the steppe was probably encamped, grazing their horses and cattle and sheep on the rich green grass in these meadows. Some of that grass was all the richer for being fertilized by Videssian corpses. And what did the barbarians think of Phos and what Videssos called good? Rhavas laughed again. He'd seen what the Khamorth did when they got in among his folk.

And had the so-called lord with the great and good mind punished them for it? Not likely! They were raping away province after province from Videssos. Phos could not favor that. If the good god couldn't, who did? Could the question have more than one answer?

Toward evening, Rhavas camped inside the edge of a stand of trees. While the light still held, he took Koubatzes' grimoire from a saddlebag and paged through it to a spell of summoning. It involved a lodestone—also plundered from the mage—and, here, some fresh clover. Rhavas was not sure if the passes he made with the chanted spell were the ones the sorcerous tome described; it didn't go into detail. As with much of the magic inside, he had to do his best to figure out how the spell should be shaped.

It worked, though. Two rabbits hopped toward the clover, which seemed to draw them irresistibly. Had Rhavas had to knock them over with stones, the spell of summoning might not have been enough to assure him of a tasty supper. But he had other ways to tend to such things. He pointed a finger at the rabbits, and they quietly died.

The supper was tasty indeed. After roasting the rabbits, Rhavas drowned and buried his fire. He wrapped himself in a blanket and slept on the ground. He didn't need to fear freezing, not here. Before Skopentzana fell, the idea of sleeping in the open would have dismayed him. Since then, he'd done it often enough to take it for granted.

No one and nothing troubled him in the nighttime. So he thought, anyway, till he woke to discover a fresh mosquito bite on the back of his left hand. That only made him shrug; the mosquitoes here were not nearly so bad as the ones farther north. One bite? One bite might as well have been nothing.

He had some bread in his saddlebags from the last town where he'd stopped. It was getting stale, but he ate it anyway, and with good appetite. Water from a nearby stream washed it down. Then he went back to the road and on toward the imperial capital.

Once the road got into the mountains, it writhed and twisted like a worm on a hot paving stone. Sometimes it ran through valleys or over hilltops. Climbing some of those slopes was hard work for the horses, but they managed. Rhavas had come to have enormous respect for the steppe ponies he'd taken from the Khamorth. The rough-coated beasts would never win any beauty contests, but they never flagged, either, which counted for more.

Sometimes, though, the slopes in the Paristrian Mountains were too steep for roads to climb conveniently. In those places, the way forward had been hacked out of the mountainside. Rhavas rode along narrow tracks with gray stone to his right and nothing but air to his left. A misstep would have sent his mount tumbling off the road, and him with it. The beast made no missteps. He was positive the steppe ponies had never faced mountains like these before, but they took them—literally—in stride.

When he met travelers going north in a narrow stretch, which happened a couple of times, one of them had to retreat to a place where two animals could get by each other without having one of them go over a cliff. It was a complicated dance, and often a bad-tempered one, but altogether necessary.

Rhavas wondered how the Khamorth had got through the mountains into the lands on the other side. There were so many places along this road where a handful of men could hold off an army.

He was picking his way through a series of switchbacks so narrow and rugged that even the steppe ponies had trouble when he suddenly realized he was a fool. As always, the realization was unpleasant. But this couldn't be the only way to the far side of the mountains, and it was probably far from the easiest. If he'd asked anyone he'd met on the road, he might well have heard where the better routes lay. He sighed, wishing he'd thought of that before getting deep into the mountains on this road. Turning around and going back now would cost him more time than just going ahead would.

Once, when all the mountains and passes ahead aligned for

a moment, he got a glimpse of the lower country to the south. Then the road bent again, and everything more than a furlong or so ahead disappeared. And once, looking down into a valley, he saw a hawk soaring *below* him. He kept that memory for a long time.

He was back on a less precipitous stretch of road—though one passing through a forest of tall pines—when he found the way ahead blocked by a barricade of tree trunks. From behind it, someone called out the age-old Videssian bandits' warning: "Stand and deliver!"

A bowstring twanged. An arrow buried its head and a good part of its shaft in the dirt a few feet in front of Rhavas' mount. The pony snorted and sidestepped nervously. Rhavas brought it back under control.

"Don't get gay with us, priest, or the next one's through your liver!" warned another bandit, this one with a higher voice.

Rhavas said, "Take what you will. I don't have much." Inside, he fumed. Here was a dangerous spot. He couldn't curse the brigands because he didn't know how many they were or where they hid. If he missed two or three, they could shoot him with ease.

And raucous laughter greeted his reply. "Likely tell!" said the bandit with the shrill voice. "Last priest we got had a pound of gold in a money belt. If it wasn't for the heft of the thing, he would have got away with it. But he didn't, oh, no." He laughed again, nastily.

"Go ahead and search me and my animals," Rhavas said, knowing they would with or without his leave. And if they all came out into the open . . . well, that gave him a chance, anyhow.

He waited. They delayed so long, he began to doubt they would come forth. But at last they did: half a dozen scrawny men, Videssians all, armed with bows and knives and one boar spear. "Get down off that horrible screw you're riding," one of them said. "We may let you keep it—not worth taking."

They did not know the worth of a steppe pony. Rhavas dismounted without a word, having no intention of enlightening them. But when one of them said, "Come on—let's scrag him now," he knew they weren't going to let him keep anything, not even his life.

"Curse you all!" he exclaimed. They twisted and crumpled and died. An arrow hissed past his head—they'd left someone back among the trees in case anything went wrong. They hadn't dreamt anything could go as wrong as it did, though. The arrow came from about the direction Rhavas had expected. "And curse you, too!" he added, and heard another man fall.

He waited tensely. If the bandits had stashed another man anywhere around there, he was still in danger. No more arrows flew at him, though. No shouts of alarm rang through the woods. This seemed to be the lot of them. He breathed a long, slow sigh of relief. Ambush remained his greatest peril.

He took a couple of steps toward the brigands' rough barricade, then stopped, feeling silly. Those logs would need more than one man to shift them. He went back to his horses instead. They stood there quietly. What had happened to the bandits meant nothing to them. They followed without protest when he led them around the barrier.

"Too bad," he murmured as he found the road on the far side. The last bandit lay a few feet to the left of it, his bow by his outstretched hand. An arrow lay there, too; he'd been nocking that shaft when Rhavas' curse struck him down. The noise Rhavas made this time was more like a gasp of relief. He'd cut it even closer than he'd thought.

But it *was* too bad, even so. The bandits were no theologians—nor would they ever be, now. They hadn't thought through what they were doing. Whether they knew it or not, though, they'd found many of the same answers as Rhavas had himself. No one who took the lord with the great and good mind seriously could have lived as they lived, done what they did, could he?

Rhavas shook his head. He didn't see how. He wished he could have had the chance to talk with them about it. They were the closest thing to converts he'd found, even if they never knew it.

His shoulders went up and down in a shrug. "Too bad," he said again, this time in a different tone of voice. If they'd given him any kind of chance, he *would* have talked with them. They hadn't, and so he'd done what he had to do.

Now they were dead and he was still alive. He vastly preferred that to the alternative. He swung back up onto the steppe pony he'd been riding. He would make converts of his own. Once he finally got through the mountains, Videssos the city wouldn't be all that far away.

*   *   *

Relatively few barbarians had got past the Paristrian Mountains, no matter what the Videssian soldiers on the other side had told Rhavas. He did not need long to see that for himself once he got down into the lower country. But that didn't mean the lower country was a land at peace. Oh, no—far from it. Rhavas didn't need long to discover that, either.

This was the land where Videssos' long civil war made its home. Stylianos aimed his forces at the imperial capital like a spearhead. And Maleinos, holding Videssos the city, did everything he could to hold back his rival. No, the Videssians did not battle barbarians here. They fought one another instead.

When Rhavas rode into a town called Develtos, about halfway across the peninsula toward Videssos the city, he found himself for the first time in a place that was strongly for Stylianos even though he'd lost a battle nearby the year before. It was so strongly for him that, for some little while after Rhavas got there, he wondered if the rebel was living in the town. That turned out not to be so; Stylianos was off with his army. But he had spent much of the previous winter in Develtos, and the locals remembered him fondly.

They remembered him so fondly, in fact, that Rhavas gave a false name and did not mention the city he'd come from when he took a room at an inn. If anyone here connected him to Maleinos, it would be disastrous. He just said he'd come from the north. Even that got him a curious look from the innkeeper. "I've heard some northern folk talk," the man remarked. "They say things like *Phaos* for *Phos*. You don't sound like that, holy sir."

"I should hope not," Rhavas said with what he hoped sounded like indignation and now alarm. "I spent years getting a decent education. Do you want me to seem like someone from the back of beyond every time I open my mouth?"

"Don't take it like that," the innkeeper said quickly. "I didn't mean to offend, by the good god."

"We'll say no more about it, then." Rhavas certainly hoped the man would say no more about it.

Some of the silver he got in change in the taproom at supper was shiny and new. That was part of what drew his eye to it, but only part. He knew all of his cousin's coins, and had got used to seeing images of a man with a long face not too different from his own on Videssian money.

Not on these coins. The Avtokrator they showed was round-faced, even plump. Tiny letters around the rim said "STYLIANOS AVTOKRATOR." The rebel had his own silver. Rhavas wondered if he had his own gold as well. When Rhavas turned the coin over, he saw a sword, a spear, and a bow in place of the usual Videssian sunburst. "BY THESE," said the lettering on the reverse.

A good many rebels had put out coins. It was a way to pretend (or to proclaim, depending on the point of view) that you were a legitimate sovereign. But Stylianos' money, unlike some older rebels' coins Rhavas had seen, was obviously minted to the same standard as ordinary currency.

Develtos had a large monastery. Several monks came into the taproom together. They started drinking heavily and then started singing songs. Several of the ones they chose were, to say the least, unmonastic. The ones that weren't about Stylianos and the slaughter he would work on Maleinos were about women, and showed they had more experience with them than monks had any business owning.

In spite of everything that had happened to him, Rhavas found himself scandalized. That these monks should behave so—! Then, after a little thought, he smiled. If the monks were doing Skotos' work . . . well, so much the better. He went back to his own supper.

"Hey, you!" one of the monks called after a while. "Yes, you, priest!"

Rhavas looked up. "Do you want something of me?" he asked in tones that would have produced chills in Skopentzana colder than winter.

Those tones had no effect here. "'D'you want something of me?'" the monk echoed mockingly. His comrades laughed. He went on, "Yes, I want something of you. I want to know what you think of us."

"I've been trying not to," Rhavas answered, which was nothing but the truth.

The drunken monk needed a bit to realize he might have been insulted. "What's that supposed to mean?" he asked angrily once the idea had sunk in. "Are you trying to put us in disgrace?"

"I could not," Rhavas said, hoping the monk would take that for an apology and go back to his swilling.

For a moment, the fellow seemed on the point of doing just

that. But then Rhavas' odd turn of phrase sank in. "Eh? You couldn't do that, you say? And why couldn't you?" the monk demanded.

"Because you already disgrace yourselves," Rhavas replied—yes, he still had all his old stern discipline, even if now turned to a new cause.

The monks shouted furiously. Three or four of them surged to their feet. "Now you're for it, holy sir," said a man at a table next to Rhavas'. "They like to brawl as much as they like to drink, and they like to drink a lot."

Rhavas also rose. "Any man who troubles me will pay dearly," he said in tones that permitted no contradiction. "Does your holy abbot know that you come into this low place looking for tavern brawls?"

One of the monks, the biggest one, took a single step toward Rhavas. Then he noticed his friends weren't following him. He looked at them. He took another look at Rhavas. The monk was almost as tall as Rhavas, and much wider through the shoulders and thicker through the chest. He took another half step forward, then stopped again. "What's the matter with you?" he shouted at his comrades. "What are you afraid of?"

"That fellow's trouble, Garidas," one of the others said.

"Trouble?" Garidas laughed a theatrical laugh. "I could break him in half without any help from the lot of you."

He took another half step forward. None of the other monks followed him. Rhavas stood waiting. He did not know what the monks saw in him, but he did know he'd meant what he said. If they attacked him, it would be the last thing they ever did. Whatever explaining he had to do afterward, he would.

Garidas started to take another step toward him, but then awkwardly swung around so it turned out to be a step back toward the rest of the monks. "Cowards!" he bawled at them. None of them said anything. "Cowards!" he shouted again. "You're all nothing but a bunch of spineless cowards! He's got a priest's robes. So what?" He shook his fist at them.

They neither moved nor spoke. Cursing more like a stevedore than a monk, Garidas stormed out of the taproom. More quietly, the other monks followed in his wake.

Rhavas sat down. The man at the table next to his stared in disbelief. "Phos!" he said. "How did you do that, holy sir?"

"If they know you'll cause trouble, sometimes you don't have to," Rhavas answered.

"No offense, but how much trouble could you cause? There they all were, and they were drunk and mean. That Garidas is one nasty customer. He *likes* brawling in here—you were dead right about that. And I looked to see you dead, or halfway dead, anyways. But they walked out instead. How come?"

"Don't you think you would do better asking them?" Rhavas said.

The man at the next table looked at him. Again, Rhavas didn't know what the fellow saw, but whatever it was, it was plenty to make him grab for his cup and drain it in a hurry. "Maybe I've got some kind of notion after all," he said. Leaving a coin on the table, he too made a hasty exit.

He hadn't even got to the door before Rhavas ran a hand over his face. No blood stained his palm. He bore no brand of which he hadn't been aware. But something must have shown to both the bad-tempered Garidas and to the inoffensive man at the next table, something that said, *If you trouble this man, you'll be the one who's sorry.*

What was it? Had Rhavas' new knowledge done something to him? He felt his face again, and again found nothing out of the ordinary. Mirrors were few and far between, but he resolved to stop when he passed by a calm pond and to look down into it. He'd often thought himself a fairly formidable fellow, but more intellectually than physically. Maybe he'd been wrong.

"I don't know whether to thank you or to tell you to go to the ice, holy sir," the tapman said from behind the bar.

"How's that?" Rhavas asked.

"Well, we didn't have a fight, and that's good, on account of it would have torn up the place," the man answered. "But you couldn't have cleared the room any better if you'd tossed a polecat into the middle of it. Can't make any money if there's no people here, now can I?"

"I suppose not," Rhavas admitted. "I can't say I'm too sorry, though, all things considered."

"Didn't figure you could," the tapman said, "seeing as how you were going to be on the bottom end of it."

Monks who battered anyone presuming to disagree with them had featured prominently in several synods. Establishing doctrine by knocking people over the head worked at least as well as doing so through reasoned argument. Rhavas didn't necessarily approve of that, but recognized its reality. He wouldn't have cared for rowdy monks pounding on him, though.

He started to tell the local what a peaceable fellow he was. He couldn't remember the last time he'd been in a brawl. But how many men had he killed since the Khamorth swarmed into Videssos? He couldn't have put a number on it. *And one woman,* he added to himself. *I've killed one woman.*

A man who looked like a farmer come to town to sell asparagus stuck his head into the tavern and blinked a couple of times when he saw Rhavas was the only customer in the place. After blinking, he came in himself. "Looks like I won't have to wait for a cup of wine," he remarked.

"That's the truth, friend. You won't," the tapman told him.

"There. You see? Nothing permanent," Rhavas said.

"A good thing, too," said the man behind the bar.

"It could have been worse," Rhavas said, and the tapman had no idea how right he was.

Rhavas rode out of Develtos with nothing but relief. Neither Garidas nor any of the bruiser's fellow monks troubled him anymore; if they got drunk and quarreled while he was in the town, they did it in some other tavern. But the combination of such aggressive devotion to Phos and such aggressive devotion to Stylianos oppressed him.

He did his best to spend all the coins with Stylianos' face on them. Having them wouldn't be illegal when he came to country that favored Maleinos; their quality was as good as that of the money the legitimate Avtokrator issued. But they might prove embarrassing. He didn't want to give the impression that he favored the rebel.

The road west from Develtos was a real highway. By comparison, all the roads north of the Paristrian Mountains were nothing but rutted tracks. Rhavas understood why, too. The road west from Develtos ran straight to Videssos the city. Those north of the mountains went nowhere in particular. So it looked to a man born and raised in the capital, anyhow.

Before long, he sniffed and wrinkled his nose. He recognized that smell of old corruption; he'd run into it on the other side of the mountains. Here, though, the reek was stronger, which meant the battlefield was bigger. This had to be where Maleinos beat Stylianos. When word of that fight came up to Skopentzana, Rhavas had thought everything would be fine.

He laughed hoarsely. That only showed how foolish he'd been.

Some of the corpses on the field had been tumbled into hasty graves—mounds that grass and shrubs and flowers still covered incompletely. Others lay where they had fallen. Those would be rebels, of course; the victors would have buried their own. No one had bothered with either side's dead horses. Their larger skeletons were more readily visible through the burgeoning new growth than those of men.

Rhavas frowned a little. On the field north of the Paristrians, neither side had buried its dead. What did that mean? Probably that neither side had won anything even close to a victory. They'd killed till they got sick of killing, and then they'd gone away.

"And both sides must have thanked the lord with the great and good mind afterward," Rhavas said. He laughed again, the mirth bitter as wormwood in his mouth. How could anyone with an ounce of sense believe Phos had anything to do with such slaughter? Whatever happened on these fields, it didn't involve goodness.

No, what happened in places like these was surely Skotos' affair, not Phos'. It seemed so obvious to Rhavas now. He marveled that he'd been blind to it for as long as he had. He marveled even more that so many Videssians were blind to it still.

If they came out and examined this field, they wouldn't be, not anymore . . . could they? No one who had seen what was left on a battlefield after the battle was done could possibly believe the lord with the great and good mind controlled everything that went on in the world . . . could he? The mere idea insulted the intelligence . . . didn't it?

Shaking his head at the follies, the foibles, and the self-deluding ignorance of mankind, Rhavas rode on. The battlefield stench lingered in his nostrils for quite some time. A man with a good nose could tell the difference between roasting pork and beef. Could that same man use his good nose to tell rotting soldier from rotting horse? Rhavas wouldn't have been surprised, but had to admit he wasn't connoisseur enough to make the distinction.

The highway didn't carry much traffic. Normally, he thought, any road that led to Videssos the city should have been crowded. But these were not normal times. Fear of rival armies—and probably fear of bandits as well—kept people indoors, or at least off the road.

Most of a day's travel west of Develtos, Rhavas rode up to a checkpoint on the road. It didn't look like much: half a dozen soldiers on horseback off by the side of the highway, with a like number of dismounted archers standing around by the other side. Casually, but not in a way that brooked any argument, one of the horsemen said, "Stop right there, holy sir."

Rhavas realized all the soldiers were more alert than they seemed. He wasn't sure he could curse them fast enough to kill them all before at least one of them shot him. Doing his best to make his voice mild, he asked, "By what right do you stop me?"

"In the name of the Avtokrator," the cavalryman replied. "Answer some questions and you can go on your way."

In the name of which *Avtokrator?* Rhavas wondered. The soldier had made a point of not telling him. He forced himself to nod. "Say on, then."

"Who are you, where are you bound, and where have you been?"

"My name is Koubatzes; as you see, I am a priest." If these were Stylianos' men, as seemed likely, Rhavas didn't want to give his own name. He went on, "I'm from Podandos, in the northeast. I managed to get away from bandits when I came through the mountains, and I am on my way to Videssos the city." He didn't want to say that, but thought the soldier would reckon him a liar if he tried to claim anything else; anyone heading west from Develtos was likely to be bound for the capital.

The horseman frowned. "Any of you boys know much about this Podandos place?" he asked his comrades. To Rhavas' relief, no one spoke up. That could have been awkward. The soldiers' attention swung back to him. "Who is the rightful Avtokrator of the Videssians?"

Now *there* was an interesting question. It was likely these were Stylianos' men, yes, but it wasn't certain. That a wrong answer would be fatal *was* certain, as certain as anything in this world could be. In a peevish voice, Rhavas said, "I don't care." That astonished not just the man questioning him but all the horsemen and foot soldiers. He proceeded to embroider on the theme: "I'll tell you what I do care about, I will. I'll tell you what Podandos cares about. First man who drives off the stinking Khamorth, *he's* the rightful Avtokrator, far as Podandos is concerned. The other fellow? A plague take him."

He waited, hoping that performance was good enough. If it wasn't, he didn't think he could give a better one. "You've got your nerve, don't you?" said the soldier who was doing the talking. "What's your business in Videssos the city?"

"My business? Why, the synod, of course." Rhavas sounded like a man who knew exactly what he was talking about. One synod or another was almost always going on at the capital. If this cavalryman didn't know which one, that just made him an ignorant lout.

The man eyed his companions again. Some of them were smiling. A couple seemed to have trouble not laughing out loud. The horseman waved. "Pass on, priest. And Stylianos will rout out those nomads, just as soon as he finishes winning this war. You can count on it."

"May it be so." Rhavas urged his horse into motion with his knees. He didn't even let his shoulders slump to show how relieved he was. He had the feeling any sign of weakness would bring the soldiers down on him. His back itched, and kept on itching long after he got out of arrow range.

And how many more checkpoints would he have to talk his way past before he got to the capital? Stylianos had won near Imbros, west of here, and presumably still controlled that stretch of territory—Rhavas hadn't heard that Maleinos' men had driven him back from it. But Maleinos ruled in Videssos the city. He would also hold some land beyond the city. His soldiers would be snoopy, too.

I can give them my own name and rank, Rhavas thought. *That's something, anyhow.* But he would have to make certain they were his cousin's men. He didn't want Stylianos' soldiers to seize him and hold him hostage.

He laughed a sour laugh. They wouldn't get much use out of him if they did. Maleinos would tell them to do whatever they pleased, and would go on about his business without losing a moment's sleep. Rhavas hadn't seen his cousin since going off to Skopentzana, of course, and they hadn't been close before that.

Maleinos was a careful, conscientious administrator, but no one had ever accused him of scholarship, and nothing else mattered to Rhavas.

Besides, Rhavas knew it was hard for an Avtokrator to get close to anyone, even—or maybe especially—a family member. So many people were ambitious, the ruler had to assume everybody was. If he didn't, he'd be sorry. Maleinos had trusted Stylianos as far as an Avtokrator could trust a general—and look what that had got him. If he survived the civil war, he would never make that mistake again.

He relied too much on Phos, and on the power of goodness. Slowly, Rhavas nodded to himself. The more he looked at the world, the more the new pattern he'd found seemed true. He nodded again, this time toward the west, toward the capital. Yes, he would have a lot of preaching to do when he got there . . . and plenty of examples to draw on when he did preach.

Up in the northeast, cities were few and far between. Skopent-zana was—or had been—the exception, not the rule. Things were different south of the Paristrian Mountains. Crops were far richer and more abundant here than on the Empire's periphery. And Videssos had ruled these lands for close to a thousand years. Compared to them, the north country was an afterthought.

And Maleinos treated it like one, Rhavas thought grimly. The way he'd pulled garrisons from the towns showed he didn't care if the worst happened—and made it more likely the worst would. And Stylianos was just as bad. Taking men out of the frontier fortifications . . . Videssos would be paying for that for years, if not for centuries.

The long journey Rhavas had made showed how true that was. The short remaining journey he was making showed him how unlikely the Avtokrator was to care. Here, relatively close to Videssos the city, things looked almost normal. This was what Maleinos saw. If Stylianos triumphed, it would be what he saw, too. How likely was either man, comfortably ensconced in the capital, to venture forth and try to set things right? Not very, or so it seemed to Rhavas.

Even if the Avtokrator *did* venture forth, what could he accomplish? How many soldiers had the civil war eaten up? How many had the Khamorth already slain? How many could Videssos put in the field? Enough? Rhavas didn't know. He didn't think his imperial cousin—or, for that matter, the rebel general—did, either.

A peasant weeding in a field waved to Rhavas. He waved back. A blackbird swooped down on a clod of earth the peasant's hoe had thrown aside. The bird flew off with a worm in its beak. The peasant called, "Bless me, holy sir."

Rhavas sighed. He was getting sick of that request. But the peasant was bound to come after him with a hoe if he gave the kind of blessing he really thought fitting. And so, mindful of his own hypocrisy, Rhavas sketched the sun-circle and intoned, "May the lord with the great and good mind watch over you, my son."

The peasant presented arms with the hoe as if it were a foot soldier's pike. "I thank you for your kindness, holy sir," he said, and went back to grubbing out weeds.

Kindness? Rhavas shook his head as he rode away. That wasn't what he would have called it. And yet . . . Didn't a lot of priests feel like hypocrites when they delivered a blessing? They had to know people took sick and died or committed horrible crimes in spite of their well-meant words. They seldom paused to wonder what that might mean. *I have the courage to go where logic leads me*, Rhavas thought.

Going there was one thing. Now he had to persuade others to follow him. He looked toward the capital again. That was why he was on his way.

Quite a few peasants worked in the fields. If they didn't plant and plow and weed and harvest, neither they nor the townsfolk would eat. Because Rhavas saw them, he needed a while to realize he didn't see many cattle or sheep in the meadows. He wondered why not, but he didn't wonder for long. Armies had been marching and countermarching along this highway since the civil war began. Either they'd already eaten or driven off the local livestock or the peasants were hiding it so they wouldn't.

As they would have anywhere, the farmhouses had vegetable plots nearby. Most of the time, the peasants' wives and daughters would have tended them. Rhavas also needed a while to notice he saw next to no women. What he did not see, armies going by would not see, either.

He sadly shook his head. How long would it take for life in the Empire of Videssos to come back to normal once this miserable war finally ended? Over how much of the Empire would it never come back to normal? How could the victorious Avtokrator, whoever he was, hope to expel the Khamorth with the straitened resources he would have at his disposal?

"And they say this is the good god's will," Rhavas murmured scornfully. "They say this is the great test of life." His laugh was all vinegar. "They cannot see what lies in front of them. This is a god at work, yes. But which god is stronger? I am not afraid to face the truth."

He rode through the next town without stopping for the night. Dolikhe was a sorry place, barely big enough to boast a wall, full of people who would have been failures anywhere bigger. By the rundown state of the shops and taverns, a lot of them were failures here.

Stylianos' small garrison seemed to care only about the gates— where the highway came into town and went out again. The soldiers questioned Rhavas, who gave them the same answers as he'd used before at the checkpoint. None of these men seemed to have any trouble understanding why he didn't want to linger here.

"Go on, then, holy sir," one of them said. "By the good god, I wish I was going with you, too."

Rhavas camped for the night in oak woods off the highway. He had bread and cheese. A small stream chuckled through the forest. Its water was sweet and cold. He had no doubt it was healthy.

He made no fire. Flames might draw bandits. Besides, nothing that he ate needed cooking, and the night was mild. Next to some of the nights he'd been through after Skopentzana fell, almost any night south of the Paristrian Mountains was mild. He would have thought this one pleasant even when he lived in Videssos the city, though. Oh, a few mosquitoes whined through the air, but mosquitoes always whined when the weather was warm. He wrapped himself in a blanket and went to sleep.

As he twisted to try to find a position where no pebbles dug into his torso and legs, he remembered how uncomfortable he'd been sleeping in a bedroll when he and the mages from Skopentzana so spectacularly failed to drive the Khamorth away from the city. Now he took it in stride. He took all sorts of things in stride now that he hadn't been able to imagine last Midwinter's Day. One last twist, a grunt of satisfaction, and his eyes closed. In mere minutes, he was snoring.

When he began to dream, it was one of those dreams where he

did not know he was dreaming. Everything seemed perfectly real, perfectly distinct. The landscape was golden, the most beautiful he'd ever seen. A few clouds floated by. He noted without much surprise that they floated by below him, not above. That he was drifting through the air felt as natural as anything else.

Other people—men, women, children—drifted along with him. He took that in stride, too. They were going somewhere. He knew where—knew well enough so he didn't need to call out to anyone else and ask. Even the idea of calling out seemed strange. He wasn't sure he could. But it didn't matter. He wasn't supposed to.

Ahead, something appeared in the goldenness: a thin line leading upward. Even as Rhavas drew closer to it, it grew no wider. He accepted that as readily as anything else. It was part of the way things should be.

He and the others drifting along with him formed themselves into a queue. No one bumped or shoved or elbowed. They all had their places, and they all accepted them. That was as least as remarkable as anything else here, but Rhavas also took it in stride.

Shapes that were not men or women flashed around that never-widening line ahead. Instead of drifting, they truly flew. Some were so bright, they left glowing afterimages on his sight. The others were blacker than midnight, blacker than charcoal, blacker than soot.

A chill ran up Rhavas' spine. Now he knew where he was, and why that line always stayed so narrow. It was the Bridge of the Separator. Those who crossed it attained to paradise, and Phos' shining messengers would escort them thither. But those who fell off . . . For them, Skotos' demons awaited, and so did the eternal ice.

One after another, the assembled souls essayed the Bridge. A few, it seemed to Rhavas, succeeded in the crossing. The demons seized far more, though.

Inexorably, his own time of trial grew ever closer. As it did, panic seized him, panic not only over what would happen to him but also over why he was here at all. *This is where souls are judged*, he yammered frantically, there in the fortress of his mind. *I am no soul! I live! I breathe!*

But he still could not call out. If some cosmic mistake had

been made, only he knew about it. No one else, not the souls drifting forward with him, not the bright messengers, and not the demons out of the darkness, seemed the least bit interested. He might as well have been a merchant trying to persuade tax assessors to lower his required payment without documents to support his claim.

The soul ahead of his stepped onto the Bridge of the Separator. Onward and upward it went, but not for long. Its despairing wail as it tumbled off chilled Rhavas to the marrow. So did the demons' laughter as they bore it away.

And then Rhavas set foot on the Bridge. It seemed infinitely long, infinitely narrow. He swayed. If he stayed where he was, he was lost. He could sense that. To have any hope of crossing it, he had to go ahead.

Go ahead he did. He heard, or thought he heard, encouraging whispers from Phos' messengers. *They* wanted him to pass into paradise. The demons did not whisper. They shouted. They screamed. They cursed. Every sin Rhavas had ever committed dinned in his ears now. And every time a demon named one, Rhavas wobbled on the Bridge. Those encouraging whispers helped steady him, but less and less after each demonic shriek.

Still, he went forward. He tried to go faster, to cross as quickly as he could, so he might get to the other side before all his sins were named. Paradise awaited if he did. He was getting close. . . .

"Ingegerd!" a great black demon roared in a voice like thunder.

Rhavas swayed. His arms flailed. He felt himself tilting. He felt himself . . . falling. How the demons laughed!

He woke . . . in darkness. But before he started screaming, before he started the screams that would last for all eternity, he saw it was not the darkness that accompanied Skotos' ice. It was only the nighttime darkness of the woods, with moonlight and starlight filtering down through the leafy branches overhead.

"Oh," he said: one soft word full of wonder. "A dream. Nothing but a dream."

A mosquito buzzed by his ear. He welcomed the sound, as belonging to this world. He was also glad to be able to hear it above the frightened thudding of his heart. The longer he lay awake, the more the fear subsided. If he was right, if Skotos was stronger than Phos and would triumph at the end of days, wasn't the good god's heaven an illusion anyhow? Sooner or later, by that logic, everyone and everything was going to the ice. And if that was so, what difference did sooner or later really make?

He twisted again, almost the way he'd twisted on the Bridge in his dream. At last, he managed to get away from the little rock that was digging into his hip. He settled toward sleep again.

Even as drowsiness overcame him, though, he remembered how terrified he'd been when he began that endless fall into darkness.

Seeing the sun once more was a relief. Getting back on the road was a relief. He kept going over his dream again and again as he rode west. The more he thought about it, the more convinced he was that he'd interpreted it the right way. Skotos' power was coming. Nothing anybody could do would change that. The dream was both a foretaste and a reminder of it.

The terror? He shrugged and did his best to make light of it. The terror was part of the death throes of his old way of thinking. The sooner he got rid of it, the sooner everyone got rid of it, the better.

That almost made him forget how frightened he'd been. Almost.

A farm boy in a colorless homespun tunic ran across a meadow toward him, calling, "Holy sir! Please stop, holy sir!"

Rhavas reined in. "What is it? What do you want?"

The boy pointed back toward his house. A thin plume of smoke rose from the hearth through the hole in the middle of the thatched roof. "My mother's awful sick, holy sir. Will you pray over her? We don't have a lot of money, but we can give you food for the road."

Before his revelation, Rhavas knew he would have done it. He still had to pretend to be what he had been then. Hoping he didn't sound too reluctant, he nodded. "Lead me to her."

"Just follow me!" The boy dashed back the way he'd come. Rhavas tugged on the reins and led the steppe pony he was riding and the packhorse after him.

A man stood in front of the farmhouse: a bigger, bearded, anxious-looking version of the boy. "The lord with the great and good mind bless you, holy sir!" he said. "Anything you can do for my Rhipsine, I'll get down on my knees and thank you for it."

"No need for that," Rhavas said. "Take me to her."

"Come on, then." The peasant held the door open for him. He ducked inside. The house reminded him of some of the ones in which he'd sheltered on the way down from Skopentzana. No need to fear freezing to death here, though. The man pointed to the woman twisting feebly on the bed. "There she is. She's still breathing, anyway, Phos be praised." He drew the sun-circle over his heart.

"Yes." Rhavas was no healer-priest. Nor was he a physician. He needed to be neither to see at a glance that the woman was desperately ill. When he set his palm on her forehead, he had to fight to keep from jerking it away—she burned with fever. Her pulse was fast and weak and thready. She moaned, but it was only gibberish. She had no idea where she was or who was with her.

"What can you do, holy sir?" the peasant said. "She means everything to me and my lad."

"I do not think a healer can help her now," Rhavas said, and the man groaned as if stabbed. Behind him, the boy started to cry.

Gathering himself, the man asked, "What is there to do, then?"

"I see two choices," Rhavas answered. "You can let her go on as she is, let her go on suffering, or you can ease her pain."

"Knock her over the head like she was a horse with a busted leg?" The peasant made a horrible face. "I couldn't do that. I'd want to drown myself as soon as I did."

"I can," Rhavas said. "It would be very quick, very simple, and then she would be at peace."

"No." The farmer shook his head. "I wanted you to cure her, by Phos, not kill her. What kind of priest are you, anyways?"

That was a better question than the weathered man knew. Rhavas had to hope his face did not betray him. "Have it your way, then," he said, and stalked out of the hut. The peasant's question still burned in his ears. "Curse you all," he muttered under his breath.

The woman had been moaning, the man praying beside her, and the boy still snuffling. Sudden silence slammed down inside the house. Rhavas had been about to remount his Khamorth pony. Instead, he looked in once more. Now the woman lay quiet. Her husband sprawled beside her, equally still. The boy had fallen nearer the door.

Rhavas shrugged. Now they were all at peace. The farmer had asked what kind of priest he was. He couldn't tell the man, so he'd shown him instead. And none of the family would ever need another lesson.

This time, Rhavas did climb onto the steppe pony. He rode away without a backward glance. What were three more bodies behind him? Skopentzana lay on his conscience. *On my head be it*, he'd said, and on his head it was. Ingegerd lay on his conscience, unless she counted as part of Skopentzana. The same applied to Koubatzes. And that priest in Podandos lay on his conscience, too. Tryphon had also wanted to know what kind of priest Rhavas was. Like the peasant and his family, he'd found out. Also like the peasant and his family, he hadn't had and wouldn't have the chance to do anything with what he'd learned.

Wearing the blue robe of a priest of Phos when he no longer believed in the good god's primacy had irked Rhavas. Now, all at once, he laughed. There were spiders that looked like the flowers on and among which they sat. Insects never suspected them till too late. Was it not the same with him?

He came up to yet another checkpoint of Stylianos'. The soldiers there did not seem to want to let him go on. That bothered him not only because it was a nuisance but also because it upset his sense of logic and order. "Why hold me back when so many of your men have let me go forward?" he exclaimed.

"You *say* you've been through other checkpoints," one of the men said.

Rhavas resented being reckoned a liar over such a small thing, especially when he was actually telling the truth. "Look at me!" he said angrily. "Haven't I been traveling for some little while? *Smell* me, if looking at me won't give you clue enough. How could I have come along this highway and *not* gone through a swarm of your miserable checkpoints?"

Stylianos' soldiers muttered among themselves. Finally, with some obvious reluctance, they let him go. "You're not a spy," said the man who'd spoken before. "You wouldn't make such a mouthy nuisance of yourself if you was a spy."

"Were." Rhavas automatically corrected him.

"See what I mean?" The soldier rolled his eyes and jerked a thumb to the west. "Go on. Get out of here."

Thus encouraged, Rhavas did. He found more trees in which

to encamp that evening. Not long after he went off the road, a troop of eastbound horsemen trotted along it. He counted himself lucky that they hadn't seen him.

He didn't know whether he found himself lucky to be falling asleep in the woods again. If he kept dreaming about falling off the Bridge of the Separator . . . No, he didn't want to do that more than once. He hadn't wanted to do it once, in fact.

Because he was so nervous about it, he lay some time awake. But when he did fall asleep, he slept soundly. No dreams troubled him. The next thing he knew, sunbeams sneaking through the branches overhead woke him.

He ate the last of the bread in his saddlebags, then started riding again. Before long, he came upon . . . a checkpoint. He felt like cursing the soldiers there just because they were an annoyance. Then one of their officers asked, "What do you want, priest, coming out of the rebel's territory?"

"You favor Maleinos?" Rhavas said in glad surprise.

"Yes, we do. But what about you?" the horseman growled.

Another officer stirred and stared. "Very holy sir! Don't you know me, very holy sir?"

A lump of ice like Skopentzana winter formed in Rhavas' belly. He nodded jerkily. "Yes, I know you, Himerios."

✦ IX

Himerios and Rhavas rode toward the city of Videssos side by side. To Rhavas' dismay, Himerios had no trouble getting leave from his superior. The other officer just said, "Yes, go on—do what you need to do."

"I know Skopentzana is lost," Himerios said now. "That news came down here some time ago. I had heard you'd got free of the sack, but did not know if it was true. I praise the good god to find it is."

"Er—yes," Rhavas said cautiously. If Himerios already knew he'd got out of Skopentzana, the former garrison commander might also know he'd got out with Ingegerd. He had to watch what he said.

"You will know what happened to my wife . . . ?" By the way Himerios said it, Rhavas couldn't tell if it was statement or question.

Rhavas looked down at the steppe pony's mane. "Yes," he answered, and then, "I am afraid the news is not good. I grieve from the bottom of my heart to have to say this, but it is so."

"Go on," Himerios told him. "I feared it would be so when I saw you ride up alone, but tell me more. Tell me everything you can."

"There is not much I can tell," Rhavas said, and that was true in more ways than he hoped Himerios ever found out. Before he could continue, the sound of hoofbeats behind him made him look back over his shoulder. A couple of men from the troop Himerios had been with were catching up to them. He shrugged to himself. Maybe they had business in the capital, too. He did need to think about what to tell Himerios. The story he'd given Koubatzes wouldn't do. It hadn't done then, in fact. But the jolt of running into the officer dismayed him.

The other riders—not very soldierly looking men, either one of them—came up by Himerios. Rhavas looked a question at him. Himerios nodded. "They're my friends. They can hear whatever you have to say."

"However you like." Rhavas shrugged again. "Ingegerd and I escaped from Skopentzana. We made our way south together for several days." That was all true enough. Rhavas looked over to Himerios to see how he was taking it. Himerios' face showed only intent interest. Rhavas went on, "After we got to Tzamandos, we fell in with some other fugitives—merchants and such—and went south with them."

Himerios nodded once more. "Yes, I had heard that, too. What happened after you joined them, very holy sir?"

How much had Himerios heard? More than Rhavas wished he had, plainly. How much news *had* come down from the north? Naturally, the officer would have looked for anything he could that had to do with Skopentzana, and especially with Ingegerd. Who were his companions? Whoever they were, he didn't mind their listening to what Rhavas had to say.

"We were attacked by Khamorth," Rhavas said—which was true. "We took refuge in a stand of trees." So was that. Then he parted company with the truth. "We got separated in the woods. I managed to escape, but"—he bowed his head in a good counterfeit of sorrow—"I do not know what became of your wife after that."

"No, eh?" Himerios looked not to him but to the two men who'd ridden up after them. With a jolt of dismay, Rhavas realized who—or rather, what—those men had to be: mages tasting the truth of what he said. Ever so slightly, one of them shook his head. Himerios turned. "No, eh?" he repeated, his voice harsher. "Suppose you tell me now what *really* happened, very holy sir."

How much did he already know? Had someone found Ingegerd's body in that farmhouse? No way to tell for certain who had ravished her—it might have been the Khamorth. But if those wizards were listening to make sure Rhavas couldn't lie and get away with it . . . "Curse you," Rhavas said, almost casually, and Himerios fell off his horse.

"Phos!" one of the wizards exclaimed. The other sketched the sun-circle over his heart. The one who'd spoken stared at Rhavas in horror. "You're mad!"

He shook his head. "Not I. I know better than to cling to the weak and the outworn." He focused his will on the mages. "Curse both of you, too."

Their faces twisted in torment, but they did not fall. Koubatzes hadn't, either, not right away. Rhavas was braced for their resistance. As Koubatzes had, they tried to work magic against him. He felt it, but it hindered him no more than cobwebs hinder a man crossing a dark room. He knew his own powers now, far better than he had when he faced off against the Skopentzanan sorcerer.

"Curse you!" he said again. "To the ice with both of you!"

Anguish filled their cries. Rhavas looked back over his shoulder, but they'd gone too far for the men back at Maleinos' checkpoint to hear. It was him against them—and he was stronger and more determined. He cursed them once more, and they, like Himerios, slid from their horses and sprawled in ungainly death.

Rhavas had left Koubatzes where he lay, dead in the snow. He couldn't do that here: this road would be used again, and soon. Dismounting, he dragged the bodies behind some bushes. Even that wouldn't do for long; their stench would soon give them away. But he would be long gone by then—and how could one priest slay a stalwart officer and a pair of wizards? For that matter, why would a priest want to do such a savage, senseless thing?

"He has his reasons," Rhavas muttered. "Oh, yes. He does indeed."

He led the other horses for two or three miles. A soldier coming the other way along the road gave him a curious look, but said nothing. Rhavas almost struck him dead, too, but in the end refrained. One more death on this highway would say where the trouble was going.

When Rhavas spied horses grazing in a meadow, he stripped the saddles and reins from the animals he led and let them go mingle with the others. He did not think the man who tended those beasts would mind suddenly acquiring three new ones. Whoever the fellow was, he wouldn't even have to look them in the mouth.

It's over, Rhavas thought as he rode on. *I dreaded it, and it's over.* Everything seemed so very simple, so wonderfully simple. But then Rhavas realized it was not over, and it was not simple, either. He had left bodies behind him. Someone would remember Himerios had ridden off with a priest. Someone would very definitely remember two mages had ridden after them. When none of those people returned or sent word of their whereabouts . . .

No, it was far from over.

Plucking at his beard, Rhavas kept on toward Videssos the city. How was he supposed to show the Empire—show the world—what needed showing without leaving this trail of corpses in his wake? Of course, the corpses were part of the point, but he didn't think the people with whom he'd be talking would appreciate that.

But what can I do about it? he wondered. Himerios, not unnaturally, had hounded him over Ingegerd. Now no one was left—no one outside of Halogaland, anyhow—to dog him about her. But plenty of people would worry about an imperial officer. Maleinos himself might do that. And those two wizards . . . Rhavas hadn't even learned their names. He'd just overpowered them and slain them.

And that was not something the ordinary priest of Phos, or even the ordinary prelate, either would or could do. People would worry about the wizards, too. Rhavas wished he hadn't killed them. Like a lot of wishes, that one came too late to do him any good.

What will I say when I get to the capital? he thought. *Would I do better simply trying to disappear?*

Stubbornly, he shook his head. He remained convinced he had found the truth. Like any Videssian convinced of the truth, he was also convinced the rest of the world needed to know it and to adopt it. The only way he could make that happen was through the ecclesiastical hierarchy.

I will persuade them, he told himself. *I will persuade them, or they will die in my trying.*

Here close to Videssos the city, refugees crowded every town, every inn. Some were those who, like Rhavas, had been lucky enough to escape from the far northeast. He even came across a couple of Skopentzanans, though none who had worshiped regularly at the chief temple in the fallen town.

Most of the fugitives, however, had started their flight south of the Paristrian Mountains. The fighting between Maleinos and Stylianos seemed to have dislodged even more peasants and townsfolk than the barbarian invasions had. Rhavas gradually realized that what he saw didn't have to be the same as what was so. Many of those who'd fled from the northlands hadn't lived to fill the inns near the capital.

Survivors were not shy about saying what they thought. "You ask me, Skotos is running the show these days," declared a man missing most of his left ear. He didn't bother spitting after the dark god's name, either.

One of his friends hissed a warning. "Shut up, you fool! Don't you see there's a priest in the taproom?" he added.

The man with the mutilated ear only shrugged. "So what? What can he do to me that hasn't already happened?"

"You don't want to find out," his friend said. Had Rhavas kept his own orthodoxy, the fellow would have been right. As things were, he exclaimed, "Now you've done it, you silly bugger! Here he comes!"

"Let him." By the way the one-eared man spoke, he'd already taken a lot of wine onboard. "I'm not afraid."

"So you think Skotos is stronger than the lord with the great and good mind, do you?" Rhavas rumbled in his most forbidding tones.

"What if I do?" The man stuck out his chin in defiance.

"Do you not know that the holy scriptures say otherwise?" Rhavas demanded.

"What if they do?" The man in the tavern plainly wasn't long on rhetoric. But he continued, "Maybe Phos had the lead when they wrote the scriptures, but it sure looks to me like Skotos is ahead now."

Several people spat in rejection of the dark god. For his part, Rhavas stood irresolute. Here was a man who agreed with him. If he said as much, everyone in here would remember him to the end of time. When Maleinos' men came looking for the priest who might have had something to do with the deaths of Himerios and two wizards and they heard about a priest spouting blackest heresy, they wouldn't need to be geniuses to see there might be a connection.

But if he kept silent, wasn't he yielding to Phos' stifling orthodoxy by default? He and this chance-met stranger shared the same belief. How could he hide it? Slowly, he said, "I have come a long way—all the way from the far northeast. I have seen a great many atrocities, some from the Khamorth, others worked by Videssian against Videssian. These are sorry times indeed."

"And you're going to tell me I'm a heretic anyway," the man said bitterly. "Well, futter you, blue-robe!"

Rhavas shook his head. "No. I was going to tell you I agree with you. Skotos is the stronger of the two gods. No one looking at affairs of the world, affairs of the Empire, today could possibly disagree without being either blind or a fool."

The man who'd also proposed that Skotos was stronger stared at Rhavas as if he couldn't believe his ears. So did everyone else in the tavern. Eyes widened. Jaws dropped. Several men sketched Phos' sun-circle. "Heresy!" somebody exclaimed. "Heresy from a priest! We're in more trouble than I thought."

"I don't know," somebody else said. "When you look at everything that's gone wrong lately, it makes more sense than you wish it did."

"Liar! You're a heretic yourself!"

Heretic or not, the man accused of misbelief punched his accuser in the nose. That set off everybody in the tavern, like a torch flung into oil-soaked wood. People screamed at one another. They punched and kicked and bit. They hit each other with cups and then with jars of wine. The tapman let out a theatrical howl of dismay. No one paid any attention to him.

Someone stomped on Rhavas' foot. He yelled in pain. Someone yelled, "Infamous, shameless heretic!" and hit him in the stomach. He doubled over—which might have been lucky for him, because a hurled winecup just grazed the top of his scalp. If he'd been fully upright, it would have caught him in the face.

He lashed out with a foot against the man who'd hit him. He didn't quite make the fellow into a eunuch, but he didn't miss by much. The follower of orthodoxy let out a horrible shriek and fell to the floor, clutching at himself.

A knife flashed not far away. Rhavas pointed at the man holding it, who was howling out a hymn. The man's eyes glazed. The knife dropped from his hand. He slid to the floor. In the chaos, no one noticed—or cared—he was dead.

Rhavas looked around for the fellow who'd had the courage to proclaim his allegiance to Skotos. He didn't see him. Either the man had already escaped or the orthodox had brought him down. Whichever was true, Rhavas had to get away himself if he could.

It wasn't easy. With his blue robe and his shaved head, he was a target for all of Phos' followers in the tavern. He picked up a stool and swung it like a scythe, clearing a path to the doorway.

"What sort of madness is going on in there?" A crowd had already gathered outside the tavern, too, drawn by the fearful, fearsome racket inside.

"It is a riot of sinners and misbelievers," Rhavas answered. And if the crowd out there judged who misbelieved differently from the way *he* judged, he did not intend to make any detailed commentary.

A man in a torn tunic staggered out of the tavern door after Rhavas and aimed an index finger at him as if it were an arrow. "There's the heretic!" the man cried.

"Liar!" Rhavas shouted, and threw the stool in the man's face. With a groan, the fellow crumpled. Rhavas nodded to the men and women on the street. "You see how it is?"

"The nerve of that rogue, to call a priest a heretic!" a woman exclaimed. Heads bobbed up and down, there in the crowd.

Another man, this one with blood running down his face from a cut over his left eye, lurched out of the taproom. He could still see out of his right eye, and glared at Rhavas. "Skotos-lover!" he screamed.

"To the ice with you!" That wasn't Rhavas—it was one of the men in the crowd. He ran forward and punched the bleeding man in the face. The fellow with the cut on his forehead was made of stern stuff. He grappled with his new opponent, threw him down, and kicked him in the ribs.

Two other men from the street tackled the bleeding man, stretched him out in the dirt, and started kicking *him*. Someone else came out of the tavern and tried to rescue his friend. That really started the brawl in the street.

Rhavas didn't laugh, not out loud. But it was funny just the same. The people on the street and most of the people inside the tavern were on the same side. They didn't know it, though, and they lit into one another too ferociously to give either group the chance to find out.

After spending a little while watching the chaos he'd helped spawn, Rhavas went back to the stables. He planned to tell the attendants that he'd decided to lodge somewhere else. He found nobody to tell, though. The stable boys and hostlers had all rushed up to join the fighting. Rhavas rode away.

Instead of choosing another inn, he rode out of town. He was too likely to be recognized and remembered if he stayed. He'd ridden for a bit before realizing he was likely to be remembered even after he left.

Too late to worry about that now. He had to hope the Avtokrator's backers would soon have more urgent things on their minds than a priest around whom strange suspicions accrued. It was spring. The campaigning season was about to begin. Maleinos' men would be on the move. So would Stylianos'. And so would the invading Khamorth.

With all that going on, who could get too excited about one priest? Nobody—or so Rhavas hoped.

Villages, towns, and fair-sized cities clustered ever more closely together as Rhavas neared Videssos the city. More people were on the road in that populous, relatively secure part of the Empire, too. Rhavas had no trouble losing himself in the crowds. He rode on in high spirits. He'd escaped, and the capital awaited him.

No one challenged him when he got to the next town. He was just another priest there, nobody to get excited about. By now, he was far enough inside Maleinos' territory that no one even thought he might have come from Stylianos', let alone the rude northeast. His accent played no small part there. Even after so many years in Skopentzana, he still talked like what he was: a native of Videssos the city. And Videssos the city still belonged to Maleinos.

"Hello, holy sir," an innkeeper said when Rhavas stuck his head into the man's establishment. "Looking for a meal and a bed?"

"And a cup of wine," Rhavas answered.

The fellow smiled and put his hand on a dipper that would go down into a big jar of wine set under the bar. "Well, I think we just might be able to arrange something along those lines."

"Good." Rhavas came in. The taproom wasn't too crowded. That was a point in its favor. Nobody in it was arguing theology right this minute, either. That was another point, though Rhavas didn't know how long the lull would last—even in a small, nondescript town like this, you never could tell.

No barmaid took his order, but a downy-cheeked youth who looked a lot like the innkeeper. The youth brought him wine and bread and cheese and then left him alone—something not every server had the wit to do.

As Rhavas ate, he pored over the grimoire he'd taken from Koubatzes. The more he learned, the better off he would be. For one thing, he wanted to be able to do more than simply curse people and watch them fall over dead. Archers used different kinds of arrowheads, depending on whether they were after birds or deer or men in mail. The more different weapons he could use, the less he would have to rely on the single brutal one.

And neither Koubatzes nor the mages who'd ridden up to join Himerios had fallen over dead as fast as he'd wished they would. They'd had some kind of defense against his weapon. It hadn't saved them, but it might have if they'd been better prepared—or if they'd been stronger sorcerers.

He couldn't guarantee he wouldn't run into a wizard like that. He flipped through the parchment pages of the codex, looking for warding spells and for what to do about them.

As usual with Koubatzes' grimoire, Rhavas had to try to piece together the things the mage wasn't saying and add them to those he was. Koubatzes had been a man of considerable sorcerous knowledge. He'd known enough to take a lot for granted. That made things harder for an inexperienced would-be mage like Rhavas to follow.

"Excuse me, holy sir, but would you like a lamp for your table?" the innkeeper's son asked. "It's getting dark out."

"Why, so it is," said Rhavas, who'd been putting his nose ever closer to the pages. He got to his feet. "Why don't you take me to my room instead, and give me the lamp there?"

"I'd be glad to," the youth said, and he did.

The room—hardly more than a cubicle—was what Rhavas had expected. It had the usual bed, stool, chest, pitcher, basin, and—under the bed—the usual chamber pot. If smaller than most of the rooms in which he'd slept lately, it was also cleaner than most.

Back in Skopentzana, Rhavas would have lit as many candles and lamps and torches as he pleased. Even then, reading after sunset hadn't been pleasant. By the feeble light of one oil lamp, it proved impossible.

All at once, he laughed at himself. If he couldn't make light, what kind of wizard was he? He remembered a charm early in the grimoire for doing exactly that—and when he remembered something, he remembered it completely and accurately.

One of the things he remembered was that the spell called on Phos. His lip curled. Fixing that would be easy enough. The spell as Koubatzes had written it suited the mage's ignorance. Rhavas, convinced he knew better, intended to revise the cantrip to focus it on the real chief power in the world.

He began to chant. At the appropriate times, he substituted Skotos' name for that of the good god. He held his hand out over the grimoire, so that light could flow from it once he finished the incantation—and that moment was fast approaching. "Let it be accomplished!" he declared.

Darkness flowed out from his hand.

He had always thought of darkness as a mere absence of light, something to be dispelled by sun or moon or torch or lamp or candle. He had thought that way—but now he found himself mistaken. The darkness his spell called up swallowed the lamplight, swallowed whatever moonlight and torchlight came in through the shuttered windows, and left him in night absolute. For all that he could see, his eyes might have been plucked from his head.

No, that wasn't true—he did see one thing. He saw the mistake he had made: if he wanted light, he should not have called on the dark god to produce it.

He wondered if this palpable, aggressive darkness held sway in his room alone or if it somehow spilled out and covered the whole inn, the whole town, the whole Empire. What had he done? After a moment, he realized he heard no screams of terror and dread, so the darkness seemed his alone. That was something, if only a small something.

He began the spell again, this time exactly as it was written in the grimoire. He had no idea what he would have done if he hadn't had it memorized. Either stayed blind forever or gone to a mage and confessed what he'd done, he supposed. In that case, the last light he saw would have been that from the flames consuming him for heresy.

"Let it be accomplished!" he said again, and hoped *something*, at any rate, would be accomplished. And something was. Light returned to the chamber: lamplight and what little filtered in through the shutters. He breathed a sigh of relief. He had, at least, managed to cancel what he'd done.

Now . . . Would repeating the spell the right way give him the light he'd craved from the beginning? He yawned. A day's travel and the magic he'd already worked had taken too much out of him. He closed the grimoire, lay down on the bed, and blew out the lamp.

Darkness descended again, but not darkness absolute, not darkness impenetrable. He could still make out the spaces between the slats of the shutters. A little light came in under the bottom of the door. Normally, he might not even have noticed it. Now, though, every tiny scrap of light seemed precious.

Rhavas closed his eyes. Even that darkness was less inky, less pitchy, than what he'd conjured up. He knew there was light on the other side of his eyelids. Before, it might have vanished from the universe. Knowing it would be there when he woke up helped him drop off.

And when morning came, he *did* know it. Knowing it felt good, too. He went downstairs to breakfast in a distinctly happy mood.

He got happier when no one else spooning up barley porridge and drinking the day's first cup of wine complained of going blind for a little while the night before. He hadn't *thought* the miscast spell went beyond his own room, but being proved right came as a relief.

The stable boys had groomed his Khamorth ponies till they looked as fine as they could—which wasn't very. No, they weren't much to see when set alongside the horses Videssos bred. But looks didn't matter so much to Rhavas. He'd seen that the steppe ponies could keep going long after bigger, handsomer horses would have foundered.

When he rode out the south gate, the guards there asked his blessing. He gave it, and wondered whether it would do them the good they'd hoped or turn on them the way his spell had turned on him when he substituted the dark god's name for that of the lord with the great and good mind. He shrugged. Again, he would be gone before he could find out.

Farmers and herdsmen waved to him as he rode by. He waved back—why not? Every so often, he would turn and look northeast over his shoulder. No, no sign of anyone coming after him. He smiled. Either they hadn't found Himerios and the wizards yet or they hadn't figured out he had anything to do with their untimely demises. The same also seemed to hold true for the man he'd felled in the tavern brawl.

It was funny, in a way. He represented a greater threat to long-established Videssian customs than even the civil war between his cousin and Stylianos. No one but himself knew it, though, or cared.

Threats . . .

For a long moment, he paid no attention to the horsemen letting their mounts graze in the middle of a broad meadow. He was looking ahead toward the Long Walls. He couldn't see them yet, but he knew they couldn't be far. And after the Long Walls, Videssos the city.

But those horsemen . . . They weren't Videssians. They were Khamorth, in the nomads' usual furs and leathers. They rode the same sort of shaggy ponies as Rhavas did himself. They made no move toward him. It didn't look as if they were there to murder or to plunder. They were just . . . there, as wild animals might have been . . . there. But they were no wolves or ravens. They were men.

And they'd got through and behind all the imperial defenses as if those defenses not only didn't matter but didn't exist. Rhavas had heard people say the nomads roamed close to the capital. He hadn't believed it, not till now—any more than he'd believed Skotos was more powerful than Phos till now. In both cases, though, what he saw made him change his mind.

He thought about cursing the plainsmen, but what was the point? More he couldn't see would be close by. If these stayed where they were, sooner or later soldiers or even assembled peasants would drive them off. Shaking his head at the sorry state of the Empire, he kept riding.

For that matter, the Khamorth saw that evil was more powerful than good. Maybe that made them closer to him than he'd thought. Maybe it made them closer to him than most of his own countrymen were. There was a truly dispiriting thought.

"I can show Videssos the truth," he said, as if someone had denied it. "I can show the temples the truth."

Before too long, a troop of horsemen in jingling mailshirts under blue surcoats trotted up the road past him. He wondered if the Khamorth still rested in the field. If they did, the imperial cavalry would make them sorry. But the nomads had already made the Empire much sorrier. And Rhavas didn't think that would end any time soon.

When Rhavas rode up to a gateway in the Long Walls, his heart hammered in apprehension. If his name and description had got there ahead of him, the guards might try to seize him. They might even have a sorcerer with them, a man strong enough to help them lay hands on him.

If he was going to get to Videssos the city, though, he would have to run this gauntlet sooner or later. Sooner, he judged, was better. The longer he waited, the longer word about him could spread.

A sentry sketched the sun-sign over his heart. "Good morning, holy sir," he said as Rhavas rode up. "Where are you from, and where are you bound?"

"Phos' blessings upon you," Rhavas said, savoring his own hypocrisy as he too drew the sun-circle. "I was lucky enough to escape from the far northeast, and plan on returning to Videssos the city."

"You've been on the road a long time, then," the guard remarked.

"Oh, by the good god, haven't I just!" Rhavas answered.

Not only was that true, it made the gate guard laugh, as Rhavas had hoped it would. The fellow said, "You were lucky to come through all the trouble along your way, too."

"Yes, I know I was," Rhavas said, more soberly this time. "The lord with the great and good mind let me do it, though. I shall thank him as he deserves when I get to the capital." *Just as he deserves*, Rhavas thought.

"I have a question for you first." The sentry swung his pike horizontally across his body to block the way. "Who is the rightful Avtokrator of the Videssians?"

"Why, the Avtokrator Maleinos, of course," Rhavas said without a moment's hesitation. He also believed that to be true.

So, plainly, did the guard at the gate. With a broad grin, he swung up the pike once more. "Pass on, holy sir!"

"My thanks." Rhavas made sure the words didn't sound as if they ought to have *you chucklehead* attached to them. A man of sardonic temperament even before the disasters of the past six months, he didn't find that easy, but he managed.

The country inside the Long Walls—and, indeed, some of the country just on the other side of the Cattle-Crossing as well—counted as suburbs for Videssos the city. Villages and towns clustered thickly. Many on the farms raised fancy fruits and vegetables for the city trade. Here and there stood villas where grandees from the capital maintained country households. Maleinos owned several. Rhavas' family had had one, too, but it lay by the sea and wasn't on his way to Videssos the city. He remembered it fondly.

He remembered everything that had to do with Videssos the city fondly—sometimes a little too fondly. He remembered how hot it got in and around the capital in summertime. In Skopentzana, cool at best and frequently frigid, he'd warmed his hands over those memories more times than he could count.

What he hadn't remembered was that it got muggy when it got hot, and doing anything—or even nothing—on a hot, sticky day quickly turned unpleasant. Sweat streamed off him. The sun beat down on his shaven head with savage force. Now that he thought about it, he remembered a sunburned scalp, too. He wished he could have forgotten.

He'd also remembered how big the capital was, and how many people it held. Skopentzana was a large city, for one out in the provinces, but you could have dropped it into *the* city without making many people notice. And the countryside around Skopentzana was much more thinly populated than that inside the Long Walls.

Now, on his return, Rhavas saw again that there were mixed blessings in what he remembered. Even before he got to the capital, the surrounding suburbs started seeming unpleasantly crowded. People were everywhere. What were they doing? How could it matter, even to them?

One of the things he hadn't recalled was how mercenary they were. He asked a man standing by a fork in the road which was the shorter way to Videssos the city. The man didn't say a word.

He just held out his hand, palm up. He didn't know how close a brush with death he had just then. Fuming, Rhavas gave him a copper—and got his directions.

Something like that never would have happened in Skopentzana. People there wouldn't have expected a reward for anything so small and simple. They would have gone out of their way to help, in fact. Had folk by the capital always been like this? Thinking back on it, Rhavas decided they had. Why would anyone come to Videssos the city or stay there if he didn't have his eye on the main chance?

What would a peasant do if a priest expected payment for a blessing? Fork over? Maybe. But Rhavas thought most of the peasants he'd seen were more likely to break a hoe handle over a greedy cleric's head than to cough up a copper, let alone give over gold.

Toward evening, another peasant called to him as he rode by: "Want supper and a bed here, holy sir? Better and cheaper than what you'd get in town."

That, now, that was legitimate business. Rhavas swung his horse toward the man. "I thank you very much, and I'll take you up on it."

The peasant hadn't been lying. His plump wife served up a fine chicken stew. He had a son whose beard was just beginning to sprout and a daughter a year or two younger than that. People told jokes about peasants' daughters. Rhavas wondered if any of them were true. Eyeing her, he didn't think so—not in her case, anyhow. *Too bad*, he thought.

Were he a more accomplished wizard, he might have brought her to his bed while the rest of the family slept. He might have arranged it so she either didn't remember what had happened or liked it—was made to like it—so well she never told her kinsfolk. He might have . . . but he didn't know how. That grimoire of Koubatzes' would repay more study.

As things were, he tried to take a spot near the hearth and leave the peasant family to their beds. They wouldn't hear of it. The young man curled up on the floor by the fire. Rhavas slept in his bed. It *was* more comfortable than what he was likely to have got at an inn, just as the stew made a better supper than most inns would have served up.

Next morning, the peasants woke at dawn. Rhavas wasn't far

behind them, not because they were noisy but because only the very wealthy and the very degenerate stayed in bed for long after the sun came up. Daylight was for living; lamps couldn't really push darkness back far enough to make a proper substitute.

"Thank you kindly, holy sir," the farmer said when Rhavas paid the scot. "We enjoyed having you here, and that's the truth. Would you be kind enough to set a blessing on us, too, before you ride away?"

Rhavas looked up to the heavens. "Give these generous people what they truly deserve, and may they truly deserve well of you," he said, a prayer that did not name Phos. He finished with the usual, "So may it be," and hoped the farmer and his family wouldn't notice what was missing.

Luck—or perhaps some power—was with him, for they did not. Maybe they so expected to hear Phos' name, they thought they did even when they didn't. That made as much sense to him as anything else.

He swung up into the saddle and rode away. As he did, the farmer of the farm family headed for the fields, a hoe on his shoulder like a foot soldier's spear. The son went to the barn to tend the livestock. The mother walked back into the farmhouse to start the day's baking and washing and spinning and weaving. The pretty daughter went down on her hands and knees in the vegetable plot by the house and began weeding.

Rhavas sighed. *So many better things she might be doing,* he thought. In his mind, the better things were all lewd. He sighed again, at the waste. But he shrugged and kept on riding. It wasn't as if she were the only pretty girl ever born. He would find plenty more—he was sure of that.

Thus heartened, he rode on for most of the morning. He didn't suppose he should have been surprised when his thoughts came back to Ingegerd, but somehow he was. She hadn't been a pretty girl; she'd been a beautiful woman. She'd admired him and trusted him—and what had it got her? Ravaged at his hands; slain by his curse.

He wondered if her death was part of the curse he'd called down on his own head. Did it count as part of the fall of Skopentzana? It certainly sprang from that fall. He'd never dreamt the Khamorth would get into the city. He'd never dreamt one of the peasants he'd helped to stay in the city would open it to the barbarians.

No matter what he'd dreamt, though, the black hour had come, and he'd made it his responsibility.

Here under the warm southern sun, he shivered as if caught in a Skopentzana blizzard. He'd cursed others, and they'd fallen. There stood a shepherd watching his sheep and lambs. *If I point a finger at him, he dies*, Rhavas thought. Beyond a doubt, that was true. But he had pointed at himself, up there in Skopentzana. He still lived. He still breathed. Even though he did, he could not believe—however much he wished he could—that he would escape unscathed.

Here came a merchant riding a swaybacked horse and leading three donkeys with thick canvas sacks lashed onto their backs. "May the good god bless you, holy sir," he said as he went by.

"The same to you," Rhavas replied. Up in the north—and, for that matter, in the westlands, too—traders commonly grouped themselves into caravans and hired guards to keep themselves safe from bandits and raiding barbarians. Here, close to the capital, this fellow felt safe enough to travel on his own.

Ideally, that should have been the way things worked all through the Empire. If the civil war and the Khamorth invasions went on much longer, it might not be true anywhere—Rhavas remembered all too well the pair of barbarians in the middle of the meadow not far north of here. They would cheerfully despoil this fellow here, and even more cheerfully murder him.

Slowly, Rhavas nodded to himself. Was that not yet another sign of what he'd first seen up in the north? Was a new might not rising in the land? If Phos had been the leading power, as so many theologians had believed for so long, he was no more. So it seemed to Rhavas, at any rate, and so he intended to show the whole world.

Being so close to the capital, he hurried toward it like a lover hurrying to his beloved—not a priestly comparison, perhaps, but not an inapt one, either. Scribblers wrote romances that largely consisted of the roadblocks fate and villains put in the way of a lover hurrying to his beloved. Rhavas had always looked down his long nose at romances; they were frivolous, and he'd never had time for frivolity.

Now, though, fate seemed to be putting obstacles in *his* way. When he stopped in a town achingly close to Videssos the city, he found himself waylaid by a local priest. He couldn't even tell the man to go to the ice and leave him alone, not without stirring up scandal; he'd taken his vows together with Arotras.

"By the good god, Rhavas, is that really you?" Arotras exclaimed when he saw Rhavas buying some sausages from a man in the market square.

Rhavas needed longer to recognize his old friend than Arotras had to know him. The other man had a big, comfortable belly, a much rounder face than he'd owned all those years before, and a beard that tumbled in gray waves past his chins and down his chest.

But his voice rang a bell. That hadn't changed so much. "Arotras!" Rhavas said. They embraced: the man who'd kept his faith and the man who'd seen his change.

"You were up—somewhere in the north," Arotras said. Rhavas hid his annoyance: to a man who'd never gone far from Videssos the city, even a town as important as Skopentzana was nothing but a part of the distant, trackless wilderness, and not such a big part, either. Arotras went on, "Phos, you must have needed a wagonload of miracles just to get down here in one piece!"

"Well, so I did," Rhavas allowed. If he didn't think those miracles came from Phos, Arotras didn't need to know that.

His old friend took him by the arm. "Come on, then. You're not going to disappear into Videssos the city—you can't fool me; I know where you must be bound—without sitting down and drinking with me and telling me your story. Come on, I say! I don't aim to take no for an answer."

The only way Rhavas could have detached himself was by making Arotras fall over dead in the street. He didn't want to do that. He didn't suppose he wanted to do that, anyhow. And so he let the priest steer him into a tavern and order wine for him. Along with the wine, Arotras ordered olives and pickled asparagus and almonds and a honey cake topped with candied apricots. By the way he and the taverner chaffed each other, he came in here often.

"You live well," Rhavas remarked.

"Not too bad," Arotras said. "No, not too. I can't screw, but there's nothing in the holy laws that says I can't stuff myself." He ate one of the asparagus stalks, then popped an olive into his mouth and spat the pit on the floor.

Priests were supposed to control all fleshly impulses, not just sensual lust. Rhavas was in a poor position to criticize Arotras, though. He ate an olive himself, savoring the rich, vinegary brine. "How have things been down here?" he inquired.

Arotras raised a bushy eyebrows. "I thought you'd rip me up one side and down the other for letting myself run to fat," he said. "You were always like that in the old days—not an ounce of give anywhere."

"I still am," Rhavas said. "But if you don't think I've seen worse things than a fat priest lately, you're wrong."

"Well, I believe *that*," Arotras admitted. "You asked how things were? They're bad. I suppose they're worse up north, with the barbarians running everywhere, but they're pretty cursed rotten here, too."

"It's . . . not good up there," Rhavas said. "Skopentzana—the place is dead, I think, and I doubt it will come back to life. The Khamorth were sacking it when an earthquake knocked it flat." He didn't tell Arotras he'd had anything to do with either of those disasters.

The other priest clucked sympathetically. "You were lucky to get away with a whole skin. We'd heard something about all this here, but you know how news is when it's come a long way. Who can tell what to believe and what not to, especially when you hear four different stories?"

"I certainly do know," Rhavas said. "With news from the north, though, it's pretty simple: the worse things sound, the more likely they are to be true."

"That's a bad business. It's what I was afraid of, but it's a very bad business." Arotras waved for more wine. When the tapman filled his cup again, he raised his hands to the heavens and spat on the floor. Then, in a low voice, he went on, "Things are just about as bad down here. The civil war goes back and forth. The soldiers slaughter each other and plunder the peasants. I tell you, Rhavas, it's enough to make you wonder whether Phos is looking the other way."

Rhavas stared at him in astonishment. That a priest of Phos should say such a thing—and to another priest! Rhavas himself had had such thoughts, of course, but he hadn't dreamt anyone else had.

Arotras turned red. "I knew I shouldn't have told you anything like that," he muttered, misunderstanding why Rhavas was amazed.

"You always took to doctrine the way ducks take to water. If you want to flay the hide off me now, you can go ahead and do it."

If Rhavas spoke in the right ears in Videssos the city, he could do worse than that. He and Arotras undoubtedly both knew it. He could cost the other priest his place here. He could have him tortured for heresy, maybe even for apostasy, and exiled to Prista, the lonely outpost across the Videssian Sea from which the Empire kept an uneasy eye on the Pardrayan steppe.

Much good that did us, Rhavas thought bitterly. But Prista was far from the border between the Empire and the nomads. No one there could have known of the frontier disaster till too late.

Now he had to think about what Arotras had said. He picked his own words with care: "As it happens, some of the things I have seen have also made me wonder about what the lord with the great and good mind is doing—and whether he is doing anything at all."

"You?" Arotras sounded as if he couldn't believe his ears. "Forgive me for saying so, very holy sir, but you are perhaps the last person from whom I would have expected to hear that."

Rhavas shrugged. "A year ago, I would have said something different. A year ago, I would have thought differently. With what I have seen since then ... A man might reasonably wonder, I believe, who holds the greater power in this world."

He waited. He hadn't said he thought Skotos was mightier than Phos. But even saying there was room to wonder, room to doubt, made him a heretic, subject to anathema and, in the eyes of the ecclesiastical hierarchy, bound for the ice. If Arotras wanted to shout curses at him now, how could he answer—except with curses of his own, curses that would show where the strength lay?

Arotras still eyed him as if unable to believe what he was hearing. "You say this, very holy sir? You, who were always such a pillar of perfect orthodoxy?"

"I say it. I mean it. With what I have seen, the only thing I do not see is how I could say anything else," Rhavas replied. If Arotras shouted of heresy ... well, so what? When Rhavas got to Videssos the city, ecclesiastics far more prominent than Arotras ever dreamt of being would shout the same thing, and shout it louder and more ferociously.

"You sound like a man ... Meaning no offense, Rhavas, but you sound like a man who has lost his faith," the other priest said.

Rhavas shook his head. "I have not lost it. I have had it turned into a new channel. Faith abides. Faith always abides." Some of his earliest lessons also abided, lessons so early he had no conscious memory of them.

Now Arotras looked around nervously and lowered his voice. "Do you say you would sooner reverence . . . him?" He did not name Skotos, but spat on the floor to show whom he meant.

"I have not said anything of the sort," Rhavas told him. "And I have said more than a little, and you not nearly so much. How do *you* feel about these things? What do you think about them, I should say? For it is only through thought that we can hope to come to understanding."

Arotras looked unhappy. He hadn't wanted to be put on the spot. Rhavas had a hard time blaming him for that—who did? But the other priest said, "Answers for answers—only fair, I suppose. How can anyone look at everything that's happened lately and say the lord with the great and good mind surely rules the world and just as surely will triumph at the end of days? Other things"—he spat on the floor once again—"are bound to be going on."

"I agree," Rhavas said crisply. "We have been blind and deaf to this for too long. If we cannot see it after the madness of civil war and the barbarian invasions, though, when will we?"

He'd jolted Arotras again. The other priest glanced fearfully toward Videssos the city. "If we say that there, very holy sir, they will make us sorry we ever opened our mouths."

"I am not afraid," Rhavas said, which overstated the case more than a little. "If we tell them the truth, they will have to see it."

"Nobody has to do anything." Arotras spoke with great and mournful certainty.

"Coward!" Rhavas said scornfully. "I have the truth behind me, and those stodgy ecclesiastics can tell me otherwise until they are blue in the face. They will not persuade me."

"They won't care, either." The other priest sounded even more mournful—and even more certain—than before. "They'll anathematize you, they'll scourge you, they'll excommunicate you, and they'll burn you. That's what happens when they decide you're a heretic—especially when they decide you're *that* kind of heretic."

"They will not do that to me," Rhavas declared.

"You think they won't? You think they won't on account of you're the Avtokrator's cousin?" Arotras was given to repeating himself. "They won't care, not if you're *that* kind of heretic."

He was probably right; Rhavas' family connections alone wouldn't be enough to save him. Rhavas shrugged even so. "Oh, I expect I can find one way or another to persuade them. Will you come with me and help guard my back? The truth needs all the defenders it can find—and we both know what the truth is, don't we?"

Arotras licked his lips. "You must be mad if you think you can persuade people the dark god is stronger than the light one. You'll die, that's what'll happen, and you'll take a long time doing it. I want to live a full life. If you don't, that's *your* business." He shivered theatrically.

"Do you not have the courage of your convictions?" Rhavas demanded.

"I believe what I believe," Arotras said. "I'll tell you something else, too: one of the things I believe is that you're not going to change these people's minds. They're too set in their ways. And besides, they live in the imperial city, and everything is normal there, or as normal as it is anywhere. You might as well try telling them the world is round."

Rhavas had had the one thought himself. He laughed at the absurdity of the other. Every so often, ships would sail east from Kalavria, the easternmost island the Empire owned. None had ever come back. If they hadn't fallen off the edge, what had happened to them? No one had any idea. No ship had ever come out of the east from foreign lands, either.

"You know what I mean," Arotras said defensively. "Converting them won't work. You can't make it work."

"I can. I intend to." Pride rang in Rhavas' voice: the pride of an ecclesiastic who knew what he knew, and also the pride of a scion of the imperial family, a man who knew others would pay attention to him simply because of who he was.

"Well, good fortune go with you," Arotras replied. "If orders come from Videssos the city to stop believing one thing and start believing another, you can be sure that I will. If they don't, I won't, not where it shows. I'm sorry, very holy sir, but I haven't got the stuff of martyrs in me. I like life too well to want to end it, especially that way." He shuddered again.

"No god cares for a lukewarm worshiper," Rhavas warned, but Arotras only shrugged. Rhavas wondered if he ought to curse the other priest. With some regret, he decided not to. If he cursed everyone who was lukewarm, half the Empire would perish. Once he did what he set out to do, Arotras would be free to turn into what he was supposed to be.

Arotras probably had a good idea of what he was thinking. In slightly sullen tones, the plump priest said, "You want to be right more than you want to be safe. I'm sorry, Rhavas, but I've never been that way."

"We *are* right, you and I and those who think as we do—and there are bound to be many of them." As usual, Rhavas spoke with great conviction. "And, because we are right, we have the right—no, we have the *duty*—to bring our truth to everyone in the Empire." Missionary zeal blazed in him.

In him, yes, but not in Arotras. "As I say, good luck to you. I will stay where I am, stay a small man, and try to stay a safe man."

"Follow what is true wherever it leads you," Rhavas said.

"I know what I think," the other priest said unhappily. "And I know what will happen if the wrong people find out what I think. What I don't know is how I ever had the nerve to open my mouth to you." He got to his feet. "I don't know that things will turn out just the way you hope they do. I fear they won't, and I'm sorry for that. I'd better go now." With a shy dip of the head, he scurried out of the tavern.

"You didn't do anything to the holy sir, did you?" the tapman asked. "We like him here. We don't want any trouble for him."

"Neither do I," Rhavas said. "We have the same doctrine. He just doesn't want to follow it as far as I do."

"I don't care about his doctrine," the tapman said, which, if true, came close to making him unique in the history of Videssos. "But he's a good fellow, and I don't want anything bad happening to him."

"I told you—neither do I. And nothing will, nothing that has anything to do with me," Rhavas said.

"It had better not." The tapman ran a damp rag over the polished wood of the bar, giving himself a chance to think. Rhavas had seen that gesture from more tapmen than he could remember. This fellow went on, "Tell you what, holy sir. If you want to, you can spend the night here, and spend it on the house."

The attempt at a bribe was about as subtle as a kick in the teeth. Rhavas thought about saying so, but kept quiet. The tapman was doing what he could, offering what he had to give. "That's very kind of you," Rhavas replied after his moment of thought. "I do believe I'll take you up on it."

"Good. That's good!" The tapman looked relieved. "I thought you looked like a sensible fellow. Is there anything else I can get you while you're here so you'll have a better time?"

Rhavas wasn't about to demand anything a priest wasn't supposed to have—not in so many words he wasn't. He shrugged and said, "Why don't you surprise me?"

"Well, holy sir, I'll see what I can do," the man said. "You just leave everything to me."

He served up a huge bowl of beef-and-barley soup—a supper Rhavas might have had up in Skopentzana, too. The bowl held several bones with lots of rich, fatty marrow inside. Rhavas sucked it out. The tapman only smiled at his slurping noises.

When Rhavas went upstairs, he found his room not much better or worse than others he'd taken at inns across the Empire. He was settling down for the night when someone knocked on the door.

At some of the places he'd been, he wouldn't have opened the door if his life depended on it. This wasn't one of those. When he swung the door open perhaps a palm's breadth—ready to slam it shut in a hurry if he had to—a woman looked back at him from the hallway. "What do you want?" he asked.

She shook her head. "No, holy sir—what do *you* want? Melias said to make you happy, if you felt like that."

"Melias?" Rhavas found himself at sea.

The woman pointed downstairs. "The tapman."

"Oh." With the name and the person joined, things made more sense. "He told you that, did he?"

She nodded. "Can I come in?"

He opened the door wider. She stepped into the room. She was pretty in a haggard way, and had probably been prettier before hard living took its toll. Rhavas asked, "Did he tell you I was a priest?"

She looked at him. "Does it matter? If it matters, you'll throw me out. If you don't throw me out, it doesn't matter."

He'd heard the same cynicism from the first barmaid he bedded. "It doesn't matter, not like that," he said roughly.

"All right, then." She pulled off her long tunic. "Let's get on with it."

When they lay down together, Rhavas learned a few things he hadn't known before. That wasn't because she was anything out of the ordinary, or he didn't think it was, anyway; more that his own experience was still scanty. She didn't take pleasure in it herself, and didn't bother pretending she did. When it was over, he asked, "What do I owe you?"

"Nothing. It's taken care of." She got out of the bed, dressed quickly, and left the room. As her footsteps faded down the hall, Rhavas realized he'd never asked her name. Melias was doing everything he knew how to do to keep Arotras from finding trouble. The tapman might even be able to blackmail Rhavas if he turned on his fellow priest.

Rhavas had never intended to do that. He'd told Melias as much. The man hadn't listened to him—and how often did anyone ever really listen to anyone else? This time, Rhavas had got a fine supper, a room, and a woman because the tapman wouldn't listen. To him, it seemed a good exchange.

He slid toward sleep. He'd almost got there when a sudden thought brought him back to wakefulness. How often *did* anyone ever really listen to anyone else? When he got to Videssos the city, *would* his fellow ecclesiastics pay attention to the new doctrine he brought them?

"Of course they will," he said, there in the silent darkness of his room. "They will have to, because I am right." Thus reassured, he resumed his interrupted journey into slumber.

When he came downstairs the next morning, Melias the tapman gave him a knowing smile and said, "I trust you passed a, mm, pleasant night?"

"Pleasant enough, thanks," Rhavas answered. "I would like half a loaf and some oil and a mug of wine to break my fast, if you'd be so kind."

"Of course." Melias gave him what he asked for, and eyed him as he began to eat. "You're a cool one, aren't you?" the taverner said with what sounded like reluctant respect.

"I try to be," Rhavas answered in his usual matter-of-fact tones. "And I will tell you one other thing: after all I have seen, all I have been through, all I have escaped, what happened last night is not so much of a much."

To his surprise, that made Melias laugh. "All right, holy sir. I think I hear what you're saying. You sound like somebody from Videssos the city talking about any place in the world that *isn't* Videssos the city."

Rhavas laughed in turn. "I suppose I do. And I *am* from Videssos the city, and I do talk about every other place that way."

"I've never known anybody from the capital who didn't," Melias said. "I've been there a few times, and plenty of people who've never set foot outside the walls in their lives talk the same way."

"I wouldn't be surprised." Rhavas finished his breakfast. When he reached for his belt pouch to pay, the tapman waved for him not to bother. Pleased but hardly surprised, he went out to the stable to get his horses. They had oats and hay in their stalls, and they'd been well tended and groomed. Again, Rhavas was pleased without being astonished.

He'd already ridden out of the stable—in fact, he'd already ridden out of the town—before he realized how much for granted he took horsemanship these days. Just after escaping Skopentzana, he'd been a thoroughly indifferent rider. No more. As with anything else, practice brought improvement.

Even with cursing, he thought, and—smoothly—rode on.

Rhavas felt like cheering when he saw the walls of the capital ahead. For a moment, forgetting himself, he felt like offering up a prayer of thanksgiving to Phos. Not altogether happily, he shook his head. He could never do that again, not without hypocrisy.

He'd thought he would be excited to return, after so many years away. And he was, but not in the way he'd expected. Too much had happened to him—and to the Empire. He'd seen too much in the years since he'd gone, and especially in the past year. This didn't feel like a homecoming. Instead, Videssos the city seemed a new place, one he would have to conquer afresh.

It seemed a formidable new place, too. It occupied a triangle of land, two sides surrounded by the sea; the third, the one he faced, protected by the most formidable walls the mind of man could conceive. Videssos the city was the most of one thing or the other in any number of ways. Thanks to the Cattle-Crossing, trade routes running east and west, north and south all converged here. Videssos the city, then, was the richest city in the world, and the largest, and the most ambition-filled. Men from towns like Skopentzana and Amorion came here to see if they could succeed competing against the best and toughest from all over the Empire and beyond. Plenty of people of placid spirit stayed where they were, content to be tall trees in a garden of bushes. Those who wanted to find out how their trunks measured up against the rest of the tall timber came to the capital.

Before, Rhavas' birth and family had shielded him from all that. With his cousin wearing the Avtokrator's red boots, of course he would succeed. He was able; he knew that. But ability wasn't the only thing that had let him rise so swiftly through the ecclesiastical hierarchy. Who he was had counted for even more than what he was.

Things would be different now. Now he would be trying to succeed in spite of what Maleinos believed, not because of it. Now his own ability would count for everything. He had to persuade a hostile world that he knew a truth of which it was ignorant.

"I have to—and I will," he declared, and urged his horse forward.

He rode in through the Silver Gate, the grandest one in all the city. He could not have chosen a lesser entrance. The drawbridge was down, to let people into the capital. Rhavas took that for a good sign: Maleinos didn't fear Stylianos would try to sneak in soldiers, anyhow.

Guards did give everything and everybody a careful once-over. The fellow in front of Rhavas led several donkeys festooned with leather sacks. He had to open them up to show what he was carrying. The guards poked through his woolens—which looked utterly ordinary to Rhavas—as if they expected to find either jewels or weapons to help Stylianos' supporters in the city rise against Maleinos. Discovering neither, they finally let the man go forward.

One of them gave Rhavas a look anything but friendly. "And who in blazes are *you*, holy sir?"

"I am Rhavas, prelate of Skopentzana and cousin to Maleinos, Avtokrator of the Videssians," Rhavas replied. He had decided he wasn't going to sneak into Videssos the city. Maybe people were looking for him by name because of what he'd done to Himerios and the mages. More likely, though, he judged, they were after *a priest from Skopentzana*, or perhaps just *a priest from the north*. And in that case, they would never dream Maleinos' cousin was the man they sought.

He sounded haughty enough to make his claim convincing to the guards. They almost injured themselves coming to stiff, creaking attention. The one who'd scowled at Rhavas shed his toploftiness like a lizard wriggling out of its skin. "Pass on, holy, uh, very holy sir," he said.

Rhavas inclined his head. "Thank you very much," he said, and urged his steppe pony forward. The guards saluted as he rode into Videssos the city.

His horse's hooves and those of the packhorse drummed on the timbers of the drawbridge, then struck more softly when they reached solid ground again. The sun disappeared from the sky. Rhavas traversed a bricked-in tunnel between the outer and inner walls. Men leered down at him from murder holes, ready to rain boiling water or red-hot sand down on attackers. Several portcullises could fall, one at a time or all together, to delay or even halt assailants.

The works protecting Videssos the city were the mightiest men could devise. No foreign foe had ever stormed them. Rhavas doubted a foreign foe ever could. That did not mean the capital had never fallen. Now and again, in civil strife, it had. Not even the strongest fortifications could hold out treachery.

Treachery, Rhavas thought. *The great Videssian sport*. Love of controversy, love of surprises flourished inside the Empire. That being so, betrayal also flourished. No wonder Maleinos' guardsmen so carefully scrutinized a mere merchant's goods.

But who scrutinized the guardsmen? There was the really important question. Rhavas could see as much. No doubt his cousin could, too.

Light at the end of the tunnel . . . At another time, Rhavas would have thought about Phos triumphing over Skotos. In fact, such thoughts did still rise to the surface of his mind. His habits had formed over many years. He could not abandon them in the blink of an eye, no matter how much he wished he could.

He scowled, there in the gloom. If he had trouble changing his own way of thinking, how did he dare hope to persuade others

to change their minds and recognize that Skotos, not Phos, pre-
vailed in the world? Wouldn't simple habit make people go on
believing the way they always had?

His laugh echoed and reechoed along with the clopping of the
horses' hooves. "Let them look around," he said. "If they cannot
see after that, what are they but blind men?"

The more Rhavas looked around, the more obvious it seemed—to
him, anyway. How would it seem to the comfortable ecclesiastics
who'd lived here for years if not for their entire lives? They had
not seen Skopentzana fall. They had not seen men robbed and
murdered, women raped and murdered. They had not seen the
Empire's whole northeast fall to demon-loving savages monstrously
good at war, savages whose sorcery outdid anything the proud
Videssian mages aimed at them.

But I have, he thought, *and I will make them see.*

Part of him wondered why he couldn't just go along with what
everyone else in Videssos believed. But, for one thing, it was only
a small part. If Videssians were given to controversy, they were
also given to the conviction that they were right and they needed
to bring the benighted rest of the world around to their point of
view. And, for another, how many others in the Empire already had
quiet doubts about the way things were? Arotras did. He couldn't
be the only one. Most folk, though, even if they thought such
things, would not have the nerve to say them out loud. Rhavas
had, if nothing else, the courage of his convictions.

They'll burn you, he thought, *or take your head, or maybe,
because you're the Avtokrator's cousin, they'll just exile you to
Prista, where no one will care what you say.*

He laughed again. Not very long before, he'd thought that Videssians loved surprises. Well, he had a few of his own to show the
assembled ecclesiastics and theologians of the Empire. Yes, they
might have a little trouble working their will on him—they just
might. Laughing still, he rode on into the capital.

At the same time, Rhavas remembered Videssos the city very well and had forgotten a great deal about it. He knew that Middle Street ran west from the Silver Gate to the High Temple and the Amphitheater and the palace quarter. He knew the squares through which the capital's chief boulevard would pass. The buildings all seemed familiar to him.

What he'd forgotten were the people. Videssos the city was *much* larger than Skopentzana. Swarms of people packed Middle Street. They shouted and cursed and elbowed, everyone trying to get ahead of everyone else. His tonsure won him no special respect. "Watch where you're going, holy sir!" was one of the kinder things people yelled at him.

Because everybody wanted what he wanted when he wanted it, the jams were even worse than they would have been otherwise. People and wagons thrust out from cross streets when and as they could. If they'd waited for openings, they might have waited forever, or at least till nightfall. Instead, they charged forward and made everyone else wait for them.

From the Silver Gate to the palaces was only a couple of miles. Rhavas needed close to two hours to get where he was going. By the time he did, he was shouting and waving a fist at the idiots all around him as if he'd never been away.

The city's biggest market square, the plaza of Palamas, lay just east of the palace quarter. That let cooks and other servitors get what they needed with the greatest possible convenience. But the square wasn't just for the Avtokrator's staff. Everyone in the capital either bought or sold there—often both.

In rapid succession, men tried to sell Rhavas cabbages, amber beads, pewter spoons, silver spoons, gold spoons, vinegar, wine, rope, lamps, olive oil, onions, fermented fish sauce, and their allegedly beautiful alleged sisters. "No," he said. "No!" he exclaimed. "*No!*" he shouted. But nothing held back the tide of hucksters.

And then, after what seemed like forever, he reached the Milestone, the black stone column from which all distances in the Empire of Videssos were reckoned. The Milestone also had another function: the heads of executed miscreants were displayed there as a warning to others not to do likewise.

When Rhavas had lived in the capital before, the occasional murderer or robber found at least part of his final resting place at the base of the Milestone. But the Empire was at peace then. Now the Milestone seemed like a tree with a great crop of fruit in front of it. And the placards below almost every head on display said, "Traitor."

If so many were traitors—and Rhavas was sure a good many did back Stylianos, which was bound to look like treason to Maleinos—how much were these heads doing to deter treason? Not much, not so far as he could tell. He wondered if his cousin would feel the same after hearing an explanation of that point of view. Converting Maleinos to the worship of Skotos would probably be easier.

Then Rhavas rode into the palace quarter. The hubbub of the plaza of Palamas faded behind him. People who did not belong in this part of the city knew better than to venture in. For the first time since passing through the Silver Gate, Rhavas found himself not trapped in a surging crowd. These paths through lawns and gardens and elegant buildings were quiet, almost deserted.

A man whose hairy arms were white to the elbows with flour—a baker—nodded to Rhavas. "Can I do something for you, holy sir?" he asked—politely, but with the air of a man who needed to like the answer he heard if there wasn't going to be trouble afterward.

"I certainly hope so," Rhavas said. "I am his Majesty's cousin, escaped from the sack of Skopentzana and newly returned to the capital."

The baker's jaw dropped. Whatever he'd expected by way of reply, that wasn't it. "The Avtokrator's . . . cousin?" he said, as if unsure he'd heard correctly.

"That's right." Rhavas gave his name and station.

"I've never heard of you, uh, holy, uh, very holy sir," the baker said. Then he decided he'd better hedge his bets: "That doesn't mean anything, of course. Why don't you, uh, go on to the throne room? They'll know what to do with you there. You know how to find the place?"

"Yes, I know," Rhavas answered, not rising to the challenge. If he didn't know how to get to the throne room, he wasn't likely to be the Avtokrator's cousin. And if he *wasn't* the Avtokrator's cousin, they would know what to do with him—and to him—there. He wouldn't enjoy it, though.

"Here, why don't I come with you anyway?" the baker said.

"All right—why don't you?" Rhavas said agreeably. "You won't get a reward for proving me a fraud, though, because I'm not."

"I didn't say you were." No, the baker wasn't taking any chances with someone who might really turn out to be important.

He also had a little more shrewdness than Rhavas would have guessed. He didn't guide the newcomer to the throne room, but followed Rhavas' lead, his own features carefully blank. If Rhavas didn't know the way, he would betray himself. But he truly did. If the baker was impressed, he didn't show it.

The splendid bronze doors to the throne room were closed. Guards in mail stood in front of them. The men watched impassively as Rhavas dismounted, tied up his horse, and walked over to the base of the stairway. He asked, "Is anyone in the throne room who has served his Majesty since the earliest days of his reign?"

"Who wants to know, and why?" one of the soldiers asked with studied insolence.

Rhavas answered as he had with the baker. The guard lost a good deal of his high-and-mighty air. He put his head together with his comrades. Then he tugged at the handle to one of the doors. It swung smoothly on silent hinges despite its great weight. He ducked inside.

When he came back, he was followed by a dignified, gray-bearded man in a splendid silk robe. Rhavas bowed to the official. "Good day, Markianos," he said. "It's been a long time, eminent sir, hasn't it?"

Some of Markianos' dignity fell away. "It really *is* you, Rhavas!" he exclaimed. "When the guard told me a priest who claimed to be his Majesty's cousin was here, I hardly dared believe it. We learned some time ago of Skopentzana's piteous overthrow. Welcome home, by the good god!" He sketched Phos' sun-sign.

So did Rhavas, as he knew he had to do. "Piteous indeed, however much I wish it were otherwise," he said. "But here I am, home, as you say, at last."

Both the guard and the baker who'd accompanied Rhavas to the throne room stared in amazement. *They* hadn't believed him. Their eyes got even wider when Markianos swept down the stairs and embraced him, saying, "His Majesty will be glad to hear of your arrival. You may be sure of that—every bulwark against the rebel he can find means much to him."

"Yes, I believe that," Rhavas said. "I rode past a couple of battlefields. The smell of death hovers over them even now."

"Times are hard." Markianos paused. "They are, but you have come here, and we should rejoice. Would you have me inform the Avtokrator of your arrival?"

"If you would be so kind, eminent sir." Rhavas bowed again. The rituals of politeness at the imperial court were much more elaborate and much more exacting than anything in Skopentzana. Rhavas hoped he could remember enough not to embarrass himself with some gaffe that would make him out to be a bumpkin, a ruffian, a country cousin in the flesh.

"Well, why don't you come with me, then?" Markianos said. "I believe his Majesty is in the imperial residence right now."

"Should we disturb him?" Rhavas asked. The imperial residence was the only place where the Avtokrator of the Videssians got even a semblance of privacy. Everywhere else he went, he was on display. Had Rhavas been in that predicament, he would have hated it. Judging other men by his own standards, he assumed his cousin hated being on display, too.

But Markianos said, "When he learns you've come home again, he'll be glad to stop whatever he's doing and greet you." He looked sly. "In fact, I expect a reward for bringing him the news."

"You do me too much honor," Rhavas murmured. Markianos shook his head. Rhavas didn't argue with him; what point to it? But whatever reward the courtier got, Rhavas judged he wouldn't keep it, not after the returned ecclesiastic made his theological opinions plain.

Markianos told the guards to see to Rhavas' horses. Rhavas knew that meant one of the guards would go get a groom and then resume his post. That was all right. A groom would do a better job with the steppe ponies than a soldier was likely to.

More guards stood in front of the residence, which was dwarfed by the throne room and the Hall of the Nineteen Couches, the great formal dining hall. Elegant dinners in the capital were eaten reclining. That was a formality much less common in the provinces, and one Rhavas hadn't missed in Skopentzana.

The guards nodded respectfully to Markianos as he went up the low, broad stairs. Rhavas waited below. Markianos pointed down to him, no doubt explaining who he was. The courtier did not presume to enter the residence unaccompanied. One of the guards ducked inside to fetch a chamberlain. The chamberlain, a hook-nosed man with a thick black beard—probably a Vaspurakaner, from the western land constantly disputed between Videssos and Makuran—escorted Markianos inside.

Rhavas stood in the sunshine. It was warm on his shaven skull. After so long in Skopentzana, he did not think he would ever complain about heat and humidity again. He was probably wrong, but that was how he felt now.

"*Is* he?" That voice from the entranceway was familiar. "By the good god, he is! Welcome back, cousin!"

"Your Majesty," Rhavas said. He was not just cousin to Maleinos II, Avtokrator of the Videssians. He was also Maleinos' subject. He had to show the Avtokrator he understood that. He prostrated himself before Maleinos, going down on his knees and then on his belly, knocking his forehead against the ground. "Your Majesty!"

"Rise, rise," Maleinos told him as quickly as ritual allowed. Had the Avtokrator made him grovel there for some time, it would have been a sign of imperial displeasure. As things were, Maleinos hurried down the stairs and embraced him as soon as he was on his feet. Rhavas kissed his cousin on both cheeks. Maleinos returned the greeting in just the same way, another sign that Rhavas was in high favor. "I feared you lost," the Avtokrator said.

"More than a few times, your Majesty, I feared myself lost," Rhavas replied.

"You look—older." Maleinos laughed a sour laugh. "And so do I, worse luck. Fifteen years will do that to you." Actually, Rhavas didn't think his cousin looked fifteen years older. They were close to the same age. Maleinos' beard had about as much gray in it as Rhavas', but his hair was still dark, and had hardly receded at all, even at the temples; Rhavas would have been balding even if he weren't tonsured. Nor was Maleinos' face—a little broader, a little fleshier than Rhavas'—heavily lined. At first glance, the Avtokrator seemed nearer thirty than past forty.

But when you looked at Maleinos' eyes . . . When you looked at his eyes, he seemed closer to sixty. There he had crow's feet, and heavy dark pouches under the lower lids. Being Avtokrator wasn't easy. Being Avtokrator in troubled times had to prove doubly wearing.

"You haven't had it easy lately," Rhavas said, and couldn't help adding, "The Empire hasn't had it easy lately."

"Isn't that the sad and sorry truth!" his cousin exclaimed. "If I could have the last couple of years to do over again . . ." He ruefully shook his head. "Phos doesn't grant wishes like that, however much I wish he did. I don't suppose I can blame him. If he did, he'd stay too busy to tend to anything else."

"No doubt," Rhavas said tonelessly.

Maleinos didn't notice anything wrong with the way he sounded. The Avtokrator slapped him on the back. "Come into the residence with me. Drink some wine. Tell me about your journey. You saw the downfall of Skopentzana?"

"I did, your Majesty," Rhavas replied. "I was in the middle of it, and lucky to get out. I hadn't been out for long before an earthquake, ah, finished the city's overthrow." *Did I summon that earthquake? I didn't believe it then, but I do now.*

"Terrible thing," Maleinos said. "The lord with the great and good mind only knows how we're going to set things right up in the far northeast. I curse Stylianos to Skotos' ice for pulling the garrisons from the frontier forts." He spat between his feet.

So did Rhavas, a beat slower than he might have. Again,

fortunately, the Avtokrator didn't notice. Rhavas said, "It isn't just the far northeast, your Majesty. North of the Paristrian Mountains, the barbarians do as they please."

"Curse Stylianos," Maleinos said again. Unlike Rhavas', his curses had no effect. Rhavas had not seen the rebel general since some time before leaving to become prelate of Skopent-zana. He had no idea where in the Empire Stylianos was. All that being so, he hadn't tried a curse of his own, judging it unlikely to succeed.

His cousin led him up into the imperial residence. Alabaster panels set into the ceiling let in a pale, cool light that gave the corridors the feel almost of being underwater. Hunting mosaics picked out in bright tesserae of stone and gilded glass brightened the floor under his feet.

On tables and on the walls were trophies of past Videssian triumphs: a helmet belonging to a Makuraner King of Kings that Stavrakios had captured when he seized Mashiz, the bow case of a Khamorth chieftain, a pair of huge two-handed swords from Halogaland. Just for a moment, Rhavas thought of Ingegerd, of what might have been, of what should have been. He shook his head. What point to regret now? It was over. It was done. It was as it had been.

On my head be it. He shook that thought aside, too.

Also hanging on the wall was a portrait of Stavrakios: a tough-looking, bandy-legged man who, but for his gilded armor, seemed more like a veteran underofficer than an Avtokrator. Maleinos' eyes flicked toward it, too. He said, "I often wonder what he would do in a mess like this."

"He didn't have to fight a civil war," Rhavas said.

"He didn't know how lucky he was, either," Maleinos said bitterly.

"No doubt you're right, your Majesty," Rhavas said. "If only you could have defeated the rebel quickly—"

Maleinos rounded on him. "Not you, too!" the Avtokrator snarled. "You weren't anywhere close by when his men and mine fought, and you still have the nerve to tell me what I should have done? You were raised in this city, all right. You're as fickle as everybody else who comes from here, too."

Rhavas did the only thing he could: he ate crow. Bowing, he said, "I beg your pardon, your Majesty. I meant no offense; I

swear it." He bowed again, ready to go through a second pros-
tration if he had to.

But his cousin, after scowling for a moment, shook his head
and sighed. "Let it go, Rhavas; let it go. I've had too many people
playing general around me—that's all. It's always easier to brag
afterward about what you would have done than it is to make
sure beforehand that everything works just so."

"I understand." Rhavas understood that pushing it would be a
mistake. He also understood that the Avtokrator, while less successful against Stylianos than he wished he were, was also more
successful than he might have been. People said Stylianos was the
best soldier Videssos had known since Stavrakios' day. Even staying in the field against him was no small achievement. Maleinos,
of course, was unlikely to see things from that point of view.

"Here." The Avtokrator waved Rhavas into a small dining
chamber that looked out on a courtyard full of flowers. A servant
brought a jar of wine and a pair of golden cups. The man poured
for Maleinos and Rhavas, then bowed and silently withdrew.

Both men raised their hands to the heavens. They spat in ritu-
alized rejection of Skotos. Like the chameleon—a lizard common
here but unknown in Skopentzana—Rhavas took his color from
his surroundings. He raised his goblet and drank. The golden
vintage sliding down his throat startled him out of his hypocrisy.
"Thank you, your Majesty!" he exclaimed. "I'd forgotten there
were grapes like this. They don't come up to the north, believe
me. It's like sipping sweet sunshine."

"I like that. You always did know how to turn a phrase."
Maleinos drank, too, and smiled. "You make me enjoy it more on
account of the thoughts you put in my mind. Sweet sunshine—a
pretty conceit." He took another sip and savored it, then leaned
across the small, marble-topped table and got down to business.
"Tell me how Skopentzana fell. Tell me how you escaped. Tell
me what you saw on the way south. You passed through lands
the rebel held, eh?"

"Yes," Rhavas admitted cautiously. Would the Avtokrator blame
him for that?

"Tell me about what you saw there, too," Maleinos said. "Tell
me *all* about that. What are his soldiers like? Is their discipline
good? What about their morale? Do the people seem contented,
or would they rise against him if they saw an excuse?"

"You may or may not know by now that he is minting his own coins, with the claim that he is Avtokrator," Rhavas said.

"I did know that, as a matter of fact," his cousin said grimly. "Well, a son of a whore is still a bastard no matter what he claims to be. But you did well to tell me. For now, on with your tale."

"It will take some time," Rhavas said. *And some selection*, he added, but only to himself.

"I have the time," Maleinos said. "Go on."

Rhavas did. He left out anything that had to do with his curses, and especially with what they might mean. He emphasized the way the Khamorth were spreading over the countryside, adding, "Some of the towns still in Videssian hands when I passed through them likely belong to the barbarians now."

Maleinos growled, down deep in his chest. The noise reminded Rhavas of the sound an angry bear might make. "One day, the lord with the great and good mind willing, I'll find a way to set this right," the Avtokrator ground out.

"I hope you do, your Majesty. North of the mountains, though, Videssian authority has for the most part simply collapsed," Rhavas said. His cousin growled again; Rhavas wasn't sure Maleinos knew he was doing it. He also wasn't sure the Avtokrator understood how complete the collapse was, and how little chance he might have of doing anything about it. Rhavas gave a small mental shrug. Till the civil war ended—if it ever did—neither Maleinos nor Stylianos could do much about the plainsmen's incursions.

When Rhavas got to his journey through the territory Maleinos' imperial rival held, his cousin questioned him sharply about every tiny detail he had seen. Despite his anger at what the Khamorth had done north of the Paristrian Mountains, Maleinos was more interested in Stylianos and his backers. They were closer—and they were Videssians.

At last—not least after mentioning the Khamorth he'd seen in the meadow just outside the Long Walls—Rhavas fell silent. He'd drunk enough wine to lubricate his throat, enough that it also left his head on the edge of spinning.

Maleinos poured his own goblet full. He nodded across the table to Rhavas. "You have a good eye, very holy sir. I remember you always did note the telling detail. The gift, plainly, has grown and not receded since you went north. You are the better for it."

"I thank you, your Majesty. These are hard times for the Empire, as I said before."

"Hard times? Phos!" Maleinos muttered. "We haven't known times like these since . . ." He shook his head. "To the ice with me if we've ever known times like these before. If a quarter of what you say is true, we'll have Skotos' own time reclaiming the far northeast."

"Yes, that may well be so," Rhavas answered cautiously. No, the Avtokrator didn't see the whole picture. Rhavas had no idea how Videssos would reconquer any of the land north of the mountains. The far northeast, up where Skopentzana lay, was only a small part of that.

Maleinos gulped the wine. He filled the goblet yet again, then gulped that, too. Shaking his head, he said, "You will doubtless think me a horrible sinner, cousin, but I tell you straight out there are times when I wonder if Phos hasn't gone to sleep and let Skotos loose in the world." He spat in rejection of the dark got, then let out an embarrassed—and drunken—chuckle. "Now go ahead and scream *Heresy!* at me. It's not like I haven't earned it."

Instead of screaming, Rhavas stared at the man who'd ruled the Empire of Videssos for the past twenty years. "You are not the first man I have heard say such a thing," Rhavas said slowly.

"No, eh?" Maleinos chuckled again. "My bet is, I wouldn't envy the last poor bugger who was dumb enough to open his mouth like that where you could hear. He's probably still sorry he did."

"Your Majesty . . ." Rhavas hesitated. He wished he hadn't poured down so much wine himself; he wanted clear wits for this. The Avtokrator might—*might*—be able to get away with joking about theology. A prelate would have a much harder time of it. Yet if Maleinos could be won over to his cause . . . "Your Majesty, I have wondered about this myself."

There. He'd said it. He waited for the sky to fall, or for Maleinos to shout for the guards and have him thrown out of the imperial residence on his ear. That didn't happen. What did happen was that his cousin the Avtokrator stared at him in turn. "*You* have had this thought, very holy sir?" Maleinos echoed.

"So I have, your Majesty," Rhavas replied.

"I can hardly believe it," Maleinos told him. "Everyone knows you're a pillar of orthodoxy."

"I am not a blind man. I can see what goes on around me. I have to think about what it means," Rhavas said. "If evil prevails, if good falls back . . . What can that possibly mean?"

"It can mean trouble. It will mean trouble. The ecumenical patriarch has declared that it means the lord with the great and good mind is testing our resolve," Maleinos said. "I must tell you, I incline this way myself—in public. To say the other, to maintain it openly, is to invite madness into the Empire."

"Madness is here, whether we invited it or not," Rhavas said. "Shall we pretend nothing has gone wrong in Videssos and everything is the same as it was a couple of years ago?"

"Videssos is already upside down in too many other ways," Maleinos said. "I don't want priests getting unruly and throwing things at each other, too. Stylianos would start screaming that *I* was a heretic, and I can't stand that. I can't afford it, either. Do you understand me?"

"Your Majesty, are we not right to follow the truth wherever it leads?" Rhavas asked stiffly.

The Avtokrator glared at him. "You are trying to cause a scandal." He might have been a father laying down the law to a scapegrace son. Rhavas wouldn't have cared for that tone even from an older man. It really rankled from someone his own age. Oblivious—or maybe just indifferent—to his anger, Maleinos went on, "There will be no theological scandals while I rule here. There most especially will be no theological scandals started by a kinsman of mine while I rule here. Whatever else happens, that had better not. Do I make myself plain enough, cousin?" His voice was heavy with menace.

"You are unmistakably plain, your Majesty," Rhavas answered.

"Good. We'll say no more about it, then." Maleinos was confident he could have his way when and as he chose. Such confidence was part of what being Avtokrator of the Videssians was all about.

And Rhavas did say no more about it . . . then.

Coming back to Videssos the city meant coming back to the High Temple. To Rhavas, that was much more important than coming back to his cousin, though he had the good sense to make sure Maleinos knew nothing of his opinion.

The High Temple's beauty was only part of its appeal. Every

time Rhavas saw its grand—even grandiose—shape shouldering its way over other buildings to dominate the skyline, he sneered at the temple in Skopentzana where he'd served so long. A ridiculous, provincial structure, and one surely downfallen now, to the Khamorth and to the earthquake that had finished the ruination the barbarians had begun.

Just as the temple in Skopentzana had been at the center of Rhavas' life in the far northeast, so the High Temple lay at the center of the ecumenical patriarch's life—and at the center of theological life for the whole Empire. Maleinos granted Rhavas quarters in the imperial residence. He would go that far for a cousin. After their first meeting, though, the Avtokrator had little to do with him. Maleinos had more urgent things to worry about. Like a spider at the center of its web, he kept all his senses alert for the slightest touch of Stylianos.

Left to his own devices, Rhavas became a theologian again. As prelate, he hadn't had the time to do as much serious theological work as he would have liked. The book he'd written up in Skopentzana was as dead as the murdered city and, probably, the scribe who'd put the fair copy down on parchment. He missed it less than he'd expected to. His thoughts had gone in different—radically different—directions since.

Before long, Kameniates summoned him to the High Temple and the patriarchal residence. He was not too surprised; his name would have been bandied about as a possible successor to the patriarchal throne even while his body was far, far away. What with his accomplishments and his ancestry, that seemed inevitable as the sunrise.

Kameniates was in his late sixties, his long white beard wispy as clouds on a breezy spring afternoon. He had big, bushy eyebrows, too, and tufts of hair growing out of his ears, which Rhavas found repulsive. The present holder of the patriarchate had neither disgraced himself nor covered himself with glory; he seemed more a placeholder than anything else.

"Most holy sir," Rhavas murmured, respecting his office if not his person. He bowed very low. "It is a privilege to make your acquaintance at last, after so many years so far from the heart of the Empire."

"I am also pleased to meet you," Kameniates said, though Rhavas hadn't mentioned anything about pleasure. The patriarch added, "Even though you were translated to a distant city, your name was ever in my ear."

By the way he said it, Rhavas might have been translated into a foreign language rather than another ecclesiastical situation. And Kameniates had probably listened with no small worry whenever Rhavas' name came up, too. If the present patriarch annoyed the Avtokrator enough, he could become the former patriarch in the blink of an eye. And Rhavas was the logical one to succeed him.

"It's good to be back in the imperial city," Rhavas said now. "Even so, I would rather have stayed in Skopentzana. That would mean the Empire was still strong beyond the mountains."

"Your sentiments do you credit," Kameniates said.

Hadn't Ingegerd told him something like that? How much good had his sentiments done her? None at all, as he knew only too well. But Kameniates didn't need to know about Ingegerd. There were, in fact, quite a few things Kameniates didn't need to know about. Rhavas didn't intend to tell him, either. All he said was, "I thank you, most holy sir."

Kameniates coughed once or twice. "You will forgive me, very holy sir, but some of the stories that come out of the north speak of doctrines being preached there that are, ah, not completely orthodox."

Maybe the ecumenical patriarch already knew about some things of which he should have been ignorant. Rhavas said, "You will forgive *me*, most holy sir, but stories speak of all sorts of things."

Before Kameniates could reply, a young priest brought in wine and honey cakes covered with chopped pistachios and almonds. Up in Skopentzana, the same recipe would have used walnuts, and probably butter in place of oil. Rhavas went through the ritual of wine without a flaw, conscious of Kameniates' eye on him. The patriarch ate with every sign of enjoyment. He said, "Some of the stories are truly strange."

"Many things that have happened in the north since the civil war began are truly strange," Rhavas answered. "I could begin with the abandonment of the frontier forts and go on to speak of the fall not only of Skopentzana but also of many lesser towns and cities. The Empire has spent centuries carrying civilization to that part of the world. Much of what we did, I fear, is lost forever."

"Surely you exaggerate," Kameniates said around a mouthful of honey cake. "Once this civil strife does finally end, we'll set our house in order soon enough."

He sounded comfortably certain. And why shouldn't he be comfortable? Nothing bad had happened here, and he hadn't gone where anything had. Rhavas said, "Most holy sir, you would have an easier time unscrambling an egg than you would restoring life the way it was north of the mountains."

"Well, you may be right," Kameniates said—an infuriating way to change the subject. Actually, he didn't change it, but swung it back toward what he'd been talking about before: "The stories I've heard from up there, though, haven't got much to do with the Khamorth. They have more to say about our own priests."

"Ah?" Rhavas made a noncommittal noise, and forced himself to follow it with a chuckle. "I'm one of those priests. Maybe the stories are about me."

Kameniates laughed uproariously. "I beg your pardon, but what I'd heard of you didn't make me think you were such a funny fellow," he said. What he would have said had he known Rhavas wasn't joking was no doubt very different. As things were, he went on, "I doubt you're a priest who slays by dark sorcery. I doubt you're a priest who's turned his back on the lord with the great and good mind." What did that prove? Only that what he'd heard about Rhavas—what he knew he'd heard about Rhavas—bore little relationship to the truth.

Rhavas said nothing about sorcery of any sort. He did say, "Most holy sir, I am going to call for a general synod of the priests and prelates and monks and abbots within the Empire."

"You are?" Kameniates looked at him in astonishment. "Why?"

Yes, that was comfort speaking. Comfort brought with it the inability to understand what might bother a man like Rhavas, a man who had seen the worst both his own folk and the barbarians could do. "Why, most holy sir? Because recent events have compelled me to reevaluate the fundamental relationship between the lord with the great and good mind and the dark god."

That put it as abstractly as Rhavas knew how. He waited to see what Kameniates would make of it, and to see how long the ecumenical patriarch needed to realize exactly what he was saying. The longer Kameniates took, the stupider Rhavas reckoned him.

Much more slowly than he should have, Kameniates finally figured out what Rhavas' innocuous-sounding words had to mean. When he did, he got it into a handful of words of his own, blurting, "You worship the dark god!"

"No," Rhavas said, meaning, *Yes*. "But I do think our easy lives in the Empire have left us complacent. We have taken Phos and his power for granted for a very long time. As we gain more experience with the world as it really is, shouldn't we use that experience to help us understand who the stronger god is?"

"Heresy!" Kameniates sketched Phos' sun-sign and spat in rejection at the same time, as if he urgently needed to do both and couldn't decide which to take care of first.

"Asking a question is not heresy." Rhavas kept his voice mild.

"Asking this question is," the ecumenical patriarch declared. "Don't play logic-chopping games with me. If you say Skotos may be stronger than Phos, what do you do but undermine the faith?"

He was right. Rhavas knew as much. He gave back the only answer he could: "What if I speak the truth in saying that, most holy sir? Everything I have seen lately makes me believe I do."

"What if you speak the truth? Well, so what?" There was cynicism to rock even Rhavas. "So what?" Kameniates repeated. "Do you want people going around robbing and raping and killing because they think the dark god wants them to? Do you want them thinking they've got nothing to look forward to but the eternal ice when they die? Does that do anybody any good? I don't think so, and neither do you, not if you've got a copper's worth of sense."

Rhavas had raped and killed, thinking Skotos wanted him to. He still thought so, and he still thought it was important. He said, "I am the prelate of a city of the first rank." The Empire of Videssos had six or eight of those. *The* city was not one of them; it was in a class by itself. Rhavas went on, "Because of what I am, I have the right to call for a synod on doctrinal matters. I have the right, and I intend to use it."

"I have the right to tell you you're a troublemaking idiot, and I intend to use *that*," Kameniates retorted. "Go ahead. Put out your call for a synod. You'll get one. It's within your rights, as you say. And you'll be sorrier afterward than you ever thought you could be. Do you understand that? You will be asking your fellow ecclesiastics to condemn you for the worst heresy we know. And they will. Being the Avtokrator's kin won't save you, not if you try to worship Skotos. Nothing will save you if you do that."

"We'll see." Rhavas thought about telling him what Arotras had said, and about what Maleinos had. In the end, he held his peace. Arotras was too small a fish to matter, and too vulnerable. And the Avtokrator could speak for himself in his own good time. It wasn't Rhavas' place to speak for him. If Rhavas hadn't understood that himself, Maleinos had made it very clear in short order.

"If you go forward, you are the one who will see," Kameniates said. "What you propose is madness."

"There, most holy sir, we agree," Rhavas replied. "Madness has swallowed the world. You want everyone to think that isn't so. You want people to believe things are the way they've always been. You want them to think everything is fine, and all they need to do is go on the way they always have. I'm sorry, but that won't do the job any more."

"Nothing else will," Kameniates said. They eyed each other, both of them realizing they'd been doing nothing but talking at cross purposes.

"We'll see," Rhavas said once more. "Oh, yes. We will indeed."

When Maleinos summoned Rhavas into his presence, Rhavas was glad to go. He even prostrated himself before his imperial cousin without the slightest notion anything was amiss. Even going down on your belly before the Avtokrator of the Videssians was a singular honor: most people never had the chance to do so.

Maleinos spoke to his servants: "I would talk with my cousin alone. Leave us." Watching them shuffle out of the audience chamber in the imperial residence made Rhavas prouder yet. Then Maleinos looked at him with a face full of winter and said, "You bloody fool."

"What?" Rhavas blinked.

"That's, 'What, your Majesty?'" Maleinos snarled. "Get on your belly again, *cousin*"—he turned that into a curse—"and tell me why I shouldn't take your head this instant."

He wasn't joking. Rhavas realized that, and did prostrate himself again. He was groveling in front of his cousin before he remembered that he had but to say the word, and Maleinos was a dead man. Whether he himself could survive saying the word was a different question.

With his forehead knocking against the floor, he quavered, "What—what's wrong, your Majesty?"

"Phos!" Maleinos exclaimed. "Are you really that naïve? I think you may be. I wouldn't believe it if I didn't see it with my own eyes. Get up, you miserable idiot, and I'll tell you."

Cautiously, Rhavas rose. "Yes, your Majesty?"

"You've decided to have a synod convened," Maleinos growled.

"Yes, your Majesty." Now Rhavas was on firmer ground.

"No, very holy sir," the Avtokrator said. "No. I didn't think you were such a blockhead, especially after we talked before. What will happen when the synod comes to order? I'll tell you what. Stylianos will start screaming, 'Look! Maleinos' cousin worships Skotos! Maleinos must worship Skotos, too!'—*that's* what. And that would do me a whole lot of good, wouldn't it?"

Once that was pointed out to him, Rhavas saw it plainly enough. "But you said—" he began.

Maleinos cut him off with a sharp chopping motion of his right hand. If he'd held a sword, he might have taken Rhavas' head with it just then. In tones of infinite disgust, he said, "What I tell my cousin over wine when we're both getting sozzled is one thing. If I don't want to remember it the next morning, I don't have to. What I say publicly, or what anybody in my family says publicly, is something else again. We talked about *that*, too, but you seem to have forgotten it. Now do you follow me, very holy sir?"

"Yes, your Majesty," Rhavas answered. "But there is something you may not see."

"Oh?" An ominous rumble came into the Avtokrator's voice. "And what, pray tell, is that?"

"The truth is the truth no matter whether we're talking about it over wine with no one else around or in front of a crowd in the market square—or in front of priests and prelates in the High Temple," Rhavas said.

His cousin scowled at him. "I told you what the truth was. The truth is, no kinsman of mine is going to cause that kind of trouble right now. I can't afford it, and the Empire can't afford it, either. Do I make myself plain enough?"

Rhavas gathered himself. He had always favored Maleinos

in the civil war, not just because they were kin but because he himself was—well, he had been—a sound conservative by nature, opposed to change in general and to usurpation in particular. He was still opposed to usurpation. Change in general... "Your Majesty, I honor you and I obey you to the extent I can, but here I will go where my studies of the good god and of the dark lord take me. I do not see what else I can do, not if I want to cleave to the truth."

"You... defy me?" Maleinos sounded as if he couldn't believe his ears. People didn't defy the Avtokrator of the Videssians every day.

"I do not wish to defy you, your Majesty," Rhavas replied. "I only wish to follow the truth."

"Piss on the truth—and piss on you, too," Maleinos snapped. "You are no cousin of mine. I disown you. I cast you out. Take whatever you have out of here: you, your goods, your horses—your shadow, too. You are no part of this family. You never shall be, not again. Go." He pointed dramatically toward the door.

If Rhavas hadn't been his kinsman, the Avtokrator would have ordered him slain. The ecclesiastic was sure of that. He said, "As you wish, your Majesty. I am Rhavas, a priest. It is enough."

"You will be Rhavas the anathematized. You will be Rhavas the excommunicated. You will be Rhavas the condemned. I wash my hands of you." Maleinos actually did make hand-washing motions. "If you call for a synod, none of what happens to you will be my doing. It will not need to be. You will do it to yourself."

"I'll take the chance," Rhavas said.

Maleinos didn't answer. He just stood there, pointing toward the door. And out the door Rhavas went.

Having always been a wealthy man—having always been the Avtokrator's cousin—Rhavas knew little about how the poor in Videssos the city lived. Suddenly, he was one of them. He could have stayed at a monastery for nothing for as long as he was willing to work, but he fought shy of that. It smacked of hypocrisy. Monks gathered together to worship Phos. Rhavas aimed to uproot that worship and replace it with something... *with something truer,* he thought.

If he ran out of money altogether, worrying about hypocrisy

would become a luxury he couldn't afford. For now, he indulged it.

He sold the steppe ponies. Now that he'd come to Videssos the city, he couldn't imagine wanting to leave again. The first dealer he approached looked dubious—a look he probably practiced every morning in front of a mirror. The man said, "Don't know that I can give you much for 'em, holy sir." He sounded artistically mournful as he went on, "Who'd want such shaggy little beasts?"

"They are Khamorth ponies. You will know what they are and what they can do at least as well as I do. You waste my time and you insult my intelligence if you pretend otherwise." Rhavas' voice was icy cold. "You waste my time at your peril—please believe me. Shall we go on from there, or shall I find a trader who is not so full of himself?"

The horse dealer blinked. He wasn't used to blunt talk like that. He licked his lips. Something in Rhavas' talk put the fear of Phos in him, a fear he'd thought long forgotten. What tried to be a laugh came out sounding more like a raven's croak. The man asked, "Well, what do you want for 'em, holy sir?" Rhavas told him what he wanted. The dealer started to laugh again, but thought better of it. Instead, he said, "I'll give you half that."

Rhavas said, "I told you not to waste my time. Few men get more than one warning from me. You can count yourself lucky—or you can go on being a fool. Was my price fair, or not? Will you make a profit when you sell after buying at that price, or not?"

When the dealer started to come out with the usual bluster, he had the good fortune to look into Rhavas' eyes first. What he saw there made him give back a pace, sketch the sun-sign, and mutter, "Phos!"

"That is not an answer," Rhavas said implacably. "What *is* your answer?"

"I'll—I'll pay what you want, holy sir. Just don't—don't do anything." The horse trader's voice rose to a frightened whine.

"I am not doing anything. I have not done anything. I will not do anything." Rhavas could even make demonstrating verb tenses intimidating. He held out his hand. The dealer gave him what he'd asked, down to the last copper. When Rhavas went away, the man let out a sigh of relief.

"What's with you?" one of his competitors asked. "You look like a goose walked over your grave."

"I wish it was only a goose," the man exclaimed. "It felt more like one of those long-nosed beasts from across the Sailors' Sea."

"An elephant?" the other trader said.

"That's it." The dealer nodded. "Maybe two of 'em."

Rhavas' landlord, a professionally nosy man named Lardys, didn't understand him. Why wouldn't a priest stay in a monastery instead of taking a room over a tavern? Rhavas didn't try to explain. After he took a barmaid to bed, Lardys stopped asking questions. He thought he knew what kind of priest Rhavas was.

By contrast, Rhavas did not think he was that kind of priest at all. His moral code remained as stern as it ever had—compromise was not a word often found in his vocabulary. But the premises from which he reasoned had changed. If Skotos was more powerful than Phos . . . People in the Empire said, *When you come to Videssos the city, eat fish.*

As with anything else, convening a synod required several formal steps before the wheels started rolling. An expert on ecclesiastical law, Rhavas was intimately familiar with them. The demand had to be made publicly. He chose the most public way he knew: he went to the High Temple to do it there.

The service was as rich and magnificent as he remembered. Priests swung censers, perfuming the air with costly frankincense and myrrh. The patriarch's golden robes, encrusted with pearls and precious stones, were almost as grand as those the Avtokrator wore. The Temple itself was even more splendid than the rituals it housed. The pews were of cedar and sandalwood and other rare and costly timber. The walls showed Phos' heavens, picked out in turquoise and glowing rose quartz and glistening mother-of-pearl.

And in the dome above the central altar, the image of Phos looked down upon his worshipers. Small windows pierced the base of the dome, admitting rays of light that made the gold tesserae of the mosaic sparkle and shimmer. The sunbeams also made the dome seem to float above the rest of the temple, as if it were a true piece of the heavens insubstantially tethered to earth.

Phos himself had a gaze that made anyone who tried to meet it think twice. The good god was stern in judgment. His dark and shadowed eyes warned that men were not worthy of him. Always before, when Rhavas had lived in Videssos the city, that divine stare had frightened him and made him wonder, *Am I worthy of heaven?* Now . . .

Now he wondered if Phos was worthy of heaven. Having changed allegiance made him see the divine liturgy in a whole new way. It might have been the shrill crying of children frightened by the darkness. But the darkness was *there*, whether it frightened them or not. Didn't they see that? Better to admit as much and go on than to hold up useless candles and pretend their feeble light stretched everywhere. Wasn't it? Rhavas thought so.

Kameniates preached a sermon almost frighteningly unmemorable. Rhavas knew he himself made a better theologian than a preacher. He also knew he could have outpreached Kameniates in his sleep. The present ecumenical patriarch had no great name as a scholar, either. He was an ecclesiastical bureaucrat, a functionary who could have been replaced by a dozen other functionaries without changing much and, indeed, without having many people notice.

As men began rising from their seats—up in the grilled-off gallery, women would be doing the same—Rhavas also rose, calling out, "Most holy sir!"

"Yes? What is it?" Kameniates made a mistake by recognizing him and letting him go on. The patriarch realized as much a heartbeat later. His mouth twisted in dismay. It was too late for that, though. Now he couldn't step away from the altar and pretend he hadn't seen the other ecclesiastic.

"I am Rhavas, prelate of Skopentzana, newly returned to Videssos the city through chaos and war." Rhavas pitched his voice to carry, and the High Temple helped him. Perfect in so many other things, it was perfect in acoustics as well. No one in the building had any trouble hearing him.

"From Skopentzana? He's come all the way from Skopentzana?" He heard exclamations like those from near and far, even from the women's galleries. He thought he caught flashes of motion from behind the grillwork in the balcony as women crowded close to get a better look at him.

Most reluctantly, Kameniates asked, "And what would you, Rhavas of Skopentzana?" He might have ignored Rhavas even yet, but he couldn't ignore that buzz of excitement and interest.

"I would call for the convocation of a synod of priests and prelates and monks and abbots to examine the premises of our holy faith, as is my right as a prelate," Rhavas replied proudly.

That set off a fresh buzz. Men and women chattered among themselves. Videssians who weren't professional theologians were passionate amateurs. As soon as Rhavas talked about looking at how the faith was put together, he had their interest, if not their support.

"And how do you propose to alter the definitions we have accepted for so long?" the ecumenical patriarch inquired of him, as if he did not know. Kameniates might not make much of a theologian, but he was a clever bureaucrat. He knew what would likely draw popular backing, and what would not.

Rhavas also knew that if he said, *I want to cast out the worship of Phos and start giving reverence to Skotos instead*, his audience would become a mob and tear him to pieces right there on the floor of the High Temple. Kameniates, no doubt, would cheer them on, if he didn't join in and grab one of Rhavas' ankles for a hearty yank of his own.

He didn't say that, then, even if it was what he meant. What he did say was, "I would like the assembled ecclesiastics to consider how our view of the constant struggle between dark and light is to be measured against events, and what support there is in the holy scriptures for the alterations I shall propose."

At that, Kameniates looked alarmed. Being no great scholar, he wouldn't know off the top of his head what texts might support Rhavas. He did know Rhavas had the gift for scholarship he so conspicuously lacked. If the prelate of Skopentzana implied there were texts to bolster his views, then that might well be so.

People started buzzing again. Unlike the patriarch, they didn't know what Rhavas had in mind. Some of their guesses were good, others wildly foolish. But they didn't sound furious and outraged, the way they would have if he'd been more explicit. They sounded . . . intrigued.

Kameniates heard that, too, and looked even less happy than he had when he answered Rhavas' call. He said, "I see no good reason to change the doctrines that have served us well for so long, and—"

"Is the truth not reason enough?" Rhavas broke in loudly.

By the patriarch's expression, it wasn't. By his expression, it didn't come close. But men started calling, "Yes, by the good god!" and, "What are you afraid of, most holy sir?" After horse racing, theology might have been the most popular spectator sport in Videssos.

"Yes, most holy sir, what *are* you afraid of?" Rhavas jeered.

Kameniates turned very read. "I fear nothing—nothing, do you hear me?" His voice rose to an angry shout. "Do you want your synod, your cursed synod, Rhavas? Well, by the lord with the great and good mind, you can have it! Do you want to be anathematized and excommunicated? You can have that, too, and you will. I told you as much before in private, and now I say it in public. To the ice with you, you vile heretic, and the sooner the better!"

Now the men around Rhavas stared at the ecumenical patriarch in astonishment. Like most bureaucrats, Kameniates was not normally a man of strong character. Such an outburst from him shook his congregation like an earthquake. Remembering the earthquake that had shaken Skopentzana down, Rhavas wished he'd found another comparison, but he couldn't help that now.

And Kameniates' fury was only approaching its peak. He pointed toward the entranceway. "Get out!" he cried. "Get out, I say! You are banned from the High Temple until the synod that condemns you—and it will."

Rhavas thought about cursing and killing the patriarch then and there, just for the sake of the chaos it would cause. He thought about it, but then shook his head. Why kill Kameniates when he'd just goaded him into promising to convene that synod? If Kameniates fell over dead now, a new patriarch wouldn't be in place for weeks, if not for months. When he was, he wouldn't necessarily feel bound by his predecessor's promises. Rhavas would have to figure out how to irk him into doing what he wanted.

Instead of giving Kameniates death, then, Rhavas gave him his most elegant courtier's bow. Kameniates gaped, plainly not knowing what to make of that. "Let it be just as you say, most holy sir," Rhavas told him. "If you fear to go where the truth may lead you until you have the force of a synod all around you, well, that may be a pity, but it is also your privilege. My own view is that you are a coward, but I suppose I could be wrong."

Kameniates got redder yet. Rhavas smiled; he hadn't thought

the patriarch could. Kameniates was too angry to do anything but gobble incoherently. Guessing the only thing that could inflame him further would be to leave quickly and quietly, Rhavas started to do just that.

He hadn't taken more than a few steps, though, before a man asked him, "Very holy sir, where do you think our present doctrines are mistaken?"

"After civil war, after disaster in the north, I'm surprised you need to ask that question," Rhavas replied.

The man frowned. "What do you mean?"

"About what you think I mean," Rhavas told him. "Look at the state of the world, such as it is. An answer will come to you. If you are honest with yourself, I expect it will be the right one."

He left the fellow expostulating in his wake. But he hadn't gone far before another man asked him almost the identical question. He gave this one almost the identical answer. Where the first man had floundered and refused to follow Rhavas' response to the only place where it could lead, the second man took the point at once. He took it, but he didn't like it. Turning pale, he exclaimed, "You can't mean that!"

"With all proper respect, sir, I not only can, but I do," Rhavas said. "And now, if you will excuse me . . ."

He gave his explanation twice more before leaving the High Temple. He didn't linger to see whether those men understood him. In the end, what difference did it make? Some people knew what he was saying. They would spell it out so even fools could see. And gossip spread faster than wildfire.

No one followed him back to his lodging. That was a relief. He wondered how long he had before people would, and how long before rocks and softer, smellier things started flying in through the window. Then he wondered if such things would content the people who disagreed with him. They might try to set the tavern and the rooms over it on fire instead.

Those who set fires were madmen. Everybody knew that. Fires ranked right up there with earthquakes as the worst things that could happen to a city—and fires came far more often. With so many open flames in a place like Videssos the city, it was probably a miracle they happened as seldom as they did. When a fire got loose, any kind of breeze could push it faster than people could put it out. And if a fire got loose when a gale was blowing . . . Rhavas shuddered. Great swaths of a city went up in flames at times like that.

Of course, those who set fires to prove their theology were not likely to care if a quarter of Videssos the city burned, as long as Rhavas' ashes were among the rest. Rhavas bared his teeth. As a matter of fact, he felt the same way about those who disagreed with him. If he burned them all, though, who would be left to worship along with him?

When he walked into the taproom, Lardys sent him a quizzical look. "You don't look so real happy, holy sir," the taverner remarked. "Feel like a mug of wine to take out some of the kinks?" Before Rhavas could answer, he added three words torture couldn't have pulled from him most of the time: "On the house."

"Thank you," Rhavas said. "I don't know if that will help, but I don't see how it could hurt."

Lardys dipped up a mugful. "What's eating you, anyway?" he asked, and held up a hasty hand. "You don't want to talk about it, you don't have to. Sometimes it helps, sometimes it's nobody's business."

"I don't mind talking." Rhavas explained, as he had on the floor and in the narthex of the High Temple.

When he finished, the innkeeper whistled softly. "You don't think small, do you?" He paused, considering. Doing what he did, he'd seen a lot of the world's evils here in this taproom. "Makes a deal of sense when you think about it, eh?"

"Seems that way to me," Rhavas said. "The ecumenical patriarch, you understand, has a different opinion."

"Well, curse the ecumenical patriarch," Lardys said gaily.

"Yes, curse him," Rhavas agreed. He suddenly finished the wine at a gulp, wondering what he'd done, wondering if he'd done anything. He hadn't intended to, but what did that prove? One way or the other, he would know before very long.

"Dig up his bones!" Lardys added, pouring wine for himself. That was the traditional Videssian cry of riot and rebellion. More often than not, it was aimed at the Avtokrator, but anyone who got on the wrong side of the city mob could face it.

"Dig up his bones," Rhavas echoed. Would Kameniates' bones need digging up before long? If they did, would people make the connection between him and Rhavas? Would a mob gather in the street here shouting, *Dig up Rhavas' bones!*? Before long, again, Rhavas would find out. "Let me have another," he told the tapman. This time, he set a coin on the bar.

"Here you go." Lardys finished his own cup and poured another for himself after giving Rhavas a refill. "I've got a question for you, holy sir: if things are the way you say they are, does that mean we all go to the ice after we die?"

"I haven't worked that out yet," Rhavas said uncomfortably—it was a better question than he'd expected. "It would seem to follow, though, wouldn't it?"

"Ah, well." The man behind the bar shrugged. "The company's bound to be better there than up above, then, isn't it?"

Eternity didn't seem to bother him. Maybe the idea of it was too big for him to grasp. Maybe, on the other hand, he hoped to find a loophole so that he would end up in Phos' heaven even if everyone else went to the ice. Rhavas didn't think either Phos or Skotos had loopholes like that; each was, in his own way, perfect.

"If bad is good and good is bad, so to speak, we're going to have to change a lot of the way we behave," Lardys observed. "You see a pretty girl you want, you just go ahead and jump on her. Why not? What difference will it make?"

He had a way of penetrating to the essence of things. Rhavas wished he would have chosen a different example. What had happened with Ingegerd still weighed on his conscience. Logically, it shouldn't have. Rhavas knew that. His own reasoning had already followed the innkeeper's. He wasn't comfortable with it, though, no matter how logical it was. He hadn't grown up thinking that way. Once he'd reformed the temples' doctrine, others would. They would think and feel the way they were supposed to under the new dispensation.

How to put that into words? Rhavas did his best: "I expect things will sort themselves out. It will take time, that's all."

"Ah, well," Lardys said again. "What doesn't?" He gestured toward Rhavas' mug. "Drink up, holy sir, and I'll pour you some more. Next one's on me. You've given me something new to chew on, and that doesn't happen every day."

"Thank you very much," Rhavas answered gravely. "You are a clever man. You might have done well to go into the priesthood so you could use your wits to best advantage."

"No, thanks." Lardys shook his head. "You use your wits plenty keeping an inn going, believe you me you do. And—meaning no offense, mind you—I don't reckon I'd make much of a priest on account of I like using my prick too well."

Having become acquainted with the pleasures of the flesh, Rhavas found that hard to gainsay. He wondered how he'd done without for so much of his life. The only answer he could see was that he hadn't known what he was missing. He supposed that was why priests took their vocations as youths. If they got experience first, they wouldn't want to abandon women—or, some of them, boys.

"The rules there will likely change, too," he said.

"I bet they would!" The innkeeper's laugh was raucous and lewd and rude. He eyed Rhavas with a strange, almost a morbid, curiosity. "Do you really think you can make the temples turn everything upside down, holy sir, or are you just talking to hear yourself talk?"

"What I say I can do, I can do," Rhavas declared, maybe a little louder than he needed to. "The truth is the truth. If I see it more clearly than others, I can make them see it, too—and I have a duty to make them see it."

"Better you than me, pal. That's all I've got to tell you." Lardys whistled: a low, mournful note. "Yeah, better you than me. You take on something that big, you're bound to lose whether you're right or you're wrong. You understand what I'm telling you? If the mouse runs into the tree or the tree falls on the mouse, the mouse loses either way."

"I am not a mouse," Rhavas said, and plucked at his bushy beard. "You can tell because my whiskers are different."

The taverner laughed louder than the joke deserved; he'd been drinking, too. The next round, Rhavas bought for both of them. They ended up killing a good part of the afternoon, and tried to solve the secrets of the universe while they were at it.

Out in the streets, people started yelling about something or other. "I wonder what's going on," Rhavas said, more than a little blearily.

"To the ice with 'em." Lardys giggled. "To the ice with everybody who doesn't come in and buy some wine. To the ice with ... everybody." He giggled again.

But then someone *did* come in, and they both demanded, "What's all the fuss about?"

"You haven't heard yet?" the man said in amazement. He rolled his eyes when they both shook their heads. He rolled his eyes, but he told them: "The patriarch is dead!"

Rhavas woke with a hangover the likes of which he hadn't had since . . . He couldn't remember when, if ever, he'd woken with such a thick head. *Yes, curse him*, he'd said, not meaning very much by it—and Kameniates breathed no more.

Groaning, Rhavas stood up. That made his head hurt more. So did bending to reach under the bed for the chamber pot. He tried to piss away all the wine he'd drunk the day and the night before, but it was still working its will on him. "Coming out!" he called—croaked, really—and threw the slops out the window. An irate screech from below said he hadn't given the people in the street long enough to get clear. That was a hazard of city life anywhere. It happened—well, it had happened—in Skopentzana, too.

He was none too steady on his feet as he went down to the taproom. He blinked and squinted. It was no brighter in there than it had been the day before—less so, if anything, for the morning was cloudy—but it certainly seemed as if it were. Lardys was already down there behind the bar. He looked more than a little the worse for wear, too.

"Wine," Rhavas said in a ghastly voice. "A cup of wine and some raw cabbage, if you have any. Maybe that will get some of the thunder out of my head."

"I have cabbage, if you want it." The taverner didn't doubt he would want a hair of the dog that had bitten him. A mug already stood in front of the man. As he dipped up another, he went on, "Or I have tripe soup. A bowl eased me—some."

"Tripe soup *and* cabbage, maybe," Rhavas said. "But wine. Oh, yes. Wine." Automatically, he went through the proper Videssian ritual. Several other people were having breakfast in there. A hungover priest was one thing—something to smile at, in fact. A hungover priest who didn't seem to reject Skotos . . . Rhavas didn't want to have to start killing so early in the day.

His hands shook as he raised the cup to his lips. When the wine hit his stomach, he wondered if it would stay down. He gulped a couple of times and told his inside to behave themselves. To his relief, they did. He crunched cabbage and spooned up the greasy, spicy soup. Little by little, his headache receded.

"Better," he said when he got to the bottom of the soup bowl. "Not good, but better."

"I know what you mean," Lardys said in tones almost as mournful as his own. The man's laugh had a distinctly hollow ring. "See if *I* ever curse anybody again for the rest of my days."

Rhavas stared. The fellow actually thought that *his* curse had killed Kameniates? Rhavas started to laugh, too. Once he started, he had trouble stopping. By the time he managed to bring the spasm—almost the seizure—under control, everyone in the place was looking at him.

"You all right, holy sir?" Lardys asked doubtfully.

"I . . . suppose so," Rhavas answered, still wheezing. A couple of tears trickled from the corners of his eyes. "Oh, dear. I'm sorry. If I didn't laugh, I would weep."

"The most holy Kameniates deserves our tears," an old man said, sketching the sun-sign. "Who now will lead the temples in this troubled time?"

That was as good a question as any the innkeeper had asked. If Rhavas hadn't quarreled with his cousin, *his* name likely would have headed the list of three candidates Maleinos presented to the small synod that would choose Kameniates' successor. They would know exactly which of the three the Avtokrator expected them to choose, too.

I was a fool, Rhavas thought. If he were the ecumenical patriarch himself, he could have presented his views on the faith from a position of strength. As things were, he would have to throw them in the faces of the ecclesiastical hierarchy.

He shook his head. One of the reasons old Neboulos sent him to Skopentzana all those years ago was to teach him to get along with people. That hadn't worked out so well as the old patriarch would have wished.

No help for it now. He was what he was, and he believed what he believed. He believed he would prevail despite everything. Oddly, he felt more convinced of it than ever, despite all the things that hadn't gone the way he would have liked.

"What do you know of the prelates and clerics, holy sir?" the old man asked him. "Who do you suppose will succeed the most holy sir?"

"An interesting question," Rhavas answered. "I've been out of the city for a while, though, and I don't know the important men in the temples as well as I should."

"I know who it would be if the barbarians hadn't jumped on us," Lardys said. "Doesn't the Avtokrator have a cousin or a nephew who's a priest up in one of those places? Agderos, I think it is. To the ice with me if I remember what the fellow's name is."

"Skopentzana. It was Skopentzana," Rhavas said. Agderos was even farther north: a small port on the Northern Sea. Not much point to having a big port up there, not when the ocean itself froze most winters.

"Was it, holy sir? I didn't think so, but I won't argue with you," the taverner said. "Wherever it was, that nephew would be the chap with the inside track. But he's probably dead now, what with everything up there being such a mess."

"Yes, he probably is," Rhavas said.

But maybe not. Maybe Maleinos would decide blood was not only thicker than water but also thicker than bad doctrine. *I ought to try to see him and find out*, Rhavas thought. *Maybe I can persuade him I'm milder than he thinks I am. Maybe I can persuade him I'm milder than I really am, too.* The worst Maleinos could tell him was no. And if he heard no, how was he worse off?

✦ **XI**

"**N**o," Maleinos said, looking Rhavas in the eye.

"But—" Rhavas began. They sat in the small audience chamber where Rhavas had made the mistake of talking about calling for a synod. Their wine—or at least Rhavas' wine—was noticeably less fine today.

"No," his cousin repeated. "You've already gone and made yourself into a scandal. I don't want scandal on the patriarchal throne. I can't afford it, not when I'm going to take the field against the rebel in a few days. And so I'll pick someone safe. Do you—did you—know Sozomenos?"

"I knew him, yes, your Majesty," Rhavas replied. "He is a most holy, most pious man." He spoke nothing but the truth there. Sozomenos was a man of the sort Kveldoulphios the martyr must have been: one whose holiness would be remembered and honored for centuries after he died. What amazed Rhavas was that he hadn't died long since. "He must be . . . close to ninety now, yes?"

"Somewhere around there." Maleinos shrugged. "So what? His wits are still sound. No one can possibly question that. And he's a safe choice. No one can possibly question *that*, either." He glowered at Rhavas. "On the other hand, anybody—especially Stylianos—could question *you*. I don't aim to give him the chance."

Rhavas had never been wounded on the battlefield. He imagined that had to feel something like this. He bore it as bravely as he could, inclining his head and saying, "You are the Avtokrator."

"I aim to *stay* the Avtokrator, too, by the good god." No matter what Maleinos had said in a casual chat, at bottom he still followed Phos. "Once I hang Stylianos' ugly head on the Milestone ... Well, if Sozomenos walks the Bridge of the Separator after that, maybe I can think things over again. Maybe. If you can learn to keep your mouth shut in the meantime." Maleinos looked Rhavas straight in the face again.

There it was: the bargain. Keep quiet now, become ecumenical patriarch later. But what would happen then? Slowly, Rhavas said, "You would expect me to keep my mouth shut—about that—after you put me on the patriarchal throne, too."

"Hasn't the Empire seen enough trouble the past few years to last for the next fifty?" Maleinos returned. "Why do we need more?"

"Because of the truth?" Rhavas suggested.

Maleinos shook his head. The sunlight coming in through the window played on the lines and shadows around his eyes, making him look older than his years. Thinking about it, Rhavas decided Maleinos' eyes made him look older than his years anyhow, even if the rest of his face seemed young. Wearing the red boots ground a man down before his time, and Maleinos' eyes were where it showed. The Avtokrator said, "If it is the truth, someone else is bound to find it one of these days. Why hurry to shove it down people's throats?"

"Because it *is* the truth," Rhavas replied. His cousin was a political animal, one who worried about what would work, what was expedient, what was practical. Rhavas wasn't, never could be, never would be. Here again he discovered his inability to compromise even when compromise would have done him a lot of good.

Being a political animal, Maleinos saw the same thing, and likely saw it before Rhavas did. Sighing, the Avtokrator shook his head once more. "No, I'm sorry—I don't think it will do. You are a man who will eat fire even if you have to kindle it yourself. I can't have that kind of man presiding over the High Temple. It's more trouble than it's worth." There was that word again.

"Even with Kameniates dead, the synod will go forward," Rhavas said stubbornly. "I had the right to demand it. Sozomenos himself would not deny that."

"Let it go forward." Maleinos sounded altogether indifferent. "It will fall down on you like a brick building in an earthquake. It will serve you right, too." He paused, eyeing Rhavas. "There have been some funny reports out of the north. I don't suppose you . . ." He shook his head. "No. I'm just saying that because I'm not happy with you."

Funny reports out of the north? Rhavas wondered. Ingegerd? Kaboutzes? The priest who'd fallen over dead in that town?—Rhavas couldn't even remember his name. Himerios and the mages? Rhavas knew the trail he'd left behind him. Fortunately, his cousin didn't connect Kameniates' sudden death with any of the others.

"We have given all the time we can spare," Maleinos said. When an Avtokrator started using the imperial *we*, that was a sure sign he didn't want to listen any more. Maleinos didn't have Rhavas escorted from the imperial residence this time, but that was the only sign of greater warmth he showed.

As Rhavas left, the Vaspurakaner steward led a sun-darkened man with a scarred face toward the audience chamber. The officer—for such he obviously was—dipped his head and made the sun-sign as he walked past Rhavas. Ironic that a man whose trade was slaughter should have more faith than a prelate.

Rhavas laughed, appreciating the joke. He doubted whether the scarred and leathery general would. And he was sure the Avtokrator wouldn't.

As Maleinos had said he would, he rode off to war a few days later. He sent Rhavas no special invitation to watch him go. But criers went through the imperial city, calling on the people to come to the parade that would see him off. Videssians in general—and those who dwelt in Videssos the city in particular—went wild for spectacles of any sort.

Although Rhavas got to Middle Street before sunup, he had to elbow his way to somewhere near the front of the crowd so he could see the street itself. If he hadn't been taller than average, even the place he won wouldn't have helped him.

"Wine! Anybody want some wine?" "Sweet cakes!" "Get your chickpeas here! Hot off the grill!" "Fried squiiid!" Vendors made their way through the crowd. When the fellow selling fried squid came near Rhavas, he spent a couple of coins for the morsels. He hadn't eaten squid in all those years in Skopentzana. They were as chewy as he remembered, and as nearly tasteless.

Roofed colonnades helped shield Middle Street from the sun. People scurried about up on the roofs, jostling one another for a better view. It sometimes happened that people—usually young men—fell off and landed on their heads on the cobblestones below. Rhavas heard no shrieks today. People were being careful.

The adventurous ones atop the colonnade got the first glimpse of the approaching procession. "Here they come!" they called, and jostled even more. "They're on the way!" A blast of bugles and flutes and drums from the direction of the palace confirmed that.

A herald came first, to tell the people what they'd see—as if they didn't know. "Forth comes Maleinos, Avtokrator of the Videssians!" the leather-lunged man roared. "Forth comes the Avtokrator, to punish the wicked rebel and usurper!"

Men and women near Rhavas burst into applause. Did that mean they favored Maleinos, or just that they wanted to be seen favoring Maleinos? Rhavas wondered how many of them even knew, and how many of them cared.

Standard-bearers carried the Videssian banner: gold sunburst on blue. Behind them marched the royal bodyguards. Some of those men were Videssian archers and pikemen. Others were Haloga soldiers of fortune. The big blond men carried long-handled war axes. They wore their hair in long blond braids bobbing behind them. Ever since Stavrakios' day, the guards had had a Haloga contingent. From the imperial point of view, that made good sense. The barbarians were personally loyal to the ruler, who was also their paymaster. Other ambitious Videssians were less likely to seduce them away from their allegiance to the Avtokrator.

Their pale eyes, pale hair, pale or sunburned skins, and blunt features set them apart from the Videssians among whom they dwelt. So did their inches and the scowling suspicion with which they eyed the crowd. To them, everyone was a potential assassin. In a time of civil war, they might well have been right. They watched their Videssian counterparts, too, and the Videssians watched them.

"Maleinos! Maleinos! Maleinos!" The rhythmic chant had every sign of being started by a claque to impress the larger crowd. "Many years to the Avtokrator! Dig up Stylianos' bones!"

Some of the ordinary people around Maleinos joined the chanting, but more didn't, though some of the ones who didn't chant did clap for the Avtokrator. Maleinos wore gilded mail and a gilded helm with a gold coronet soldered to it. A scarlet cape shimmered out behind him. His red boots were very red indeed, and showed up all the better because he rode a white horse.

Beside him and half a pace to the rear rode the scarred general. He looked tough and capable. Past that, Rhavas didn't know who he was. Back when Rhavas was last in Videssos the city, he hadn't been anybody in particular. Rhavas wondered how he liked going up against Stylianos, who had been somebody for a very long time. No way to ask him, of course, not without risking arrest for treason.

More horsemen in blue surcoats rode after the Avtokrator and his general. The horses' hooves clattered on the cobbles. At an officer's signal, the men all shouted, "Maleinos!" together.

And if Stylianos won the war, would they shout his name just as enthusiastically? Most of them probably would. Pikemen on foot followed. The foot soldiers also roared out the Avtokrator's name. Were they also likely to roar out *any* Avtokrator's name with equal zeal? Again, it looked that way to Rhavas.

Then they were gone, heading off toward the Silver Gate, off toward Stylianos' army, off toward civil war. What had they left behind? A memory of loud shouts and a lingering aroma of horse manure—not that that wasn't a strong motif in Videssos the city at any season of the year.

If they cut down Stylianos' men . . . Videssos suffered. If the rebel's men slaughtered them instead . . . Videssos suffered anyway. Civil war was a nasty business. Whichever side won, the Empire lost.

Somewhere off beyond the Paristrian Mountains, would Khamorth khagans laugh when they heard the Avtokrator and the rebellious general were going at each other again? Without the civil war, the barbarians couldn't have got into Videssos in the first place. Rhavas had no doubt they were all for it.

They warred against one another, too. Back in happier days, Videssos had used bribes and gifts of weapons and trade to keep the nomads squabbling among themselves, and to keep them too busy and embroiled to cause the Empire trouble. Now the Khamorth would play the same game with Videssos.

Beside Rhavas, somebody said, "Well, you can call that a parade if you want to, but I've seen plenty better."

That seemed to be the general mood. Maleinos wouldn't have been very happy had he heard what his subjects were saying. Odds were he *would* hear, sooner or later. If he didn't have agents in the crowd listening to what ordinary people said, he was missing a trick. Rhavas didn't think his cousin missed many tricks of that sort.

The crowd slowly dispersed. The vendors headed back to the several squares in the city, where they could always find crowds of people who might want to buy. Pickpockets and cutpurses probably did the same.

"Holy sir?" a nondescript little man said to Rhavas.

"Yes?"

"Holy sir, are you a healer, by any chance? I've got this nasty ulcer on my shin, and I was wondering—"

"I'm not a healer. Sorry."

"Could you try?" the little man whined.

"I wouldn't do you any good," Rhavas told him. "Go look for a priest who really is a healer, if you want help."

"Oh, come on. You can do it." The man had found a priest. Finding *another* priest must have seemed like too much trouble to him—this in a city where you could hardly walk a block along Middle Street without running into one.

Rhavas' temper began to fray. "I told you, I am not a healer-priest. Please go away and leave me alone."

"But my leg . . ." the man whimpered.

He seemed spry enough to Rhavas. But he went on whining and fussing. He wouldn't take a hint and go away. At last, Rhavas lost patience altogether. "All right," he said, exhaling angrily. "*All right*. Come in the alley with me, and I'll give you what you deserve."

"Took you long enough," said the man with the sore on his shin, not noticing the way Rhavas put that. Into the alley he went, limping only a little if at all. "Here. Bend down and you can see it."

Rhavas did bend down. The alley was narrow and dark. Moss and something slimier than moss grew on the bricks of the houses to either side. Middle Street had cobbles, but the alley was all dirt and mud. Flies buzzed. The city stench seemed stronger here than on the main boulevard.

"See?" the man said. That was the last word that ever passed his lips. He let out a soft sound of surprise and then fell over dead. Rhavas did not even bother to rifle his belt pouch. He left it there to surprise and please some scavenger who would stumble across it.

On the way back to his inn, he found himself whistling. He had a marvelous talent there in the ability to curse. And if he couldn't use it every now and again to rid himself—and the world—of an annoying nuisance, what good was it, anyway?

In due course, Sozomenos was installed as ecumenical patriarch. Rhavas went to the High Temple to watch his investiture. Sozomenos hardly seemed to have changed since Rhavas left for Skopentzana. He'd been an old man then, his face lined, his beard long and tangled and white as snow. He looked just the same now.

The patriarchal robes were heavy with cloth of gold and their encrustations of semiprecious and precious stones. Sozomenos' shoulders, already stooped, had trouble bearing the weight. He looked out at the crowd in the Temple.

When he spoke from the pulpit, his voice was clear and strong despite his years: "My friends, I never expected or wanted the honor his Majesty has chosen to bestow upon me. I would rather contemplate the lord with the great and good mind than seek to govern unruly men. But, this having been asked of me, I shall bear the burden to the best of my ability."

He looked out over the crowd. Rhavas remembered his gaze as being almost as penetrating as that of the image of Phos in the dome above him. So it still seemed now. "We live in troubled times," Sozomenos continued. "Some would say the times are troubled because the dark god puts forth his strength to make them so. Even some respected ecclesiastics have been heard to make such claims. They will have their chance to prove them—if they can."

Did he know Rhavas was in the High Temple? Rhavas had no trouble recognizing him, but would he know Rhavas after so long? The new patriarch did know Kameniates had had to order a synod convened, and did not seem to object to it. That was all to the good, as far as Rhavas was concerned.

"Myself, I have no truck with such newfangled notions," Sozomenos said. "I believe in the faith I learned at my mother's knee a lot of years ago. I trust in that faith. It has held me up through thick and thin. I think it always will."

He smiled then. Light didn't radiate from him, the way it did from the windows set into the base of the dome. It didn't, but it might as well have. He was not lying when he spoke of his faith. It shone on his face.

Smiling still, he said, "I could be wrong. I admit I could be wrong. If the synod decides I am . . . I expect I will lay this burden down, and gladly." Did he mean he would resign the patriarchate? Or did he mean he would quietly die? With a man of his years and his obvious determination, either seemed possible.

Rhavas wanted to persuade him. He called on the patriarchal residence the next day, and was admitted in due course. After bowing to Sozomenos and congratulating him on his accession, he said, "Most holy sir, I was lucky enough to escape the fall and the sack of Skopentzana. What I saw there, and what I saw afterward . . . You don't know how lucky you are to live in Videssos the city. Much of the evil in the world has passed this city by—so far."

"There is a struggle. I would not deny it. How could I, when the faith ordains it?" Sozomenos seemed content with the world as he found it. "But the faith also ordains that goodness and light shall triumph at the end of days, and darkness be cast down. This I still believe."

"Even after our own evil allowed the Khamorth to enter the Empire and work their outrages?" Rhavas demanded.

"Even then," the patriarch said placidly. "Men can be knaves and fools. Men often *are* knaves and fools. But even knaves and fools have Phos' light within them. It raises them above brute beasts."

"Does it?" Rhavas told Sozomenos some of the things he'd seen. He almost told him some of the things he'd done, but held back at the last minute. Not even holy Sozomenos needed to hear that. Rhavas finished, "If you ask me, these things do show us to be separated from the beasts. We are below them. They act as they must, but we act as we choose."

"Yes, as we choose. And we can choose the light. We must choose the light." Sozomenos sent a gesture of benediction toward Rhavas. "*You* must choose the light, very holy sir. It is there, for you as for anyone. That you have known hard times should not make you shove your faith aside."

"The world knows hard times," Rhavas insisted. "Times are so hard, Phos cannot hope to triumph. The idea that he could is a snare and a delusion."

Sozomenos sadly sketched the sun-sign over his breast. "I will pray for you. I will pray for you with all the strength in me. May the lord with the great and good mind grant you peace in the end."

Rhavas almost cursed him where he sat, just for being so secure and comfortable in what was obviously—but, it was clear, not obviously enough—an outworn creed. But no; it would not do. Sozomenos was an old, old man. His passing would not astonish anyone . . . most of the time. If two ecumenical patriarchs died within days of each other and within hours of quarreling with Rhavas, though, eyebrows would be raised. And rumors from the north had already reached the capital. So far, not even Maleinos connected those rumors to his cousin. Two dead patriarchs, however, and plenty of people might start making that connection.

Rising, Rhavas bowed to the white-bearded man who seemed so out of place in his gaudy robes. "Most holy sir, I will see you at the synod. The assembled ecclesiastics will be there."

"So they will," Sozomenos agreed. "But I hope to see you before that. I hope you will come and worship at the High Temple and pray for your faith to be restored. Sometimes sitting under the eye of that marvelous mosaic Phos will work a miracle of its own."

"Perhaps you will see me there." Rhavas did not care to refuse or insult Sozomenos to his face—such was the personal power the patriarch had. With another bow, the younger man strode out of the patriarchal residence.

A secretary of some sort was waiting for an audience with Sozomenos. "Holy sir," he murmured politely as Rhavas walked past him.

Rhavas nodded back. The pen pusher knew only that he was a priest, not that his beliefs were at odds with everything the temples taught. Somewhere out there, though, couriers were riding through the Empire (or that part of it not lost to the Khamorth, or maybe just that part of it not lost to the Khamorth and to Stylianos). They were summoning priests and prelates, monks and abbots to the city for this synod. After it was done, Rhavas told himself, things would be different.

But what if they weren't different? What if the synod just ratified the faith as it stood now? Bright sunlight made Rhavas blink. He scowled up into the sky—Phos might have been telling him he wasn't as smart as he thought he was. Phos might have been, but he didn't think Phos was.

If the assembled ecclesiastics didn't go along with him . . . In that case, there would be some sudden and unexpected demises. There might even be some at the synod itself. If people refused to look at what was obviously true, he would just have to rub their noses in it. After that, with a little luck, the survivors would have better sense.

If there were any survivors, of course.

The patriarchal residence opened on the plaza of Palamas. Rhavas had to make his way through it to go down Middle Street to his definitely less than fashionable inn. As far as the city's great market square went, the civil war might as well not have existed. Somewhere not far away, a vendor hawked fried squid. Rhavas' stomach growled, though the last one he'd eaten hadn't been especially good.

Fish caught in nearby waters gleamed under the sun. Customers sneered at the quality. Fishmongers swore at customers. A thieving cat ran off with a fat prawn hanging out of its mouth. The man who owned that stall flung a rock after the cat. He missed. The rock bounced off the cobbles, skipping crazily before coming to rest at last.

A juggler kept a fountain of balls and knives—and another fountain of stale jokes—in the air. A bowl with a few coins in it sat at his feet. Rhavas wondered if he'd put the money in there himself to encourage others. A singer accompanied himself on the lute. He used a hollowed-out calabash instead of a bowl. A scribe wrote a letter for an angry-looking peasant. A soothsayer offered to tell anyone anything—for a price. Rhavas turned away from him. He wanted nothing to do with soothsayers anymore. And if this soothsayer really could see the future, he probably wouldn't want anything to do with Rhavas, either.

Stolid grandmothers (some, actually, grimmer than stolid), their heads covered in bright scarves, sold green beans and onions and asparagus and dill and thyme and fennel and a dozen other vegetables and spices from baskets in front of them. They haggled with customers and gossiped among themselves. A couple of them watched Rhavas thread through the crowd. One sketched the sun-sign. In the interest of remaining a chameleon, he returned the gesture. Satisfied, she nodded.

He could have bought books or knives or puppies or rope or jewelry or a woman or a boy or an icon or olives or olive oil or a charm guaranteed to make him do better with the woman or boy he could have bought or a medicine guaranteed to cure whatever he caught from the woman or boy he could have bought or a belt or a belt pouch to wear on it or a tunic or the dye to change a tunic's color or (had he been a secular man and not an ecclesiastic) a trim for his beard or a manicure or a chicken or a toy oxcart or a full-sized one or a ball or a pair of stout boots with which to kick it or a pound of prawns or the scale to weigh them on and a set of weights to go with it or prunes or dried apricots or poppy juice to close up his bowels after the fruit opened them or . . .

The square had been like that before Rhavas left Videssos the city, too. If you wandered around cataloguing everything you could buy, you might end up spending all your time wandering and none of it buying. Plenty of people did. Their glazed eyes gave them away. There wasn't another place to shop like this in all the Empire.

Rhavas resolutely worked through it. He felt like patting himself on the back when he reached Middle Street and started up it. The main boulevard was itself lined with shops and with buildings devoted to the imperial administration. Though it had temptations of its own, it wasn't a patch on the plaza of Palamas.

When he turned off Middle Street and found his inn, the innkeeper gave him a peculiar look. "Ask you something, holy sir?" Lardys said.

"You can always ask. I don't promise to answer," Rhavas replied.

"Well, I'll see if I can loosen your tongue a bit." The taverner dipped up a mug of wine and slid it down the bar to Rhavas. "Have some of that, why don't you?"

"Let me get you a mug, too." The coin Rhavas set on the bar

ensured that the taverner wouldn't regret his own generosity or
resent Rhavas as the object thereof.

"You're a gent, holy sir." Lardys wasn't shy about drinking on
the job. He poured wine for himself, spat in rejection of Skotos
(so did Rhavas), and drank. After a long pull at the mug, he
inquired, "Is what people say about you true?"

"I don't know," Rhavas said. "What do people say about me?"
He tried to keep his tone light, but could not help a stab of
fear. If news from the north had attached itself to his name after
all . . .

But what Lardys said was, "I heard you were some kind of
kinsman to the Avtokrator. Is that so? Can that be so?"

"Anything *can* be so." As usual, Rhavas was relentlessly precise.
"As a matter of fact, though, that does happen to be so."

Lardys stared at him in owlish amazement. "Phos, man, in that
case what are you doing *here*?"

"Staying here. Sleeping. Eating. Drinking wine. The kinds of
things people usually do at an inn," Rhavas answered. *Taking a
barmaid to bed now and then*. But his tonsure kept him from
talking about that, if not from doing it.

The innkeeper went right on staring. "But . . . But . . . Why are
you doing it *here*, holy sir? Why aren't you in a fancy room in
the palace quarter eating suckling pig off golden plates? Doesn't
the Avtokrator need all the help he can get? Kinsmen, now, kinsmen are beyond price, on account of he can be pretty sure they'll
stay loyal. So why aren't you there?"

"Well, for one thing, his Majesty isn't all that fond of suckling pig," Rhavas said. Lardys made an impatient—and very
rude—gesture. With a shrug of his own, Rhavas went on, "For
another, his Majesty isn't all that fond of *me*."

"Oh." Having digested that, and having decided Rhavas was
serious, Lardys said, "That's pretty stupid."

"Of his Majesty? I doubt it." Rhavas knew how much he'd done to
antagonize his cousin, even if a lot of it had been inadvertent.

Impatiently, the other man shook his head. "No, no, no—of
you, for throwing a connection like that over the side. Think of
everything you could have done with it." Glorious dreams of what
was probably larceny made his face shine.

"You may be right," Rhavas answered, which was one of those
things you could always say without offending anyone, but which

had no real meaning. It could also be a polite way of saying, *Well, to the ice with you,* which was how Rhavas intended it this time.

Not realizing that, Lardys said, "You'd better believe I am. How could it not matter? Tell me that, my brilliant friend."

Rhavas didn't care to be baited. He said, "If Stylianos wins the civil war, my connection with his Majesty won't matter a counterfeit copper—unless it sets me up for the headsman's sword."

"Oh." The taverner looked foolish. "Well, there is that, isn't there?"

"You might say so. Yes, you just might." Rhavas went upstairs with the satisfaction of the last word. He didn't tell Lardys that associating with the Avtokrator's cousin could set *him* up for the headsman's sword if Stylianos won the civil war. If the fellow couldn't figure that out for himself, he was in the wrong place and the wrong line of work.

With some ecclesiastics cut off from Videssos the city by barbarian invasion and perhaps slain, with others unable to cross from land Stylianos held to that controlled by Maleinos, and with still others caught by marching and countermarching armies, priests and prelates, monks and abbots were slow to come into the capital for the synod Kameniates had convened.

Delay, here, worried Rhavas not at all. It gave him more time to pore over Phos' holy scriptures to find texts that would bolster the examples the world provided only too abundantly. And it let him study the late Koubatzes' grimoire. Little by little, he began to gain control of the magic the wizard had been able to work.

He even began to alter and improve the spells Koubatzes had devised. The mage, he slowly started to realize, hadn't been such a clever fellow after all. The grimoire might as well have been a cookbook; Koubatzes had his recipes, but he'd rarely got playful with them.

By contrast, Rhavas enjoyed variations on a theme. He not only used the dead mage's spell to rout cockroaches from his room, he improved it so that the bugs left marching in formation, as Maleinos' soldiers had when they tramped along Middle Street on the way to war against Stylianos.

Of course, Maleinos' soldiers had marched down Middle Street only once. Rhavas had to expel the bugs from his room again and again. Even when he worked another spell to keep roaches expelled once from returning, enough new ones got in to keep him busy repeating the cantrip.

He also used the conjuration that filled a room with darkness rather than light to persuade moths and flies and other insects fonder of illumination than was the most pious priest to go elsewhere. As with the other one, he had to repeat that charm again and again. He minded less than he might have; he knew he could use practice with his sorcery.

A few at a time, ecclesiastics did come into the capital. Most traveled in from the westlands, where the civil war burned less fiercely, or from the countryside close to the capital, which still lay in Maleinos' hands. A few priests and prelates did reach Videssos the city from towns that Stylianos held. Maybe they'd sneaked out in spite of the rebel's garrisons—or maybe his men had let them go to make sure the Empire stayed religiously united even while politically split. Did Stylianos and his officers have that much sense? Rhavas could hope so without being convinced or certain.

He wondered whether Arotras would come to the capital for the synod. He didn't see why the priest shouldn't. Arotras' temple was in a town not far away, and Rhavas' former seminary colleague had also had his doubts about Phos' ultimate triumph. Wouldn't he try to see that the temples' theology reflected his own? Rhavas dared hope so, anyhow.

Along with the priests and prelates, monks started coming into Videssos the city. Rhavas had never had much use for monks or monasteries. To his way of thinking, monks didn't pull their weight. They withdrew from the world without devoting enough of themselves to the divine. Their scholarship, when they had scholarship, struck him as narrow.

When they had scholarship, indeed. Monks didn't always reason their way toward the truth. Sometimes—often—they decided what it was and then thumped everyone who presumed to disagree with them. That had happened at more than a few synods.

It didn't look unlikely here, either. A swarm of monks paraded up Middle Street toward the High Temple. Some of them brandished bludgeons. Others held up jars of wine. Quite a few were drunk. They all bawled out hymns proclaiming Phos' glory. Some of them yelled curses aimed at anyone who might have another idea.

"Anathema to the accursed heretics!" they shouted. "Anathema! Anathema! Let them be anathema! Dig up their bones! Curse them all to Skotos' ice!" People cheered as they went by, whether from agreement or in relief at having them gone, Rhavas could not have said.

A monk who reeked of wine glared at him out of eyes as blood-shot as a boar's. "*You're* not one of these accursed—*accursed*—heretics, are you, holy sir?" the man demanded blearily.

"What if I were?" Rhavas asked in mild tones.

"Well, in that case, pal, to the ice with you." The monk, a stout—even beefy—man, raised his club as if to send Rhavas there on the instant. "In that case, pal, curse you and everybody who thinks like you."

Rhavas looked around. Nobody seemed to be paying any special attention to the monk or to him. Why should people in Vides-sos the city notice one monk or one priest more or less? Why, indeed? Still mildly, Rhavas said, "No, curse *you*, pal."

Outrage started to form on the monk's face. Then surprise replaced it. And then his features went blank. The club slipped from his hand. It landed on his foot, which should have made him jump and swear and hop . . . if he weren't already a dead man. Rhavas waited to see if anyone would pay attention to his collapse. But no one did. If anyone saw the fall, it was doubtless taken for just another drunken monk going down.

Whistling, Rhavas went on his way. He wondered what would happen if he had to do something like that at the synod to get his point across. Would the assembled priests and prelates, monks and abbots, pay attention to him then? Would they decide his theology had something behind it after all?

He whistled some more. If they didn't, they'd be sorry.

Soldiers kept laymen away from the High Temple. "Phos!" one of the pikemen complained. "This is liable to be more dangerous than going out and fighting Stylianos' boys. Leastways you know what you're up against with them."

The soldiers did not keep club-swinging monks from crossing their line. Rhavas hadn't expected them to. The monks belonged in the synod. So they were convinced, anyway.

When Rhavas walked into the High Temple, he found priests and monks arguing with one another. Here a priest wagged a finger under a prelate's nose. There an angry monk brandished his bludgeon. The priest at whom he shook it told him it would have an unlikely final resting place if he presumed to swing it. The monk expressed a certain amount of disbelief.

The commotion made Rhavas smile. For one thing, this was what synods were supposed to be like. And, for another, the mere fact of at least some disagreement encouraged him. He'd wondered if everyone would automatically oppose him. It didn't seem that way, anyhow.

Behind the pulpit stood Sozomenos. He watched the assembled ecclesiastics, and listened to them. He did not try to bring them to order, not just then. Maybe he couldn't. Maybe he simply didn't want to. Rhavas wasn't sure which the answer was, though he hoped for the former.

More and more priests and prelates and monks and abbots came in. Sozomenos waited and watched. At last, for no reason Rhavas could see, the ecumenical patriarch raised both hands in a gesture of benediction, and also—not incidentally—one that brought every eye to himself. An imperial commissioner heading up an important assemblage would have had a gavel with which to control his group. Sozomenos had only the strength of his will. As things turned out, that was more than enough.

"We are ready to begin," Sozomenos said. They hadn't been. They hadn't been anywhere close. Suddenly, though, they were, for no better reason than that the patriarch said they were. In spite of himself, Rhavas was impressed.

Another small group of ecclesiastics walked into the High Temple. Seeing everyone in front of them quiet and orderly, they ducked into pews not too far from the altar and sat ready for whatever would come next. They might have been schoolboys not quite late but not anxious to draw the master's eye even so, lest he reach for a switch.

Sozomenos had no switch, any more than he had a gavel. Plainly, he did not need one, either. "I thank all of you for your presence here this morning," he said. "One of our brethren had called upon my illustrious predecessor, the most holy Kameniates, to convene this synod to examine our faith and its most fundamental workings. That is his privilege, and, Kameniates no longer being among men, I have the honor of conducting this resulting assemblage. On your prayers, on your belief, and on your reasoning rest our direction for years if not centuries to come. I am confident you are up to the job."

He said nothing about what Rhavas' challenge really meant. He also said nothing about his own view of Rhavas' belief. Again, Rhavas was impressed. Sozomenos presented at least the appearance of scrupulous fairness. He would, no doubt, find some way to make his views felt—but then, so would every other ecclesiastic at the synod. That was what synods were for.

Hands still upraised, Sozomenos began to intone the creed: "We bless thee, Phos, lord with the great and good mind, by thy grace our protector, watchful beforehand that the great test of life may be decided in our favor."

All the clerics in the High Temple repeated the words after him. They came echoing back from the dome, as if the image of the good god picked out in mosaicwork there were also saying them. A tight smile on his face, Rhavas joined in the creed. Sozomenos had ways of showing which side he was on, sure enough.

But then the ecumenical patriarch said, "The task before us is nothing less than to decide whether that is still an appropriate summary of belief for us in this day and age. Think well on it, my colleagues: has goodness failed?"

"Of course not!" The prelate who boomed out that response was a plump, red-faced man in regalia almost as magnificent as Sozomenos'. He seemed much more accustomed to it than the ecumenical patriarch did, too; he wore it as if entitled to it, not as if surprised by it. Rhavas did not know him. He must have risen to prominence since Rhavas went to Skopentzana, and by his accent came from the westlands, which had not suffered barbarian attack, and which had had only a limited share in the current civil war. Since he knew little of suffering, he thought the same had to be true for the Empire of Videssos as a whole.

Fool. Fat, pompous fool, Rhavas thought. *You'd sing a different tune if you ever set eyes on a Khamorth.*

More than a few other ecclesiastics were nodding along with the pompous prelate. His was the comfortable road, the safe road. If they went along with his views, they wouldn't have to change their own.

Sozomenos held up a hand. "Do not decide too soon. Consider that you may be mistaken. Consider that we all may be mistaken. Consider well, my friends, my colleagues. Decide on the basis of the faith of our holy scriptures, not on account of your own prejudices."

Rhavas heard that with astonished respect. He knew Sozomenos disagreed with him—disagreed with him down to the very core. Yet the ecumenical patriarch could not have presented the case more evenhandedly. He urged, he invited, the assembled ecclesiastics to settle it on its merits, not on their preconceptions. Rhavas wondered whether he could have, would have, done the same had some other prelate come before him with a doctrine of which he so strongly disapproved. He had his doubts.

Would it matter, though? That plump, powerful prelate rumbled, "This is all a waste of time, most holy sir."

"Time spent studying the faith is never wasted, very holy sir," Sozomenos replied. "We shall examine the truth, we shall define it, and we shall refine it. May the lord with the great and good mind . . . and, ah, any other interested deity . . . aid us in our deliberations. So may it be." He lifted his hands to the heavens once more.

"So may it be," intoned most of the ecclesiastics in the High Temple. Several of them, however, spat in rejection of Skotos instead.

A couple of men who stood by the outer wall did not, to Rhavas' eyes, seem to be ecclesiastics at all. It was not so much that they dressed in nondescript mufti. It was the way they watched the proceedings. They were more interested in the ecclesiastics as people than as priests or as theologians.

Who are they? What are they doing here? Rhavas wondered. *Are they keeping an eye on things for Maleinos?* But the Avtokrator would surely have priests here to keep him up to date on what was going on—and to help keep things from going wrong.

One of the strangers happened to meet Rhavas' gaze. Swords might have clashed, there in the quiet under the dome. Power rang off power. *Whatever else he is, he's a mage,* Rhavas realized.

The man leaned toward his comrade and whispered something to him. The other layman stared at Rhavas. He was also a sorcerer. Rhavas did not think of himself as any such thing. How his power might seem to a pair of wizards . . . He would find out.

He did not fear them. He had cursed mages before, cursed them and watched them die. If he had to, he could and would do it again.

"Dig up the heretics' bones!" a monk shouted.

In an instant, the cry filled the High Temple. It echoed from the dome, as the creed had before. Phos himself might have condemned heresy.

Sozomenos raised a gnarled hand. Silence fell. In due course, even the echoes faded. "Whoever shall not agree with what this synod decides, whoever shall fail to accept it, will be a heretic indeed," the ecumenical patriarch said. "But until someone says that he will not accept it, we are all brethren together. This being so, I expect we shall all act toward one another as toward brethren. Do I make myself plain?"

No one told him he did not. The sway he held over Videssos' unruly ecclesiastics made Rhavas marvel once more. *Could I ever lead them so?* He hoped the answer was yes, but was too remorselessly honest with himself to find that likely.

"Question, most holy sir, if I may?" Even the plump prelate from the westlands was polite with Sozomenos.

"Go ahead, Arkadios," the patriarch replied. "Questions are always welcome. They help clarify the faith."

"It seems to me, most holy sir, that the question before us here does not clarify the faith, but rather undermines it. If we do not take the good god's ascendance on faith, what have we got left?"

"Well said!" The words came from half a dozen men scattered all over the High Temple.

"I shall not try to answer that. Instead, I shall yield the floor to the prelate who caused this synod to be convened," Sozomenos replied. He gestured toward Rhavas. "Here is the very holy Rhavas of Skopentzana. I trust he will be able to give you what you require. Very holy sir?"

"Thank you, most holy sir." Rhavas got to his feet. He bowed to Arkadios. "Very holy sir, my view is simple. A faith that goes unexamined, unquestioned, is in fact no faith at all. Only examination yields truth. We have gone a very long time without a proper examination of what we believe. The times we live in argue that this examination is long overdue."

Arkadios snorted. "You want to bow down to the dark god"—he spat between his feet—"and you are looking for a synod to tell you it's all right."

"No. That is not true." Rhavas shook his head. "I have never *wanted* anything less in my life. But I have the nerve to follow the truth wherever it leads me. Can you say the same?"

"I know what the truth is. I don't need any fancy examination to tell me," Arkadios declared. "And I don't need somebody who hides corruption behind a lot of fancy phrases."

Rhavas bowed again. "Thank you, very holy sir. Your objectivity does you credit."

"Do you mock me?" Arkadios demanded angrily. "Do you dare mock me? You have your nerve, all right, you heretic dog!"

"That will be enough of that." Sozomenos did not raise his voice, but had no trouble making himself not only heard but heeded. "Arkadios, you were the one who first resorted to personal attack. You cannot—or at least you should not—be surprised if you find it coming back at you. And if you resort to it again, you will find you are not too prominent to be expelled from this gathering. Do I make myself plain? Please apologize so we may proceed."

The prelate from the westlands bowed his head. "I am truly sorry, most holy sir." For a wonder, he sounded as if he meant it.

Even so, he did not satisfy Sozomenos. "You need not apologize to me, for I did not suffer under your harsh words. The very holy Rhavas, on the other hand, did."

Arkadios turned red with anger. He managed a most perfunctory bow toward Rhavas and muttered, "Very holy sir, I'm sorry."

"I'm sure you are." Rhavas answered one untruth with another. He bowed to Sozomenos once more. "Most holy sir, I believe the relevant passage from which we should begin our discussion is the third verse of the thirtieth chapter of our holy scriptures. I will quote it for the benefit of any who cannot call it to mind without help."

"How generous of you," Sozomenos murmured. Rhavas hadn't thought he had such sarcasm in him. Some priests and prelates muttered angrily at Rhavas' assumption that they could not quote chapter and verse for themselves. Others showed by their blank and anxious expressions that they needed all the help they could get. The ecumenical patriarch must have seen as much, for he added, "Well, go ahead, then, very holy sir."

"And so I shall." And Rhavas did: "'Now at the beginning the two gods declared their nature, the good and the evil, in thought and word and deed. And between the two, wise men choose well—not so the foolish.'"

"There!" Arkadios cried. "Out of your own wicked mouth you convict yourself!" He shouted toward Sozomenos: "Let him be anathematized now, so we can go home and tend to our own business."

"What have you to say to this?" Sozomenos asked Rhavas.

"Why, that the very holy Arkadios has proved himself . . . foolish, of course," Rhavas replied calmly.

Arkadios was anything but calm. "To the ice with you, Rhavas!" he roared. "I curse you in Phos' holy name!"

If Rhavas cursed Arkadios in return, there would be a death on the floor of the High Temple. That would give those two mages something to think about! But he was not ready to do that, not yet. In fact, he consciously restrained himself from doing anything of the sort. All he said was, "The very holy sir needs to consider whether he has in fact chosen well in choosing Phos. That is what we all need to consider today."

He would have gone on, but shouts of fury from every corner of the High Temple drowned out whatever he might have said. Then Sozomenos raised his hand again. Again, he won silence from the assembled ecclesiastics. Into it, he said, "You are welcome to disagree with the very holy sir. But you must do it through reasoned argument. Bellowing like a bull has no place here."

Rhavas wondered what the bludgeon-bearing monks thought of that. Bellowing had had its place at a great many synods in Videssian history. So had breaking heads. No matter what the ecumenical patriarch had to say, such things might also come into play at this one.

For now, though, Sozomenos' force of character—his holiness, to use a word Rhavas increasingly mistrusted—carried the day. He said, "The prelate of Skopentzana has the floor. He may speak as he wishes. Should you think it wise, you will have the opportunity to rebut him: of that, you may rest assured. For now, though, very holy sir, you may proceed."

"Once more, most holy sir, I thank you." Rhavas looked out at the sea of hostile faces around him. "I am going to ask you, gentlemen, holy sirs, to consider the state of the Empire of Videssos in deciding whether choosing Phos was wise or foolish. Which god has shown himself to be the more powerful?

"How many bloody battles have the Avtokrator and the rebel general fought against each other? How much have those fights accomplished, except in killing Videssians who would better be left alive? Who laughs, who triumphs, in a civil war? Phos? Give me leave to doubt it."

Arkadios, who seemed to have decided that he was the chief spokesman for orthodoxy, threw back his head and laughed theatrically; his big gray-streaked beard bounced up and down. After the theatrics were done, he said, "The Empire has had trouble before. Trouble is not enough to turn all of us into accursed Skotos worshipers." He spat again. So did most of the ecclesiastics in the High Temple.

"When there is room to doubt, I am in favor of giving the benefit of the doubt," Rhavas said. "I do not see that there is room to doubt anymore. Can you, Arkadios—can any of you, holy sirs—deny that Videssos today rules only half the land she ruled a year ago? Can you deny she is liable, even likely, to lose more land still?"

"Half the land?" Now Arkadios shook his head, for all the world like a bull bedeviled by flies. If he could have flicked his ears back and forth, he would have done that, too. "You lie, very holy sir."

"In saying this, very holy sir, you prove two things. First, you come from the west, and do not understand the north and the east. And, second"—Rhavas planted his barb with a certain ferocious glee—"you are an ass, and an ignorant ass at that."

Now Arkadios bellowed like a bull, a bull one of those flies had bitten. How long had it been since anyone presumed to stand up to him in argument? Quite a while, plainly; and, as plainly, he did not relish the experience now. "Why, you bald-arsed son of a whore!" he roared. "I'll thrash you with my own hands!"

He stormed toward Rhavas. No doubt he could have done it. He was taller than Rhavas (who was not short), twice as wide through the shoulders, and twice as thick through the chest. Rhavas, however, did not intend to take a beating. If Arkadios swung on him, that would be the last thing the prelate from the westlands ever did.

"Stop!" Sozomenos' voice was as sweet and clear as a silver bell. And Arkadios *did* stop. That made Rhavas wonder for a moment—but only for a moment—if Phos still could work miracles after all. The ancient ecumenical patriarch pointed a trembling forefinger at Arkadios. "Resume your place, very holy sir. I told you before that no unseemly violence would mar this synod. Resume it, I say!"

"But, most holy sir, he—" Arkadios pointed toward Rhavas. Even as he did, though, he began to obey Sozomenos' command.

"I had not finished." Sozomenos himself turned in Rhavas' direction. "Neither will there be any crude and crass insults heard. As much as violence, they taint our holy faith. Do you understand me, very holy sir?" He sounded very stern indeed.

"Yes, most holy sir. Please recall that I was insulted before I gave back the same coin," Rhavas said.

"That will be enough from both of you," Sozomenos said. "Are we ecclesiastics, or only so many squabbling tradesmen? If reason cannot prevail, why did we come together here?"

I don't know. Why don't you ask the monks with clubs? But Rhavas didn't say it out loud. He bowed to the ecumenical patriarch and said, "I shall remember your wise words, most holy sir."

Sozomenos looked in Arkadios' direction. With obvious bad grace, the prelate from the westlands mumbled, "And I, most holy sir."

"Excellent. I thank you both." From most men, that would have been nothing but a polite, insincere phrase. Sozomenos obviously meant it: one of the character traits that made him so impressive. He nodded to Rhavas. "You still have the floor."

"Thank you." Rhavas looked around the High Temple. "I say again that more than half the Empire is lost to us. I say also that it will be difficult if not impossible to win it back. Think on how many priests and prelates are not here, for their cities and towns were overrun by the Khamorth.

"I could speak for hours about the atrocities and massacres the barbarians have perpetrated against the people of Videssos, and this despite the countless prayers for thanksgiving and salvation those people offered up to the lord with the great and good mind. I know whereof I speak. I led many services calling on Phos to save his people from the onslaught of these savages who know him not. I led them, yes, and what good did they do us? Why, no good at all, as anyone can see, for I also watched the Khamorth sack Skopentzana. I watched them kill. I watched them rape. I watched them plunder. I saw nothing to make me think the lord with the great and good mind restrained them in any way.

"And how was it that they were able to enter the Empire in

the first place? Was it because the lord with the great and good mind invited them in? Do any of you think so, my fellow priests and prelates, monks and abbots?"

He waited. No one shouted out such a belief. Only silence came echoing back from the good god's image in the dome. Rhavas dared hope it was a troubled silence.

Into that silence, he continued, "You also know how and why the barbarians came into the Empire. The rebel emptied the frontier fortresses, leaving the border bare so he could better battle the Avtokrator. And how did the savages win such successes once they were inside? Why, the Avtokrator had emptied the city garrisons so he could fight the rebel. Tell me, holy sirs, is this a truth or am I trying to deceive you?"

Rhavas paused again. Again, no one screamed that he was a liar. Nobody screamed at him for criticizing Maleinos and Stylianos impartially, either. In the Videssian civil war, there was plenty of blame to go around. No one with eyes to see could doubt that.

Since no one was screaming at him, Rhavas continued, "We have to ask ourselves what this means, don't we? Does it mean the lord with the great and good mind truly is watchful beforehand that the great test of life may be decided in our favor? If it does mean that, how do we demonstrate it?"

Another pause. More silence. Maybe the assembled ecclesiastics of Videssos were thoughtful. Maybe they just thought Rhavas was a madman. Either way, no one tried to respond.

And he went on, "To my way of thinking, holy sirs, any explanation of these events that involves Phos also involves much convoluted thinking, much twisting of the facts to fit preconceived notions. I am not saying these notions are ignoble; on the contrary. But I am saying that notions which fail to fit the facts must be viewed with suspicion.

"What seems to me to be the truth may be—is—less pleasant to contemplate, but does that make it any less true? How better to explain the events of the past couple of years than in the most obvious way? We have given reverence to the lord with the great and good mind for centuries, but what has he done for us? Anything at all? If he has, is it visible? The works of his opponent are all *too* visible, for better and—mostly—for worse. Is it not the plain truth, then, that Skotos is stronger than Phos?"

There. He'd said it. He waited for the storm to burst around his head. And this time, he did not have long to wait.

"Heretic!" was the kindest thing the priests and prelates and monks and abbots yelled at him. They went on from there. "Infamous heretic!" was popular. So was "Apostate!" Quite a few liked "Skotos-lover!" and "Filthy Skotos-lover!" Some of the more ingenious ecclesiastics invented obscene variations on that theme. Other men, less clever or more furious, roared out wordless rage, like so many wild beasts.

Rhavas had looked for nothing different. Hoped, yes; looked for, no. No one physically attacked him. Sozomenos must have impressed the other ecclesiastics no less than he'd impressed Rhavas.

But, though the assembled clerics obeyed the ecumenical patriarch's injunction against violence, they would not come to order when he tried to calm them. Their rage had to break loose, it seemed. Had they held it in, they would have done themselves an injury.

To Rhavas' astonishment—and, he thought, to that of everyone else in the High Temple—the patriarch pulled a bugle from a shelf under the pulpit, raised it to his lips, and blew a long, not particularly musical note. The noise pierced the hubbub of human voices and bought Sozomenos a moment of something close to silence.

"Holy sirs, you have made your opinion plain," Sozomenos said. "You have, perhaps, made it too plain. The very holy Rhavas argues from Phos' holy scriptures, and from his interpretation of recent events. You may find his interpretation erroneous. Shouting insults at him, however, will not demonstrate that it is."

"Why do we even need to refute him, most holy sir?" Arkadios cried. "He refutes himself out of his own mouth. He shows himself to be accursed by Phos." He pointed a dramatic finger at Rhavas. "Accursed you are, and accursed you shall be forevermore, until the eternal ice at last takes you for its own!"

A storm of applause followed his impassioned words. Like the earlier outrage, it echoed from the High Temple's dome. Phos himself might have cheered on Arkadios' curse. The good god might have, yes, but Rhavas remained upright. He went on breathing, he went on thinking, not affected in any way he could sense by what the other prelate had said.

"How do you intend your curse to strike, very holy sir?" Rhavas inquired with exquisite, ironic politeness. "Will it perhaps bore me to death? It seems incapable of doing anything else."

Arkadios shouted angrily and waved his fist at Rhavas. "Let's see you do better, you lying sack of turds!"

Rhavas bowed to him. "As you say, so shall it be." He bowed to Sozomenos. "He has claimed a power—arrogated a power to himself, I should say. I too claim a certain power, or claim that it is stronger than the one he embraces. His demonstration, I believe, failed. Now for mine." He pointed to the other prelate. "Curse you," he said.

And Arkadios fell over dead.

Now there was silence in the High Temple: absolute, complete, horrified silence. A moan broke it, a moan from someone standing only a few feet from Arkadios' crumpled form. "He's . . . gone," the man quavered. He too fell over, Rhavas hoped only in a faint.

Tumult erupted. All the ecclesiastics close to Rhavas edged away from him, as if afraid he might level one of them next, or maybe more than one. Priests and prelates automatically sketched Phos' sun-sign. Some of them stared at their hands afterward. They might have wondered if the gesture was as apotropaic as they'd always believed.

The two mages at the outskirts of the gathering were arguing with each other, and getting hotter moment by moment. One of them pointed at Rhavas. That wasn't a curse—or if it was, it didn't bite. But Rhavas thought the man was only identifying him. And he still wasn't afraid of wizards: less so than ever, now.

Ecclesiastics also began pointing at Rhavas. "Sorcery!" one of them shouted. In a moment, many took up the cry: "*Sorcery!*"

"No." Rhavas shook his head. "I used no special wizardry. Arkadios claimed his god spoke through him. When he was put to the great test of life, though, all he found in truth was emptiness—wind and air. I have told you, holy sirs, that I believe the other god to be stronger. I asked him to speak through me, to answer Arkadios' lies and insults. I asked him to, and he did."

"*Sorcery!*" They hadn't listened to him at all. He hadn't really expected them to. He kept looking at the two wizards. One of them was nodding, Rhavas thought in agreement with what he'd said. The other kept shaking his head, though with less conviction than he'd shown before.

To Rhavas' surprise, Sozomenos was looking toward the mages, too. "Well, gentlemen?" the ecumenical patriarch asked them.

"Most holy sir, it is at least possible that he speaks the truth," said the one who'd been nodding. The other one looked very unhappy, but didn't disagree with him, at least not out loud. The mage who had spoken continued, "I found him to have used no ordinary spell, at any rate."

"I see," Sozomenos said heavily. "Or perhaps I see." He spoke to the assembled ecclesiastics: "Holy sirs, I adjourn this session of the synod. We shall convene again in three days' time. In the meanwhile, I charge you to speak to no one of what has passed here today."

That, Rhavas knew, was asking waves not to roll in from the sea or the sun not to rise in the east. What had happened in the High Temple would be all over Videssos the city before an hour went by. He supposed Sozomenos had to make the effort, though.

The ecumenical patriarch turned his way. "Will you do me the courtesy of staying to discuss this matter?"

"Of course, most holy sir," Rhavas said. "I am at your disposal."

Ecclesiastics flooded—they fairly flew—out of the High Temple. A couple of the priests who had attended Arkadios dragged his body away. The other man who had fallen must have got up again during the chaos, which meant he had only passed out. Rhavas was more pleased than not. He hadn't intended that priest to die.

Sozomenos descended from the pulpit. He seemed to abandon some of his patriarchal dignity as he did so. Approaching Rhavas, he seemed only a sad old man. "You did not have to kill Arkadios," he said in a deeply mournful voice.

"I am sorry it upset you, most holy sir," Rhavas said—he would not say he was sorry for what he had done. "The man insulted me and called me a liar. How else was I to show him to be mistaken?"

"Killing is easy." Sozomenos sighed. "If we have learned anything lately, we have learned that. When you can give back life as readily as you take it, taking it may perhaps be justified. Until then?" He shook his head. "Until then, no."

"We see things differently," Rhavas said.

"In many ways," the ecumenical patriarch agreed. "If you think you can frighten people into reverencing the dark god, I must tell you that I believe you are wrong."

"That is not why I did it," Rhavas answered. *Not all of why I did it, anyhow.* "He said I did not have the power. He said the dark god did not have the power. He cursed me. I cursed him. You see which of our curses was the more decisive."

"No, not yet," Sozomenos said. "Sometimes these things play out more slowly than it seems at first."

"Have it your way, then, most holy sir," Rhavas said dismissively. "I am alive. He is dead. I draw my own conclusions from that."

"I suppose you would." Sozomenos eyed him. "I suppose you are also the priest who has left a trail of blood in his wake from the northeast down to Videssos the city. I prayed it was not so, but I fear there is no longer much room for doubt, is there?"

"I admit nothing," Rhavas said. "Nor do I think your assertion is susceptible of proof."

The ecumenical patriarch let out another sad sigh. "I wish you had simply said, 'No, I am not the man.'"

Rhavas wished he had said that, too. He could say it now, but Sozomenos would not believe it. Sozomenos probably would not have believed it had he said it before. What he did say was, "I wish life were as we wished it. I wish I had not been forced to the conclusions I have reached. But life is as it is, and I believe what I believe—and I believe I have the evidence for that belief."

"There we differ," Sozomenos said. "The dark god may speak through you." He spat in rejection of Skotos—but he did it almost apologetically, as if to remind Rhavas it was his duty. "He may speak through you, yes, but you must always remember that he lies."

"I have other evidence of his strength than what he does through me," Rhavas said, "and those who oppose him would naturally say he lies."

"Perhaps you will persuade the assembled clerics," Sozomenos said. "Perhaps—but I would not care to bet on it."

"We shall continue, as you commanded, in three days' time." Rhavas bowed to the ecumenical patriarch. "Until then."

"Yes," Sozomenos said, sadly still. "Until then."

✳   ✳   ✳

When Rhavas came to the High Temple for the next session of the synod, the two wizards who'd been there before waited in the narthex. He bowed to them as he'd bowed to the patriarch. "Do you want something of me, sorcerous sirs?"

One of them flinched. The other one asked, "How did you do what you did to that other prelate? It was no ordinary spell." He looked daggers at his colleague, as if defying the other mage to tell him he was wrong.

"The god spoke through me," Rhavas said. Let them make of that what they would. He bowed again and went on into the High Temple.

A few priests came up to him and even fawned on him. That he had some supporters warmed him. But they were not the men he wished they would have been. He knew only a couple of them. One was a drunk, the other notorious for taking his vows lightly. The rest struck him as being of similar stripe. The sober, sensible prelates he would have wanted at his side did not care to join him. He shrugged. As he'd told Sozomenos, life was the way it was. Expecting it to be otherwise was asking for disappointment.

Sozomenos called the session to order with the usual prayers. Most of the ecclesiastics seemed more eager to offer them up than they had when the synod opened. Rhavas found that funny. He'd frightened them into piety.

Debate resumed. No one insulted him to his face, as Arkadios had done at the first session. No one insulted him, no, but next to no one spoke in agreement with him, not even the men who'd fawned on him.

He argued on. If he was to be alone against the world, then he was, that was all. It made the challenge larger. The ecclesiastics who argued against him kept on being much more polite than the late Arkadios had been. They would not agree, but they would not revile him for his opinions. He almost wished they would have. Killing a couple of them might have taken the edge off his own rising temper.

Those two mages kept watching him and muttering back and forth. He wondered what they were saying. He didn't worry overmuch—he'd told them the unvarnished truth—but he did wonder.

Some sort of commotion started outside the High Temple late

in the afternoon. Occasional shouts and outcries made their way into the immense building, though Rhavas could not make out words in them and didn't think anyone else could, either.

Then a man burst into the temple, crying, "Holy sirs! Holy sirs! I have news, holy sirs, important news!"

"Say on," Sozomenos told him from the pulpit, as if warning it had better be important.

And it was. "There's been a battle north of here," the man shouted, his voice filling the High Temple. "There's been a battle, and Stylianos has beaten and slain Maleinos! The new Avtokrator is marching on the city!"

✦ XII

Stylianos—now the unchallenged Avtokrator Stylianos—came into the capital six days later. A few officers had thought about resisting him. They couldn't do it in Maleinos' name anymore; one of them would have had to declare himself Avtokrator in turn, and start a new round of civil strife. That proved the sticking point. None of the ambitious men seemed willing to let one of his fellows get ahead of him. They all preferred to accept Stylianos rather than one of their friends and rivals.

So rumor said, at any rate. None of the officers summoned Rhavas, either to curse a rival or to curse Stylianos himself. Maybe they didn't believe what had happened to Arkadios. Or maybe they feared losing with or without Rhavas, and didn't want associating with him to count against them.

Sozomenos suspended the synod again till things grew more stable. None of the assembled ecclesiastics complained. Facing the ideas Rhavas presented—and facing Rhavas himself—was more daunting than the usual sort of theological disputation. Facing Rhavas and his ideas meant facing issues of life and death.

Lardys stayed cheerfully cynical. "None of it really matters, holy sir," he said. "None of it matters for beans. To the likes of me, what difference does it make who wears a crown?"

"It makes a difference to me," Rhavas said.

"Well, yes, I suppose it would," the innkeeper allowed. "You going to light out for the tall timber? Figure Stylianos'll do the same for you as he did for your cousin?" Lardys remained cheerful as he drew a finger across his throat. Why not? *His* wasn't the throat that would really be slit.

Rhavas only shrugged. "No way to know ahead of time."

"I guess you're right," Lardys said. "Well, you'll find out pretty soon, won't you?"

Like any new Avtokrator, Stylianos staged a triumphal entry into Videssos the city. His soldiers came in the day before he did, and secured Middle Street from the Silver Gate all the way to the palace quarter. The capital's garrison did not presume to quarrel with the newcomers. They knew which end of the loaf they would dip into oil.

Heralds announced Stylianos' arrival, just in case anyone in the capital had somehow missed the news. Rhavas had watched Maleinos ride out to battle. Now he saw Stylianos come in after winning that battle.

Rhavas was, in fact, in about the same spot on Middle Street as he had been when his cousin went off to war. Stylianos' parade was almost identical to that of the fallen Avtokrator, the main difference being that he went from the Silver Gate to the palaces, not the other way round.

The acclamations were different, too. People shouted Stylianos' name and "Stylianos Avtokrator!" and "Many years to the Avtokrator Stylianos!" Those same cries had greeted every Avtokrator who preceded him—Maleinos included—and would no doubt greet all his successors as well.

A man standing beside Rhavas nudged him with an elbow. "How come you're not yelling, holy sir?" he asked.

"I've got a frog in my throat," Rhavas answered in a husky whisper. "I can hardly even talk." Satisfied, the nosy man nodded. Maybe he was keeping lists of people who weren't celebrating enough. Plenty of new Avtokrators made lists like that. Rhavas wasn't worried about them, or not very much. He assumed he was already on whatever lists Stylianos had.

Here came the new Avtokrator, behind his standard-bearers. Stylianos rode a fine white horse, as Maleinos had before him. Along with his gilded armor, that set him apart from his officers. Though he was round-faced, he looked harder and more weathered

than Rhavas had expected: certainly harder than Maleinos. Rhavas'
cousin had spent most of this time in the imperial city, while
Stylianos lived in the field.

I could point my finger . . . Rhavas thought. But what good
would that do? It wouldn't bring Maleinos back to life. It would
probably just set off another round of civil war, or maybe more
than one. Rhavas looked down at his own hands. Even the power
to kill had limits. Who would have imagined that?

Stylianos was gone, bound for the palaces. The servants would
tend to him as they'd tended to Maleinos. Nothing ever happened
to them, no matter who ruled Videssos. They were indispensable,
and they knew it.

Stylianos' soldiers looked like . . . soldiers. Rhavas couldn't see
that they were any different from the men Maleinos had led. For
all he knew, some of them *were* men Maleinos had led. Stylianos
commanded all the soldiers in the Empire now, and would until
and unless some new rebel rose against him.

A few city folk trailed after the soldiers, singing their praises
and their master's. Most just went on about their business once
the parade passed them by. Avtokrators came and went. The
people of the capital praised them when they took the throne
and generally jeered them afterward. Every once in a while, an
Avtokrator would respond to scorn with massacre. That seldom
stopped more scorn from raining down on him, and commonly
gave him a black name in history.

Rhavas made his way back to the inn. He half expected to find
soldiers there, men waiting to haul him up before Stylianos. But
there were none. He pointed to the taverner. "You didn't want to
see our new sovereign?"

"Not me." Lardys went on pouring olives from a jug into a
bowl. "I'm no highborn mucky-muck. Why should I care whose
face goes on the goldpieces, as long as I can spend 'em?" He set
down the jug, reached under the bar, and pulled out a rolled-up
piece of parchment. "Fellow brought this here for you."

"Thanks." Rhavas took it. The image stamped on the seal was a
good copy of the portrait of Phos in the High Temple. *Sozomenos*,
Rhavas thought. He broke the seal—he took a peculiar pleasure
in breaking the seal, in fact—and unrolled the parchment.

The ecumenical patriarch's handwriting was thin and spidery,
but clear enough to be easy to read. *You would do well to think*

of disappearing, Sozomenos wrote. *The synod will surely condemn you, and you will as surely face the most severe punishment. Is it not better to be refuted while absent than to subject yourself to the rigors of the new regime?*

Walking over to the hearth, Rhavas tossed the note into the fire. The parchment charred and crumpled and burst into flame. In no more than a handful of heartbeats, it was gone. Its memory, though . . . That lingered. Sozomenos opposed Rhavas with all his heart—with all his soul, in fact. Even so, the patriarch did not seem to want to see him dead.

That sort of magnanimity . . . made no sense to Rhavas. Were he ecumenical patriarch and Sozomenos his theological rival, he would have done everything he could to destroy the other man. Did Stylianos' soldiers have orders to arrest any priest caught trying to sneak out of the city? Rhavas wouldn't have been surprised.

"What was it, holy sir?" Lardys asked. "What was that all about?"

"Nothing," Rhavas answered. "Nothing at all."

In due course, the synod reconvened. The soldiers outside the High Temple eyed Rhavas with mixed scorn and caution. The caution won: none of them had the nerve to mock. The story of what had happened to Arkadios plainly had lost nothing in the telling. Who would want to take a chance that the same thing might happen to him?

Priests and prelates drew aside from Rhavas when he walked into the High Temple. Yes, he might have been carrying some loathsome disease. *And so I am,* he thought. *The truth. There are none so deaf as those who will not hear.* And, now, he also carried the wrong blood in his veins, which only made things worse.

Sozomenos stood there talking with a couple of ecclesiastics. He broke away from them as soon as he saw Rhavas. "Very holy sir!" the patriarch called, hurrying toward him. "Did you not get my letter?" His face was a mask of distress.

"I got it," Rhavas said coolly.

"Then why did you not heed it?"

Rhavas looked at him—looked through him. "I think that should be plain enough, most holy sir."

"No." Sozomenos shook his head. "No, it is not plain at all. Unless—" He broke off, bowed his head, and covered his face with his hands. When he looked up again, tears glinted in his eyes. "I did not—I truly did not—believe the dark god had taken up residence in your heart, to make you mistrust those who would be your friend even if they think you mistaken." When he spat in rejection of Skotos, it was with obvious sorrow.

Of all the things in the world Rhavas could not stand, being pitied stood perhaps highest on the list. "Curse you, Sozomenos," he snarled, his voice clotted with hate. "Curse you to death."

And nothing happened.

Astonished, Rhavas stared at the ecumenical patriarch. He'd felt no resistance to the curse, as he had with Koubatzes and the mages who rode with Himerios. It simply . . . had not touched Sozomenos—and for the life of him, Rhavas could not understand why not.

"I will pray for you, very holy sir," the patriarch said quietly. "Those who are lost are not always lost forever." He gathered himself. "Since you are here, we shall have to proceed with this whole unfortunate business. If you will excuse me . . ."

"Wait," Rhavas said, and Sozomenos did. "Curse you, why don't you fall?" There. He'd said it again, and meant it with all his being.

Sozomenos gave him a sad little shrug. "You, it seems, have your god, in whose powers you trust. Can you not see I have mine as well?"

He walked off toward the pulpit. Had Rhavas been less steeped in the certainty of his own rightness . . . But he was what he was. He was sure he understood why the world worked as it did. And anything that happened to contradict that? He did not—he would not—see it.

As courteously as if Rhavas had not tried to kill him, Sozomenos gave him the floor and let him do his best to persuade the assembled ecclesiastics of his new doctrine. He did his best, piling more—and more graphic—examples and more quotations from Phos' holy scriptures atop the introduction he had given in the synod's earlier session. He alarmed them. He horrified them. He persuaded them . . . not at all.

Some of their counterarguments also came from the scriptures. Others were more pragmatic. "What will the Avtokrator Stylianos give us if we fall into this black heresy?" a plump abbot asked rhetorically. "He'll give us the sword, that's what, and put all our heads on the Milestone. If the very holy sir wants his head there, that's his business. If he wants ours up there with his, that's a different story."

"Even if Phos did rule the world, as you mistakenly believe, your cowardice would be plenty to send you to the ice," Rhavas sneered. "And it's a pity the ice is not fire, for you would burn very well."

"That will be enough, both of you." Sozomenos might have been reproving a couple of small boys, not two of the most powerful clerics in the Empire of Videssos.

The abbot, his face brick red, gobbled and sputtered but—no doubt luckily for him—did not manage to put his protest into words. Rhavas merely gave the ecumenical patriarch a stiff bow and returned to the theological attack.

Some time during the morning, a newcomer entered the High Temple. He seemed to have been there a while before Rhavas noticed him. He was neither ecclesiastic nor wizard. He leaned against a column sheathed in moss agate with the air of a man who'd drawn a soft duty but intended to fulfill it as if it weren't.

One of Stylianos' henchmen, Rhavas thought, *here to keep an eye on the synod for him.* Rhavas had a pretty good notion of what that meant. If the assembled ecclesiastics didn't condemn him on their own, the Avtokrator would take care of things for them.

Bitterness rose up in him like a cloud. Maleinos had shared his view. So had Arotras, a priest himself. So did Lardys. They all believed as he did—yes. Would any of them publicly admit it? Not a chance, not in all the world.

"Hypocrites!" he cried furiously. "You're all nothing but hypocrites, and you will get what hypocrites deserve!"

They would not believe him—or, perhaps more likely, they would not admit they believed him. That only made him angrier. He pictured priests and prelates nodding to themselves while they shook their heads for the world. He wanted to break those empty heads to let truth into them. That was the only way he could see to get the truth in there.

If he shouted, *Curse you all!* . . . what would happen? They would go down in windrows, like barley before the scythe. But even if they did, what then? Who would replace them? Men who thought as he did? Men, for that matter, who thought at all? Or would the new ecclesiastics just be more muttonheads indistinguishable from the ones he'd slain? That seemed altogether too likely.

A priest not far away pulled a loaf of brown bread and a chunk of pale yellow cheese out of a large belt pouch. Ignoring the debate and the occasional catcalls that filled the High Temple, he began to eat his lunch. That probably meant his mind was made up. It certainly meant he had a practical bent.

Not too much later, Sozomenos adjourned the synod to let the rest of the ecclesiastics eat. As they filtered out of the High Temple and down to the nearby plaza of Palamas to see what they could find, the ecumenical patriarch beckoned Rhavas to him. Warily, Rhavas approached.

"You are still here." Sadness filled Sozomenos' voice.

"Yes, of course I am," Rhavas said.

"But you are making a foolish mistake," the patriarch said, "a mistake even more foolish than I thought before I wrote you a few days ago. I met the Avtokrator yesterday. His Majesty would not be pleased with you even if you were not related to, ah, his predecessor. He seems to be a man of hasty temper, and one not easily swayed from anger."

"The synod will do as it will do. The Avtokrator will do as he will do. And I—I will do as I will do," Rhavas declared. "Does no one understand that I am as sure of my rightness as anyone else is of his?"

"*I* believe you are, very holy sir," Sozomenos replied. "I believe you—but I also believe your sincerity to be mistaken."

"And I feel the same about yours," Rhavas snapped. He did not care to think about how and why Sozomenos still stood. Since he didn't care to, he didn't.

"No doubt you do." Something in the ecumenical patriarch's stance and gaze put Rhavas in mind of a gentle grasshopper. Sozomenos went on, "The difference is, the synod will not condemn me when the time comes for it to define the faith. Nor will I be bound over for punishment. You wage a war you cannot win."

"Come the end of days, the war will be won," Rhavas said. Sozomenos frowned and shook his head. Rhavas ignored him. "The war may be won well before the end of days, too. Skotos is loose in the world, most holy sir. That you do not see it only shows you do not leave Videssos the city."

"Skotos is loose here, too," Sozomenos answered calmly, spitting in rejection of the dark god—as Rhavas had not done. "Skotos is loose everywhere—which does not mean we should embrace him."

"Why not? If he is the stronger, should we lie and say he is not?" Rhavas asked. "The Khamorth graze their ponies by the Long Walls—maybe inside them now, for all I know. Skopentzana is dead, along with so much else."

"I would believe as I believe if the barbarians rode their horses up the aisle of the Temple to the altar here," Sozomenos said. "I do not know when the end of days will come. I do not believe it will come soon. The struggle has a long way to go."

Rhavas scowled at him. "My prayers died unheard. My curses are fulfilled ten times over. Phos is deaf and blind and weak. Skotos hears me. More—Skotos speaks through me."

"Are you really so enamored of spectacle, very holy sir?" the patriarch asked. "I believed you a man of thought."

"And so I am," Rhavas answered, stung. "But thought that does not look at the world and what goes on in it is pointless. You will not see that, for you refuse to open your eyes."

"We talk past each other," Sozomenos said mournfully. "I wish it were otherwise. You were once the faith's strongest friend. I think you strike at it more from disappointment than from reason."

"I tell you, you are mistaken," Rhavas growled. Sozomenos only shrugged. Rhavas said, "The synod will do as it will do, as I said before. But its acts will be preserved. Those who come after us will see which side was in the right. I do not fear that."

"It will be a long time before anyone surely sees. Until that day of days comes, you must have faith. This is what you do not see," Sozomenos said.

"The day of days is coming sooner than you think. And I do have faith, most holy sir. This is what *you* will not see," Rhavas replied. Sorrowfully, the ecumenical patriarch turned his back on him.

Imperial guards seldom came to the inn where Rhavas stayed. They had their own dives, fancier and closer to the palace quarter. When they did come, they were even less likely to be accompanied by a pair of mages. Without much surprise, Rhavas recognized the men who had kept watch on him in the High Temple. But the wizards stayed in the background. It was one of the soldiers who pointed a gnarled finger at Rhavas in the taproom and declared, "Priest, you are summoned before his Majesty, the Avtokrator Stylianos."

"Am I?" Rhavas said mildly. "And if I don't care to come?"

"We are ordered to do whatever we need to do in that case," the soldier answered.

How much did he know? That he and his men had mages with them suggested they knew more than a little. How much could the sorcerers do to stop Rhavas if he chose to curse them—or Stylianos? He wasn't sure. He would have bet they weren't, either.

He shrugged and rose from his stool. "Never mind," he said. "Take me to the palaces."

Did the soldiers look relieved or disappointed that they didn't have to do whatever they needed to do? Rhavas couldn't tell, which was a tribute to their stone faces. Stylianos had chosen his men well.

A priest, a few soldiers, a couple of wizards—not such an unlikely group to walk west along Middle Street toward the palaces. "Bless me, holy sir," called a man with a cataract clouding one eye.

"You have my blessing, for whatever it may be worth to you," Rhavas said. The man bowed in thanks. He hadn't noticed that Rhavas didn't use the sun-sign or even name the good god.

"Why did you do that?" one of the mages asked. "By all the signs, you don't believe in blessings."

Rhavas shrugged. "It was simpler. If I'd said no, he would have raised a fuss."

The mage's right eyebrow quirked. "You don't worry, of course, about the fusses you raise yourself." Rhavas inclined his head, acknowledging that the other man had scored a hit.

The usual frantic hubbub of Videssos the city faded behind them when they entered the palace quarter. Gardeners trimmed shrubbery with long-handled shears. A washerwoman carried a basket of clothes on her shoulder. Two secretaries with ink-stained fingers argued about some piece of bureaucratic inconsequence as they strolled down the flagstones of a path between splendid buildings.

Rhavas had expected Stylianos to meet him in the throne room. That way, the new Avtokrator could have tried to awe him with the overwhelming majesty of the imperial office. Stylianos might well have assumed no Videssian, no matter how heretical, was altogether immune to that. He might well have been right, too.

But he decided otherwise. As Maleinos had when Rhavas came to Videssos the city, Stylianos chose to meet him in the imperial residence: as close to informality as ceremony-hedged Avtokrators could find. The furry-bearded Vaspurakaner steward who had served Maleinos now served his successor. No, who ruled the Empire made little difference to those who served the ruler.

"Come with me, please, very holy sir," the steward said when Rhavas had climbed the low, broad stairs. Remembering Rhavas' ceremonial title was the only sign he gave of ever having seen him before.

Along the winding corridors of the imperial residence they went. Rhavas nodded to himself as they walked past the high gilded helm of a Makuraner King of Kings, the one Stavrakios had brought back. People said the conquering Avtokrator had put the dent in it himself, with a mace. Rhavas didn't know if that was true. From everything he'd heard about Stavrakios, though, he wouldn't have been surprised.

Stylianos met him in the chamber where Maleinos had received him not so long before. Did the new Avtokrator know? Had he asked the stewards? Had they been happy to tell him? Rhavas didn't know that, either, which was probably just as well.

"Your Majesty." Rhavas prostrated himself, as he had before his own cousin.

"Get up, get up." Stylianos sounded as harsh and impatient as he looked. He waved Rhavas to a stool, then went on, "We can kill each other at a word. If that doesn't make us equals, what would?"

"A point." Rhavas knew he could slay Stylianos at a word. Could the Avtokrator really return the . . . favor? He might well need to summon a swarm of mages and soldiers, but odds were he could manage.

A servant came in with a silver pitcher of wine, two goblets, and a plate of pistachio-topped honey cakes on a tray of rare dark wood. After the man had bowed his way out, the Avtokrator poured wine for both of them. Stylianos went through the usual ritual. Rhavas ignored it. Stylianos eyed him. "You really want to make things easy for me, don't you?"

"What difference does it make?" Rhavas returned. "I'm Maleinos' cousin. How likely am I to get to Sozomenos' age?"

"Nobody's *likely* to get that old." Stylianos' chuckle held a grim edge. "Some people are less likely than others, of course. You're dead right about that." He laughed again. "*Dead right*'s about it. But if you go on spouting heresy every time you open your mouth, I don't even have to find an excuse to get rid of you."

Rhavas shrugged. In its own way, Stylianos' blunt candor was refreshing. "Try to tell people a plain truth and see the thanks you get," Rhavas said, doing his best to match it.

"Telling people the plain truth is one of the best reasons I know for roasting somebody over a slow fire," Stylianos observed. "Without some honey smeared over it"—he picked up a cake—"life wouldn't be worth living most of the time."

"No!" Rhavas shook his head. "Enough hypocrisy!" He almost said, *To the ice with hypocrisy!* Old habits of thought died hard. He went on, "Too many will not admit what is only too plain: which god is really the stronger."

"How would life be any different if they did?" Stylianos asked, and took a big bite out of the cake.

"How? We would be honest, that's how!" Rhavas exclaimed. "We could herd all the Vaspurakaners into pens and slaughter them for the sport of it, and the men who did it would cry out that it was Phos' will. A wizard could melt a city into a puddle of glass and sing a hymn to Phos in his glory, as long as the city was filled with people who didn't believe as he did. Another mage could poison the very air his foes breathed, watch them choke and die, and say the lord with the great and good mind delighted in their agonies. Enough of lies! We do evil. We enjoy doing evil. We take pride in doing evil. We always have. We always will. Time to tear away the veil!"

Calmly, Stylianos finished the honey cake. He pointed to the plate. "Have one. They're good." He waited. When Rhavas only sat there, he shrugged. "Or don't, then—whatever suits you. We do evil, yes. We enjoy it, yes. But do we take pride in it? *Should* we take pride in it, eh?"

Rhavas remembered how he'd felt after ravishing Ingegerd and then cursing her to keep her from killing him. Had he been proud of himself? Hardly. He'd been heartsick instead. But, he told himself, he'd still been struggling against the truth then. Now he understood it and accepted it. He said, "Why shouldn't we, your Majesty? It is part of what we are, just as much as—more than—good is. We have to be taught good, from the time that we are tiny. If we aren't, we grow up knowing it not. Evil, though, evil comes forth of itself."

Stylianos studied him again, this time for some little while. The Avtokrator's eyes were hooded, opaque; they seemed more likely to have been carved from jet than to belong to a living man. "Well, very holy sir, you are more dangerous than I gave you credit for," Stylianos said at last. "The synod will see to it, though. You were brave, to try to persuade Phos' priesthood to bow down to Skotos." He spat—reflectively, Rhavas judged, rather than from reflex, before continuing, "Foolish, mind you, but brave."

"The truth is there," Rhavas insisted. "People *will* see it."

"It's always been there," Stylianos said with a shrug. "The sun has always been there, too." He didn't sketch Phos' sun-sign; Rhavas found the omission interesting. Stylianos went on, "If we look at the sun too long, it blinds us. Then we don't see anything at all. If we look too closely at what people are really like, we throw up our hands—or maybe just throw up—and run away. How can we help it? That's why we have faith, I think: it lets us console ourselves by thinking we might be better than we are. We might be, yes, but we're bloody well not."

"You are a better defender of Phos than most of those in the High Temple," Rhavas said slowly. "Did you study for the priesthood before you started soldiering?"

"Not me. Not a bit of it." Stylianos made his denial sound absurdly cheerful. "But I've been around a long time"—he plucked at his beard, which was grayer than Rhavas'—"and I've seen a lot of shit. And a lot of what you see in my trade, very holy sir, *is* shit, believe you me it is. I've seen it, and I've thought about it, and this is what I've come up with."

"You will make a formidable Avtokrator," Rhavas said. "You may make a better one than my cousin did." He'd never dreamt he would think such a thing, let alone say it. But he'd barely met Videssos' new sovereign before today.

Stylianos only shrugged. "We'll see. I hope so. That's why I rose up against him, anyway."

Rhavas wondered what the Avtokrator would do if he were to renounce the doctrine he'd preached at the synod and in this little dining hall. He didn't wonder for long. Stylianos would find some other reason to condemn him. Or maybe Stylianos wouldn't find any reason he publicly announced. That didn't mean Rhavas would stay alive even a heartbeat longer. He couldn't go without sleep. He couldn't watch his back all the time.

He could—he thought he could—kill Stylianos now. But if he did . . . so what? The synod would still condemn him. The Empire would fall into chaos—*worse chaos*, he corrected himself. Rhavas had already seen as much. It seemed even more painfully clear now.

By Stylianos' small smile, he'd seen it, too. "This *is* how things work, very holy sir," he said, something approaching sympathy in his voice.

"They shouldn't," Rhavas said. "In the acts of the synod, the truth will be set forth for all time. Those who come after will see it for themselves. They will be persuaded. It will triumph."

"Dreams are nothing but dreams, no matter who dreams them," Stylianos said. "Yours will crumble, too."

"We shall see, your Majesty. Unlike you, I do have faith, even if it is not the sort of faith you might prefer," Rhavas said. The Avtokrator laughed and laughed. That might have been the funniest thing he'd ever heard.

Back at the High Temple, Rhavas listened to one ecclesiastic after another denounce him. The priests and prelates probably would have done the same even with Maleinos still on the imperial throne. With Stylianos' fundament warming that seat, they thought they had a license to assail Rhavas—and, no doubt, they were right.

The ecumenical patriarch remained courteous, and kept giving him chances to respond. Though Rhavas began to see they would do him no good, he used them anyhow. "Any man who can look at the state of the world and then declare that good will surely triumph is either a liar or a fool—most likely both," he declared.

Boos and hisses and catcalls filled the air around him. Someone flung a rotten squash at him, as if he belonged to a bad Midwinter's Day mime troupe. The flying vegetable missed him and smacked another priest instead. It came from behind Rhavas. Whoever hurled it hadn't wanted his face seen, lest he be cursed.

Rhavas bowed in that direction, sarcasm steaming from his good manners. "And in which chapter of Phos' holy scriptures do you find that response?" he inquired. Only more jeers answered him, these from all around the High Temple.

"Shall we proceed, holy sirs?" Sozomenos could make the assembled ecclesiastics pay attention to him. "Shall we proceed in something at least approaching order?" If *he* had to resort to sarcasm, things had come to a pretty pass indeed. When he got enough calm to satisfy him, he pointed to a scrawny, clever-looking young priest. "I recognize Seides. You may proceed, holy sir."

"Thank you, most holy sir. I wish I did not have to," Seides said. "But we have seen murder done here on the floor of the high Temple—yes, even here. And I am sorry to have to report to you—to report to you all, my fellow ecclesiastics—that this is not the first murder worked by Rhavas, who no longer deserves to be deemed a very holy sir. I speak with regret, but also with conviction. And conviction is what this man who has abandoned his soul to darkness deserves."

Sozomenos, as usual, turned to Rhavas. "Will you deny, very holy sir? Will you extenuate?" He sounded as if he hoped Rhavas would. He probably did. Rhavas saw as much, even if it baffled him.

"He has said nothing yet," Rhavas said. "By the time he has finished, he will have said the same. As for Arkadios, I deny that was murder. A duel, perhaps, but not murder. He called on the power he respected. I called on mine. I still stand here. He does not."

After another of his sad sighs, Sozomenos nodded to Seides. "You may proceed, holy sir."

"I thank you, most holy sir. As I say, this appears not to be the first murder the prelate of Skopentzana has perpetrated. He rode off in company with a certain Himerios, an imperial officer, and two mages. The bodies of these men were discovered behind bushes. They had been there some time, and scavengers had been at them. No one is *certain* what became of them, mind you, but they are dead, while the very holy Rhavas lives on. This Himerios, be it noted, lived for long and long in Skopentzana, where he commanded the imperial garrison. He and Rhavas could not have been unknown to each other."

"He commanded the imperial garrison, yes," Rhavas said. "He commanded it for Maleinos, and fought for Maleinos against Stylianos, as did these mages. This being so, how can anyone here care about their deaths under any circumstances?"

That produced a sudden and thoughtful silence in the High Temple. Priests and prelates and monks and abbots had to bear in mind who their new sovereign was. Those who couldn't shift with the changing tides would be left behind—or something worse than that would happen to them. Rhavas almost laughed out loud. This Seides knew a lot, but he wasn't as smart as he thought he was.

Then the priest said, "You may make whatever denials you like in this case, very holy sir, but it is also a fact that you were in the company of this Himerios' wife, a fact we know from a merchant, a certain Arsenios, who traveled with you and the woman for a time. And it is a fact that the woman was found dead, with no obvious reason that she should be dead, in an otherwise deserted farmhouse north of the northern town of Kybistra."

Arsenios! Rhavas had forgotten all about him. But the merchant evidently hadn't forgotten about Rhavas. Who would have thought he could reach Videssos the city?

"And a Skopentzanan mage, a certain Koubatzes, was found dead, with no obvious reason that he should be dead, in the snow south of Kybistra," Seides went on. "Arsenios has stated that the said Koubatzes was not satisfied with your explanation of this woman's fate, and that he rode after you on the morning you departed Kybistra."

Curse you, Arsenios, Rhavas thought furiously. He had no idea where in Videssos the city Arsenios was. But he hoped—and he thought—the curse would find the miserable wretch.

Nor had Seides finished. "There is also the question of the priest Tryphon, who expired for no obvious reason while debating theological questions with you in the town of Podandos. And there is the question of the most holy Kameniates, the recently deceased ecumenical patriarch, who expired for no obvious reason not long after rejecting the wicked and heretical doctrines you have propounded at this synod. What have you to say for yourself in regard to these matters, very holy sir?"

Rhavas was tempted to curse Seides, too. The man was more clever than Rhavas had thought he was, clever enough to be dangerous. But if Rhavas did curse him, his demise would only prove his point. Had Seides figured that out? Did he count on it? If so, he was very clever indeed—and very dangerous, too.

"What do I say?" Rhavas needed a moment to decide just what he *would* say. "I say these are lies. I say this is nothing but scandalmongering, an effort to blacken my name so impressionable fools"—*which means most of you*—"will look away from the truth in my words."

"I have the written reports from Kybistra," Seides said calmly. "The men who wrote them knew nothing of your doctrines, such as those are. I have the written report from Podandos as well. And Arsenios' deposition was taken before he learned why it was of interest. Further, your innkeeper, a certain Lardys, states that you cursed the late Kameniates at about the time of his unexpected and otherwise inexplicable demise."

He cursed him, too. Did he say that? But Rhavas couldn't ask the question, not without betraying himself. "You are too blind and too afraid to acknowledge the strength and power of the doctrine I have presented to you," he declared. "If you make me out to be a villain, you don't have to."

"You have made yourself out to be a villain. I merely report your deeds." Seides spread his arms to the assembled ecclesiastics. "Holy sirs, I speak with regret, but I also speak with certainty. This Rhavas has shown himself to be not only an infamous heretic worthy of our condemnation but also a common, vicious murderer deserving the full penalties of the law. Shall the synod now call the question on his misguided and pernicious doctrines?"

"Yes! Let us call the question!" That shout came echoing back from the dome, as if straight from Phos' lips.

"The question shall be called." Sozomenos did not sound exultant at the prospect of seeing Rhavas defeated. Instead, he seemed sad things had come so far. But he pressed ahead nonetheless: "Let those who agree with the doctrines propounded by the very holy Rhavas so signify by a show of hands."

Defiantly, Rhavas raised his own right hand. He wondered whether any other ecclesiastics would have the nerve to do likewise. To his surprise and pleasure, a few more hands did go up, all around the High Temple. A few, yes, but not nearly enough.

"Will the patriarchal secretary please inform me when he has completed his count?" Sozomenos said. A priest came up and whispered in his ear. "Thank you," the patriarch told him, and then raised his voice once more: "Let those who oppose the doctrines propounded by the very holy Rhavas so signify by a show of hands."

A forest might have suddenly sprung up, there inside the High Temple. Arms in blue sleeves, arms in cloth-of-gold sleeves, arms in sleeves that had fallen down . . . Arms by the hundreds rose. Sozomenos' was one of them.

"Will the patriarchal secretary please inform me when he has completed his count?" the old man repeated. The priest needed longer this time; he had many more arms to count. At last, he approached Sozomenos once more. The ecumenical patriarch bent to hear his whisper, then nodded. "The very holy Rhavas' doctrinal innovations having failed to win a majority, the true and orthodox faith remains defined as it was before this synod was convened."

A storm of cheers rose from the assembled ecclesiastics' throats. With the cheers were jeers: "Anathema to Rhavas!" "Rhavas the heretic!" "Dig up Rhavas' bones!" "To the ice with Rhavas!" Rhavas stood there calmly, listening to his foes exult. *Let them yap*, he thought. *They have no power to do anything else, while I . . .*

Sozomenos raised both hands in the air. Little by little, silence returned to the High Temple. "Calm yourselves, holy sirs," the patriarch said. "Those who have been found to be in error shall still have the chance to restore themselves to the fold. You priests and prelates, you monks and abbots who voted for the doctrines found not to be acceptable, will you not recant your errors and do penance for them?"

"I recant!" someone called.

"And I!" someone else added. One by one, other ecclesiastics abjured what they'd favored only minutes before. Rhavas knew what drove them: fear. If they persisted in what had been ruled heresy, they would suffer for it. If *he* persisted, the assembled ecclesiastics would do their best to make him suffer, too.

At last, it seemed that every cleric but Rhavas himself had renounced the view that Skotos was or could be more powerful than Phos. Sozomenos looked out to him from the pulpit. "Very holy sir, I appeal to you: return to the true and orthodox faith," the ecumenical patriarch said, stretching out his hands in supplication. "Return to the light, which is your true home. I beg of you, bend your proud neck and agree with the ecclesiastics assembled here."

Bending his proud neck was the last thing Rhavas cared to do. If anything, he was prouder in defeat than he had been while still hoping for triumph. "The light has failed," he said. "Darkness covers the face of the world. You who will not see it, you are the eyeless ones."

"Anathema!" "Heresy!" "Excommunicate him!" The cries rose up again, like the baying of a pack of wolves.

Again, Sozomenos raised both hands. Again, he needed some little while to win quiet. Once he had it, he spoke in somber, even sorrowful, tones: "Those who will not recant must be condemned. You do understand that, very holy sir?"

Rhavas laughed a laugh with knives in it. "This synod has not the power to condemn me," he said. "You are yourselves condemned as madmen, blind men, and fools. Those who will not see the truth in this life will surely learn of it in the next, and I wish you joy of it."

The rising roar of rage was music to his ears. He pointed at the thickest crowd of clerics, intending to send as many of them as he could to the next life right away. If Arkadios hadn't driven home the lesson, this would.

But it didn't. He never got the chance to use his curse. During the long, dangerous ride down to Videssos the city, he'd thought several times about monks who decided synods with bludgeons. He'd paid no particular attention to the monk standing behind him: just one more blind man among a great swarm of them. But the man was not blind; he could see more than well enough to swing.

Stars exploded against the side of Rhavas' head. He groaned, or thought he did. Then the stars went out and everything spiraled down into blackness.

This wasn't the Bridge of the Separator. At first, that was all Rhavas knew for sure. He thought he was dead, but he wasn't so sure about that. Wherever this place was, it was dark, and it was freezing cold.

"Ah, my friend, my disciple. Welcome. I did not expect to see you so soon." The voice was deep and slow. If a voice could be dark and freezing cold, then this voice was.

"Where . . . where am I?" Thinking about the ice in the abstract was one thing. Living it, experiencing it, *knowing* it—that was something else again. But why, if he was in Skotos' hell, couldn't he remember falling off the Bridge? Surely he would have had to go through that before meeting . . . this.

"Where do you think you are?" Had the voice known how, it would have sounded coy.

"This . . . has to be the ice," Rhavas said with such courage as he could muster. Being brave was cold comfort indeed.

"Well, if it does, are you ready to make the most of it?" the voice asked.

"Make the most of it?" Rhavas wondered if he'd heard right. How could he or anyone else make the most of an eternity of torment, of punishment?

"You are still of the world, if not precisely in it," the voice said. "Go back, if you care to, to work for me. You can serve me well, and win time for yourself beyond any mortal's dreams. Or you need not leave this domain at all, ever again. The choice is yours, and yours alone."

Already, the dark and the cold were shriveling Rhavas' soul. He wondered if there was another choice: to leave them behind for light and warmth. No sooner had that thought begun to form than laughter rolled around him, rolled through him. *There* was something the voice found truly funny—and Rhavas' soul shriveled even more. The answer to his question seemed only too clear.

"I'll go back!" he gasped.

"Why am I not surprised?" Oh, yes, that struck the voice funny, too, not that Rhavas was in any position to appreciate the mirth. Its laughter made the most terrible peals that had ever burst from his or any other merely human throat seem cries of delight absolute and unrestrained. "Very well, then. You may . . . wake up!"

"Wake up!" Someone threw a bucket of water in Rhavas' face. The water was stale, almost stagnant. He coughed and spluttered, half-drowned. "Wake up!" the voice shouted again.

Rhavas did, and wished he hadn't. His head felt as if a boulder had fallen on it and driven him into the ground up to his neck. But the shout came from a merely human throat, not from . . . anything else. He frowned, trying to remember. Had that been only a dream? He wasn't sure. He wondered if he ever would be.

He also wondered if it would matter one way or the other. His head pounded so much, he wished he were dead. A moment later, he shook his head. He regretted it immediately afterward, for the motion brought fresh shooting pains and made him want to be sick. But he did *not* wish he were dead. However miserable he was, he wanted to live.

Another bucket of musty water soaked him. "On your feet, you cursed heretic! By the lord with the great and good mind, you're going to get every bit of what's coming to you."

On my feet? Rhavas thought. He had to remember how to make them work. He couldn't just rise, the way he would have if he hadn't just been clouted over the head. Each individual motion took intense concentration. Putting the motions together took even more. After some little while, he stood, swaying like a tall tree in a bad storm.

He realized he was in a cell. Stout iron bars separated him from his tormentor. The man who'd drenched him stood there laughing in the corridor—*he* had no trouble staying upright. He would have been safe from any ordinary victim. Whatever else Rhavas was, ordinary he was not. "Curse you," he growled, and waited for a measure of revenge.

But the man did not fall. Rhavas swore under his breath. Were his wits still too scrambled to let him curse? He wouldn't have been surprised.

Then the man sketched the sun-circle over his heart. "Phos!" he exclaimed. "You're as strong as they said you were, and more besides. They put every kind of ward under the sun on me, and you still almost knocked me over."

That made Rhavas feel better—the first thing that had. He started to curse the—guard? sorcerer?—again, but checked himself before he did. There would be others. If they came in and found this one dead, it would go worse for him . . . assuming it *could* go any worse. And killing this wretch wouldn't get him out of the cell. He wondered if anything would, save the last walk to face a headsman's sword, or perhaps the stake.

"Every time you try to curse somebody from now on, we'll clobber you again," the man said cheerfully. "Before long, you won't have enough brains left to keep from pissing your drawers—and you wouldn't be able to do any more than you did just now anyway, so you'd better save your strength for praying."

Rhavas wasn't so sure of that. With all his wits about him, he could curse more powerfully than he had. Could the Videssian wizards' wards also grow stronger? He didn't know, but he was inclined to doubt it. Even so, he nodded as if he understood and accepted the other man's words. That made daggers of pain stab him again, but he set his teeth and endured them. Whether his foes knew it or not, he had something in reserve.

"We'll be well rid of you," the fellow said. "Even the patriarch thinks so, and he's soft as a pile of goose down."

Sozomenos had needed no wards to withstand Rhavas' curses. They hadn't almost knocked him over, either; as best Rhavas could tell, they hadn't affected him at all. Rhavas still didn't understand—didn't want to understand—that, but he did understand one thing: the ecumenical patriarch, whatever else he was, was far from soft.

If Rhavas' foes did not understand one another, that was something else he held in reserve. He kept quiet, one of the hardest things any Videssian could do.

The guard, by contrast, went right on gloating. When he had something to say, he talked. When he didn't have anything to say—he talked anyway. "They'll anathematize you," he said, anticipation bubbling in his voice. "They'll excommunicate you. And then they'll execute you. With your cousin on the throne, you might have got away with the sword. Now that Stylianos is Avtokrator, though, I figure they'll burn you. How do you like that?"

"Not very well," Rhavas answered. The guard only laughed at him. Why not? He'd said something funny. As if how he liked things would matter a bit! "Where am I?" he asked, a reasonable question for somebody who'd been knocked over the head.

That only drew more laughter from the man in the corridor. "Don't even know, eh? And you were the fellow with all the answers in the synod. Except they didn't much like your answers, did they?"

"Fools don't know wisdom when they hear it," Rhavas said.

"No, you don't, do you?" the man retorted—a better comeback than Rhavas had looked for from him. The fellow went on, "As for where you're at, you're in the prison under the patriarchal residence. Where else would they stow an arch-heretic till they're ready to get rid of him for good?"

Rhavas hadn't known there *was* a prison under the patriarchal residence. He would have bet Sozomenos hadn't known about it, either. But someone had: probably Sozomenos' sakellarios. The patriarchal secretary always knew where the bodies were buried. He was also the man who kept an eye on the patriarch for the Avtokrator. Did Sozomenos have a new sakellarios these days? Or was the old one just . . . flexible?

That was, quite literally, the least of Rhavas' worries right now. He asked, "May I have some water to drink along with what you gave me to swim in?"

"Oh, you are a funny fellow," the guard said with another laugh. "We'll see how funny you are when they light the woodpile under you. You'll laugh out of the other side of your mouth then, by Phos." But, to Rhavas' vast relief, he went away after that, perhaps even to get the water.

Rhavas took the chance to look at his cell. Three walls were of stout masonry, the fourth of iron bars. The lock was beyond his reach. The cell held only a canvas mattress cover stuffed with straw and a brass-bound wooden bucket whose purpose was depressingly obvious.

What light there was came from a couple of torches in sconces on the far wall. Rhavas was glad there wasn't more; even looking at the flames made his headache worse. That monk had almost caved in his skull for good.

Here came the guard. Two archers accompanied him. "Get back against the far wall," he snapped. Rhavas obeyed, dimly flattered the man thought him so dangerous. While the archers aimed at Rhavas, the guard reached into the cell and set a cup on the stone floor. "Here you are." He drew back and waved Rhavas forward.

The water wasn't cold and wasn't especially fresh. It might have been the same stuff that had drenched Rhavas. He didn't care. He drank eagerly. "Thank you," he said when the cup was empty.

"It's all right," the guard said. "Drink as much as you please. It won't be enough to put out the fire when the time comes. So long." Away he went, the archers at his heel. Rhavas wanted to throw the mug at his head. He didn't, and afterward wondered why. What could he do now that would get him in worse trouble than he was already?

✳   ✳   ✳

Like so much else in Videssian life, anathematizing and excommunication had a ceremony all their own. Guards heavily reinforced by mages came to get Rhavas out of his cell. He thought about striking at them, but again held back. He didn't think he could slay them all, and anything less than that would do him no good. If they wanted to hold a ceremony with him in the starring role, they could do that. He still thought he might be able to take his revenge on them later on.

For now, they were too alert—as alert as if he were a lion coming out of a cage. "No false moves, priest, or you won't live long enough to be sorry!" barked one of the guards who warily unlocked the iron door confining him.

"Here I am," was all Rhavas said. "The priests and prelates and patriarch make a mistake condemning me."

"One of you says yes. All of them say no," the guard answered. "I expect that pretty much settles it."

Rhavas shook his head. "How many are mistaken makes no difference. How many have the truth is another story. I have the truth. You would do well to remember that, and learn from me."

"No, thanks," the guard said. "I'll take my chances with the whole rest of the world, I will." He laughed.

He thought he was a wit. Rhavas thought he overestimated by a factor of two. "The more fool you," Rhavas said.

"I'm not the one getting anathematized. I'm not the one getting excommunicated," the guard replied. "You cursed well are, and cursed you will be. Now get moving, not very holy sir, or we'll bloody well drag you."

He had nerve, if not much in the way of brains. Rhavas didn't fear curses from the ecclesiastical hierarchy. What the priests and the wizards would do to him after the formal condemnation was liable to be a different story. Admiring the guard's cheek, he accompanied the man without any more argument.

When he came up, it was evening. That surprised him; he'd been looking to see sunlight one more time. But night was falling, with the nearly full moon in the east casting a pale glow across Videssos the city. A few birds sang the last sleepy songs of day. As more and more stars came out, the birds fell silent.

The vast bulk of the High Temple blotted out a good many stars.

It covered more of the sky than the Paristrian Mountains had till Rhavas drew quite close to them. Men with torches moved ahead of him and behind him, so that he never got out of the light.

"Keep moving, you!" the guard told him, again as if he were a dangerous beast that might turn and bite if it got the chance. *And so I might, too*, he thought, not without pride.

Torches and fat, perfumed candles and innumerable olive-oil lamps made the High Temple's narthex almost as bright as day. Almost. During the day, the light came from one source: the sun. Here, with all these lamps and candles and torches blazing, a million shadows danced and jiggled and swooped and competed. The light was bright, but daylight it was not.

"Keep moving!" The command came again. Rhavas obeyed it. Walking from the narthex into the High Temple itself was passing from light into near-darkness. Half a dozen great beeswax candles burned near the altar; here and there, they raised ghostly golden twinkles from the tesserae in the dome mosaic. But half a dozen candles, no matter how large, could not begin to illuminate the vast space under that dome.

Here and there, the candlelight also raised golden echoes from the ecumenical patriarch's rich robes. Sozomenos still sounded sad when he called the session to order: He did not want to condemn Rhavas. But where what he wanted and what he judged his duty conflicted, he would do his duty.

"We are met this evening in the matter of the very holy Rhavas, formerly a priest of Videssos the city, formerly prelate of Skopentzana, who has refused to put aside beliefs declared heretical by the synod recently convened," Sozomenos said. "Very holy sir, will you not renounce your misbelief and return to the bosom of the true and orthodox faith?"

"I do not believe it to be misbelief, and I will not renounce it," Rhavas said firmly. He also did not think renouncing it would do him any good. If he did, the assembled ecclesiastics would rejoice for his soul—and turn him over to Stylianos, so the secular authorities could dispose of him for his crimes against imperial law.

A sigh rose from the priests and prelates and monks and abbots in the High Temple. The ecumenical patriarch gestured to someone Rhavas could not see. That worthy stepped forward and used a bronze snuffer to put out one of the tall candles.

Sozomenos gestured again. A chorus invisible in the gloom sang out: "Anathema to the heretic! Let him be excommunicated! Let him be cast into the outer darkness! So may it be!"

The beautiful rendition contrasted chillingly with the dreadful words. Hardened as Rhavas thought himself to be, he couldn't help shivering. The condemnation sent him . . . *Where I already am*, he thought, and made his back stiffen.

"Will you not renounce your mischievous belief that the power of Phos has receded in this world, while that of Skotos has advanced?" Sozomenos inquired.

"I do not believe it to be misbelief, and I will not renounce it," Rhavas replied. He knew how this ceremony would go. He knew how it would end—or rather, how it was supposed to end. He had in mind a dénouement somewhat different from the one the patriarch envisioned.

Another sigh rose from the almost invisible ecclesiastics in the High Temple. Was it a sad sigh or a hungry one, an anticipatory one? Rhavas knew what his opinion was. Sozomenos' gesture, though, was beyond question sorrowful. The priest with the snuffer extinguished another candle. The chorus sang out again: "Anathema to the heretic! Let him be excommunicated! Let him be cast into the outer darkness! So may it be!"

Three more times Sozomenos asked Rhavas to return to orthodoxy and renounce his newfound faith in Skotos. Three more times Rhavas refused. The snuffer put out three more candles. The chorus sang of Rhavas' condemnation three more times.

Only one candle remained alight in the High Temple. Sozomenos asked one more ritual question. Rhavas did not answer right away. When he didn't, the patriarch said, "Very holy sir?" with fresh hope in his voice. Maybe even at this last instant Rhavas' soul might be saved.

Rhavas still did not think his soul needed saving, not from the likes of the ecclesiastics assembled in the High Temple. He had been otherwise occupied, watchful beforehand (he smiled at the conceit) that they would not have the chance to lay their hands on it, so to speak. Sozomenos' final ritual question interrupted him.

When he reached a place where he could speak again, he said, "My apologies, most holy sir. I do not believe my doctrine to be misbelief, and, for the last time, I will not renounce it."

"For the last time, indeed," Sozomenos said sadly. Sadly, he gestured for the last time to the priest with the candle snuffer. For the last time, the priest used it, and the High Temple plunged into darkness. For the last time, the chorus sang out: "Anathema to the heretic! Let him be excommunicated! Let him be cast into the outer darkness! So may it be!"

There in the darkness, Rhavas was not idle. He had begun a spell while one candle still burned, and was in the middle of it when Sozomenos asked him that last question. He'd had to wait till he finished a softly murmured stanza before he could speak again. Once he'd refused to admit he was in error, he raced through the rest of the spell. Only a heartbeat after the last candle died, he muttered, "Let it be accomplished!"

As it had at the inn in the town east of Videssos the city, darkness flowed from his fingers. This was *true* darkness, darkness as the enemy of light rather than just its absence. It was the darkness you got when you called on Skotos in place of Phos. It swallowed sight, swallowed the very idea of sight. Back at that inn, Rhavas had cast that spell by way of experiment, to discover what it would do. Now he knew, and had practiced with as many variations as he could dream up. He sent it forth with all his strength—and, maybe, with the dark god's strength flowing through him as well.

After the ceremony of excommunication was complete, priests and acolytes should have raced through the High Temple lighting lamps and torches and candles, bathing the interior of the great building with light to show the condemned man what he would have to do without forevermore. Perhaps they started, but how could they go on when blackness drowned even the tapers they carried? Their cries of alarm were the first ones to ring out inside the Temple.

Theirs were the first, but far from the last. "Light! Where is the light?" someone called urgently.

The light has failed! Rhavas exulted. He almost shouted it aloud, but swallowed the words at the last instant. Why give his foes a clue about where he was and what he was doing?

"Sorcery?" someone with a shrill voice shouted. Someone else cried, "Skotos is loose in the High Temple!"—and that, in the Videssian phrase, spilled the perfume into the soup.

Somebody reached for Rhavas. He thought it was one of

the wizards who'd come up with him from the prison under the patriarchal residence—or it might have been one of the guards. Whoever it was, the fellow missed Rhavas, blundering past him in the darkness impenetrable and seizing someone else. "Ha! Got you!" the mage or guardsman exclaimed. A scuffle broke out.

Not far away, another sorcerer began a low-voiced counterspell. That was the last thing Rhavas wanted; it might strip his protection from him. He pointed toward the sound of the quick, quiet chant. "Curse you, mage!" he whispered fiercely. "Curse you to death!" The chanting stopped. The mage groaned. Rhavas heard the sound of a body falling. Whatever wards the man had had, they weren't enough, not now.

Yes, the light has *failed!* Again, he wanted to shout it. Again, he made himself hold back. And, even if he no longer believed in the power of the light, he still needed it, or a little of it, to make good his escape. He murmured another charm, a new one, to lift the absolute blackness from his own eyes but no one else's. He was still not an accomplished mage. He couldn't be sure how a spell would go till he tried it.

This one accomplished everything he wanted from it. Even to him, it remained dim inside the High Temple. The lamplighters had got to only a couple of fixtures before realizing something was dreadfully wrong. But he could see again. And it was very clear that all the other assembled ecclesiastics—and all the soldiers and wizards as well—remained blind.

"Where is he? Catch him!" somebody yelled.

They tried. He watched them try. If he hadn't been so busy getting away, he would have giggled as he watched them. They staggered this way and that. Whenever two of them bumped together, they both shouted, "Here he is!" and tried to tackle each other. It reminded him of the best Midwinter's Day mime skit of all time.

Someone bumped into him, shouted, "Here he is!" and tried to tackle him.

"No, you idiot!" Rhavas said, wrestling free. "He's over there, closer by the altar."

"Oh. Sorry, holy sir," his would-be captor said, and let him go. The man blundered away and wrapped his arms around someone else a few heartbeats later. "Here he is!"

When Rhavas neared the narthex, he paused. He wasn't sure the darkness he'd sent forth reached so far. He worked his spell again, this time aiming it in that direction. Startled shouts from the antechamber said the light there had suddenly died. Rhavas worked the other spell again, too, the one that let him see in spite of the sorcerous darkness.

The narthex, to his relief, wasn't nearly so crowded as the floor of the High Temple. Before Rhavas went out the door, he again sent darkness out ahead of him. Some of the soldiers posted outside the High Temple might recognize him. They would surely wonder how and why he was walking out of his own condemnation. They wouldn't worry about that, though, if instead they were wondering why they'd suddenly been struck blind.

They were rubbing at their eyes and shouting—sometimes screaming—as he strode past them. "Wizardry!" one of them cried. "Wicked wizardry!" Rhavas laughed under his breath. It wasn't as if the man was wrong.

When he saw people running *toward* the High Temple, he realized he'd passed out of the region where his sorcery was effective. "Is there a fire inside, holy sir?" one of them asked.

For a moment, he was puzzled. Then he understood they had to be seeing his darkness as thick black smoke. "Yes," he answered, doing his best to let out a convincing gasp. "It's—it's terrible in there!" He lurched and hacked and coughed, as if he'd breathed in too much smoke.

Crying out in horror, they hurried past him. They cried out again when they ran into the darkness. One of them said it smelled like smoke. That was the man's imagination working overtime, nothing more, but in an instant all the rest were yelling the same thing.

Quite forgotten, Rhavas walked out into the plaza of Palamas. He wondered how long the darkness he'd created would last. Sooner or later, it would have to dissipate as the energy that powered the spell wore off, even if the mages in the High Temple didn't manage to disperse it sooner.

Meanwhile, though, he was free. His darkness had done all he'd hoped it would, and more besides. The market square was quiet in the natural darkness of night. A few food stands stayed open under torches. A few trulls slipped from shadow to shadow, calling invitations to the men they saw. One of them called an invitation to Rhavas. He ignored her. She swore, more from force of habit than from real anger, and walked on.

Rhavas own anger was real, and growing by the moment. He turned back toward the High Temple, and toward the ecclesiastics assembled within. Refuse to hear him, would they? Condemn him, would they? Cling to their defeated god, would they? They deserved to stay blind forever, not just until his darkness broke up.

They deserved worse than that. Videssos the city deserved worse than that. Rhavas gathered himself. "I curse this city!" he cried in a great voice. "I curse it in the name of Skotos, the dark god triumphant!"

And the earth moved beneath him, *roared* beneath him.

Unlike Skopentzana, Videssos the city was prone to earthquakes. At Skopentzana, Rhavas had still been fighting to believe in Phos, and hadn't wanted to think his curse touched off a temblor. Here in the capital, he wanted nothing more. He cried out again, this time in wordless delight, altogether certain what he'd done.

That dreadful roar went on and on. It seemed to go on forever, though in fact it couldn't have lasted even a minute. Rhavas was knocked off his feet—was, in fact, knocked out of one sandal. He kept on shouting joyfully, though not even he could hear himself through the deep bass rumble of the very earth in torment.

What he did hear through that rumble were the lesser roars and crashes of buildings crumbling and falling. Much, even most, of Videssos the city was built of brick and stone, and bricks and stones shook themselves apart from one another when the ground shook beneath them.

Rhavas, who had had the sense to stand in the open before cursing the capital, hoped with all his heart he would bring the High Temple down on the heads of the ecclesiastics assembled within. That struck him as justice sweeter and stronger than the merely poetic. But when the trembling finally eased, the Temple remained intact, though the patriarchal residence next to it had fallen into ruin. Swearing under his breath, he wondered if he could lay another curse specifically on the Temple. When he reached inside himself, though, he found nothing left. What power he had, he had used, and for the moment used up.

Time to get away, then. If the men who condemned him had a chance to think, they would decide the earthquake on the heels of his sorcerously aided escape from the High Temple was no coincidence. The hunt would be on as soon as they did. And, depleted as he was, he would have a hard time resisting them. That being so, best not to linger till they gathered their wits.

An aftershock staggered him as he trotted toward Middle Street. He heard fresh screams after that, and fresh crashes as well. Moans and groans and cries of pain seemed more or less constant. How many people suffered, buried in rubble? How many more were beyond suffering?

Someone not far enough away shouted, "Fire!" That was one of the great perils in an earthquake. Fortunately for the shattered imperial city, there was no more than the barest hint of breeze to fan the flames.

Rubble clogged even Middle Street, the broadest thoroughfare in the city. Some of the roofed colonnades had collapsed. So had some of the buildings along the avenue. Rhavas spared a moment, but no more than a moment, to hope Lardys and his inn still survived.

Men and women ran here and there. Many of them shouted other people's names, trying to find relatives and friends. Others, like Rhavas, made for the Silver Gate—and, no doubt, other gates as well. Each new aftershock that rattled the city sent more folk fleeing. Spending a night in the open would have been a hardship during the winter. On a warm summer night, it seemed far better than spending that same night under a roof that might come down.

Like the High Temple, the walls still stood. Again, Rhavas had to swallow his disappointment. He couldn't do anything about it now. The Silver Gate was open. He joined the throng of men, women, and children streaming out through it. "We're safe!" someone said once outside the city.

Rhavas knew he wasn't safe yet. But neither was Videssos safe from him.

✦ XIII

The miserable excuse for a horse that Rhavas rode made
him long for the steppe ponies he'd had to leave behind in
Videssos the city. Not for the first time, he wondered if he
should have tried to retrieve them. Also not for the first time,
he shrugged. Too late to worry about such things now.

His hoofed snail approached one of the more northwesterly
gates in the Long Walls. He eyed the gateway, and the soldiers
at it, with some trepidation. Orders to seize him on sight might
well have got here before he did. Considering the quality—or
lack of same—of his mount, anything at all might have got here
before he did.

But the gate guards didn't seem unduly concerned. "Hello, holy
sir," one of them called. "Where are you bound?"

"Imbros," Rhavas answered; if he followed the road ahead, it
would lead him there. Taking a chance, he added, "I'm on my
way home from the synod."

"Phos!" The guardsman sketched the sun-circle. Rhavas gravely
imitated the gesture. The soldier went on, "We've heard something
about that, we have. They ought to string the stinking heretic up
by his toes and roast him upside down over a slow fire."

"That's too good for him." Another gate guard came up with
an even more ingenious—and even more appalling—torture.

"He will get his just deserts in the world to come," Rhavas said gravely. That was bound to be true, but his view of what those deserts were surely differed from that of the gate guards.

They all nodded. "No doubt you're right," one of them said, "but we'd like to see him catch it in this world, too." He paused for a moment, then added, "You're heading to Imbros? You'll want to be careful on the road, holy sir. There's Khamorth loose, and they like sporting with travelers they catch. *They* like it, but you wouldn't."

"Thanks for the warning. May you be blessed for your kindness." If Rhavas was going to play the role of a priest who believed in Phos, he would play it to the hilt. "Perhaps I can even convert them to the worship of the lord with the great and good mind." He drew the sun-circle over his heart again.

All the guards who heard him started to laugh. "Don't try it unless you aim to end up dead in a hurry," one of them said. "Most of these fellows are from the clan of Kubrat, and that's about the meanest bunch of Khamorth there are. They suck up to Skotos, they do." He spat in the dirt of the roadway.

So did Rhavas. If he hadn't, he might have roused suspicion. "May I pass through?" he asked.

"Go ahead, holy sir," one of the soldiers answered. "Don't say we didn't warn you, though. That road's not safe—not even close."

"My faith will protect me," Rhavas said. This time, several gate guards sketched the sun-sign. He supposed that meant they admired his piety. And he *was* pious, or so he felt himself to be. But the god he revered and the one to whom they clung were not the same. "*Get* up!" He booted his horse forward. It plodded through the gate and out past the Long Walls. The guardsmen smiled behind their hands at the miserable beast.

"His faith better protect him," one of them said, not quite softly enough. "The good god knows he can't run away from trouble."

"We told him," another one replied. "If he doesn't want to listen, that's his funeral—and it's liable to be."

Rhavas rode on. He wondered whether the Kubrati really were more ferocious than other Khamorth, or whether they were simply the barbarians the guards knew best. After what he'd seen in the far northeast, he would have bet on the latter.

He also wondered whether, before very long, grim-faced horse-men would ride up the road after him. Though word hadn't got to this gate, he was outlawed in the Empire of Videssos, fair game for anyone who might bring him down. He was far more dangerous than any single pursuer—he was a host in himself, in fact—but he was only one man. He had to sleep, and he couldn't look every which way at once. The clout in the head he'd taken in the High Temple brutally reminded him of that. He still got headaches more often than he wanted.

Despite those headaches, he wondered if the monk hadn't done him a favor. When he first woke up in the cell under the patriarchal residence, he'd thought of the dream he'd had while unconscious as nothing but . . . a dream.

The longer he contemplated it, though, the greater its importance seemed to grow. He slowly became convinced it *was* more than a dream: a vision, even a covenant. Some very holy men claimed to have found a mystical communion with Phos. Rhavas, always hardheaded, had had trouble believing those claims, chiefly because he'd never experienced anything like that himself. Now . . .

If he hadn't come to an agreement, made a bargain, with Skotos after the monk's truncheon let—made—him slip the bonds of consciousness, what had he done? Years, many years, in exchange for dedicated service to the dark god's cause . . . That struck him as fair enough, and more than fair enough.

He would have given Skotos dedicated service even without the promise of more years with which to do it. He was loyal, unless forced not to be by overwhelming weight of circumstance. He would give the dark god the same fierce allegiance he had formerly lavished on the lord with the great and good mind. Skotos could surely see that. And it was in Skotos' interest to grant him as much time as he needed to carry out his work.

The horse paused, looking longingly toward some tall grass by the side of the road. Rhavas glanced back over his shoulder. No Videssian cavalrymen pounded up the road after him. No Khamorth in sight, either, come to that. He slid down from the saddle, led the horse over to the grass, and let it graze. Why not? It wasn't *much* slower standing still than in alleged motion.

As the animal grazed, Rhavas wondered whether pursuers *could* do anything to him: whether he needed to worry at all, in fact. If Skotos had promised him many years, wouldn't he get them come what may?

He didn't need long to decide not to take foolish chances.

Sozomenos' warning that the dark god lied had nothing to do with his decision, either. So he told himself, and he thought it was true. If he found a cliff and jumped off it, he wasn't so foolish as to imagine Skotos would take him in his arms and bear him up. He would hit the ground and die, regardless of any promises. If Stylianos and his soldiers and mages caught him, he might also die. That seemed only too clear. He *could* live for many years, but he would have to earn them.

When he mounted once more, the horse snorted indignantly and sent him a resentful stare—the most animation he'd seen from it. If it had been more animated when he wanted it to move, he would have liked it better. It didn't want to leave the grass, any more than a man would have wanted to leave an eatery where he was enjoying himself. With reins and bit and stirrups, Rhavas had means of persuasion he couldn't have used on a man. Still unhappy, the horse went north.

A breeze carried the salt tang of the Videssian Sea to Rhavas. He hadn't realized how much he'd missed it in Skopentzana till he had it back. He wondered if he would have to leave it behind again. He hoped not.

He rode on till the sun sank low in the west. A village lay not far ahead, but he did not dare try the tavern there. If recognized, he could be killed while asleep. He'd camped in the open many times on the way from Skopentzana down to Videssos the city. He could do it again. He could, and he did.

Bread and cheese and an onion made a spare but tolerable supper. He had more in his saddlebags. He washed down the food with rough red wine. If he had to, he could drink water. He'd got used to the bed at Lardys' inn, but bare ground wasn't impossibly hard, not when he was swaddled in a couple of thick wool blankets. He yawned and twisted and fell asleep.

When he woke, the eastern sky was gray. He felt elderly as he unrolled himself from the blankets. His back had some pointed things to say about the way he'd treated it. He wasn't a young man anymore, and waking up after a night on the ground reminded him of that. He ate more bread and cheese and wine as blue replaced black in the west, the stars faded, and the east went from gray to pink to gold. He was riding north again by the time the sun came over the horizon.

In the early morning, he didn't fear the village. A couple of dogs ran yapping toward his horse, but a peasant on his way out to the fields shouted at them and scared them away. The man waved to Rhavas. "You're up and about early, holy sir," he said.

"So are you," Rhavas answered.

"I'm up early every day—well, except sometimes in the winter, on account of I can't do anything then," the local answered. "But I mostly wake up at sunrise anyways, just on account of I'm used to it." He eyed Rhavas. "You're a city man yourself, unless I miss my guess."

"That's so, yes." Rhavas admitted what he could hardly deny. "I'm bound for Imbros."

"You want to be careful. I hear there's savages on the road. Haven't seen 'em here, Phos be praised"—the peasant sketched the sun-sign, and Rhavas had to remind himself to do the same—"but they're around. Now that we've got us a new Avtokrator, maybe things'll get better. 'Course, maybe they won't, too." Peasant fatalism was older and often stronger than faith in the lord with the great and good mind.

"I do not fear the heathen," Rhavas said. "Perhaps I can convert him."

The peasant thought he meant converting the Khamorth to the worship of Phos. He made the sun-circle again, and again Rhavas imitated the gesture. "Good luck go with you, holy sir, but I wouldn't push it too hard. The barbarians are supposed to have a nasty temper when they're roused."

"Well, so do I," Rhavas said, and the local guffawed. The fellow sketched a salute, as if to a general, and then went on his way. The work wouldn't wait. Work never waited.

A woman gave Rhavas a sack of dried apricots as he rode through the village. A man handed him a slab of smoked salmon. Plainly, his fears the night before had been for naught. Word of him had not come to this place, not yet. He gave back blessings, for all the world as if he still favored Phos.

On he went, at his horse's shambling walk. He eyed every stand of trees by the side of the road with suspicion. He remained vulnerable to ambush, as he did to surprise by night.

But there was no surprise, no ambush, when he met the Khamorth. He rode up to the top of a low rise and saw a barbarian encampment ahead, cattle and sheep grazing in a field of grain, tents of hide and felt pitched nearby.

They had sentries out, of course. One of the plainsmen pointed toward Rhavas, who saw he was very visible as he came over the rise. The Khamorth were too far off for him to hear them calling back and forth. They must have done it, though, for three of them trotted his way on horseback. He could imagine their laughter—look at the silly Videssian, too stupid even to run!

Rhavas didn't intend to run. Maybe that made him silly, but he didn't think so. He pointed in the direction of the riders and said what he'd wanted to say to his own miserable horse: "Curse you, beasts."

All three steppe ponies fell over dead at the same time. One faint startled squawk reached Rhavas' ears. Two of the Khamorth rose at once. The third had caught a leg under his horse. The other barbarians pulled him free. He could walk, but not well: he hobbled over to a big gray boulder and sat down on it.

What would the other two do? If they came forward on foot, Rhavas knew he would have to kill them. He didn't want to do that; it would antagonize the rest of the clan. But if he didn't, they would certainly try to kill him.

One of them started to head his way. The other one grabbed his intrepid friend's wolfskin jacket. The Khamorth who'd done the grabbing pointed to the horses. Rhavas couldn't hear what he was saying, and wouldn't have understood it if he could. He could made a pretty good guess just the same. *That could have been us.* That was what he wanted the barbarian to be saying, anyhow.

After a short argument, the plainsman in the wolfskin jacket gave in. He and his pal helped their limping companion back toward the encampment. Slowly and warily, Rhavas also rode in that direction.

His back tingled. If the Khamorth wanted to, they could slip men around behind him to try to shoot him from ambush. They might get away with it, too. He kept looking back over his shoulder to make sure they didn't. He reined in well away from any cover. With their extraordinary bows, though, he wasn't sure he was far enough away.

He waited, painfully aware of how vulnerable he was. In due course, a single barbarian rode out of the camp toward him. The man drew his sword, waved it so the blade caught the sunlight, and tossed it down onto the grass. He slowly turned his steppe pony in a circle to let Rhavas see he had no bow case. Heart pounding with nerves, Rhavas waved him forward.

The Khamorth pointed to the dead steppe ponies. "What you do?" he shouted in bad Videssian. "How you do?"

"I could have killed the men on them instead," Rhavas answered. The Khamorth nodded to show he understood. Rhavas kept looking back over his shoulder. He didn't aim to let the fellow in front of him lull him. Still seeing no one, he went on, "I spared them so I could talk with your chieftain."

"Me chieftain." The nomad jabbed a thumb at his own chest. "Me Kolaksha. Who you? You wizard? Wizard from Videssos not even piss pot." He spat to show his contempt.

"No, eh?" Rhavas pointed at Kolaksha as he'd pointed at the other Khamorth and their ponies a while before. He smiled when the barbarian flinched. Smiling still, he went on, "I am stronger than your shaman. If you do not believe me, I will fight him with magic."

He had to go back and forth with the chieftain several times. Kolaksha did not speak much Videssian at all. Rhavas, of course, knew not a word of the Khamorth tongue. *I suppose I'll have to start learning it*, he thought in surprise, the first time the notion had even crossed his mind.

Kolaksha laughed when he understood. "Why you want? Lipoksha kill you if you try. You priest of Phos, yes? Yes. Phos puny god. Puuuny." He seemed to fancy the word, and stretched it out lovingly.

Lipoksha, Rhavas gathered, was the name of the tribe's shaman. Kolaksha, for his part, had packed a lot into a few words. "Why?" Rhavas echoed. "To lead you, to lead all the Khamorth, against Videssos. Videssos is my enemy now." The Empire having cast him out, this was the best way he'd come up with to gain revenge. Despite being cast out, he remained very Videssian indeed in his hunger for it.

Revenge, plainly, was a notion Kolaksha understood. Just as plainly, he wasn't much taken with Rhavas' chances. "You priest of Phos," he repeated. "Phos weak."

"I am not a priest of Phos," Rhavas said deliberately. "I am a priest of Skotos. Shall I curse your horse, the way I did those?" He pointed to the dead animals not far from the one the chieftain rode.

"No! This good horse!" Kolaksha laid a protective hand on his steppe pony's mane. He sneered in Rhavas' direction. "Gooder than ugly buzzard bait you ride."

"Any buzzard that ate this horse would puke afterward," Rhavas replied. He waited to see whether Kolaksha would get that. When the barbarian threw back his head and laughed, Rhavas knew he had.

"Funny man. Funnnny." Kolaksha stretched that out as he had *puny*. He eyed Rhavas' mount again. "Horse funnnny, too." The chieftain plucked at his beard, which was full and curly to the point of shagginess. "Skotos . . . Skotos is god who fight Phos?"

"That's right." Rhavas nodded. "Skotos is the god who is beating Phos. And Skotos is using the Khamorth, using your people, to beat Videssos."

Kolaksha scowled. "But Skotos wicked god, yes? Khamorth not wicked. Khamorth good. *I* good." He jerked a thumb at his own broad chest again. "Videssos have it coming." He added something in his own language. If it wasn't more of the same, Rhavas would have been amazed.

He almost laughed in the plainsman's face, as Kolaksha had laughed at his sardonic crack. Only worry about angering the chieftain held him back. No one was ever a villain in his own eyes. That seemed as true among savage steppe nomads who robbed and raped and killed for the fun of it as it was among suave, sophisticated Videssians . . . who robbed and raped and killed for the fun of it.

Rhavas wasn't a villain in his own eyes, either. He was a reformer, a man denied his rightful place by the willful blindness of those with a vested interest in keeping things as they were. Videssos . . . had it coming. He was no more able to look at the black things he'd done than Kolaksha was to examine *his* deeds—and he was also no more able to realize that he couldn't look at them.

The Khamorth chieftain eyed him, eyed the dead horses, eyed the vultures and ravens already starting to circle above the carrion. Kolaksha nodded to himself. One way or another, he'd made up his mind. "You come," he said, and waved back toward the nomads' camp. "Come, yes. You fight Lipoksha. Why not? After he kill you, we go on."

"A truce until he and I fight?" Rhavas asked.

"Yes, yes." Kolaksha nodded impatiently, as if to a little boy who was nagging him about something unimportant. "We not bother you before. Let Lipoksha take care of you."

His certainty was daunting. *But I can't let him daunt me, not now*, Rhavas thought. His head came up. He stared at—stared through—the chieftain. "And if I take care of him?"

"Then we listen to you." Kolaksha laughed. "But you not do that."

"We'll see. My god supports me," Rhavas said. The Khamorth chieftain laughed again, louder this time, as if Rhavas had told him a funny story. Rhavas didn't think it was funny. Angrily, he went on, "Bring me to this Lipoksha. And look well on him when you do, for you will not see him again." His bragging only made Kolaksha laugh even more.

When Lipoksha emerged from his tent, he was not at all what Rhavas had expected. Instead of being an even rougher, hairier, more barbarous version of Kolaksha, Lipoksha could almost as easily have been a woman as a man. His face was scraped smooth, and his dark hair flowed down over his shoulders. Moreover, the Khamorth shaman moved with a woman's grace and delicacy. He wore tunic and trousers of deerskin adorned with fringes on the chest and back and at the elbows and wrists and knees and ankles—and at the crotch.

When he spoke in his own language, his voice was high and light: not quite a woman's voice, but not quite a man's, either. Rhavas snapped his fingers. Something he'd read a long time before came back to him. "You're an *enaree*!" he exclaimed. The last word sprang from the plainsmen's language, for Videssian had no equivalent.

Lipoksha did not seem to know any Videssian. Kolaksha, who did, jerked in surprise at hearing a word in his speech from Rhavas' mouth. "How you know of this?" he demanded, his voice hard with suspicion.

"I've read of it," Rhavas answered. But that made no sense to the nomad, who did not know the Videssian words for reading or writing or books. *A barbarian indeed*, Rhavas thought. *Do I really want to live among these people?* A moment later, he bleakly answered himself. *What choice have I got? I cannot live in Videssos any more, not until the Empire falls.*

Finally, Kolaksha gave up trying to understand. Lipoksha spoke again, in that epicene, effeminate voice. *Effeminate.* Rhavas nodded to himself. That was the word he remembered—an account of a trader's journey deep into the Pardrayan steppe used it to speak of *enarees.* The chieftain translated for his shaman: "He say, you not like Videssian wizards, not like Videssian priests."

"That is true," Rhavas agreed gravely. He supposed Lipoksha meant he was not like them. But if the *enaree* had actually said Rhavas did not like them, that would have been no less true.

Lipoksha said something else. Were those high, thin tones natural for him, or had he acquired them by practice? Rhavas could not ask, for Kolaksha's gruff, surely natural baritone followed: "You want his place, yes?"

"Yes," Rhavas said.

More twittering from Lipoksha. More growls, more or less in Videssian, from Kolaksha: "You want to be like Khamorth, you fight in Khamorth way, he say. You go together into felt tent. You fight there." The chieftain frowned. That wasn't what he'd wanted to say. His heavy features looked surprisingly thoughtful for a moment. Then they lightened. He'd found the words he needed. "The of-you *spirits* fight." He'd made hash of the Videssian possessive, but his meaning came through. Casually, he added, "One come out of felt tent. The other . . ." His gesture needed no words to get the meaning across.

"How do our spirits fight in the felt tent?" Rhavas asked. The trader's tale had spoken of this ritual, too, but he couldn't bring back the details.

Kolaksha blinked. When he translated Rhavas' words into his own language, Lipoksha seemed startled, too. "Ignorant foreigner," Kolaksha said scornfully. He might almost have been a Videssian sneering at barbarians. "All folk know of the tent where breathe in hemp smoke." He flared his nostrils and inhaled noisily to show what he meant.

"Not all folk do, for I did not," Rhavas said with ponderous precision. That only made both Kolaksha and Lipoksha sneer more, which annoyed him. He asked, "What can breathing in hemp smoke possibly do?"

After the chieftain translated, the *enaree* spoke volubly in his guttural language, waving his hands for emphasis. Kolaksha turned his words, or some of them, into Videssian: "Put you in spirit world. You want magic fight, should be there."

"Ah." Rhavas fought down a stab of unease. Maybe hemp smoke was some sort of drug, then—or maybe the plainsmen, with barbarous ignorance, imagined it was. Lipoksha plainly wanted the sorcerous duel on his terms, not Rhavas'. *Are you confident in what you are doing, or not?* Rhavas asked himself. He nodded. He was. And even if he weren't, it was much too late to back out now, and he had nowhere else to go if he did. As firmly as he could, he nodded again. "Let it be as you say, then. The felt tent."

The Khamorth eagerly set up the felt tent. It was smaller than the rest of the tents in the encampment, for it was not meant as a dwelling place, only as one of ritual. Unlike the tents in which the nomads lived, this one had no smoke hole at the top; the smoke inside was supposed to be trapped. Rawhide lashings could tightly close the tent flap, also to keep smoke from escaping.

The flap had lashings on both inside and outside. From Kolaksha's bits of Videssian, Rhavas gathered breathing in hemp fumes was entertainment as well as the stuff of sorcerous confrontations. Today, though, only the interior lashings would be used. The winner of the duel would have to untie them when he emerged.

With no smoke hole and with the flap shut, it was dark inside the felt tent. Lipoksha brought in a lamp along with the brazier atop which the hemp seeds would burn. The lamp smelled odd. After a moment, Rhavas realized it was burning sour butter rather than olive oil. He sighed. Yes, he was among barbarians.

But they, at least, give me this chance, he thought savagely. *That is more than my own folk did.*

With gesture, Lipoksha had him sit crosslegged on one side of the brazier. The Khamorth shaman took his own place opposite Rhavas. Rhavas' knees creaked; the *enaree* took the posture for granted. There wouldn't be room for stools in the nomads' tents, Rhavas realized. When Khamorth sat, they sat on the ground or on carpets. Of course they would be more limber than the average Videssian.

Lipoksha gave Rhavas a seated bow. Rhavas inclined his head in return. Gestures of respect had their place before any struggle. The *enaree* nodded to himself, satisfied that Rhavas had given honor for honor. Lipoksha took from his belt a small sack. Even

in the dim, flickering lamplight, Rhavas saws that it was made of
leather. Videssians probably would have used linen instead. But
the plainsmen used almost exclusively the products of their flocks
and of the hunt. The only cloth they had was the wool they spun
and what they got from Videssos by trade or theft.

The shaman undid the rawhide cord that held the sack closed.
He murmured a few incomprehensible but rhythmic sentences. *A
prayer of sorts*, Rhavas thought. Then Lipoksha poured the seeds
in the sack down onto the hot brazier.

A cloud of smoke rose and filled the tent. It stung Rhavas' eyes
and made him cough. The smell wasn't unpleasant: spicier and
more pungent than wood smoke. But he wouldn't have cared to
be trapped in a tight place with a smoky campfire, and he didn't
much care for this, either.

He tried to breathe as little as he could. Lipoksha, by contrast,
inhaled noisily, sucking in great draughts of smoke. Then Rhavas
made himself do the same, even if he felt as if his throat were on
fire. Whatever power the smoke had would not help the shaman
without helping him.

A foolish grin spread across Lipoksha's face, almost but not
quite the grin he might have worn after too much wine. Rhavas
found it hard to maintain the hatred of the world that had sus-
tained him for so long. His body felt lethargic, while his mind
was more interested in itself than in anything around him.

His will, though, still drove him. He pointed at Lipoksha, sitting
there on the far side of the brazier. "Curse you," he said.

He could *see* the curse leave his fingers. It was as if he existed
on two planes at once, the normal mundane world and the world
of the spirit, the world of power. He saw the curse fly toward
Lipoksha, and he saw the shaman's spirit sidestep it so that it
went on out uselessly into the void.

"Is that all you can do?" In the spirit realm, Rhavas had no
trouble understanding the Khamorth. Lipoksha's spirit-self waved
contemptuously. "Here is a curse with *bite*."

Behind Rhavas, something growled. His spirit-self whirled,
though his physical body sat unmoving. A great wolf advanced
on him. Fire blazed in its eye sockets; its teeth were jagged as
old saw blades. He knew without being warned that it would eat
his soul if it could—and it could.

"Begone!" he cried. The wolf's tongue lolled out. It laughed a doggy laugh at him and padded closer, the fire in its eyes burning brighter. "Curse you!" Rhavas said, as he had when he aimed death at Lipoksha. But death had missed then, and it missed now. He was not sure the spirit-wolf lived, not as the material world understood the word.

The wolf's jaws gaped wide, wide enough to swallow Rhavas at a gulp. Lipoksha's spirit-self giggled. "Good-bye, little man. Good-bye, little fool," he said gaily.

Rhavas wondered if he could run. But, he sensed, as in the material world, so here: a lone wolf could always outrun a lone man. He ran, then, but *at* the wolf. It reared back in surprise. "Skotos take you!" he roared. "Darkness eat you forever!"

And the wolf was gone.

Lipoksha stopped laughing. Rhavas' spirit-self turned back toward the shaman. "I did not think you could do that," Lipoksha remarked.

"Life is full of surprises," Rhavas said. "You called on your powers, and I called on mine. Here is another taste of them, and see how you like it!" He shouted out the spell he had used in the High Temple, the one that would have brought light if used with Phos' name but sent blackness across the world when made with Skotos'.

Again, that blackness flowed from Rhavas' hands. Here in the spirit realm, it seemed more alive, more aware than it had in the material world. It streamed toward Lipoksha's spirit-self, as if to drown him in darkness. As Rhavas had against the shaman's summoned wolf, Lipoksha stood his ground. A drum appeared in his hands. He beat out a rapid, intricate rhythm. The leading edge of the darkness writhed. He was trying to seize control of it for himself, maybe even to turn it back against the one who had sent it.

"Skotos!" Rhavas whispered, both his spirit-self and his physical body. He pointed toward Lipoksha, he turned his will toward Lipoksha—and the darkness obeyed him.

As it engulfed the shaman, Lipoksha let out a startled, frightened wail. Above it, or perhaps behind it, Rhavas thought he heard—imagined he heard?—a dark, cold laughter. The *enaree* might have heard—or imagined?—the same thing, for the wail from out of the darkness rose to a high, desperate shriek. And then it was gone, gone forever. The laughter? There on the spirit

plane, the laughter rolled on forever, as eternal and resistless as
the tide.

Little by little, Rhavas came back to himself, or found himself
once more in the material world alone. Was there a difference?
He could not have said. The hemp fumes still clouded his brain.
They still clouded his eyes as well. But there was no mistaking the
corpse that slumped down on the far side of the brazier from him
for a living man. No man alive could have achieved that boneless
posture—and luckless Lipoksha's bowels had let go, adding a fresh
stink to the pungency of the hemp fumes in the felt tent.

Head spinning, Rhavas crawled to the tent flap. His fingers were
clumsy on the rawhide lashings that held the flap closed; he had
to fumble at the knots before they finally came free. When they
did, and when he saw daylight again, he wished he had a shield
to protect his eyes from the sudden and unexpected brilliance.
No, he was not Phos' creature anymore.

Kolaksha and several other Khamorth waited expectantly outside the felt tent. When they saw Rhavas emerge, their faces were
comic studies of astonishment and dismay. "Where Lipoksha?"
the chieftain demanded, as if that weren't, or shouldn't have
been, obvious.

"In there." Rhavas pointed back to the tent. He also added what
was, or should have been, obvious: "Dead." His eyes adapted to
the light outside, a bit at a time; he was not doomed to be an
owl, then, and blind by daylight. He added one thing more, the
first thing on his mind: "I'm hungry."

Kolaksha spoke in his own language. One of the other plainsmen shouted. A woman, gold hoops in her ears and bracelets
jingling on her wrists, hurried up with a wooden tray piled high
with roast mutton and unleavened wheat cakes and a drinking
horn that looked to have been shaped from a real cow's horn.
She seemed very ready. Maybe Lipoksha would have been hungry,
too, had he come out.

Rhavas ate like a starving wolf. The Khamorth flavored mutton
with mint, not garlic. It was strange, but it wasn't bad. The butter on the wheat cakes was going off, or had gone. That plainly
didn't matter to the Khamorth. In Rhavas' famished state, it didn't
matter to him, either. The horn held something thin and sour,
but at least as strong as wine.

When Rhavas asked what it was, Kolaksha answered in his

own language: "*Kavass*." That helped Rhavas not at all. Kolaksha gathered his fragments of Videssian and did his best to explain. Eventually, Rhavas gathered that he was drinking fermented mare's milk. Not so long before, the news would have turned his stomach. Now all he did was hold out the drinking horn for more.

The woman who'd served him refilled the horn from a skin full of *kavass*. That would have revolted Rhavas, too; he was used to pitchers of pottery or metal. But the nomads had to travel light. Something that could be stored in very little space like the skin suited them better.

"How you kill Lipoksha?" Kolaksha asked when Rhavas' feeding frenzy at last gave signs of slowing.

"How?" By then, the mare's milk had risen to Rhavas' head—or maybe he still felt the aftereffects of the hemp fumes. Grandly, he answered, "Because I was the stronger. I said I would be, did I not?"

"But—you Videssian." That summed up the chieftain's attitude in three words.

"Not anymore." Rhavas did not try to make his voice grim. It came out that way by itself, which made it more effective than any histrionics could have. He went on, "The folk who raised me are my enemies now. And I will do what anyone with enemies would try to do: I will have my revenge on them."

As Kolaksha had before, he understood that now; higher sentiments might have baffled him. "You want us to help you with revenge, then?"

"Not just help me." Rhavas remembered reading that belching was a sign of good manners on the plains; it showed a man appreciated his food. He let out what he would have suppressed in Videssian company. Kolaksha's smile showed he'd done right. "Not just help me," he repeated. "Oh, no. I want you to share in my revenge. How would you like to take Imbros, for instance?"

Kolaksha understood that, too; a greedy light kindled in his eyes. But then it faded. "Take town slow business. Not get over wall. Videssian soldiers come," he said sorrowfully.

"If I give you Imbros, will you finally believe I am all I say I am?" Rhavas asked.

"I believe," Kolaksha said. "You not beat Lipoksha if you plain old pissant Videssian priest." He paused. That greedy light came back. "You give us Imbros, I believe *more*."

Just for a moment, Rhavas almost wept. This barbarous chieftain was willing, even eager, to let what he saw, what he experienced, influence what he believed. Could the priests and prelates of proud and civilized Videssos say the same? *If they could, they never would have condemned me*, Rhavas thought bitterly. He scowled. If he couldn't show them one way that evil was loose in the world, then he would have to show them another.

And he would show Kolaksha, too. Kolaksha would enjoy the demonstration. The priests and prelates of Videssos? That would be a different story.

Kolaksha sent riders to several nearby bands of nomads with connections of blood or marriage to his group of Kubrati. How such alignments worked among the Khamorth Rhavas did not know, not in any detail. He did gather that the other plainsmen would ride with Kolaksha's men against Imbros. If the city fell, they would share the spoils. Kolaksha would accrue greater glory for providing it—and for discovering Rhavas.

If, on the other hand, something went wrong . . . "You make I look bad before other khagans, I make you pay," he warned Rhavas.

Rhavas only nodded. He did not tell the chieftain he could kill him at a word. Make a man afraid and you also made him dangerous. All he said was, "You want to do this. I want to do this. Together, we will."

"How?" Kolaksha asked.

"Soon enough, you will see," Rhavas said.

Kolaksha fumed, but decided not to press it. "You say you kill Lipoksha, then you kill him," he said, as if reminding himself. "I not think you can do that, but you do. You say you do to Imbros, too. Maybeso you do it."

That was something less than a ringing vote of confidence, but he didn't nag Rhavas anymore afterward. Plenty of Videssians in positions of authority would have. Kolaksha might have been—*was*—a barbarian. That did not make him stupid, or a fool. Rhavas had not understood the distinction before he came to live among the Khamorth. He did now.

The plainsmen were *people*, not monsters. He hadn't grasped that before, either. They were husbands and wives, fathers and mothers, sons and daughters, brothers and sisters, aunts and uncles and cousins, friends and lovers and enemies, inferiors and superiors. Among members of their own tribe, they behaved as people ordinarily did. Some of their rituals differed from the Videssians', but they *had* rituals. They used them, with diminished force, among other Khamorth as well. To them, though, Videssians simply were not human beings. The word they applied to Videssians was related to the one they applied to mussels that used self-made strings to fix themselves to rocks in a river.

At first, that dismayed Rhavas. But what did Videssians think about the Khamorth? Nothing good. They called them plainsmen and savages and barbarians. They sometimes called them other things, too, things that suggested the Khamorth showed their livestock undue affection. Rhavas had believed that was so, or could be so. He saw no sign of it. In due course, being ever curious, he asked Kolaksha about it.

"Oh, yes, we know about that," the chieftain said matter-of-factly.

"What do you do about it?" Rhavas asked.

"We kill man. Kill animal, too. Animal have bad spirit in it. Let spirit out," Kolaksha said. Videssian shepherds also faced the death penalty for bestiality. Videssian sheep, however, remained immune from punishment.

Riders went back and forth between Kolaksha's tribe and those of his friends and allies. They were on Videssian soil, but they did not appear to know it, or to care. A few towns in the area still had imperial garrisons. The plainsmen avoided them but otherwise ignored them.

Plainsmen drifted closer to Imbros. Except for Kolaksha's band, none of them came *very* close. They were ready to pitch in if things went well. They were also ready to leave in a hurry if things went wrong. They wanted proof before they gave Rhavas more in the way of confidence. They wanted to see what he could do.

Yes, they were people, all right.

Dressed in nomad furs and leathers, Rhavas surveyed Imbros. Shedding his priest's robe felt oddly final. He might have been a snake shedding its skin. But what would come forth, he judged, was more different from what had gone before than the new snake was from the old.

Imbros was smaller than Skopentzana, larger than Develtos. Its garrison seemed alert. Once, when Rhavas rode too close, a catapult on the wall shot a dart at him. It missed, but the whoosh of the thing as it flew past made him hastily draw back out of range.

After fright came anger. He told Kolaksha, "Tomorrow, Imbros falls to the Khamorth, to the Kubrati who have trusted in me."

"How?" the chieftain asked once more.

"The walls will fall—much of the city will fall—and you can go in and take what you want, do what you will," Rhavas answered.

Kolaksha looked at him, as skeptical as any Videssian might have been. "Just like that?"

Rhavas looked back. "Just like that," he said. "Remember Lipoksha, Kolaksha. What I say I can do, I can do."

Kolaksha grunted. "We see." After a moment, he added, "We be ready. All Khamorth be ready." If this did go off as Rhavas said it would, he intended to take advantage of it. If it didn't, he no doubt intended to make Rhavas pay if he could. He probably could. Rhavas was even more alone among the nomads than he had been among his own people. *Who would have imagined I could be?* he thought.

He spent the night gathering himself. He knew what he had to do. He'd done it before. Once more. Once more, and he could start paying Videssos back for spurning him. When dawn came, he went looking for Kolaksha. The chieftain, as it turned out, was also looking for him: the sort of mishap that made people laugh in a Midwinter's Day skit. By the time Rhavas finally found Kolaksha, he was fuming, not laughing. "Are your men ready?" he demanded. "Are the other Khamorth clans close enough to join in after the walls fall?"

"I come to ask same question to you," Kolaksha said. "I come to ask, you are ready? We are ready. We wait. Now you do."

"Waiting is at an end. Follow me." Rhavas ordered the chieftain around like a prelate telling a newly ordained priest what to do. Kolaksha muttered to himself in his own language, but follow he did. He had a stumpy, splayed-out gait, his feet wide apart. Like a lot of Khamorth, he was bowlegged. Rhavas wondered if that sprang from all the time the plainsmen spent in the saddle. But he could worry about that later, if he worried about it at all. He pushed aside some bushes and pointed ahead. "The walls of Imbros."

"Yes, walls of Imbros," Kolaksha said impatiently. "How we get *inside* stinking walls of Imbros?"

"Like this." Rhavas pointed again. Bringing forth all his strength, he cried, "Accursed and downfallen be the city of Imbros, accursed and downfallen in the name of Skotos, lord of darkness and master of the world!"

Kolaksha shouted when the ground began to shake. He shouted again when the walls of Imbros broke to pieces and tumbled down. A great cloud of gray-brown dust shot up into the air, obscuring what was happening inside the city. But the grinding crashes that came through the roar of the earthquake itself said that Rhavas' prophecy was being fulfilled.

When the shaking stopped, Rhavas nodded to the Khamorth chieftain. "Send in your men. Let all the tribes send in their men. Did I honor my promise, or did I fail you?"

By way of reply, Kolaksha folded him into an embrace and kissed him on both cheeks. Rhavas would have liked that better if the barbarian had bathed anytime in the past year. Since he couldn't do anything about that, he endured it. "You do! You do!" Kolaksha bawled in his ear, capering like a bowlegged puppy. Rhavas could have done without that, too. He told himself the plainsman's heart was in the right place, anyhow.

Watching Imbros laid low, Rhavas felt his own heart leap and soar. He would have been happier were it Videssos the city, but he had done what he could do. *This* would tell Stylianos and Sozomenos and everyone else who had condemned him that he hadn't gone away. They'd thought they could get by with punishing him and ignoring him. They'd thought so, but they needed to think again.

"Come!" Kolaksha yelled. "Forward!" He lumbered toward the ruins of Imbros. Khamorth, mounted and afoot, approached the city from all sides. Rhavas didn't see how he could hang back. He'd watched the barbarians sack Skopentzana. He'd watched in horror and despair. *On my head be it.* Even now, the curse he'd called down on himself still bit him.

Here, though, he wouldn't be watching a sack. He wouldn't be trying to escape a sack. He would be joining a sack. And as for the Videssians whose homes and lives he'd just shattered—well, too bad for them.

Cry out to Phos, he thought. *Go ahead. See how much good it does you. As much good as it ever did me.*

An arrow hissed past his head. Someone in the wreckage was

trying to fight back. Rhavas ducked. By the time he did, of course, the shaft was long past. Plainsmen started scrambling over the stones of the shattered wall. There had been screams inside Imbros before. Now new ones erupted.

An aftershock staggered him. He had some control over the first shaking. Once that passed, his earthquakes behaved like any others. Aftershocks from this one would go on for months, if not for years. Some of them would be big enough to do damage in their own right. When this one ended, he ran on toward the wall.

It had come down even more completely than he'd hoped. As he approached, he saw why: it was worked stone inside and out, but had a rubble core. It wasn't solid, mortared stone all the way through. *Build on the cheap, will you?* Rhavas laughed. *You get what you pay for—and what you deserve.*

Although not a particularly athletic man, he had no trouble climbing over the wreckage and into Imbros. Some of the buildings inside the town had fallen; others still stood. Rhavas laughed again to see steeples topped by gilded sun-globes toppled in the streets. Phos' temples had not proved immune to Skotos' powers. He had expected nothing different, and rejoiced to be proved right.

Iron belled off iron as a Videssian soldier who'd somehow survived the collapse traded sword strokes with a plainsman. Another Khamorth used both hands to throw a chunk of rock at the Videssian. It caught him in the ribs and almost knocked him off his feet. The nomad with whom he'd been dueling slashed his throat before he could recover. Gurgling and clutching at the gushing wound, the Videssian sank to his knees. There was nothing sporting about the way the Khamorth fought. Effective? That was another story.

But the plainsmen were after loot as much as blood. They descended like locusts on a jeweler's shop, and came away festooned with gold and silver chains and rings and bracelets. Rhavas wondered where the jeweler was. Buried in the ruins? Or just sensible enough to realize his gauds weren't worth his life?

A woman shrieked, high and shrill. Rhavas knew that sound. Sure enough, several plainsmen had her down and were doing what they pleased. Seeing him in clothes like theirs, they waved for him to join them.

For a moment, he thought of Ingegerd, and of his self-disgust afterward. But that was different. He'd really cared for her, and she *should* have cared for him, especially after all he did for her. Besides, then he hadn't understood the way the world worked as well as he did now.

This luckless Videssian? What was she but a body to him? Nothing at all. He nodded to the Khamorth and lined up with them. His turn came fast. It was soon over, too. He rose, fumbling at his trousers. A nomad took his place. That couldn't have made any difference to the woman.

He wondered if they would let her go once they finished their sport or get a last fillip by cutting her throat. He wasn't curious enough to stay around and find out. Whether the barbarians did the one or the other might not matter much to the woman, either.

A ragged-looking Videssian man still in his nightshirt pointed at Rhavas and cried, "You damned barbarian, curse you to Skotos' ice forevermore!"

Rhavas pointed back. "No, curse *you*," he said. The local had just enough time to realize a supposed nomad spoke perfect Videssian before falling over dead.

Taverns also proved favorite targets for the Khamorth. The plainsmen poured down wine as if they thought they would never see it again. Remembering the taste of the fermented mares' milk that was their usual drink, Rhavas had trouble blaming them.

Some of them, plainly, were out to drink themselves blind as fast as they could. Maybe they had friends who would watch over them till they revived. Or maybe they just didn't fear anything the Videssians of Imbros could do. Maybe they thought there wouldn't be enough Videssians left alive in Imbros to worry about.

And maybe they were right. Along with drinking and theft, the Khamorth delighted in slaughter. They shot, slashed, stabbed, or broke in the heads of Videssians by the hundreds—no, by the thousands. And they exulted in what they did in ways that would have turned the stomach of the most hardened Videssian bandit. Some of what they did turned Rhavas' stomach, and he'd worked worse than any Videssian bandit ever born.

This is what you wanted, he reminded himself. *This is what all of Videssos deserves.* He nodded. He knew that. Knowing it and seeing it acted out before him proved two very different things.

A few Videssians got away. He saw them running off to the east and south. In a way, that was good: they would tell the other imperials what the barbarians had done here today. But in another way, it was not so good: they would bring back soldiers to seek revenge. Rhavas went looking for Kolaksha.

The chieftain listened to him, then shrugged a broad-shouldered shrug. "We leave when we leave," Kolaksha said. "If soldiers come, we run or we fight. No soldiers now. Looting now. Killing now. Women now. Wine now." He thrust a jar of wine at Rhavas.

"You are a chieftain. You can give orders. . . ." Rhavas' voice trailed away. Kolaksha *couldn't* give orders, not the way a Videssian general or even a Videssian captain could. He had no force of law behind his commands, only force of character. If the other plainsmen—especially those not of his tribe—didn't feel like listening to him, how could he make them? He couldn't, and he knew it. Rhavas hadn't fully understood it, but he did now.

He felt betrayed. What good was a leader who didn't really lead? Not much, not to him, although the Khamorth didn't seem to mind. But what did they know? They were just barbarians.

They are an instrument, he thought. *I have to play them.* But how? No two strings on this instrument vibrated the same way. How could he get a tune out of it?

While he wondered, the nomads went on doing what they wanted to do. To his horror, he realized that was what they'd been doing all along. They'd got him to knock down Imbros' walls for them. Then they did what they would have done if they'd got in some other way. They were playing him, not the other way round.

He turned away from Kolaksha and left the ruined city. Not all his pleasure in Imbros' fall was slaked; he did have a measure of vengeance against Videssos. But it was not enough to satisfy him fully. He wanted something less savage, something more sophisticated, at his beck and call: something like Videssos turned upside down and worshiping Skotos.

For a moment, he thought of journeying to Makuran, the only other civilized land Videssos knew. Not without regret, he shook his head. The long voyage was only a small part of what deterred him. The Makuraners had their own faith, that of the Four Prophets. Like any other Videssian, Rhavas reckoned it so much nonsense, but, from what little he knew of its ideas, it was full of the same foolishness as Phos-worship. It would not be easy for a lone man, and especially a lone Videssian, to overthrow.

What then? The only other tools he had left to work with were the Khamorth and the Halogai. The big blond barbarians in the far north would have intimidated him even if not for Ingegerd. They had wild gods of their own, certainly savage enough to have crawled up from Skotos' ice, but they were not likely to hearken to a Videssian preaching to them—no, preaching at them. The tale of Kveldoulphios the martyr showed that.

The Khamorth, then. It would have to be the Khamorth. But not *these* Khamorth, Rhavas decided. Horses were tethered everywhere near fallen Imbros. Men were supposed to have been detailed to keep an eye on them. Most of those nomads, though, had gone into the city to share in the looting and drinking and rape. That didn't surprise Rhavas. The plainsmen lacked anything resembling discipline.

He found the steppe pony Kolaksha had given him to replace the miserable Videssian horse he'd been riding. He also took two others, so he wouldn't wear down the one animal. And then, on his pony and leading the others, he rode away from Imbros. The disaster that had overwhelmed it was necessary but not sufficient. He wanted—he *needed*—more and better.

A sentry who hadn't gone into the ruined city shouted at him. He shouted back, not with words but just with loud noises. Those didn't do—the Khamorth hopped up onto his own horse and rode toward Rhavas, plainly wanting to know who he was and what he thought he was doing.

With a sigh, Rhavas said, "Curse you," and the plainsman slid off his pony's tail and lay on the ground, dead. Rhavas, meanwhile, muttered under his breath. He hadn't wanted to do that. It might tell the nomads in which direction he was going. It also gave them even more reason than horse theft to want to follow him.

Dismounting, he dragged the dead man behind some bushes. The pony he added to his own string. Maybe the nomads wouldn't find their fellow for some time. Maybe scavengers would have got to him by then, so no one could see he'd died for no apparent reason. Come to that, maybe the Khamorth didn't associate death for no apparent reason with Rhavas. And maybe, when they found him fled, they wouldn't look toward the northeast.

He hoped they wouldn't, anyhow. Wouldn't they think he'd sickened of what he'd done and gone back to his own folk? It seemed reasonable to him that they should. Whether what he knew of reason and what the Khamorth knew of it were related was apt to be an . . . interesting question.

In his saddlebags were wheat cakes and smoked meat. They made a good enough supper. No doubt the plainsmen whose horses he'd stolen also carried iron rations. He could keep going for a while. And, after night came, he shielded his campsite with some of the darkness impenetrable he'd used to such effect in the High Temple. To anyone riding past, it would seem like nothing but a darker shadow under the trees.

Murmuring a prayer of thanks to Skotos for the protective shield—adapted from one he would have used for Phos—Rhavas rolled himself in a blanket and slept.

Videssos still had a presence on the Astris River. War galleys like those that sailed the seas patrolled it. The Khamorth built no boats larger than canoes hollowed out of tree trunks. Had Videssos had more ships on the river, she could have kept the barbarians from crossing. As things were, the galleys harried them when they could.

When Rhavas rode down to the riverbank, he had shed his furs and leather and redonned his priest's robe. He had also shaved his head for the first time in some little while. He wanted the galleys to recognize him as a Videssian.

He didn't encounter one till the next day. It rowed up close to the shore. One of the crew shouted, "What are you doing way up here, holy sir?"

"I am going to convert the heathen on the far side of the Astris to the one true faith," Rhavas replied, which was true, but not in the way the galley's crew would look for. He went on, "I require passage across the river."

"Those savages? They'll eat you without salt," the sailor said.

"I fear nothing, for I have my god on my side," Rhavas said loftily—again, true but unhelpful to his audience. Then he added a bit of bluff: "The Avtokrator and the ecumenical patriarch will hear of it if you fail to aid me."

Even that might not have been altogether bluff, now that he thought about it. The skipper of this galley would certainly hear about it when people in Videssos the city figured out whom he'd taken across the Astris. And the assurance with which he spoke carried weight. The war galley grounded itself on the muddy bank. A gangplank thumped down. Sailors jumped out and helped Rhavas lead his horses up into the ship. One of the men said, "Looks like you got these beasts straight from the barbarians."

"I did," Rhavas said.

That impressed the sailor. "Maybe the Khamorth really will listen to you, then, holy sir. You're a braver man than I am, though, and I'm not ashamed to admit it."

Rhavas rapidly discovered he was a braver man than the war galley's captain. The officer fidgeted like a man coming down with the runs when the long, lean vessel beached itself on the north bank of the Astris. "Hurry up! Hurry up!" he cried over and over again, his voice unmistakably frightened. "If a troop of those savages come down on us while we're stuck here, we're all dead men—but we won't die fast enough to suit us. Hurry up!"

At last, Rhavas and the steppe ponies were off the ship. Sailors strained and shoved to get the galley back into the water. They all cheered when it floated again. And they jeered at Rhavas, shouting, "So long, holy sir!" "We'll never see you again, by the good god!" "Good luck—you'll need it!"

Rhavas only shrugged. They trusted in their god. He trusted in his. He did not think Skotos would let him fall before he accomplished what he had in mind. He booted his horse forward. Before long, he left the Astris—and the Empire of Videssos—behind and rode out onto the Pardrayan steppe.

Videssian writers often likened the vast plains to the north and west of their realm to the ocean. Rhavas hadn't understood the figure of speech when he lived in Videssos the city or Skopentzana. Now, seeing the terrain, he did. Everything was green and gently rolling. When the wind whistled through the tall grass, it made it bend and rise like waves skimming across the surface of the sea.

And, like the sea, the steppe was vast. When Rhavas sailed to Skopentzana, he was rarely out of sight of land. Even so, he got a vivid sense of the sea's immensity. That same feeling struck him now. The steppe swept on for what might as well have been forever. It looked the same in every direction. He might have been all alone there, alone as if no other human beings existed now, ever had, or ever would. There he was, by himself, under an infinite sky, moving across an equally infinite landscape.

He built a small fire when the sun went down. The wheat cakes he ate with his smoked meat seemed less stale after he toasted them. He worried that the flames might draw plainsmen, but was glad to have them when wolves began to howl in the distance. The sea had its sharks. The steppe had predators as well, and not all of them went on two legs.

When morning came, he woke undiscovered and undevoured. He mounted a different steppe pony and led the other three behind him. On across the great, unchanging plain he rode.

A band of nomads found him four days later. The plainsmen were out hunting. They thought they'd come across better game than rabbits or their neighbors' cattle. Their harsh whoops as they galloped toward him put him in mind of the croaking and cawing of ravens and carrion crows.

He cursed them. One by one, they dropped from their saddles and thudded to the ground. Their horses slowed and began to graze. Rhavas plundered the food from the animals' saddlebags and kept on in the direction he'd been going.

A week went by before he ran into another human being. The plainsman was riding along keeping an eye on a large herd of cattle. When he saw Rhavas coming toward him, he broke away from the herd. Rhavas got ready to fell him as he'd felled the other Khamorth. This nomad, though, neither aimed an arrow at him nor drew his sword. Instead, waving, he shouted something in his own language.

He sounded more curious than angry. "I don't understand you!" Rhavas shouted back in Videssian.

Hearing another tongue intrigued the Khamorth. He yelled something else. Again, Rhavas answered in Videssian. By then, the nomad was close enough to give Rhavas a good look at him. He was a young man with an open, friendly face. Jabbing a thumb at his own chest, he said, "Argippash." Then he pointed at Rhavas and mimed curiosity.

"Rhavas," Rhavas said. "I am from Videssos." He pointed south and tried to use sign language to show he'd come a long way and been traveling for some time.

Argippash exclaimed excitedly to show he understood. He used gestures of his own to invite Rhavas back to his tribe's encampment. He didn't seem like a man intent on murdering a stranger. After a moment, Rhavas figured out what he did seem like: a man who'd found something unusual and who wanted to use it to win points from his friends and neighbors. Rhavas didn't mind. He'd hoped to get a friendly reception from one of these bands, but hadn't been sure he could. This seemed his best chance.

The plainsmen's camp wasn't much different from that of Kolaksha's Kubrati. The chieftain here was a barrel-chested gray-beard named Takshaki. To Rhavas' surprise and delight, he knew a little Videssian: less than Kolaksha had, but enough to make himself understood. "Learn from traders," he said. "You trader? Got wine?" His bushy eyebrows quirked up hopefully. He knew what he wanted, all right.

"No, I am not a trader," Rhavas answered. "I am a priest."

Takshaki's face fell. "Phaos, Phaos, Phaos," he grumbled. "No want hear Phaos." He said something in his own language to Argippash. The younger man spoke defensively—something that had to mean, *How could I have known?*

"I will not speak of Phos," Rhavas promised. "If you want to hear me, I will speak of Skotos. If you do not want to hear that, I will not speak of any god. Instead, I will tell you that much of northern Videssos lies open to you nomads and to your flocks and herds."

"We hear. We on way." Takshaki cocked his head to one side. His eyebrows rose again, in a slightly different way this time. "Why you tell? You Videssos." He corrected himself: "You *of* Videssos."

"I have a feud with Videssos," Rhavas said. The Khamorth chief frowned. Rhavas did his best to explain. When Takshaki got it, he got it all at once. He understood the idea; he'd been missing the word.

He might have been a barbarian, but he was nobody's fool. "Videssos big," he said, stretching his arms wide. "You one man." He held up his right forefinger. "How one man *feud* with big?" He grinned as he used his new vocabulary.

Rhavas pointed his finger at a hawk circling above the encampment. "Curse you," he said, and the bird plummeted out of the sky. Takshaki and Argippash and the other nomads who'd gathered around to see the strange new arrival all exclaimed in astonishment. Rhavas gave the chieftain a courtier's bow. "I am one man, yes. But I am not weak."

"You do to man, too?" Takshaki asked.

"I can," Rhavas answered.

The nomad plucked at his long, thick, curly beard. "You do with this Skotos?"

"Yes, that's right," Rhavas said eagerly.

Takshaki folded his arms across his broad chest in a truly kingly gesture. "You stay," he declared.

Stay Rhavas did, for the next several months. More than a few men in Takshaki's tribe learned Videssian from him. He picked up the plainsmen's language, studying it with the same dogged persistence he'd given to his theological research back in what was now a vanished time. The tribe's shaman was a man named Budin. He dressed in a fringed costume, as Lipoksha had, but he was not effeminate. Rhavas' sorcery and doctrine intrigued him, as his intrigued Rhavas. Despite differences of birth and culture, they were kindred spirits.

"You want us to hurt Videssos," Budin said when they'd learned enough of each other's languages to be able to talk fairly well.

"I do indeed." Rhavas nodded.

Budin clicked his tongue between his teeth. "A renegade is more dangerous than a man from another tribe," he observed. "He knows his own too well."

"No doubt you are right," Rhavas said. Videssos and Makuran had used that truth against each other to great effect. He hadn't thought a barbarous shaman would be able to see it, but if the man had . . . "I aim to be as dangerous to Videssos as I can."

"Videssos has done things to you." Budin did not make it a question.

"Videssos certainly has." Rhavas nodded again.

"But what has Videssos done to Takshaki's tribe? What has Videssos done to the Khamorth?" the shaman asked.

Maybe he did not think Rhavas would have an answer for him. But Rhavas did: "Videssos has held you away from land where you could graze your animals. Videssos has held on to gold and goods and wine that could be yours. Videssos has been too strong to attack. Now Videssos is weak. Many plainsmen have already entered her." He deliberately used the Khamorth word for going into a woman. "Will Takshaki's tribe stay behind when others grow rich? You were already on your way to Videssos."

Budin licked his lips. "I think we will not stay behind. I think Takshaki also thinks this. But he wants grazing space and wine and riches and plunder. You want endless war against Videssos. These are not the same thing."

What would you have been if you'd grown up in Videssos and truly been trained in how to think? Rhavas wondered. *With your native shrewdness, you would have been formidable. You are wasted as a nomad shaman.* Budin was bound to be right again. Rhavas thought it better not to come out and admit as much. "If you want to take what should be yours, you will need to fight to seize and to hold it," he said. "That suits me, and should suit you as well."

"Time will tell if it does," Budin said—yes, he *was* shrewd.

Here, though, he was not shrewd enough. When he thought of time, he thought of one year, or five years, or ten. No man was likely to think in terms longer than those. Rhavas did. He was starting to think in terms of generations, of lifetimes. Had he not been promised years, many years, to bring his hopes and those of his new master to fruition? He had, or he was convinced he had, and he intended to take advantage of it.

A broad ditch with fortresses spaced every couple of miles along the eastern edge of it had protected the Empire of Videssos from incursions off the steppe. It had. It did not anymore. The fortresses stood empty. The edges of the ditch had begun to fall in on themselves. Takshaki's tribe had no trouble getting its flocks and herds across to the other side. No one challenged them. No Videssians were in any position to challenge them, nor had they been since the fortresses emptied so their soldiers could go fight in the civil war.

As for the Khamorth—well, the new land was wide. There was plenty of room for them to spread across it as they pleased. So none of them challenged Takshaki's entrance into what had been Videssos, either.

Sometimes the nomads guided their animals. Sometimes they simply let them wander where the grazing was good. Takshaki preferred the latter way. His cattle and sheep ambled north and east. That disappointed Rhavas; the plainsmen headed into an area far from any place where the writ of Stylianos and Sozomenos ran these days. He thought about leaving them and attaching himself to another tribe more actively engaged against Videssos. It would be easier now that he'd picked up some of the barbarians' language.

Rhavas thought about it, but then abandoned the idea, at least for a while. Takshaki's herds and flocks moved east along a river valley—snowy now, as it had been the last time Rhavas traveled along it—that grew more familiar the farther he went. It was the valley of the Anazarbos, and the livestock and the tribe were on their way to Skopentzana.

They reached the burned and battered ruins about a week later. "This was a large, fine place once," Budin said, as if he were speaking of centuries in the past and not something less than a year. Takshaki's men started combing through the wreckage, and they were rewarded. Earlier plunderers had not found everything worth stealing.

"So it was," Rhavas said. Dead weeds poked up through the snow between cobblestones now. Bushes had begun to cover the downfallen, tumbled stones that had made up the wall. He too went into the city, though what he was looking for had nothing to do with loot.

He started toward the chief temple and the prelate's residence beside it, but checked himself before he got there. That was a past life, a mistaken life, a failed life. He hadn't grasped what mattered then.

Instead, he sought out what was left of Himerios' house, where he'd first set eyes on Ingegerd, where he'd first set out on the path that made him what he was today. After some effort, he found the street. It was the fourth house. He went inside: not hard, not when the walls had fallen in on themselves. He looked out at what had been Skopentzana and slowly nodded to himself. This was where it had started, and this was how he aimed to make it end. He nodded again. Why not? Didn't he have all the time in the world?